# THE
# STORY
## OF H

# THE
# STORY
# OF H

## A NOVEL

## MARINA PEREZAGUA

### Translated by Valerie Miles

*An Imprint of* HarperCollins*Publishers*

THE STORY OF H. Copyright © 2018 by Marina Perezagua. Translation copyright © 2018 Valerie Miles. All rights reserved. Printed in the United States of America. No part of this book may be used or reproduced in any manner whatsoever without written permission except in the case of brief quotations embodied in critical articles and reviews. For information, address HarperCollins Publishers, 195 Broadway, New York, NY 10007.

HarperCollins books may be purchased for educational, business, or sales promotional use. For information, please email the Special Markets Department at SPsales@harpercollins.com.

Ecco® and HarperCollins® are trademarks of HarperCollins Publishers.

Originally published in 2015 by Los Libros del Lince, Spain, as *Yoro*.

FIRST EDITION

*Designed by Suet Yee Chong*

Library of Congress Cataloging-in-Publication Data has been applied for.

ISBN 978-0-06-266071-8

18 19 20 21 22  LSC  10 9 8 7 6 5 4 3 2 1

*To Robert Wimmer*

# CONTENTS

# AUTHOR'S NOTE

I am a granddaughter of the Spanish Civil War, a member of a very long-lived family. As a baby, I was rocked to sleep by two great-grandparents, and I have been able to have mature conversations with two great-grandparents and all four grandparents. From such direct and vivid testimonies, I understand to some degree the fear of losing one's life, the tragedy of killing a brother, the hunger and the chaos that follow a bombing. One of my earliest memories is an image: in Toledo, when it rained, red rivers flowed down the paved slopes, the rain mixing with the blood of neighbors, the baker, the teacher, who from one day to the next went from being friendly when they met one another on the street to being mixed in the flow of the same water pouring downhill. For me there was no Snow White, no Little Red Riding Hood—the stories my great-grandmothers told me were their own dramas: their husbands were soldiers who got drunk to ease the weight of their consciences; their children lay in the common graves of Spain without names on their tombstones.

When I think of the circumstances that make up this prehistory of mine, I consider the fact that I'm here right now, writing this note, to be a miracle. That all of my great-grandparents fought and survived the war in the most troubled areas of Spain, that of all the children they lost, none of them were the grandparents who had to survive to make me possible, is enough for me to confirm that my existence was improbable. And yet here I am, not only born but also having written this novel that has so much to do with the longevity of my elders. Although *The Story of H* confronts war, it moves away from the war in Spain in part as a result of that collective consciousness my grandparents gave me: I'm not just me, but the memory of all those who survived to make my birth possible. I therefore consider that writing about a war that wasn't of my land, my blood, my flesh, is to accept that every war is everyone's war.

If a girl in Hiroshima on August 6, 1945, hadn't managed to survive the postatomic radiation after the explosion reduced a large part of her school to ashes, along with her teachers and classmates, I might never have become a writer, since I began to approach writing by the hand of one of the bomb's descendants: a Japanese professor who, like me, like anyone, is a product of the miracle of surviving all of our wars.

It was that professor, a professor of art history at the Sophia University in Tokyo, who made the kintsugi technique my philosophy of life through writing. Just as pieces of broken pottery can be put back together by covering their cracks with a varnish of gold dust, so could I both in my day-to-day life and in what I write try to protect the historical and aesthetic value of scars. When I see a wound, I admire it because there, and not in our unbroken flesh, do I find the nature of being human: its vulnerability, but also the enormous energy that it requires to pick up our pieces from the ground, reunite them, and be born again. We are born as many times as we are capable of recovering. Only the belly button is a scar that proves that a woman gave birth to us. All other scars show that we are the ones who, so many other times, had to give birth to ourselves. We are all mothers when we fall, the mother who gives birth to us in each of those golden cracks that unite the mud that forms us but that has broken so many times, to be put together again, perhaps with a function more suitable to our own being, according to those desires that we weren't able to fulfill before our fall.

My relationship with Japan is also a consequence of history: my family, on my father's side, comes from Coria del Río, a town in Seville where *Japón* is a common last name, ever since the samurai Hasekura Tsunenaga was chosen in the seventeenth century to lead a diplomatic mission to the then-powerful Spain, which reached through the Guadalquivir River. A drop of that blood must remain in my family, and in myself, since I have felt a very special attraction to that country for as long as I can remember, an attraction not due to an interest in a culture that, in theory, is exotic for a Westerner. As a child, my family used to remind me that my ancestors came from Japan, and the attraction that I have always felt toward the country has been a literal, physical one, a kind of call that signifies, more than a trip, a return. When I went to Japan for the first time, on my first trip, I felt exactly that: that this wasn't my first trip, but instead was a return to a home of sorts. Later on I heard someone on TV from Coria del Río say that, unfortunately, his father had died with the sadness of not having been able to return to Japan . . . even though he had never set foot there. Maybe that's why my look toward Japan can't be one of exotic distance. When I was a child, my mother told me Japanese legends as she fed me, until I was old enough to discover for myself—with the help of *Spring Snow* and the great Yukio Mishima—that Japanese literature was the one that most corresponded to my transformation from adolescent to woman, with its eroticism of change. This novel also deals with eroticism—with bodies and transformations.

And so, finally, I want to mention that, in parallel to the

evolution of her atomic wounds, the protagonist of this novel lives out a biological drama, a drama of a sexual nature that has enslaved her in her body from the day she was born, when her parents decided that her sexual organs—debated as being those of a male or female—should be, for the rest of her life, those of a man. And they were wrong. They were so wrong in determining the sex of their daughter that only an event with the forcefulness of an atomic bomb could allow her a sort of redemption, given the particular circumstances of her case. What chance was there for a victim of the nuclear attack to express that, of all her relatives and close friends, only the bomb was able to recognize her as the person she really was? It seems a paradox that the victim of a massacre unprecedented in history comes to be grateful for some of its consequences, considering them of greater benefit to her than what was granted by the peaceful society into which she was born, a peacefulness that silenced her more than the war. In that way, the paradox is just an appearance of one. This is a novel that underscores the reality that in all acts, even in the most terrible, you can find a residue of hope, the opportunity to build a second life amid the rubble of the last bombing.

I hope you enjoy reading my story, and I'm grateful in advance for life and for those readers who, I trust, know how to desire peace between the lines of battle and of light.

—Marina Perezagua

# TRANSLATOR'S NOTE

This novel, Marina Perezagua's first after two highly acclaimed story collections, announced the emergence of an audacious and original new voice on the literary scene in Spain. The novel is an extension of one of the stories in her collection *Leche,* whose protagonist, Marina said, wouldn't let her go. As you read *The Story of H,* you will doubtless come to appreciate the truth of that. H is precisely the type of character who finds a spot in the imagination and makes herself very comfortable. She's willful, a survivor, coy and brash all at once, a seductress, and exasperating and compassionate and so full of love. She's all in one. You can almost hear Nina Simone in the background—"Ain't Got No . . ."—crooning in her gritty, complex voice how she ain't got no schooling, no home, no perfume, no uncles, no aunts, no love, not even a name. Then the song shifts and Nina chants, powerfully now, the "all" she does have—a body, a nose, her ears, her toes, her boobies, her sex. And finishes with "I've got my freedom. And I've got life . . . And I'm gonna keep it." This is the song Marina Perezagua goes to when life becomes overwhelming. And in a way it is the soundtrack of this novel that narrates how, against all odds, an intersex child who survived the bombing of Hiroshima, who lost absolutely everything in that devastating detonation—family, home, even sex—finds, at great cost, meaningful love and a family. H abides, even without a name.

*The Story of H* is an outcry for love and compassion from the center of a profoundly disturbing sensorial world, a barbaric yawp straight from the lungs of a writer for whom imagination and water are inseparable. As a vehicle for metaphors, water is a shifting mirror. It's the *fons et origo* that precedes all form. It's present not only in Marina's name and in the fluid, incantatory intensity of her prose but also in her free-diving record of lasting five minutes underwater. So saying there's a breathless quality to this novel is fairly close to a literal description. It's in the intensity of its conviction, its urgency, its fluid nature, and its constant transformation. While writing *The Story of H,* Marina trained in the Mediterranean every day and finally swam the Strait of Gibraltar. In four hours.

WATER SYMBOLIZES DEATH and rebirth, purification, eternal return, the ring. In *The Story of H,* structurally, Marina draws a magic circle, an *ouroboros,* a serpent biting its own tail. It's an ancient symbol and archetype, the basic mandala of alchemy. It signifies the assimilation of the opposite, something that is constantly re-creating itself. The construction or creative impulse from destruction, the all in one, is like a school of fish or a conspiracy of ravens. And I write this hoping to persuade readers of the fact that, though Marina's novel is powerfully creative, oceanic, and visionary in its gallery of images at once horrific and stunningly beautiful, it is not of the magical realist tradition. All that is written in Spanish and is not of a realist bent does not of magical realism come. Marina is first of all an art historian, schooled in the power of ekphrastic expression, how the written description of a visual work of art can become vivid and charged with energy. Time capturing space, describing it vividly, mapping it and bringing it to life, creating polarized opposites that spin and create a frame. She works, as Roberto Bolaño did, in reviving symbolist and surrealist techniques of pictorial imagery in the subtext of her work and in the juxtaposition of magnetic opposites like pain and pleasure or life out of death or salvation amid cruelty and corruption, empathy before a bloodthirsty world driven by violence and kitsch. "Perhaps universal history is the history of a few metaphors," Borges wrote in the opening of his story "Pascal's Sphere." He closed the story with the same sentence, slightly altered: "Perhaps universal history is the history of various intonations of a few metaphors." In between, he traced a metaphor to give a holistic idea of the universe as atom and globe, primordial form, whose center is everywhere and its circumference nowhere.

———

The epicenter of this novel is the sixth of August 1945, when we see the first atomic bomb, Little Boy, plunge from the *Enola Gay* straight at us there, sitting in class, with H, her schoolmates and teacher, and the hundreds of thousands of civilians in Hiroshima. An angel of death dangling above the city in the form of an American plane. But our H, an intersexual child whose parents choose to see her as a boy even though she identifies as a girl, survives, the only student left alive. "When I came to," she relates, "the whole school had become a big playground, a playground without monkey bars, a gaping expanse open to a gaping city. [ ... ] I watched a naked lump approach me in what had been the bathroom. It asked for water. I was frightened. Its head had swollen to three times the normal size. Only when the lump said her name did I realize it was my teacher. I ran away."

Through H's story, Marina individuates History back down

to the level of the human, to the pathos, to what it means, the tremor in the collective unconscious at the sudden murder of tens of thousands of people. The heat of the human told with enough imagination to melt the freezing effects of quantification. A poetics of beauty even in horror. Through History and Science, *The Story of H* pins the narrative to a specific time and place, to reality, like a butterfly to a board. But the imagination is set free—it is revolutionary, boundless. The oneiric world tries to make sense of all that has happened, all that has been broken by violence and war. H confesses to a murder. And the question hovers: does a society that is capable of unleashing an atomic bomb have the moral grounds to judge a woman who has murdered to defend life?

H HAS NO OTHER NAME but this letter. In Spanish, the letter *H* is silent. In English, this voiceless glottal fricative, as the *H* sound is called in the parlance of phonetics, can be silent, but it can also be aspirated. These are the felicities of translation, when a detail like this can open a new level of meaning—in this case, the sound captured in a symbol that has been culturally determined over time and historical circumstances. We have *hour* and *honest*, which are words from the French and so are silent. There is *messiah* from the Hebrew, or *rhapsody* from the Greek, silent by derivation. Or *shepherd* or *exhaust*, silent by elision, which in linguistics means merging or shortening a sound. But other words from the French have slowly acquired in English an aspirated *H*, as in *horrible, host*, or *human*. And of course, *Hiroshima*. Thanks to some strange inner mathematics of sound over time, the aspirated *H* shows up again in these words. So, readers, our H and her story jump into the English-speaking world and your imaginations outfitted with additional metaphorical possibilities. An aspirated letter for a breathless novel. There's H, who free-dives with the *amas*, the Japanese pearl divers whose tradition goes back thousands of years, and nearly succumbs to the narcotic effect of diving into the abyss, and there's the author, who swims all the way across the Gibraltar while writing H's story. H wanders the earth like an *oni,* a Japanese ghost born of destruction and sent into the world to take vengeance, like a gasp of noxious atomic wind sent whirling and churning across the planet, haunting and hunting what was taken from her—the future, the daughter, her love, her penis like a blind lizard stalking her in nightmares. But not her body: "I've got life, and nobody can take it away from me."

H CAN BE SILENT, or *H* can be an aspiration. The constellation of words in my thesaurus tells me that *aspiration* is synonymous with desire. *Hope. Longing, yearning, urge, wish.* It even says *fire in the belly* and *dream.* Keep those correspondences in mind when you read the novel. These are the joys of translation: not what's in a name or even in a word, but what's in a sound or the lack of it, spinning like a needle in that tiny little letter in the center of a magical circle. You see? You haven't even started reading yet, and already H is colonizing her space in your imagination.

THE GREAT SPANISH ART HISTORIAN and symbolist poet Juan Eduardo Cirlot, who was close to the surrealists, once wrote about an encounter with a woman in a letter to André Breton: "I am still spellbound by the moonlike pallor of her leg and her semitransparent silk stockings that allowed me to glimpse the features of her flesh and its delicate shadow of very fine down, like the seabed as seen through water, the algae and the urchins. I understood how this gray transparency, like a veil or misted glass, expressed the principle of true mystery, that it's not a matter of seeing or not seeing, but of glimpsing."

This novel is about the mystery of sexuality—its fluidity,

identity, compulsion—an exploration of the dark, broken places where sexuality manifests itself and its capacity for healing, the body as the center of everything, since without the body, the soul cannot exist. Full of the tension of its juxtaposition of disturbing, sublime images, *The Story of H* pulls the reader into a maelstrom of passion, pain, and perseverance. Cirlot, in his *Dictionary of Symbols*, writes in the entry for *scars:* "The author once dreamed of an unknown damsel (*anima*) whose beautiful face was marked by scars and burns which in no way disfigured her features." They didn't take away from her attractiveness and perhaps even increased it. "Moral imperfections, and sufferings (are they one and the same?)[,] are, therefore, symbolized by the wounds and scars caused by fire and sword." Ah, H.

BREATHLESS, FEROCIOUS, UNCONVENTIONAL, RAW, a primal scream from the depths of what is human, Marina Perezagua dives into the subconscious while her lungs compress to the size of raisins. Water is a conduit—our brains react and shift chemically when we are near water—and dopamine, serotonin, and oxytocin levels rise, while the inducer of bad moods, cortisol, drops, in the same way as when we are reunited with someone we love after having been separated. Even the sound of water causes a chemical reaction in our brain. Ishmael knew that, of course, before there was scientific proof. And H, like Ishmael, launches on a quest to find the whiteness of the United Nations whale in the shadows of the Congo. If all voyages are a homecoming, then could it be that water made humans as a way to transport itself? Are we the damp, spore-like vessels colonizing the world for it? What if our brains react to the sound, the sight, of water because, on a molecular level, water is recognizing itself in us? With H, you are in for the plunge of your life.

Sir:

The pages that follow constitute my declaration, which focuses primarily on the circumstances that led me to the crimes for which I will be judged, acts I do not regret.

This is not a confession. A confession is nothing but a weapon for people in power to coerce someone into betraying him- or herself. I won't be the one to give my own self away. You'll see that I've done everything possible to resist the powerful. If I was tarnished in any way, it's never been in their defense.

Neither is this a justification.

What you are about to read is the mark of a firebrand on a mule's rump, or a groove in a rock eroded by rain, or even a tree that's been warped by strong winds. That's right, what you are about to read is my story, the coherent reaction of a sensitive nature. A story penned by me, but set in motion by a fate that was woven on high.

As you read on, you'll see portraits of certain colleagues of yours, perhaps a relative, maybe even you yourself. If you don't like what you see, you can go ahead and break the mirror or burn the pages, but you'll never be rid of the infection, the rot that pollutes the rivers, seas, wombs, and fields. And you'll never be able to take from me the joy I've finally come to feel.

I call myself H because I've never been given a voice, and a Spanish man once told me that h is a silent letter in his language. So this letter will be my name, seeing as it's a name I share with many other mute people who might discover their voices here.

*I'm sure they'll find me before long. I won't resist, as this story is what stands as my resistance. Whoever is coming to arrest me will see the same brown river I'm gazing out at now from my African refuge, a place that has allowed me to transcribe my testimony over these days. Perhaps my captor is so near that he's watching the same hippopotamus as I am right now, in the same position, with the same bird on top, drying off in the sun as if there were no such thing as hell.*

*I penned this last note after narrating the story that follows. I'm weary now; maybe that's why you'll find in these last words that my tone has grown colder. Don't take it personally. Love has always prevailed in me. I love and have loved as if I had been born for it. If you pay attention, you'll see how love stands steadfast behind every deed. Judge me according to your laws, but consider this as my last wish:*

*Once you too have taken my voice away, if ever you should have the chance to speak in my name, don't employ the vocabulary of death. When you raise my head with your fist, everyone will know that I've killed. So if anyone ever asks, please remember H's last words were these:*

*"God knows I stood for life."*

*H*
*The Democratic Republic of the Congo*

# Zero Gravity: 1942

## WE WHO CARRY THE BOMB INSIDE OF US

The refugee camp's main tent was on fire before us. Hungry flames engulfed the tarpaulin as if it were synthetic fur. I stretched my hand out to clasp Yoro's. I noticed she was trembling and that her tremors seemed in sync with the roaring fire. As if they provided the flames with something more than sound alone: substance. Yoro and the blaze were like the sternum and spine of a single creature, two integral parts of a whole, a drum and its stick. Through her, my hand was able to perceive the swan-song hiss of a tin cup, of the metallic tubes that held the tent up. I was absorbed in these subtle details, but that doesn't mean I didn't feel for the people and things being consumed right there, though I've trained myself to resist the instinct to flee in dire situations, and not to sob or try to find a solution for something beyond my control. I tried hard to keep from blinking. Blinking too much is like hyperventilating. A steady movement of the eyelashes saves oxygen, energy, and helps keep my knees from buckling. That's how I could remain standing. That's how I could fix my gaze. Of course I was scared. Of course I felt compassion. But I held myself in check, not only because if I fell, others would come to consume me, but also because I promised never to move a muscle out of rage or despair. Not a single one. I had promised Jim that. Dwelling on these thoughts helped me keep my promise, observing from a distance the heat so close it was like my own skin. I found serenity in my own way, tugging at a string of memories to find some experience that would help me sustain my composure. I found it. The string was the death of Quang Duc, the seventy-six-year-old monk who immolated himself in front of me and a host of fellow monks on a street in Saigon. He torched himself for freedom, incinerated himself without varying his meditative lotus position; even when the flames enveloped him, he did not move a muscle. The other monks and I, we sobbed over him without opposing his will; others begged for help, wishing to rescue him, for his sake but against his will, because he had to burn in order to end persecution, to achieve peace for his brothers and sisters and others like me, who had to avoid blinking while facing a fire. Eventually I found serenity. The heat of the flaming tarp carried me to a distant place, far from the here and now, and rekindled the heat of the monk I saw immolate himself in Saigon, and the more the refugee camp's tarp burned, the further away I slipped, motionless, toward the instant of Quang Duc's death. Just as Yoro's trembling seemed to give flesh to the sound of the flames, so the sobs of we who loved the monk seemed to give sound to his silence, because the man who burned himself alive said nothing, not a moan, not a hiss to express complaint or pain or reproach.

THE FIRE CULMINATED A PURSUIT that had begun when I met Jim, exactly fifty-five years ago. Jim's story is my story. It's not that his story is linked to mine, it's not that my love for him has had a bearing on my life, it's that without him I would never have become, since *becoming*, to me, is that moment when I first dared to open my eyes and see myself for what I was. I could finally know, I could finally be—that's what I owe to Jim. I said goodbye to the skinless me, the me who lacked the body's biggest organ—the epidermis—the me who'd never claimed a right to the only hide ever offered freely. Slowly but surely I became the hunterly me tracking the prey that had been ripped from my teeth, the racing lion me pouncing, fighting to take back the stolen flesh, the lion's own flesh, not zebra or antelope, not the flesh of some other lion, but its own. I became the lioness stalking her own self. That's how I became the me that I am now—intact, golden, menacing. Jim's hand was the first to see and to stroke the earnest skin my mother delivered me in, skin that gave me back the natural protection that belonged to me. I've *become;* I see myself now as being so strong that even naked I still feel dressed in armor. Long gone are the times I used to wake up trying to fit into someone else's skin, so that by the end of the day I went to bed distraught and with throbbing joints. How wouldn't my bones grow misshapen, trying so hard to fulfill other people's expectations? But it doesn't hurt anymore. Thanks to Jim, my fingers stopped deforming by endlessly picking fruit grown for other people; thanks to Jim, my legs began straightening out once I stopped following the curves of landscapes that didn't matter to me; and thanks to him, in my dotage my back is even straighter today than it was when I was twenty.

I reckon I knew Jim's significance from the beginning, so I started scribbling a few notes, and naturally the writing accumulated over our years together. I never realized the material might come in handy later, maybe today, for reconstructing the story that gives the fire meaning. Guided by the notes, then, I'll try to articulate the long journey, which I suspect is now reaching its conclusion.

BEFORE WE MET, before ever acknowledging my role in his life, Jim had been one of the American soldiers in occupied Japan. For a long time, his days came and went, shorn of significance; he was simply an officer occupying the territory of his commission. There were only minimal assignments undertaken to help the country recover, and as a result, the changes were also minimal. There was nothing to give purpose to a soldier's life, neither in humanitarian aid—which in those days hadn't yet been defined as such—nor in terms of personal or national self-interest.

Jim didn't know at the time that these were the months when our union really began, before we ever met, when the base gave him custody of a baby in May 1950. He told me the baby had been delivered unannounced, given like any other order, like his assignment to occupy the region. At first he rejected the infant, but they bonded very naturally by the end of the first day, when he realized this almond-eyed baby just might be a catalyst for the reconciliation he'd sought for the past six years, since the Japanese shipped him off to Manila with sixteen hundred North American prisoners. Everything Jim had suffered on that ship and the misery of his captivity prior to that turned to benevolence when he felt the delicate heft of the baby in his arms for the first time. He'd never completely overcome the lasting ache of what had happened to him, but this tiny girl, this victim of the United States, was like a piece of fruit placed in a weighing dish that struck a balance in the division of cruelties perpetrated on either side.

The ship where Jim had been confined was built in Nagasaki in 1939, and was initially intended as a Japanese passenger cargo ship. It was christened with the name *Oryoku Maru*. The ship was later repurposed as a floating prison, earning the moniker "Ship of Death." Jim never liked to talk about what went on there—his memories were too disturbing—but a few years ago, some of the accounts General MacArthur had tried to destroy came to light because George Weller, the author, had stored carbon copies in his trunk. They were recovered by his son, who delivered them for publication. They helped me fill in some of the gaps in Jim's testimony.

The *Oryoku Maru*, then, was intended to transport hundreds of Japanese civilians. The American prisoners would be confined to the hold. The voyage, which the prisoners expected to take some ten days, ended up lasting seven weeks. Jim said if he had known what was in store, he would have let the Japanese soldiers run him through with one of the bayonets they used to herd the soldiers into the ship. If so, if Jim had ended his life then and there, I would have grown to be a timorous woman, obedient and gloomy, a twenty-year-old cadaver waiting forty, sixty, seventy years for someone to come and lay me to rest. But Jim couldn't imagine what was in store, and so he made it through. Of the sixteen hundred and nineteen prisoners, only some four hundred survived (the exact number is unknown). A hundred of them arrived so far gone already that they perished before being turned over to the authorities on land, and as many died in Japanese work camps. It's believed that only around two hundred of the initial sixteen hundred and nineteen actually survived through liberation in 1945. Jim was twenty-nine at the time, and one of the survivors. I give thanks for it still, every day of my life.

I MET JIM IN NEW YORK on April 27, 1960. There are four medieval cloisters in the northern part of the city, in Fort Tryon Park, brought over from France stone by stone. The gardens are carefully groomed—then as now—in the tradition of Romanesque horticulture. That day the skies cleared up for the first time after weeks of rain, and I walked from cloister to cloister following the movement of the sun. I'd emptied my mind of thought; all I wanted was to keep warm and abandon myself to the simple pretensions of a sunflower, when someone said, "The sun makes for strong bones. You need it if you spend winter in the city."

I glanced over my shoulder and there was Jim, sitting on the ground with his back against the stone wall. He was looking at me. His words must have been directed at me. I drew closer and he said, as if picking our conversation right back up from where we had left off, that according to Herodotus the Egyptians already knew the sun was good for the bones, which they reckoned was why the skulls of their dead withstood so much more than did the skulls of their Persian enemies, which could be crushed artlessly with a simple rock. Egyptians knew not to protect themselves from the sun as children, while the Persians wore turbans that blocked it out, not allowing it to strengthen their crania. The stranger said his name without asking for mine, and gracefully segued from Persian and Egyptian bones to pointing out the park's variety of indigenous birds and flowers. I was amazed at how many different species he could name when for me the world was divided in only two: plants and animals.

A few hours later in a nearby café, still chatting with the same fluid grace, he said that like me, he too was searching for something. The context of the search was the same, World War II; he had lost something in the war, while for me something had been won. The crucial word for both of us was *daughter;* for Jim it was about his missing daughter, while for me it was about a daughter that I'd never conceived. As we left the café, I could detect the velvety touch of synchronicity, an inkling that the relationship between both of our explorations might meld our two paths into one.

I found my answer as to how almost immediately, when he told me the story of his heartache. The more I learned about the daughter who was taken from him when she turned five, the more I identified his missing girl with the child I wasn't able to deliver myself. Every time Jim shared things about her, the desire to find her grew stronger in my mind and heart, and eventually in outward ways too, as in my breasts, in whose swelling came the proof that hope, under special circumstances, can produce milk just like gestation. My milk ducts reacted with a pasty liquid that dried up a few weeks later, probably obeying the messages relayed from my brain warning that the nine months of a normal pregnancy would have to extend over a much longer period of time in a case like this.

What I didn't know was that my so-called psychological pregnancy would initiate a journey that began in Japan and would end in Africa. Here was the speedy head of a spermatozoon—the atomic bomb of Hiroshima—and over there its little tail—a fire in the Democratic Republic of the Congo. Thousands of victims of the first atomic bomb on this side; a few deaths by fire on the other in a land where cadavers pile one on top of the other daily from hunger, from slavery, from illness, until their number matches the number of victims of the bomb. From wartime Japan to contemporary Africa, a seventy-year span outlined by this sperm-comet whose current flows from the Japanese genocide to where I am now in this African land, sweeping me along with it together with shrapnel from the bomb itself. I take in the view here of life spread across the continent where the first human was born only to die, over and over again.

———

I once heard a forestry expert say that woodland trees are not individual beings, but units that together form an organism that exchanges carbon dioxide and nitrogen underground through bulbs, mushrooms, and roots. The breath of one tree comes from the lungs of another. A tree's quality of life and longevity depend on the others around it. My life is rooted in Jim's story, and his life bears the marks of mine. Jim and I were—are—part of the same rhizome, trees connected through the first atomic mushroom. The weapon planted us in the same forest when it was christened seven months after they boarded Jim on the *Oryoku*

*Maru,* changing history, touching my life in such a peculiar way that today it's still hard for me to describe things from the distance I read in historians' accounts. They don't move me in their writing; they don't affect me. There's no sting when I read a history book, and I find it difficult to understand how anyone can try to explain a war without its causing heartache or provoking empathy. Historians like to say it's being impartial, but pain can be communicated from impartiality too. I call it indifference, which means being partial to the victors, doing them a service. Doing you a service. Just a few pages into my testimony and already I've forgotten that I'm writing mostly to you.

Well then, allow me to explain why I don't like history books, since this story on the whole is about history. At some point you've no doubt heard an eyewitness to some great historical event say things on the order of "I was born to bear witness for other people." History with a capital *H* could be said to have imbued his or her life with a sense of purpose. Well, sir, that is not my case. I didn't survive Hiroshima to bear witness. I survived Hiroshima because it was my duty to survive; this is why my mother brought me into this world, to observe what is in front of me, whether it be a bomb or a flock of sheep nibbling some peaceful green pasture. So simple, and yet not everyone can admit it. People need spectacular missions. Someone born in a tiny village in Provence decides it's a tedious place. What kind of mission is it to wake up and see the same rocks every day? So he or she decides to study the Spanish Civil War. Then come a few trips to Spain and conversations with survivors. The tender small-town soul can't abide such cruelty and a tear spills over a cheek, so she reads more books, let's say several books, and the rest of her life is devoted to writing paragraph after paragraph from the lens of the side she has chosen to champion. She found her source of meaning. Research. Spread the word. Maybe that's the historian's ambition after all, to act as a messiah of information. And that's all well and good, sir, it's needed.

But let me tell you something else. This kind of so-called history isn't worth a plugged nickel if it isn't written from the emotion of universal pain. A war is much more than statistics, body counts, lists of atrocities. A war is a gaping wound in a human being's sense of dignity; it's a defect, a congenital deformity that expresses a failure of humanity. The historian who hasn't lived through the episodes he or she is narrating should be writing from feelings of shame and compassion. Of course I could write a chapter on Hiroshima, not because it's my birthplace, but because even as a child I could sense this human defect stealing into everyday life until it detonated into a Hiroshima, a Vietnam, or another tributary of the mighty river of war. I swear to you: a tree is not a single being. One tree's breath comes from the lungs of another. Until a historian realizes this, his students appropriately will go on hating his classes, and what's worse, forgetting them entirely. So I'll try to give my own account, far removed from the detachment of a library-writing historian, as I lived through the events in the trenches, so to speak. I'm not sure whether I was on the winning or the losing side, and frankly I couldn't care less. What I do know is that I lived my time in the first person, which gives me an advantage over those who find themselves in the dusk of their lives believing they participated in their time on earth because they read the Sunday paper.

As I said, a few months after Jim was boarded onto the ship, the history-altering baptism took place. It was August 6, 1945. The creature had no hands to bear arms, yet annihilated more than two hundred thousand lives that day; no mouth and yet it blew houses, trees, and factories to oblivion in a single breath. Conceived outside of any human warmth, it melted steel, cremated parks, pets, and pigeons. They hadn't given it a gender either, but they did give it a name—Little Boy—and at 8:15 on a cloudless August morning, they unleashed that device over Hiroshima.

Before it was born, before it was christened with its name, Little Boy was no more than an abstract pattern in the brains of countries competing against one another to decipher it. It was so powerful and it changed my identity so drastically that for a long time I thought of it as a living being, and not of the men who created it. I imagined its gestation, how it could perceive the brain waves moving to and fro among the rival scientists racing to finish it. How it let itself be carried along the electrical currents, gliding through the neural pathways of the era's most brilliant physicists. Often I fantasized about using the image of a CAT scan in which sections of the successful brain were illuminated, the one that discovered the formula, won the race, the sharpest of them all: J. Robert Oppenheimer's. And I imagined how his little organic lantern, his firefly, must have stimulated the pleasure circuits in the satisfied physicists' brains, whose intelligence had impregnated North America with Little Boy, its favorite son (or daughter?), the atomic bomb that defended the Allies in those difficult hours and, crucially, allowed them to win the war.

Since I was still so young and immature those first few years, I personified the bomb as an extension of my own identity, but eventually I shuffled the weight of responsibility to where it belonged: the man, the manifold who were capable of creating and detonating what is still the most lethal weapon known to humanity. But I don't want my story to linger on these well-known facts. Allusions to the event are meant only as a backdrop over which something personal is being highlighted. If I can be so extravagant as to imagine a victim whom the bomb benefited, then I'm that victim. I forfeited limbs, whole chunks of my flesh, and my relatives, and though nothing could ever compensate me for these losses, I gained other important things. So my life is poised between grief over what the bomb took from me and celebration over something marvelous it gave me.

———

Morning had broken on what seemed like an ordinary day when Little Boy fell. It promised to be one of those placid, clear-skied days that lull you into thinking a place's peacefulness extends over the rest of the planet. Same as every other day on earth, thousands and thousands of mothers were spreading their legs to give birth, bearing the pain children inflict as they make their way to the outside world. Legs didn't open for Little Boy, though, but the bomb bay doors of a B-29. Many mothers were focused on breathing through contractions and the pain of labor while a bombardier was preparing the greatest contraction of them all: the global gash.

Little Boy was born and gave birth. It was at once deliverer and delivered, a nativity that gave birth to a colossal luminous mushroom-shaped cloud. For some, it meant total annihilation; for others, peace; and for all, it was light. A light so intense that people who saw it detonate before hitting the ground lost not only their sight but also their eyeballs. He (I can't help giving it a personality) watched all the people looking up as he fell. He was the last thing they ever saw. Light. His father released through the gray ink of equations an eternal light that was bequeathed to the world. The formula could have been presented with the words "Behold, my son, the light of the world." He'd never imagined it. Nobody had seen the shining until detonation, so it wasn't until after Hiroshima that we knew our race would never be in the dark again.

Oppenheimer brought the most radical promise of light. This latter-day messiah, this higher god of theoretical physics, built a formula that could never be expunged, a weapon that outlived

Little Boy, that would inseminate other countries at the speed of a rabbit, and today there are over twenty thousand bombs more potent than the one dropped on Hiroshima. Others claim there are many more than that. Whatever the case, there are at least twenty thousand rabbit-fucks and pyromaniacs who could incite a planetary inferno capable of liquidating us all in the ejaculation of a single sun, should nations get annoyed with one another. Forget Hiroshima. Little Boy's nature is being cloned into thousands of iron-skinned brothers. As long as their creators keep them hidden, these clones will remain as lethargic as a hibernating bear, but when they are awoken, all the heat of all the summers will enter the lair, and all the caves, all the houses, all the mouths will open black as a door that wasn't able to resist the heat when someone closed the oven. Then Hiroshima will be nothing but a piece of historical fluff. The time hasn't come yet, so you who think of the planet as an everlasting place will think my testament outrageous. It seems outrageous to me too, but I know the world's mechanism is being lubricated to make Hiroshima nothing more than the tangle in a strand of hair that has fallen out and been swept into the corner of that perpetually filthy house we call history.

———

Since my life and my transgressions can't be separated from Jim's story, allow me now to return to him, he who was, like me, a victim. He told me the heat in the belly of *Oryoku Maru* was unbearable, but this vague adjective does not really convey any true sense of the heat. You might get a better sense if I tell you that according to George Weller's accounts, the heat must have reached nearly 130 degrees Fahrenheit. A hundred and thirty degrees Fahrenheit. Way too high, and yet approximately 10,830 degrees lower than the temperature of the earth where the atomic bomb exploded. It's like a slow roast versus spontaneous combustion. The throats of the prisoners dried out slowly. The Japanese used panels to cover most of the hatches, so ventilation was nil. The first ones to pass out were those located at the extremes of the compartments. The only way to distinguish an unconscious passenger from a dead one was by his pulse; the heat was so intense that even the postmortem cooling process was halted. But nobody bothered to take anyone else's pulse. The more people who died, the longer the oxygen would last. Weller recounts how the prisoners removed their clothes to breathe through their skin when they weren't able to use their lungs. The ship's wood absorbed the humidity of all the men piled on top of one another and oozed droplets of sweat. When their thirst became unbearable, the men would lick the little pearls of collective sweat. When the prisoners moaned because the air was so scarce, the Japanese man in charge, Mr. Wada, threatened to seal the hatches completely. Yet when the North American aviators circled the ship ready to bomb it, thinking there were only Japanese on board, Jim said, they all mustered one last morsel of energy to panic at this new threat of death—ironically, at the hands of their own. Yet the sound of the hatches rattling under the aviators' bombs also brought hope, with fresh currents of light and air. And another thing: the Americans in the hold, delirious and half-mad by now, opened their mouths thinking it was water—or maybe they knew better—and drank the blood filtering down from the wounded Japanese on deck. Any liquid coming from the outside world was refreshing.

The accounts detail ever-increasing acts of madness as a result of the dehydration and the lack of fresh air. The Japanese finally brought pails into the hold for the prisoners to relieve themselves. But when the body breaks down, the mind adjusts its mechanisms arbitrarily, and what was once considered hideous was now material for buffoonery. Some men amused themselves by switching the pails of excrement for the pails of food—they were so alike.

JIM COULD NEVER HAVE SUSPECTED then that his true journey would begin fifteen years later, and that he'd make it hand in hand with a compatriot of his torturers. What ran through me was pure Japanese blood, not a drop of anything else that might decontaminate it for him. But the baby was as Japanese as I am, and the two of them had already sealed a pact of reconciliation, though I think the process of forgiveness was under way even earlier, when Jim had to walk among thousands of people, homeless children, roaming spaces where bedrooms had once been, carrying buckets into which they'd thrown whatever seemed even remotely attached to the memory of a loved one. Jim said they basically collected anything that wasn't dust. I think he realized that while he was agonizing on the *Oryoku Maru,* my people's humiliation was in gestation, the most devastating the world had seen to date. Walking a few months later through the ruined city among bodies maimed by his American colleagues must have allowed him to accept his daughter and then me in peace. Jim said not even the doctors in the American occupation forces were there to help. His sole mission was to observe, to study the effects of radioactivity, and they didn't intervene even in the simplest stages of reaction, like vomiting or infant diarrhea. Unawares, some of the victims were still being used as part of the investigation linked to the Manhattan Project.

My people's great misfortune caught me with a thermometer in my mouth. The fever should have kept me home in bed. I was only thirteen and it was my place to obey my mother, who preferred that I not attend school that day. But I couldn't miss recess because my friends and I had left a game unfinished the day before, and I used every excuse in the book to coax my mother into letting me go. I had no idea this little act of defiance would set in motion what a few months later turned me into what I'd always wanted to be. The thought of playing at recess, of the game, was enough motivation for me to fight with my mother, and by eight o'clock sharp, after an hour in the car traveling to school, there I was sitting at my desk. My memory of the next few days has been wiped clean. I've never been able to remember anything, but the victor's version of history offers some very precise data for reconstructing the things that went on while I sat at my desk, unaware of what was being dropped from the sky above, and a few seconds later, when I was prostrate and unconscious on the floor. I know the exact second when William Sterling Parsons, captain of the *Enola Gay*, released the bomb, checked the gauges, and began measuring the seconds it took for the artifact to fall the 31,000 feet from the plane's altitude to the estimated point of detonation at 2,000 feet. I also know the crew expected the explosion to happen within forty-two seconds of release, so at forty-three seconds they were starting to get anxious. Tension built to a peak as they tallied the seconds in their heads. The experiment worked with a three-second lag: when the forty-fifth second struck, I was blown into another room. When I came to, nothing was left standing; there were no walls. The whole school had become a big playground, a playground without monkey bars, a gaping expanse open to a gaping city. Of the 152 pupils in school that day, I was the only one left. I watched a naked lump approach me in what had been the bathroom. It asked for water. I was frightened. Its head had swollen to three times the normal size. Only when the lump said her name did I realize it was my teacher. I ran away.

For years I gathered details about exactly what took place in the air while those of us on the ground went about our daily lives. Knowing the facts about the airplane and the launch of the bomb made me think I might fill some of the gaps in my own story. I used the same method to piece together what happened just after the explosion, while I was unconscious. For several years it was the best I could hope for, to fill the gaps in my memory with reports written by the people responsible for those gaps, and for hundreds of thousands of casualties, for the sick who still today are passing their sicknesses on from one generation to the next. So you see, sir, I was clutching at straws. It's a sad method to have to put myself together with what was responsible for pulling me apart, and an impossible one too. After all, how could I lift myself up with the same tools that were meant to annihilate me? But this was what I had, and I grabbed on to it as a means to scar over part of my amnesia.

Once it released the weapon, the *Enola Gay* enacted its escape protocol, tracing a 155-degree turnaround toward the northeast. The crew put on their dark glasses and braced for the shock waves, which came a minute later, when they were nine miles away. In my case, the data was much less precise. I had no idea how long I had been unconscious or what time it was when I left the school. I remember that all the clocks had stopped at the same time: 8:16. But I have no idea how I got to the hospital. Maybe the person who brought me there doesn't remember either.

Details of the following weeks spent among the huddled masses of the wounded are fuzzy. Later we learned there had been one doctor per three thousand victims. And though I didn't know it at the time, I had burns over 70 percent of my body. My eyelids stuck together after a few days. I couldn't open them. I thought I'd gone blind. No medicines, no tranquilizers, vicious pain. My only treatment was having my position readjusted. Someone came in to turn me over every once in a while. The pain was so severe I couldn't tell if I was being placed faceup or facedown. My whole body was red-hot, in excruciating pain—my chest, my stomach, my knees, all part of the same incandescent slab with shoulder blades, buttocks, the back of my legs. Pain made my body lose texture, as if the front and back of me had melded into a single flat, uniformly blistering griddle. The first sign of recovery came when I felt the wetness of my urine. That's how I could figure out my position. If the urine dripped downward, I was faceup. If it came straight out and formed a little puddle, I was facedown. They cleaned my eyes and I could open them again, so when the pain subsided just enough for a slight effort, I picked my head up to view my raw skin and discovered that while the shape of my extremities was intact, the area from my lower abdomen to my thighs was an unrecognizable pulp. The area was so swollen that I couldn't be sure, but everything seemed to suggest that the bomb had been particularly vicious with my sex.

# First Month: 1960

## JUNGLE VERSUS MAN

I realize now as I'm writing this that you may consider certain particulars unnecessary for delivering your verdict. But believe me, your judgment is not my only concern. I wish to write certain things down without taking you into consideration, perhaps to re-experience the events, or because way down at the bottom of my heart, I would like to be understood by someone who is far removed from revenge and close to deep human emotion. These personal details serve as my defense before the powers that be, a valid defense regardless of the punishment. There's also absolution. The absolution you aren't going to grant me, though I have faith that others may find it in themselves, if they ever read what I have written.

I remember the first time I slept with Jim. We weren't acquainted enough to spend an entire night in each other's arms without feeling awkward, though he clung to me, or I clung to him, with a kind of naturalness that comes only with the passage of time. I'd never felt that way with a near stranger. It was as though he required my full presence as he slept, my full attention, yet at the same time he was fully aware that this kind of intimacy comes only by way of affection, and though he wouldn't let me pull away from him, he held me so gingerly that I slept with an uncanny sense of autonomy. I came to associate his holding me that way with something he explained later on. One of the ways insanity would present itself among the prisoners on the *Oryoku Maru*, he said, had to do with how a prisoner would suddenly seize another and grope his face, his body, like a blind person from out of his darkness frantically trying to scrutinize the features of a loved one. It's something I also read in George Weller's ship chronicles. There were so many prisoners jammed into the compartments that most of them were forced to sit with someone else nestled between their legs and that person in front of them also had someone nestled between their legs, and so on in a herringbone pattern, and the excessive clutching and groping by the crazy ones resulted in the death of more than one of them. Jim never told me whether he had needed that type of contact or had avoided it however he could, but what matters is that when I learned about it, I reckoned that this particular way of clinging to me was his manner of holding on to life itself, to whatever still breathes in the blackness of night.

Most of the experiences Jim told me about took place after the war. He spoke about them distantly; not that the events hadn't affected him, but his tone of voice, his eyes, denoted the type of distance born from years of effort. The few things he shared with me about his experiences as a prisoner of the Japanese were conveyed from inside not only of his own suffering but of the suffering of everything he named. When he described a companion scratching his flea-ridden scalp, the story had implications far beyond the idea of a companion who wouldn't let him sleep; it included all that this single flea, and not another one, suffered during the onslaught of the soldier's fingernails in its struggle to survive. In a single sentence he declared the destruction of the world order, the vibrating strings of a violin—sheep guts to cat guts—conveying wave after wave of massacre, from the hand that wields the bow to the eardrum that receives the sound and repeats the chain of sorrow like a tolling bell.

The only points of reference I had for concentration camps were the Nazi camps. But I heard Jim say several times that he found the situation with the Japanese concentration camps more perverse, partly because of the lack of awareness about what had happened in them, since most people have paid exclusive attention to the pain of the Jewish people, relegating the Japanese victims to the worst agony peace can inflict: obliviousness. This obliviousness wasn't perpetrated by the enemy, but by the Allies themselves. I remember thinking about this so many years later when I read a plaque that had been placed above one of the ovens in Ebensee, a subcamp of Mauthausen, in Austria. There were a few verses written in German by the Austrian poet Peter Rosegger, which I jotted down in my notebook. Rosegger professed himself a friend of heat and light, so he asked to be incinerated and freed of the worm that in the earth penetrates the body:

> May no slimy worm
> Drag itself across my body someday!
> May the purest part of me be consumed
> Since my love for heat and light was constant
> Burn me, and don't bury me.

This is something the Austrian poet wrote from his love of life, his love of warmth and of light, being used as an adornment for horror. That plaque must have been read by countless eyes as the cadavers were being cast into the ovens, and regardless of who read it—Germans, Jews, homosexuals, or whoever else—the context allows only a single interpretation: the first-person narrator of the verse is begging for cremation. So ironically the last thing left to be taken from the prisoners about to be incinerated was removed: not their voices in life but their voices in death, foisting upon them the desire to be cremated beside the anonymous multitude. Placing these verses above the horror of the ovens was an act of perversion, as if trying to make it seem as though not only did the Jews accept their death, unafraid, but that they were asking for it, even offered justification for it. But as fate would have it, the unsought precedence of this despairing anonymous multitude unwittingly overshadowed another disgrace: the parallel atrocities committed during the Asian holocaust.

ON AUGUST 31, 1946, a little over a year after the first atomic bomb was dropped on my city, *The New Yorker* published a piece by John Hersey in which he presented the stories of six survivors about what the bomb had done to the city and to the flesh of its citizens. I was too young at that point and hardly knew English yet, so it wasn't until several years later—maybe ten, give or take a few—that I could actually read the text. When I finally did read it, I became obsessed with victims' testimonies, whether anonymous accounts or the ones recorded in documentaries. That's how I first realized that the recurring image I frequently went back to, of unrecognizable lumps of flesh forced to say their name in order to be identified, wasn't something I had made up on my own. The sharpest, most powerful images, those that I thought were strictly my own, in fact appeared again and again in other people's testimonies. I tried to explain it in the most logical terms possible. I thought perhaps the survivors were led to share the most effective expressions precisely because of how indescribable it all was, so in this way they forged a new syntax for horror: a brand-new language that was—unlike the ones passed down over the generations from parents to children—learned in one fell swoop and passed instead from one eyewitness to another. In this language, then, "a lump whose head is swollen to three times its size" can be expressed only as "a lump whose head is swollen to three times its size." There are no equivalent expressions. It's a language without synonyms.

I was able to glean information from the material published in North American reports about what happened on the plane that dropped the bomb while I was waiting at my desk for the teacher, and in the same way I now hoped to use the other testimonies to help fill in that empty space before I opened my eyes in the hospital. I needed to know what had been going on while I was unconscious. By gathering testimony of the fact that life had continued to move forward, I might recover the days I had spent unconscious—which is to say, dead. All the testimonies seemed to be speaking for me. Once I heard a woman describe how the wounded would wander among the dead asking their forgiveness. That's how I was brought up, feeling ashamed for having survived. The printing presses and newspapers removed the ideograms for *atomic bomb* and *radioactivity,* and the government avoided the use of the word *survivor,* it said, as a show of respect for the more than two hundred thousand fatalities. In Hersey's text I read that *hibakusha* means "explosion-affected persons." That's exactly what it meant, a term that skirted not only the pain but also the miracle of having survived. A three-letter word could have made all the difference: "persons affected by *the* explosion," not "persons affected by *an* explosion," as if it were any old garden-variety bang, like the tempura batter that splatters when the oil's too hot, or a birthday-party firecracker that explodes in a careless hand. That bomb was no accident. Hiroshima was THE explosion. In my head I conjured up some words that included the definite article *the,* which could better define what others call hibakusha. I decided that if forced to choose a name for us all, I would prefer "we who carry the bomb inside," because the morning that a B-29 bomber dropped Little Boy over Hiroshima was only the beginning of the detonation. Ninety percent of the wounds the survivors suffered would come in doses of radiation, minute by minute, month by month, year by year, impregnating us with this evil that could be aborted only if we obliviate ourselves with it. I imagined a backward big bang, where every hour on the hour another little piece of the universe shrunk (shrinks?) into my body, so that on any given day, who knows when, it will finally rupture once and for all.

———

The Japanese never respected the Geneva Convention on the treatment of prisoners of war signed on July 27, 1929. It's not so unusual as history would like us to believe. It's true that for the Japanese, who exalt suicide over surrender, the value of a prisoner who would want to remain alive was below that of a street rat. But the states that actually respected the convention, despite having signed it, were the exception. Surely you must be perfectly aware of that already. I didn't yet know when Jim explained the conditions he endured as a prisoner of war that destiny would tug me along by way of a string of fake international organizations to reach the crucial element for concluding this story. As the nursery rhyme goes, these treaties are like a spider's web on which an elephant balances precariously, and when that elephant sees how it holds up, he asks another elephant to join him until finally the web breaks for the weight of so many overfed, irresponsible elephants/states.

Before arriving in Manila to be boarded on the *Oryoku Maru*, Jim had already been the victim of noncompliance with the Geneva Convention. He was one of the Allied prisoners of war the Japanese used to build the Burma Railway, which like the *Oryoku Maru* boasted a well-earned moniker: Death Railway. On June 22,

1942, construction was begun with slave labor: some 190,000 Asian workers and 55,000 Allied POWs. The British had already contemplated a Thailand–Burma railway when they governed Burma, but the terrain was so hard going that it had never gotten under way. When the Japanese invaded Burma in 1942, they decided to tackle this project to strengthen their presence there, meaning they had to secure the supply of matériel, which by sea was extremely dangerous, since it exposed them to Allied submarine attacks. On the other hand, the sheer numbers of Chinese and Allied POWs obliged them to find new ways to keep them under control, and what better solution than to use them as slave labor in this colossal undertaking.

The first 1,414 POWs died in record time, coinciding with the construction of 258 miles of tracks and eight steel bridges. This period was called the Speedo, though I'm not sure whether that was because of how fast the railway was built or how quickly those constructing it died. I have to check some of these statistics against the notes I took, as a faithful lover of one of those prisoners. But most of that data has somehow remained seared in my memory. I suppose it's just one more contradiction the war triggered in me, that I could never memorize a telephone number but the sinister statistics of fallen ranks were somehow burned right into my brain. I don't think my memory betrays me here. Not a single death more, not a single death less, the excruciating exactitude of my memory thanks to the bomb. The scrupulous mathematics of one corpse atop another.

Work in an environment like the Burmese jungle was gruesome. The Death Railway can be considered World War II's largest concentration camp, the tracks of which basically cut across the entire country. A very long, skinny concentration camp, one that destroyed over two hundred thousand lives, superseded in its destructive power only by Auschwitz. The jungle conditions were nearly as awful as the treatment by the Japanese officers. Sixteen-to twenty-hour days in sweltering heat and humidity and monsoon rains; suffering from tropical ulcers and incurable diseases, plagued by mosquitoes, snakes, and fleas; enduring dysentery, malnutrition, torture, and cholera. The jungle versus man, a conflict to see which could be more lethal. There were also numerous casualties due to airstrikes by Allied forces who couldn't distinguish the camps where their own people were interned. But at times the jungle and man came together to form alliances in which the jungle offered trees and men the idea of crucifixion. One of the few rites the Japanese took from Western tradition; as in Roman times, crucifixion became a habitual form of torture. A few crucified prisoners, Jim told me, held out as long as fourteen days because the Japanese kept giving them just enough water and food to prolong their suffering. The torture extended to the other workers, who were forced to listen to their companion screaming in agony.

THE PEACE THAT CAME after Hiroshima's destruction brought a sense of hope and promise. Surely you understand that I was a gullible adolescent then, and that's what I wanted to believe. How far I've come from that credulity, that youthful ability not only to forgive but to forget. I imagine resentment is a gene that comes into play like a survival instinct, the same as other necessary mechanisms such as the desire for copulation. A gene that activates over time and only under specific circumstances. Yet animals live resentment-free. Our capacity for annihilation has become so great that it has planted a sentiment in us that is meant to keep us from falling prey to ourselves: our ability to exterminate. I'm not privy to the mysteries of genetics. But at some point along the way humans have become absurd creatures. Our genome is made of negative genes melded with positive ones. Before we've spent even two decades on earth, that contaminated information becomes rooted and can never be changed. It's all fused together inside and we can't separate the good from the bad.

As I said, the youngest of us were able to rustle up a new sense of hope. Twenty-five girls were chosen after the war to travel to the United States for reconstructive plastic surgery, in an attempt to mitigate the disfiguring effects of the bomb. They were called the Hiroshima Maidens. I was jealous of them. I followed their every move on television, I watched them exit the airplane, demurely, heads lowered, welcomed with bouquets of flowers in a country that was trying to return the smiles it had just ripped off their faces. I wanted them to choose me, though they would never have admitted me. Yet the images of those twenty-five maidens encouraged me to start saving my money. So I salted away all the money I was given, and once I reached employment age, I worked as many hours as I could, thinking of all the operations I would eventually pay for myself. A few basic facial touch-ups, but more significant, the reconstruction of my genitals.

Many years later, I still bear some of those scars. You'll see them when I turn myself in. Without makeup. Like the gummy red keloid scar on my cheek in the shape of Africa. The bomb branded Africa onto my face. Who would ever have thought that a continent I'd thought so little about in my life, a place so radically different from where I was born, would become the place of Jim's hopes and mine for such a long time. Africa was on my face, yes, and I was enclosed within its contours and tucked away in this borrowed cabin while I write this, my last testament.

The scar, being so visible, was a constant source of problems at first. For a long time such scars were unmistakable in Japan. Because of them, and because people were afraid of radiation sickness, survivors became outcasts. Nobody would hire us, and the marriage agencies, which arranged many matches back then, rejected survivors looking for a husband or wife because everyone took it for granted that our children would be born with defects. I remember when my cousin was pregnant. Instead of swelling, her belly began to shrink in her sixth month. It was as if her womb decided to rethink the whole thing and started taking steps backward from fetus to sperm and finally that much-longed-for flatness prior to gestation.

AT FIFTEEN, I was adopted by a family and finally landed in the occupying country, as if the bomb and I were two arms of the same boomerang on its way back to the hand that had thrown it. My new friends at school wanted to be football players, astronauts, and teachers. All I wanted was to be a grandmother, but the doctors told me the effects of radiation would eventually manifest themselves, likely sooner rather than later. Besides the elective surgical procedures, I underwent others that were life-and-death, and even today I still come down with new illnesses. I've learned how to let them in the door silently, cup of tea in hand, as serene as if each one were the last. I welcomed all illnesses except one: infertility, the absence that took my womb like a presence. A loss as real as the iron purged from my body with every menstruation, periods that ceased only to come back a few years later with no medical explanation one way or the other. Loss, the negated child, showed up between my legs; in panties that for months or years showed not a trace of blood, or the opposite, a red, saturated sanitary napkin flushed down the stygian drain into which the dead and the unborn disappear in equal measure.

This absence was the perfect ground for a maternal instinct to flourish once I met Jim, and the search for his daughter substituted for the absence of my son. I seized on his daughter as if she were my own. I absorbed every detail Jim gave me of her story and retained it in my memory as if I had lived it out myself. So even though I may not have experienced it, I still remembered it, and that memory was like a suction cup on my brain's wall. It held up the memory of Jim's daughter—my daughter—and maintained it firmly, the way the pads of a lizard's feet fasten onto the wall so it doesn't fall off into the void. That was all I had for a long time. The void.

# Second Month: 1963

## DEATH FORGOT MY HOUR

I convinced Jim to take the search for his daughter to Japan, a country I'd been back to only twice, a country he'd never wanted to return to, and where—he said—he didn't expect to receive any help with our research. But I had a hard time understanding why he hadn't begun his research at what I assumed was the beginning.

We took a direct flight to Tokyo, the city where Yoro had been delivered into his care by American occupation forces on May 7, 1950, though according to her birth certificate she had been born sixteen days earlier, on April 22. The provisional military hospital where they'd done the exchange was closed down eleven years later, and by the time we arrived, it had become a wing of the Tsukiji Fish Market, Tokyo's biggest. The demand for nourishment on the part of the living had imposed itself, though not without the customary forgiveness the Japanese always beg of the dead. So a sort of respect governed all movement, all sounds in the market, as if a death cult were imbuing the fish's blood with sacred significance in the last few seconds of its life.

Having grown accustomed to my adopted country, I could appreciate some of the differences between how Jim's mind worked and my own in the way the produce in the Japanese market was presented. The fish in Tsukiji were arranged into sections according to species. On one side, the sayori, or halfbeak, and on the other, salmon. There were great green areas with countless varieties of seaweed. Occasionally a whale loaded on a truck would pass by. The way the produce was arranged in the Tokyo market made it seem like a museum, while American markets are arranged more like bazaars. And the distinctive ways of sorting content seemed to mirror the ways in which Jim and I were so different. I remember an English tourist who approached us once to ask Jim a question, obviously because he looked Western. Before walking away, he mentioned he'd overheard us speaking and congratulated Jim on his Japanese. It wasn't the first time someone had made a comment like that, and it always made me laugh because Jim and I communicated in a sort of pidgin. What the tourist heard wasn't really Japanese, but a sort of mangled language that nevertheless allowed Jim to communicate, more for the worse than for the better, in both English and Japanese. But I quit laughing when I realized how this in-between language had become a reflection of the mental limbo that both of us lived in sometimes.

At the outset, we simply didn't understand each other. Not that we didn't get along just fine. It had nothing to do with cultural differences; it was more as if our brains shared the same evolutionary stratum, but from two different planets. What might have led me into a grilling of or an argument with someone else, with Jim became a hesitation, a respectful deferral to another form of intelligence, and I would resign myself to that detachment, which I could stand for one vital reason: despite everything, we understood each other in bed from the get-go, because as you'll soon come to see, my experiences in bed are always foreshadowed by a *despite everything*.

I finger through one of my notebooks from that time. These notebooks are the only things that have followed me everywhere.

My memory. I pasted a photo of an Edo period painting on the cover. It's a whale hunt. The water must be red. But the reddened sea fades out gracefully; otherwise it would overwhelm the ocher tones of the coast. Seeing this painting reminds me of something Jim always used to say: in Japan the beauty of varnish conceals the rotten wood they use to build the homes. I granted him that, even from the hybrid state that is my identity. But I'm not glossed over with varnish. My face, all my scars, they show exactly what I am. Nothing can match the bomb for candor. The shade of the color of the kill in the Edo period painting was softened so as to temper the contrasts, but the bomb acted naturally. It revealed the hues of the whale's blood in a red-stained sea as if to say: I am the true paintbrush, the one with uranium bristles.

The rest of the notebooks on the table have gray covers. There's something else that distinguishes Hiroshima survivors. It's a sound I hear every time I see this particular shade of gray, a sort of synesthetic effect. It's in the voice, that distinctive voice of the hibakushas. While not every survivor bears the marks of the explosion on his or her skin, all of them have it in their voice. We all sound alike: we speak in a kind of cropped tone, jagged and with stretch marks, as if some dead person were clawing at a white sheet trying to rip through it to be born again. I think it's why I associate the voice of survivors with the color gray, the hue of white skin that goes ashen, the shade of inert dust advancing toward life. Something that's neither white nor black, neither dead nor alive.

I remember people telling me about those first days after the bomb, when I lay in the ruins of what had been the hospital, how people could be seen shuffling around with outstretched arms. They'd been blinded and were trying not to stumble over other survivors, though even the ones who could still see held their scorched and gummy arms out to keep them from sticking to their bodies. They weren't the living dead, but the living dying. They used canola oil, the kind used for cooking, to alleviate the burns. When that was gone, the survivors with enough strength would make their way to the train station to milk the cars like cows for the black motor oil, thick and pasty; they'd plaster it all over their faces or bodies, blackening the red blisters and the black of their charred skin.

Being in Tokyo again brought all of it back, all these images I'm describing returning as fresh as the newly delivered fish at the Tsukiji market. I jotted things down in my notebooks—impressions, descriptions that I could draw on now—but even if I was to lose these notes, I think I'd be able to re-create them anew, word for word, not because my memory is so precise, but because my senses react to these memories the same way now as they did then. I mean, I could write in these same notebooks for the first time, over and over again. Time's fish never rots in my memory. That was Tokyo. The city we re-encountered was like a huge fresh-smelling tuna that took the edge off our appetites but never actually provided nourishment. The harder Jim and I looked for Yoro, the tighter things closed around us. And so the fish's scales constricted into a slick airtight surface that slipped from our hands. Jim was right; we'd never find a lead there. Tokyo closed its doors to us; in fact it never even let us glimpse the doors.

As often happens when one is just starting out on an undertaking, before one's strength begins to flag, I had such a surfeit of energy that it clouded my ability to distinguish between fact and fancy. Since Jim had launched this endeavor much earlier than I did, he was in that place where exhaustion forced him to prioritize and conserve energy. Be that as it may, it was during this trip that the link was created between my own maternity and the search for Jim's daughter. Locating her offered the greatest chance life had manifested thus far to actually make me a mother. So the daughter of the man I'd fallen in love with at first sight also became mine, with the simplicity and truth of things that don't need an explanation. I was twenty-eight years old. He was quite a bit older. Both of us were old enough to know what we wanted.

Of course Jim knew from the start that he had been given custody of the baby only temporarily. He knew from the first time he held her in his arms that the clock was ticking toward the day she'd turn five and he'd have to give her back, no questions asked, knowing he'd never see her again. It had all been put in writing, as if the girl were a military report. Jim would be her first foster parent, and each subsequent family would know the circumstances from the get-go; Yoro would stay for the same fixed five-year period.

Yet the proscribed detachment didn't work as easily as planned, not with Jim and not—as I later came to discover—with some of the other foster families. I suppose Jim's stretch was one of the most painful but also the most beautiful in Yoro's life: a baby's first days, when she eats and grows thanks entirely to you, and the transformation, the metamorphosis from baby to little girl. Jim was never one for sharing emotional details, but every once in a while he'd let one escape in the middle of a conversation. He'd express himself with a kind of strained reserve, yet the substance of his narrative was always powerful and his subdued tone never undercut the strength of his emotion. He told me once about a night he'd gotten out of bed to soothe Yoro in her crib. He had scooped her in his arms and given her a bottle. But Yoro wouldn't be pacified. Jim spent half an hour trying to get her to suck the milk. She simply wouldn't take the bottle. Jim snuggled her in closer to his chest. He slept bare-chested in his underclothing, and while he was trying to calm her, the baby's mouth fastened onto his nipple. He was about to pull it out of the baby's mouth when he realized she was finally quiet. She slumbered and suck-led peacefully. He understood maternity in a flash and didn't care that he hadn't gestated the baby, because the contact with a mouth that wasn't hungry for milk but for human warmth was all it took to turn him into a mother.

The mission papers he had signed stated that Yoro had but one father and one mother: the army. The army, as we all know, has nipples too; it's just that they point inward. The army is a body that doesn't nurture, like a dog that instead of suckling her puppies saps the litter's strength. Jim had an impeccable military record, and from what he told me, he'd participated in other missions that had wiped him out. It's what made him such a good candidate for Yoro. But twenty-four hours was all it took to undermine an entire career as an anonymous military man. What he first accepted as just another mission quickly morphed into his worst fear. From the first day he knew it would be difficult to give Yoro up. From the second, he knew it would be nothing short of impossible.

Jim had already been looking for Yoro for five years by the time we met, and at that point she must have been around ten years old. He had been court-martialed for refusing to hand her over, but the trial was set aside because of the military's desire to keep the case under wraps. He was discharged from the armed forces for disobeying orders that forbade him from establishing an emotional bond with the baby, to avoid his wanting to keep custody of her, as of course happened. So his crime was disobeying a ridiculous order, the kind that resists being given, let alone carried out: an emotional one.

From one day to the next, Jim found himself deprived of both Yoro and a military career. But he still had friends, and thanks to them he found a string of clues that he worked down one by one for a long time, including documents proving that the girl had been given to a family in the United States. When we met in New York, he was nearing the end of his painstaking investigation, which culminated two years later with our trip to Tokyo. Yoro's foster family, or at least the last one we could find out about, was living in New Mexico. Who could have imagined my setting foot in a place like that: Los Alamos, the exact spot where the first atomic bomb had been developed and the Manhattan Project secretly coordinated.

WE LANDED IN LOS ALAMOS to call on the National Laboratory in July 1963, thanks to Jim's contacts. It was sweltering, and I couldn't help but connect that heat with the atomic bomb tests that took place that same time of year, in that same enclave. It was here that the thirty-eight-year-old Robert Oppenheimer received General Leslie Groves's proposal to head a team of the world's most brilliant scientists, nearly all of them older than he was. Jim went into detail about that mission, one of history's best-kept secrets: the race with the Germans to see who could develop the first atomic bomb.

Oppenheimer agreed to oversee the project. Nearly all of them stepped up to the challenge. Scientists and military men worked day and night shut away in that reserve, their sole obsession to find a way to bring their theoretical formulations into reality. And to do it before the enemy did. The team was highly motivated. At first the atmosphere there was something like a summer camp. It was a race, after all, and not just any old race—here the most competitive, brightest athletes were poised for a sprint. When genius is challenged to outperform genius, not even the knowledge that the result will be the creation of a monster is enough to make it stand down. Intelligence gets restless once it's engaged, eager, and ethical considerations are not going to dampen the pleasure of discovery, of cracking a highly complex problem. The opportunity to extend the very limits of the mind trumped any moral quandary.

Initially the scientists and the military clashed over ethical and political issues, but the day they found out the Germans were nowhere close to developing nuclear weapons and that surrender was imminent, it became obvious that their disagreements were only superficial. The scientists had been tasked with beating the Germans in building the most destructive weapon known to man, but had just lost their purpose. From that point on, all that mattered was how to create the monster, not in order to destroy the other one but only to see its face, to give birth to it, and unbeknownst to them at the time, to christen it among so many Japanese civilians. So Colonel Boris Pash, commander of the Alsos Mission in charge of investigating the Nazis' atomic weapons program, sent a telegram to General Groves in November 1944. I haven't had a chance to check the exact wording, but according to Jim, the telegram read something like "Mom didn't have a baby; she's not even pregnant; the doctors have declared her sterile." Germany's infertility, the fact that it was incapable of developing the bomb, left the race uncontested, wide open for the minds at Los Alamos, and winning was no longer a matter of peace but one of war. Robert Oppenheimer expressed himself after the first Trinity tests by quoting the Bhagavad Gita, a sacred Hindu text: "Now I am become death, the destroyer of worlds."

So here we are now, in Los Alamos, knocking at a stranger's door to ask after Jim's daughter, my daughter. "To catch a glimpse of her," Jim said as we drove, "just to know she's alive, that she's healthy and happy, that's all I need."

A blond woman with a sophisticated hairdo opened the door. I felt like a beggar. Surely this family was part of the same operation, expected to raise their girl without ever bonding. They probably went through the same range of emotions as Jim did. And I wasn't far from the truth. Three minutes later we were sitting in the living room, on the family couch, and the woman was telling us that Yoro was no longer with them. They'd already come and taken her away. She gave us information on her whereabouts, but it wasn't very reliable, she warned. Alcohol had debilitated her to such a degree that she lacked the strength for what could only be an impossible search—how could she or her husband find someone the military was trying to keep hidden? But she talked at great length about a project her husband had been working on before he was retired. It was called Project Orion, and she spoke excitedly, saying it'd been the only beautiful thing to come out of all those years in the industry of death.

She said her husband had worked in Los Alamos with Stanisław Marcin Ulam, the Polish mathematician who first presented the project in 1946, which the physicist Freeman J. Dyson went on to develop at General Atomics, the nuclear physics center in San Diego, keeping the dream alive even today, despite the naysayers. For most of the team, Orion was about salvation: how to avoid the extinction of the human race if it came to having to evacuate the planet. Then, as now, there was no means for reaching the distances needed to find habitable environments in space. So Orion was based on nuclear propulsion systems for spaceships that could outlast the fuel insufficiencies of chemical rockets and travel longer interplanetary distances. A series of atomic bombs were placed at the rear of a vessel so that the ripple effects of consecutive explosions could propel the craft into speeds reaching up to a considerable percentage of the speed of light. Taking into account that the human body cannot withstand prolonged periods of acceleration beyond 49 m/s$^2$, scientists calculated the number of atomic bombs it would take to reach a viable escape speed with thrust enough to punch through the earth's gravitational field. Their conclusion was two to four bombs per second, which would initially require one thousand atomic bombs only to keep it out of orbit. Most of this information, she said, had been classified as top secret in 1959. The radioactive element strontium 90 had been found in the baby teeth of children living near the nuclear test sites, and the global population was taking a stand against the arm's race and nuclear energy, just as Project Orion was proposing not a single bomb but thousands of them. And this led to another immeasurable danger, details of which could be found in the reports: alternative ways of producing nuclear materials on the cheap. Access to this intelligence could allow any country to produce atomic weapons en masse and cheaply. That's why most of the project had been kept secret aside from the relatively trivial details the woman gave, which were declassified.

Then the woman offered a more personal perspective. To her, the project meant that for once the devil's artifact that is the atomic bomb might find a positive purpose: to pluck a handful of humans away from this inhumane planet. Though she didn't number among the select few fortunate enough to abandon Earth, it was enough to know that someone would be given the chance to start anew in some faraway place, and with time our planet would turn into that blue globe people pointed at as a symbol of well-deserved abandonment. Now that she was a recluse in a world where the only thing that didn't look phony was death, Project Orion became the only outlet for her fantasy. Mateo de Paz, a close friend of her husband's, would call on them from time to time; he was one of the most lucid scientists at San Diego's General Atomics. She thought his name, de Paz (meaning *peace* in Spanish), was yet another beautiful reason for using the bomb as an instrument of survival and not of murder. She slept with him several times because of that name, and because it put her in touch with her Mexican origins. But it happened only after the treaty came along that shattered her dreams of evacuation, the so-called Partial Test Ban Treaty, or Treaty Banning Nuclear Weapon Tests in the Atmosphere, in Outer Space and Under Water. A long name she'd never forgotten.

Orion dwindled away after that, once they'd prohibited nuclear testing. I thought about her again when I read an article by Freeman J. Dyson in *Science* magazine titled "Death of a Project." What caught my attention was how Dyson had highlighted something not typically associated with the aims of the atomic bomb: the opportunity to redeem humankind, to counterbalance what the bombs had done to Hiroshima and Nagasaki. According to my notes, he wrote:

It is perhaps wise that radical advances in technology, which may be used both for good and for evil purposes, be delayed until the human species is better organized to cope with them. But those who have worked on Project Orion cannot share this view. They must continue to hope that they may see their work bear fruit in their own lifetimes. They cannot lose sight of the dream which fired their imaginations in 1958 and sustained them through the years of struggle afterward—the dream that the bombs which killed and maimed at Hiroshima and Nagasaki may one day open the skies to mankind.

Jim and I had arrived late, but at least we had a new lead that, even if uncertain, was nevertheless better than nothing. Hope was what kept all of Yoro's parents clutching at straws. But the best part of the visit was seeing photos of Yoro from her time with them. It allowed Jim to fill in the gaps, at least about her physical appearance. Apparently Yoro had had a difficult time adapting to them the first few months. She had missed her father. Being told as much was a precious gift for Jim, though back in the car he admitted it made him feel selfish; it would have been so much better for Yoro if she hadn't missed him, yet he was relieved to know she remembered him. He repaid the woman's kindness by showing her a few photos he kept in his wallet. Yoro as a newborn. Yoro at two. At three. Just before she left. Between the two of them, they composed the most current image of Yoro possible, given the circumstances.

You'll probably have asked yourself by now, several times,

why that woman considered looking for Yoro a lost cause too, why they were hiding her at all, and why at best we could track only the girl's itinerary, but never her present location. It was like some macabre race to pick up body parts scattered over a variety of geographical locations and put them together again in the hopes of bringing Yoro back to life with the final piece, the most important one, the one it seemed we would never locate before the worms had liquefied it forever. The clues seemed valuable at the time, but now I know they were just gold-plated distractions whose bogus sparkle only sidetracked us and kept us from searching for what was essential. I've even suspected we were purposefully fed false leads to slow us down, to keep us distracted and thinking that our research was actually bearing fruit. But this is all speculation on my part. I could answer the other questions too, but things wouldn't be clear for you yet, so for the time being, allow me to keep you waiting. This delay is necessary, because what you'll have found out by the time you finish reading is so hard to explain that you'd never put the pieces together unless I dole out the information gradually, allowing meaning to collect in your consciousness over time, eventually catching fire in an instant when you finally understand what can only be comprehended over time.

SO I LEARNED JIM'S STORY slowly but surely. He too fed me the information a little at a time. I'm convinced that if he hadn't gauged carefully what he told me about himself, I probably wouldn't have remained at his side. I had always figured I would fall in love with someone a little less weather-beaten than me, whose ingenuousness would help ease the weight of my own life's story. I thought if I had a preference for one type of man over another, it was the kind who had experienced little pain. So each time Jim went into his past, I would stare back silently, trying to conceal my surprise over having fallen in love with him. And I was so good at hiding my feelings that I think it would have been hard for him to identify my surprise, but still I worried that he'd realize how I felt by the expression on my face.

Sometimes an object would spur a memory and Jim would go into the details of the story. Once the object was a bicycle. Jim had always seemed to retreat into himself when he watched people riding their bikes in Central Park, enjoying a bit of exercise. One day as we were just strolling along, Jim opened up about his time working on the railway in Burma.

Neither he nor his companions had been equipped to survive the Burmese jungle. The working conditions—he assured me—were worse than combat. Besides their tanks and their weapons, the Japanese employed something else: a perfectly pacific mode of transportation meant for recreation. Slowly but surely, though, a capillary system for the blood of war was built with them: bicycles. I came to realize over time just how obsessed Jim was with bicycles. I imagined it was because of how inconspicuously they can move while still being speedy and agile. The Japanese used them to haul artillery over difficult terrain. But they had become more than just a means for transport. Having survived not only forced labor and torture but also episodes of malaria, diphtheria, dysentery, and beriberi, Jim prized the ease of the cyclist, who was always moving forward, and the idea became a fixation: a wheel moving forward toward the end of the war. At night, on edge though trying to sleep despite the humidity and mosquitoes, the diarrhea and vomiting—whether on his part or someone else's—he'd fantasize about a bike that would suddenly materialize and carry him away.

Daydreams like this were a common diversion among the prisoners, which brings me back to something Jim had fixated on nearly as obsessively as bicycles. At least a dozen times or more, he talked about ways the prisoners would alleviate the torture of hunger by exchanging recipes the way kids swap baseball cards. They'd hand them around from person to person, salivating while trading them off, as if they were real food. But just as Jim's escape bike was imaginary, the recipes were simply pieces of paper, at best with some flakes of color left on a few of them. Yet both of these objects of desire, the wheels and the inky ingredients, provided nourishment if not for the body, then for the imagination, which is what allowed my man to leave that jungle alive.

His stories made it easier for me to get a handle on some of Jim's quirks, the phobias that didn't necessarily bother me, but that I could acknowledge more affectionately once I understood where they were coming from. Spaghetti Bolognese sent Jim into a panic. Because I knew that, of course I never prepared that dish at home, but Jim would literally tremble if someone at a nearby table ordered it when we ate out. Since recipes were their escape valve, what kept their minds off the horrors of the jungle, sometimes they became the source of fights. There were rules to how they could be swapped. One of the rules was that they couldn't swap duplicate recipes—when energy flags, so does imagination, and so individuality was paramount for stimulating a person's ability to pretend. Uniqueness activates the competitive urge, the risk-taking, and even the desire to play, all of which are synonymous with life. But the game, when played by dehydrated, starving men, could become a sort of hallucination, and the prisoners would get into scrapes, bite and maim each other like a cageful of famished dogs fighting over a piece of meat. Jim told me about an incident that grew out of one of the star recipes, the most disputed: spaghetti Bolognese. Despite hailing from several different culinary cultures, apparently this particular blend of pasta, meat, and tomatoes was a favorite, and they fought like animals over it. Finally, one of the spaghetti recipe brawls ended in two deaths. Hallucinating from starvation, one of the prisoners attacked the spent bodies of his companions, whose meat was as red as the pasta that started the fracas in the first place.

Another time in Central Park, Jim told me why he was so afraid of saunas. Whenever one of the prisoners committed a brutal act, the lucid ones took it upon themselves to end the life of whoever had gone berserk. That way the Japanese could never mistake the prisoner for an animal or objectify him as a thing and torture him. It was better to end their comrade's life quickly and not be forced to cope with the dying man's screaming, the agony of an inevitable death spread out over days. The sweatboxes were the worst of all, because death took its sweet time in them. Because these were located right beside the barracks, the prisoners who had to work sixteen- or eighteen-hour shifts couldn't get any sleep thanks to the shrieking and laments at night. The sweatboxes were a form of solitary confinement, and the instant a person was in one, he began to sweat. The materials they were made of and the fact that they were hermetically sealed to keep the heat in meant that the victims would dehydrate within minutes and slowly begin to roast, as in an oven. Even many years later, Jim still couldn't enter a sauna. He couldn't fathom how anyone could derive pleasure from spending time in one of them; the torture boxes had filled with meaning all the spaces meant for sweating.

THE BRITISH ARTIST Jack Bridger Chalker drew portraits of his comrades while he was a prisoner in Burma. Jim had told me about him, but it was never clear whether they'd known each other personally. I had never asked if Chalker had painted Jim's portrait; somehow it seemed inappropriate given the collective suffering that had taken place there. But when the portraits were published some years later and I could see their faces for the first time, distinguish their true features, their gestures and wrinkles and folds, the distinctive characteristics that represented suffering on an individual scale instead of the collective, I didn't ask Jim if he was there but looked for him all the same, thumbing quickly through the book several times.

One sketch was of a standing man tied to two bamboo rods that seemed thicker than they usually do in contrast to the prisoner, who was skin and bones. A pail with what looked like a metal handle hung around the man's neck, and looking at this image, one had to question whether the guards had placed the pail that way so the victim, weakened by illness, could vomit all the more easily, or if instead the pail was of itself an instrument of torture due to its contents, which we couldn't see.

Another one of the drawings showed an ulcerous foot corroded to the bones and with pus encasing the tendons. Tropical ulcers, I heard or read, were caused by bacteria in the dirt, microorganisms that ate through flesh like acid. A scratch was enough for these invisible termites to rush in.

Another illustration that stunned me was one in which several prisoners, mouths wide open, were gathered inside a canvas tent. It looked as though they were treating one another's canker sores, and from the black oval of one of their mouths issued the screams of all the rest. That drawing too still sparks a memory of synesthesia between sight and hearing, a drawing in pencil and watercolor that penetrates my ears like an agony or lamentation.

My mind inevitably returns to the Geneva Convention whenever I think about these images, and the articles on the treatment of prisoners of war. Jim gave me a copy of it. The contrast between what Jim lived through and the articles of the convention makes me feel as powerless as when I face up to my own experiences before comparable humanitarian agreements. Going through these articles is more than just reading a checklist of what wasn't respected; it also outlines what was nullified by the process of objectifying prisoners, stripping them of any trace of their humanity. Let me quote from a few of these articles here, chosen at random. You'll see that between parentheses I offer examples of noncompliance according to Jim's experiences. May I remind you that this is but one example of how such treaties have been violated? Consider it one more piece of the puzzle that shapes my revenge once it's put together. In the end everyone will see it as plainly as a photograph.

### ARTICLE 2

"Prisoners of war . . . shall at all times be humanely treated and protected, particularly against acts of violence, from insults and from public curiosity." (Jim wasn't treated like a human being or even a sentient animal, but like a bacterium under the microscope of a curious biologist prodding it in order to observe mutations, mutilations, and death. He told me how every once in a while a guard would pass by and tell a prisoner to kneel down and open his mouth. The guard would spit in it. If the prisoner swallowed the sputum without contorting his face in disgust, the guard would continue on his way; otherwise he would slit his throat.)

### ARTICLE 9

"Prisoners captured in districts which are unhealthy or whose climate is deleterious to persons coming from temperate climates shall be removed as soon as possible to a more favorable climate." (Hundreds of prisoners died as a consequence of diseases either directly or indirectly derived from the jungle climate. Their transferal was never considered, since they had been sent precisely to that place to work.)

"Belligerents shall as far as possible avoid bringing together in the same camp prisoners of different races or nationalities." (The Japanese mixed the prisoners on purpose, forcing them to attack each other like fighting dogs.)

## ARTICLE 11

"The food ration of prisoners of war shall be equivalent in quantity and quality to that of the depot troops. . . . All collective disciplinary measures affecting food are prohibited." (The prisoners had to kill and eat rats, lizards, and worms in order to survive. All they were given to eat was one fist-sized ball of rice per day.)

"Sufficient drinking water shall be supplied to them. The use of tobacco shall be authorized. Prisoners may be employed in the kitchen." (The prisoners had to break the stems of certain plants to drink their sap. When they were given water their captors would throw pails of it at their faces to watch how the prisoners licked one another to fight the thirst.)

## ARTICLE 30

"The duration of the daily work of prisoners of war, including the time of the journey to and from work, shall not be excessive and shall in no case exceed that permitted for civil workers of the locality employed on the same work. Each prisoner shall be allowed a rest of twenty-four consecutive hours each week, preferably on Sunday." (It was a forced labor camp; there was no time of rest, let alone twenty-four hours' worth.)

WHETHER JIM WAS OR WASN'T in Jack Bridger Chalker's drawings is irrelevant now, but they proved something he'd said to me over and over again: "When the time came, death passed me by." The idea gave him an aura of divine protection that people noticed. Jim truly lived as if death had missed its date with him. We'd been spending time in a natural reserve close to the Canadian border when I received a call that they'd seen the small Cessna Jim and a friend were flying in crash on the far side of the lake.

We sped along following the trail of metal debris and charred shell, and I was ordered to remain in the jeep so as not to break down at the crash site. But there was Jim, trying to stitch up a spooked buffalo whose neck had gotten caught in a barbed-wire fence. The same thing happened every time misfortune came sniffing around. Either the whole lot got off scot-free or the bad luck touched someone else, and Jim would say, "Don't worry. Like I said, Death forgot my hour." Jim was seventeen years older than me, but he was still active and I never cared much for that image he conjured of the Grim Reaper as some absentminded creature. As it turns out, Death had not forgotten about him entirely. Or maybe I should say that Death, who certainly hadn't forgotten about me, held off just long enough for us to get to know each other so that by taking him it could kill me once again, just like that, once more, time and time again.

Whatever the case may be, back then all I wanted was to believe everything he said, to trust that he would live forever. Maybe that's the origin of a recurring dream I still have. I'm in a room with a big window. I have a book in my hand, but instead of reading it, I'm amusing myself by watching a bird in a cage. It hops from one branch to another, in that nervous way caged birds have. I observe it calmly for a few minutes. Then suddenly something happens. The bird has fallen to the bottom of the cage, where it's trembling and convulsing. So I grab the cage and run outside to look from door to door for help—a veterinarian, someone, anyone. Each person sends me on to someone else, and I keep searching, getting more and more desperate, dashing here and there, and I can see the bird is suffering. Finally someone promises me that there's a person who can help at the house on the other side of the street, but as I cross the street, a car hits me. I fall to the ground and watch as the cage is propelled into the air and the door pops open and the bird flies out safe and sound, spreading its wings at the same exact moment my heart stops beating. Jim used to say that he's the soul that leaves the body at death. Only in his case he keeps returning to the same body in time to link the last heartbeat to the new one, which becomes the first in the chain of a new existence. If only it had been that way, the eternal pulse of a free bird.

Now, how could my dreams be of any consequence to you? As I already said, I'm writing this in the faith that someone else might read it without judging me. Who knows what those specialists in forensic psychiatry will make of my dreams? Am I innocent or guilty? It's the luck of the draw when the evaluating psychiatrist won't admit that today we still can't categorize a psyche. But I know my case won't be given to any psychiatrist, something I'm actually grateful to you for. Don't think I've forgotten my fate is now in your hands—that only days remain, maybe hours, before you find me here in this cabin, this refuge where I write, undoubtedly sentenced to death, but still surrounded by life, water, beasts, vegetation.

———

I've had to look for so many things. Yoro was certainly the most precious of them all, but I'd already begun a journey of my own when I met Jim, to find other people like me who didn't feel comfortable with the ongoing notions of sexual categories. Labels made me feel as though I were being stuffed into a corset cut to fit another person, or wearing a rubber suit that made moving a hassle and required a huge amount of effort to remove. I felt good stripped bare—I mean, as a non-category—but my neutral status was never enough for people, because as you well know, affixed to the bottle of formaldehyde containing a specimen of each species of creature, there has to be a label. The problem is that labels inevitably convey an air of reassurance simply for being accepted as such and printed out in ink. Sometimes I think this is the only thing that organizes our social lives, some small group of people that bands together and is willing to pay for the letters naming their collective on jerseys and baseball caps. So there's no individuality, no space for being an outsider, since it costs too much to be a representative of one's own self. Being truly marginalized is when you don't even have a minority group to belong to. The world is composed of large minorities, but for a very long time I was radically on my own.

I remember the first vacation I took with my foster family. We went to London and spent a day in the Natural History Museum. We signed up for a guided tour of the museum's Darwin Centre, which admitted small groups of five people. Our group was made up of my American parents and sister, another visitor, and me, and we followed closely behind our guide, who was a biologist dressed in a white lab coat, to see some of the species that would later be absorbed into the wider collection. She led us to a rectangular station and closed the door. The smell of formaldehyde, of dissected death, permeated everything. It left a deep impression on me. I observed the shelves of thousands of tiny jars that the biologist said contained the simplest organisms she wanted to show us. Bacteria, invisible life-forms from the most minute to the largest, up to lichens or micro-insects. The successive rooms, always rectangular and particularly narrow, were arranged along a lengthy aisle separated by doors. And the smell intensified with each new space; as we moved along, the size of the jars increased because they were filled with larger and larger specimens. When we finally entered the room reserved for simians and I took one look at those nearly human faces preserved in fluid, the range of expressions on those faces, those hands like children's hands, I was hit with a sharp stitch of anxiety, the first panic attack of my life. My new family, the guide, the other visitor—none of them seemed to belong to the same species as me. I felt closer to any one of the animals trapped in their glass jars than to the ones observing them. That's when feverish thoughts took me over, the dread of identifying myself as a stranger in that group of humans. What if the biologist put me in one of those jars for the next group of tourists? The terror was so great that I shouted to be allowed to leave. Once I was outside, and while they tried to calm me with a glass of water, I couldn't help thinking that the incident had given me a bird's-eye view of my own despair: of the hundreds of thousands of specimens in the museum's collection, including the people I was there with, I identified with not a single one of them. The feeling of being a rarity in my species, a one-off, has accompanied me ever since, even now, when it's no longer my problem. What made it difficult was that my singularity made me invisible; I felt as though the only dignified thing about me was my absence.

These ideas about the presence of absence bring to mind my encounter with T, the first of a series of people I met who are as uncategorizable as me, and someone I never saw again. She must have been around twenty years old, and I met her on the second trip I took to Hiroshima after being adopted and carted off to the United States. Oddly enough, T declared herself asexual, and though asexuality is now considered a category, it remains a tenuous one. People have a hard time understanding absence. They're better at gauging what is excessive—overabundance, extravagant desire, a wild orgy. Hunger is assumed to be a lack of food, but few people get what it really is: a lack of something that is unreferenced, a hole that is full of hole. It's the same as asexuality, which people consider a lack of sexual desire, but not a thing in itself.

T wasn't injured by Little Boy, but by a different bomb: the rain. The thick black liquid that came down after the explosion. Everyone was drenched in it, and T, like the others, didn't think to protect herself. Nobody could imagine that the oily fluid, which some went so far as to drink, carried a bomb in each drop, like an assault rifle that shot invisible pellets of ulcers and cancer, and that would sprout one day strong as potatoes. What a spectacular ability it had to recycle itself. It went on like that for years; people were fine until suddenly they weren't. So the bomb wasn't entirely sincere: you could no longer distinguish the living from the dead by characteristics like appearance or movement. For the first six months following the explosion, T was as visibly healthy as she was silently dead. In the end she survived, though she traces the origin of her asexuality to that terrain of apathy, that field of in-difference between what is moving and what is static, what stands erect and sprouting on one side and what is limp and weak on the other. T said she lost her sexual appetite after the explosion. She was asexual in the most literal sense of the word. She felt close to other creatures that exist in nature like her, and whenever she would pronounce words like *jellyfish, starfish,* or *salamander,* something filled her mouth that I would say is akin to desire. So you see? Same as everyone else, maybe I'm incapable of seeing presence in no-desire.

———

Jim could never have imagined that after his experiences in the Burmese Death Railway and the *Oryoku Maru,* he'd be called to occupy the country responsible for torturing him. He would have preferred to go home, but there was nobody special waiting for him there, and in a way military life gave him a sense of belong-ing to a bigger picture where his presence was required. The truth is, he knew full well how dispensable he was, just the same as any other soldier, but he allowed himself to be persuaded by his commanders' spiel about the importance of individuals and found some relief in that—they'd won the war, after all, and there was no reason not to believe he'd had a hand in that himself. Might be true after all.

Jim was liberated in September 1945 by the North American

troops. The first contingent of occupying forces comprised 15,000 soldiers. Thousands more would join them over the next seven years. Jim was about as familiar with the Japanese mind-set as he could be, knowing how impossible that really was, but the Americans arriving in Japan now found themselves confronting a society they'd never before encountered. And they barely knew anything about the country. Sadao Araki, a general in Japan's imperial army, coined a slogan to describe his pride over the cultural differences between them and the invaders: "The sword is our steel Bible." Every image, every word, refuted the biblical traditionalism of the occupation forces by a people whose moral code was not circumscribed by sacred scriptures but by an imperial dynasty descended from the sun itself. Every element of the American way of life found its antithesis in Japan. My fathers, my brothers, they didn't need the words of some prophet when the heat of the sun could be felt across the continents, its power conveyed not through the ears but manifest through the skin itself, temperature as a physical, inarguable fact. The sun, the ball of fire illuminating the earth, belonged by birth to Japan alone, and my country felt itself the rightful proprietor of precepts that should extend, like rays of sunlight, across the globe. While the United States fought to expand its empire, Japan fought for the same cause but with a single difference: the North Americans justified themselves with weapons and speeches, while the Japanese only bore arms, since the fact that the sun rose every day was an authority beyond rhetoric.

Having known Jim, more than anything else having known love with Jim, turned me into a sponge that absorbed every piece of news, every story, every testimony of Japan's tragedy. Love for a foreigner is what got me interested in my own people's tragedy, since I'd been so broken by them before I met him that I'd probably have disentangled myself from my own roots, little by little. But once I met Jim, I started paying attention. I remember a government propaganda movie meant to describe the Japanese spirit that was sent to the North Americans in 1945. One of the descriptions had to do with the sun. According to the narration, the emperor, being a direct descendant of the sun, was the most brilliant, the tallest of them all, and his roles included president of the United States, prime minister of Great Britain, pope, archbishop of Canterbury, and head of the Russian Orthodox Church. Everything flowed from and was sustained by Emperor Hirohito. First-floor windows were closed when he walked down the street, the propaganda video explained, to shield houses from the radiation, as of a great star passing by. The difference between the American and the Japanese ways of thinking was evident. Though one thing remained clear: "We must try to understand Japan, since the Japanese and the Americans have been engaged in the closest of all possible relationships: war. And like it or not, we and the Japanese are doomed to remain friends for a long time."

These videos were meant to prepare the occupation troops for the years ahead. The first North Americans to land in Japan liberated their compatriots from the concentration camps and were horror-stricken at the sight of tortured bodies: the starving, the dying, and the dead. But the reaction was mitigated by what they learned of the suffering the Japanese civilians had endured. There were thousands of orphans wandering around, begging and thieving in the streets of Tokyo and other devastated cities. Food and water were scarce. Some ate sawdust for a daily ration of starch and their protein mainly came, at the behest of the government, from reptiles, rats, and insects. I heard the testimony once of a Japanese woman who lived through the occupation, Kitty Teraki, who said it had been impossible to survive on government rations. A professor tried to disprove this statement by refusing to buy anything on the black market. He died within a short time.

Another witness said the only task the living had for months was to bury the dead. The everlasting act of burial made a deep impression on me then, as it still does now. There are certain accounts one can't ever forget, whether direct or indirect. I remember a witness's narration of his feelings in a film recording of the Christmas Eve mass in Nagasaki's Urakami Cathedral in 1945. Everything around the cathedral had been destruction, wasteland, and death, but the angelic voices that rose inside the cathedral—he used that very word—created a sort of mirage in contrast to the desolation outside. Entering the cathedral, he saw women dressed in kimonos singing "Silent Night." Urakami, or St. Mary's, had been built in 1875 thanks to the robust presence of Christians living in the area, and it was totally destroyed by the atomic bomb in Nagasaki. It had originally been built at a time when the persecution of Christians came to an end. The sight of the women's serene faces, their kimonos as unsoiled as circumstances allowed, and the sound of their voices that Christmas Eve melded two different prototypes of martyr together, according to Daniel Machover: those who lost their lives defending a religion and those who lost it defending an empire. The canticles were hymns of death, beautiful, but hymns of the dead who survived only by remaining dead.

SO I INITIATED MY ADVENTURES, exploring sexual persuasions that might accommodate what were at the time still doubts regarding my identity, when I turned twenty and returned to my city, Hiroshima. The story began with T, whom I met on my second trip to Hiroshima. I started with her because I saw in her asexuality the roots of my own distress—a lack, a void not only of desire but also of allies, of models, of companions. But I had already met N before that, on my first trip. I looked her up because she was a renowned expert in sexual deviations. You see, out of loneliness I was willing to ascribe to myself whatever kind of sexual deviation necessary, as long as it would give me a label, something written, an entry in a dictionary of bizarre creatures. Out of loneliness I treated myself unfairly.

N and I arranged to meet on a bench in front of the sculpture at the center of the park. Everything was green. I was surprised because the last time I was there the trees had been utterly shorn of leaves. The earth's temperature reached 4,000 degrees Celsius at ground zero. To fully realize the scope of such a massive figure you'll likely need another point of reference. Let me offer a few statistics for comparison: the sun's maximum temperature is 5,800 degrees; steel melts at 1,500. So there are your references. My city blistered under temperatures ranging from that of liquid metal in a forge to that of the sun. Like those walking lumps with heads swollen to three times their size, other images populate my memory and the testimonies of others. The people looking skyward when the bomb fell were inevitably described in very precise terms: a verb, *to hold;* a plural noun, *eyes;* a phrasal verb, *to come out;* and a second noun, *sockets.* When I left the school on the day of the explosion, I remember walking by itinerant men and women holding their eyes with their hands to keep them from sliding out of their sockets. N's eyes—I thought the first time I saw her—were so black they looked hollow.

N wasn't a hibakusha. She'd always lived in Hokkaido and wasn't even aware of the attack when it happened. It took a week for the news to reach her, and since it was impossible to grasp the new weapon's magnitude, she gave it the same importance as she did one of the combustible bombs that had already been used to destroy 70 percent of Tokyo. Nobody who wasn't in Hiroshima that day could have conceived of a greater force than what had already decimated 70 percent of the country's largest city. N listened to my stories, but the truth is, I'd seen something she hadn't, and it made me nervous to think she'd never be able to grasp the nature of my suffering. I wanted to share my experiences, but at best all she could see was something that wasn't there anymore, like the light of a dark star. So I provided the same statistics I've given to you: over twenty thousand bombs like the one that destroyed Hiroshima are scattered across the planet.

I began by sharing some of the photos I've kept over the years. I figured it was as good a place as any. A gentle introduction, easing into the main issue that so many people find paradoxical; they're always surprised to hear me admit that the bomb actually had a positive effect on my appearance, and that I could no longer recognize myself in photographs prior to that Monday, the sixth of August. The bomb—I acknowledged as much to N as well—changed parts of me that I had detested and outlined new features I tried to fix surgically later on, once I had saved enough money. My comments might seem categorical, but the explanation is really quite simple: I was already a victim prior to the attack, and from within that milieu, the bomb alone saw me for what I truly was.

I looked beautiful in the photos. It was probably this appeal that led a visibly stunned N to ask the question she did. She asked if I'd had sex again. I told her I'd been with three men, each of whom were scared off by something they saw. I wasn't sure because I hadn't ever seen another female sexual organ for a comparison, but the procedures must not have been as successful as they had promised. From then on, I wouldn't let anyone see that part of my body, not even the doctors. That's how I know—even now—that none of my physical afflictions could have originated there. My sexual organs are as strong as an atomic shelter; the problem is that unfortunately, nobody wanted in for a very long time.

I went back to an experience I had one night on a Florida beach. Something happened that made it click from outside of myself, and I could appreciate the disorientation a man must have felt entering me. I reviewed it scene by scene. And narrated it to N in that order:

Me peeing,
Me walking through the desert,
Me squashed under a wheel.

I went out to sit quietly in the sand alone to contemplate
the sea as I often did, which is to say to contemplate nothing, to
think about nothing. My hands were sunk into the sand, probably probing for dampness on their own. It was through my
hands, I think, that I first felt something that pulled me back to
consciousness. Something was pushing against my fingers. Then
I felt the same pressure against the soles of my feet, now bare. I
jumped up. My eyes had adjusted to the dark to the point that
I could make out the little mounds of sand around me. At first
it looked like little holes were opening into the sand, but then
I realized that there were bodies inside the empty holes. Little
heads, appendages, beaks, and the shells of thousands of turtles
breaking out of the eggs their mothers had laid, now synchro-
nized by the ticking of a common biological clock. I watched
them crawling out of myriad nests all around me, circles whose
diameter must measure the exact size of an adult turtle. There
were so many that they looked like ants. Once they'd emerged
from the sand, you could see the whole turtle, though, and they
were beautiful, much lovelier than insects. I knew—because I
had once been told—that the newborns had to make their way
to sea immediately. Unlike us, who are born in the air, they must
return to the water. Each one is on its own, without help. They're
born smack into the worst threat of their lives, that space between the nest and water like an open plain full of the kind of
predators that work in borderlands. It was such a privilege to be
there at that precise moment, and I was eager for them to reach
safety.

But instead of scuttling toward the shore, they started moving in the wrong direction, toward the highway. I started to panic. I got closer and could see the trail of slime they leave behind, the viscous material that had protected them inside the egg. I was ready to shoo away any predator—a fox, a dog—with a stiff kick. But how could I save the most important thing of all, that moisture I intuited as being so essential, similar to the lubrication that dried up inside of me before saturating the man who ran away after undressing me, discovering me, seeing what not even I could explain yet. That's how they were going to cross that dry asphalt on the road separating the beach from the big city. The light pollution wasn't as bad as it is now. But the artificial lights were overbright in some stretches. The turtles were confusing the lights of the highway with the moonlight, the sound of the cars with the waves, and were swarming in a direction opposite to that which thousands of millions of others, same as them, had respected since the dawn of time. I kept still, watching their fins fumble awkwardly, poor little marine reptiles taking their first steps on land. That's how they migrated, swimming without water toward the lights of the cars whooshing speedily by in a constant susurrus, unawares of that disoriented army marching against itself. It started to drizzle. I couldn't stand the sight of it: the tiny turtles testing their new lungs in a puddle of tar, car oil, and water sans salt.

Then a solution occurred to me. If the city could give off artificial light, then why couldn't I? And from up close. So I turned on my flashlight. I pointed the light at the line of tiny carapaces and then out toward the sea. Over and over again. Nothing happened at first, but a few seconds later the little creatures began following the path of my flashlight, which I was guiding toward that body of liquid that had perpetuated their species from the first instant to the first day, from the day to the year, from the year to an era. I waded into the water up to my knees and watched as they crawled to the shore. They all reached the water safely. From the first turtle that would have been the last to reach the highway, to the last turtle that would have been the first.

I sat back down again to contemplate the sea. But this time I imagined myself crawling toward the highway, drying out, losing all my moisture along the way. I saw myself creeping along hideously, on that beach where nobody would lend a hand, nobody would point a light over my body and tell a man undressing me what I didn't want to explain, what I couldn't explain, who entered me not for an explanation, because I had none to give, but to swim in the sea, which is the same as thinking about nothing.

Of course this experience didn't help N whatsoever. She asked me to please be less allegorical, and said if I really wanted her help, I had to show her what these men were running away from. But that was impossible for me at that time. I wasn't prepared. I didn't even want to see it for myself. We said our goodbyes.

For a long time, allegory was the only level I could use to explain what was happening to me. Now, seen from a distance, I'm glad because I think the way I expressed myself then corresponded with a kind of naiveté, or perhaps modesty or bashfulness. I like to remember that I did go through that stage, same as everyone else, surely, and I'm glad in light of things that happened later, because the cruelty would come, and events would rip away the delicacy I used to have when telling my story. I learned to express things blatantly, in literal terms, direct, harsh, and painful. No sea. No water to alleviate the fever.

———

Jim often used to say that there is no relationship more intimate among men than that of war. Not love or friendship, no other relationship acknowledges like conflict the stuff that binds men together: knowledge. In war, survival is contingent upon knowing the enemy. The better you know him, the greater your chances for survival. You learn the most intimate things about people in war: what a man is capable of doing to his enemy, what he's capable of doing to his own people, his father, his son, out of the pain inflicted by the adversary. The outer war always seeps into the inner war, into the home, the heart. Jim once mentioned a prisoner who had hidden a flute in the Burmese jungle when he was interned there. At night they would ask him to camouflage the howling of the people being tortured or the moans of the sick when they grew unbearable. Once one of the girls the camp guards kept to prepare food caught him playing it. Everyone expected her to snitch; it could mean extra rations or an unguent for insect bites. But the girl returned the following night. Silently she approached the flute player and gestured to him to let her touch the flute. She covered the holes with her fingers and blew. With the first sound, she dropped it on the floor and ran away. But she came back the next night and the next. And every time she blew a little longer. It was never melodic, which prompted someone to ask her in her own language what attracted her to the sound. She said she didn't know, but the flute reminded her of a game her father, now dead, used to oblige her to play, though only wind came out of our friend's flute. Hearing that, someone snatched the flute from the girl's mouth and told her not to come back. Some days later she was seen kneeling in the sand, dirtier than usual, hair a mass of tangles, wild and unhinged. She was holding a huge lifeless lizard. Her only action was to hold the lizard's yawning mouth to her lips and carefully blow.

The story of the flute, together with the description of the voices singing "Silent Night" in Uramaki's cathedral, ties in with a series of associations and a third musical idea that relates to those years of my search for a sexual identity. This third musical connection took me by surprise a few months ago. One of the few times I was able to connect to the internet from the refugee camp, I watched a film a friend had sent in which one of the characters explains nymphomania using Bach's concept of polyphony. In the same way polyphony made it possible to play and sing several melodic lines simultaneously, a nymphomaniac views all men as one single man. When I was a child and adolescent, I could only vaguely intuit what it was like to recognize the singularity in multiple voices; I hadn't lived long enough to experience things that might overwhelm my spiritual tranquility. My doubts were always defined by an enigma, a confusion that never seemed to bother my schoolmates those first years, or even beyond the years of adolescence and youth. Everyone around me seemed so radically sure of his or her sexual identity. That's why I began looking for links that would connect me with other people as undefined as me. And it was in the shape of Japan's bridges that I found the closest simile to this idea of discerning the singular within a multiplicity. Not the flat bridges, but the arched ones, whose shape allows people to see the landscape from many different points of view as they cross over. So it's not just a matter of walking from one side to the other, but of seeing how many landscapes can be found in a single one. I wanted a view from the bridge between man and woman, a bridge in whose curvature all genders are encompassed, the infinity of sexes that exist between either side. I've walked a long way, I've observed much, I've tried to understand.

# Third Month:

## INTERSEX

By the time I met Jim I was already past being uneasy about my sexuality, but for some reason I still felt vulnerable, exposed, fragile even. I made up my mind to write him a letter and explain my issues before we had sex, a letter he kept for the rest of his life and that was returned to me when he died. The following is an excerpt of that letter. I'm skipping the heading, the closing, and a few things that skirt the central issue that prompted me to write it, the fear that Jim might be put off by me. Reading the letter will help you see how from the day I was born I was already saddled with the first of a series of inflictions that would make my life so problematic. What you can't imagine, though, is how much happiness that infliction brought, which for such a long time I'd considered in a negative light. Even now, as I'm writing this, I'm stunned by something that's just come to my attention. Something joyful and unexpected. But I'll leave the details of that for the closing of my testimony, because when I penned this letter to Jim, I hadn't the slightest inkling that there might be a compensation for all the heartache:

*I was born with a sexual differentiation disorder. That's the clinical term for it anyway. You're probably more familiar with the layman's term they use to define us: a hermaphrodite, or an intersexual person. Don't you think I've ever been confused, though; I've always been a woman, since I was a little girl, even though I was educated as a boy. At birth, the doctors and my parents decided that I was a boy and so remained indifferent to certain ambiguous features. And my female organ, a half-formed uterus, wasn't visible on the outside. I was sent to an all-boys school and raised in ignorance of the fact that for the first few weeks of my life, my sexual identity had been a source of confusion for the doctors. Until I turned twelve, my biggest troubles had to do with things like how I combed my hair, how I wore my uniform, how my teachers projected my future as a man.*

*But the older I got, the more I developed, and the greater the number of conflicts that began cropping up in other areas too—not just how I dressed and combed my hair, but the way my body was changing. I had low testosterone levels, but not enough to hinder the typical down that grows in puberty, as it did for the rest of my schoolmates, and the other visible changes that took place as my testicles began producing semen. All the simple superficial problems like clothes and hair started to morph into deeper problems until finally one morning it felt as though I had woken up in full costume. The most traumatic thing was that I couldn't remove the get-up that I had been forced to wear. Like the web secreted from the belly of a spider, these external inflictions had trapped me inside of something I wasn't. But I had range of movement from my spot in the web: my tiny penis responded to the stimulus of my left hand. The little masturbating bug explored the advantages of its new apparatus. But with the pasty milk like the membrane of an aquatic bird making a film between my fingers, I asked myself if this climaxing was going to be enough.*

*One day I considered self-mutilation. Then I started thinking about it more and more often. The thoughts could have just remained at that stage, as a sort of fantasy. So I was glad when the bomb actually made it happen. It wasn't easy to look at the scar, and I did cry for weeks over losing the penis I had hated so much. For a long time I slept on my back because I missed the feeling of that little appendage rubbing between the futon and my leg. I used to imagine it to be a lizard's tail that had been severed and was thrashing around, trying to reattach itself to my body. It wouldn't have upset me as much to imagine something charred, inert, turned to puree; but instead I saw it wiggling around somewhere, looking for me in the ruins of Hiroshima like an eyeless lizard. It's a recurring nightmare now, that blind, bewildered lizard.*

*It's been so painful for me, Jim. Ten years. For ten long years I've felt like a derelict reptile longing for the twitch of a shunned tail. My feelings swung between relief that it was gone and the ache of castration; I was in a netherworld between wanting to mutilate myself and wanting the tail to regenerate into a different organ. And on the outside, I had a doll's genitalia—neither a penis nor a vagina. The detonation had also affected my testicles; they were half their size in my scrotum.*

*Then I had my first period. It thrilled me to think that maybe the bomb had actually turned me into a woman, infused me with this fluid I'd dreamed of since I was a little girl, a means of expressing my true self to everyone. But I don't dare call that blood menstruation now, because what started as a tiny stain every couple of months turned into bouts of abundant prolonged bleeding that at times lasted up to three weeks and left me anemic from iron loss, making it impossible to carry out even*

*the smallest daily tasks. Just bending over the sink to wash my
face in the morning was a huge undertaking. My menstrual
cycle never balanced itself out, and the constant swing from a
negligible to an overabundant flow only reinforced the fact that
my body remained undefined.*

*By then I longed for motherhood. You're a father, Jim. I
know your daughter is alive, but right now, today, she's lost to
you and you suffer her absence. I was overwhelmed by the need
to be a mother, what I felt was the worst kind of presence: the
presence of what didn't exist. I can't compare your situation
to mine, but believe me when I tell you how excruciating it
can be to lose something you've never had. I followed the news
of a group of women called the Hiroshima Maidens; they
were disfigured by the bomb and selected to receive free plastic
surgery in the United States. They made public statements,
announcing how they could now become mothers thanks to their
operations. Their scars healed, they regained their figures, and
a country that had suddenly become the land of good intentions
offered constant social and economic support. The Hiroshima
Maidens were celebrated with balloons and applause.*

*I remember an episode of a television show called* This Is
Your Life. *You might have seen it. Just another example of
the countless humiliations a defeated Japan had to endure,
though it didn't diminish how jealous I was of the Hiroshima
Maidens, not a single bit. This time it was Reverend Tanimoto
who had to stomach the disgrace, since he had chaperoned
the maidens on this U.S. tour. As the reverend stood with a
frozen smile plastered on his face, the program host recounted
the events of his life story, all the way back to infancy. I knew
Mr. Tanimoto was there as a hibakusha, and like the rest of
the television audience, I was anxious to hear his testimony.
But the host held the spectators in thrall, building suspense
with each new chapter of Mr. Tanimoto's life only to break for*

*a commercial selling a brand of fingernail polish whose name,
like the reverend's, had an ecclesiastical tinge: Hazel Bishop.
It seemed utterly sadistic to me that they would advertise a
cosmetic product called Hazel Bishop to an audience awaiting
the painful testimony of a minister and Hiroshima victim.
Afflicted, the reverend waited for the young woman to buff her
fingernails and show off the hottest shades on the market—
look, no flaking! Another element of intrigue was added to
Tanimoto's story besides the abrupt segues from his life to
nail polish: a few minutes into the show, they presented the
silhouette of a man hidden behind a translucent screen. The host
spoke to the reverend concerning the surprise guest, announcing
he was about to meet someone he'd never seen before. The
silhouette finally uttered a few words and stepped from behind
the screen: "On the sixth of August, 1945, I flew over the
Pacific in a B-29. Destination: Hiroshima." Turns out it was
Robert Lewis, the copilot of the* Enola Gay *who—according
to the host—was on set that evening to shake Tanimoto's hand
before thousands and thousands of spectators, in a gesture of
friendship.*

*The reason I'm explaining all of this is to help you
understand how passionately I wanted to become a mother,
that not even insults like these were able to curtail my envy
of the Hiroshima Maidens. When I was finally able to leave
my foster family, I started undergoing a few of the easier
procedures: breast augmentation, which I had to repeat a few
years later because my body rejected the first implants, and a
potent hormone treatment meant to soften my appearance and
make me more feminine. I'd have to wait ten more years to
gather the money for a vaginoplasty and finally comply with
the bomb's verdict. Do you follow what I'm saying, Jim? I'm
trying to explain—and it's so frightening for me—that if after
reading this you might still want to make love to me someday,*

*it will likely be very different from anything you've experienced before. It's terrifying to me. The idea that you might run away from me. I'm writing these lines because I don't have the courage to wait for you to figure it out from my body.*

*I used up my savings on trips to Sweden for the procedures, since back then the United States was hesitant to authorize the kind of definitive operations I needed. I've already recuperated from the last round. Nothing hurts anymore. But I had to withstand a lot of pain, not only physical pain during the recovery period, but also just knowing that I'll never have ordinary genitalia. I had to come to terms with the fact that penetration will forever raise questions about my sexual identity, and what's worse, about my sense of self. The vaginoplasty was a complete success given the state of surgical techniques at the time, but not enough for a penis not to take issue with my vagina's shape, texture, and size. Paleolithic penises wanted Paleolithic vaginas, holes with sizes and textures that fit.*

*I was pleased with the results of the first operations. Anorgasmically satisfied, since because the glans was no longer there, the doctors couldn't construct a clitoris, though I found it psychologically less damaging than having orgasms with a member I didn't recognize. Anyway, you should know that I do reach climax now, thanks to another procedure a few years later, in which they recovered what appeared to be, and was, the internal segment of my clitoris. So now I can say that I've had orgasms as both sexes. It was a long and painful process, but I was satisfied, though over time and as an adult I had to admit that the bomb had been a little hasty. If only it had been detonated ten years later, I could have enjoyed the presence of a child in my life. That loss still causes me to grieve today.*

*There's something else I need to mention. After you have read all I've already written, this may seem petty to you, but it's not* minor to me. There's a masculine feature the hormones couldn't treat: baldness. By the age of twenty I had to wear a wig. I'll never really know if my hair loss is due to premature male-pattern baldness or simply a side effect of radiation exposure. Whatever the case, it has always been a sign of decadence to me. I'm able to deal with it a little better now, though I never allow anyone to see me without my hair, or I guess I should say without some other woman's hair.

It's not just the sexual differentiation disorder that I find so hard to explain. I've long seen myself as a woman, and thanks to the hormone treatments and operations, I don't think anyone finds ambiguity there. What I have trouble talking about is my body itself, from my hair follicles down to the marrow of my bones. How can I prepare you, Jim, to accept and desire me? And the hardest thing of all is something else. Something I'm still not sure how to articulate convincingly, for you to absorb not with your brain but with that other part of you, whatever it is, that allows us to empathize, to actually feel another person's pain. What distresses me the most is that I'll never be a father or a mother. I've been denied that forever. It's a hard fact to swallow, so much so that it's become a part of my identity, like a coarseness of the soul that I can pinpoint in my half-uterus, an organ whose dysfunction was decided in the first few weeks in my mother's womb. In my case, a specific form of congenital adrenal hyperplasia arrested the indetermination of the hermaphrodite embryo that we all are in those early weeks. Neither male nor female. Both male and female. But beyond my biological makeup, there's me, the woman that I am. I began aching for a child a few years after the bomb. At first it was just a wish, but over the following years a strong urge to get pregnant gripped me, and I still feel it today, feel it so powerfully that I'd exhaust whatever resources at my disposal to find a way to procreate.

*For years I was called a hibakusha, but if I had to give myself*
*a name it would be the nuclear parturient, because the morning*
*that B-29 dropped Little Boy on my city and on me, I was*
*impregnated with an atomic baby that I could feel but couldn't*
*see, the nightmare of a pregnancy that went beyond a nine-*
*month gestation, one that lasted a lifetime.*

*I remember my days as an adolescent masturbating my*
*penis for lack of a clitoris, and can't help wondering if it might*
*have allowed me to beget the desired child, since the penis*
*was livelier than my ovaries. I had testicles, amenorrhea,*
*mammary hypertrophy, and seminal vesicles, which meant I*
*was designed to be a father. But the bomb exploded too soon*
*and carried my penis away, my child, when I was too young*
*to want to be a mother or a father. If I could go back in time,*
*I think I would have chosen to be a father then, to be a father*
*and then a mother.*

I'm going to interrupt Jim's letter here, now that I've touched
on the most important points, to go back to something that happened with S, my friend, whom you'll get to know in the coming
pages. It took place in 2008, the last time I was in Japan, though
I didn't realize then it would likely be the last time I'd ever visit
the land of my birth.

S and I had gone to see *Okuribito,* a film by Yojiro Takita.
One of the first scenes struck me as being incredibly coincidental.
The young protagonist, together with his teacher, was about to
conduct an improvised *nokanshi* ritual. In Japan, the nokanshi is
the person who prepares the body of the deceased following the
Nokan ceremony, which involves caressing, massaging, and washing the body with a warm soft sponge and is meant as a double
gesture of tenderness, at once a goodbye and also a welcoming.
At the start of the film, the apprentice prepares the lifeless body
of a beautiful young girl before the family. The young girl seems

nearly alive, since she killed herself in a relatively gentle way, using carbon monoxide. The nokanshi admires the corpse's face. He begins caressing it. But they weren't just any caresses. We watch him softly press her eyelids, her cheekbones, her chin, as if to relieve the tension in the tiny muscles. Then he takes a wrist and pushes the rigid palm of her hand back, as if helping her stretch, preparing her extremities for physical exercise. Her body seemed to be relaxing, which made it hard to relate those exchanges with death. In fact he seemed to be preparing her for an awakening. The awakening of death, which is like the awakening of life. This is the manner in which Jim woke me up even before I had opened my eyes. The gentle touches that rouse someone from sleep are the same as those that encourage a rigid body toward death.

The next scene in the film contained the coincidence that surprised me so much because it referred so precisely to one of the chapters in my own life. The nokanshi covered the body with a kind of quilt, below which he removed the young girl's kimono, always under the watchful eye of the family. This allowed him to place his hand below the quilt and wash the girl's skin without anyone's seeing the naked body. The nokanshi dipped a small sponge in a vessel of steaming water at the girl's head, then introduced it below the cloth at chest level. He began washing the body. You could see the warm fingers working underneath the fabric, like a tiny animal stealthily burrowing a tunnel under the surface. But the hand stopped just below the belly. The little animal found something and palpated it, trying to identify what it was. Without a doubt it was a penis. The penis surprised the nokanshi, who looked in amazement at the unmistakable face of the young girl, her feminine features, the long hair. Suddenly he grasped why she had committed suicide.

I think that kind of wordless sudden comprehension of the rationale for a stranger's suicide, arrived at merely through contact with the body, was the kind of awareness I'd always looked for. Instantaneous sensitivity like that would have saved me from having to write that letter to Jim, for example. I'm unable to communicate some things through words. They can be shared only nonverbally, perhaps by way of an endoscope. It's not a metaphor. It's an endoscopy. I open my legs and speak with my mouth shut. So I think about placing a camera inside a surgical tube inserted into my vagina up to my uterus. Everyone whose understanding I need—meaning you too, sir—are seated in a room. The microcamera moves around the neck of my uterus, projecting an image on a domed screen all around us. We are the camera. Right now everything we see is pink. A pink tunnel. At the end of the tunnel is the resolution, the awareness of my conflict. But for now we wait. A pulse beats ever closer. The sound isn't coming from my genitalia or from the monitor where I see the pink walls, but from on high; it's the bomb cutting through the air as it falls. I see little numbers on the artifact indicating its weight—over four tons. I know the B-29 had difficulty at takeoff, and as a result the team had to arm the weapon in midflight. So I see the hand of the last man to touch it, Morris R. Jeppson. The hand doesn't shake, but the man is afraid. Maybe Jeppson doesn't recognize the umbilical cord that's hanging from the bomb. Looking upward, I follow the umbilical cord. It's very long, some 31,000 feet. It tickles my womb. On one side, there's the bomb about to drop; on the other, there's me, waiting. We're all waiting along the umbilical cord suspended from the sky, from a bomb that is approaching and in its free fall through the air begins to make out a block of uneven streets. As it advances in a nosedive, it starts to comprehend Hiroshima. To comprehend me. So I want the cord to dock in my uterus. I see the epicenter of the detonation and understand the sudden incineration of the void: a baby's spinal column sucks in everything around it with the tides of a vortex. A spine without marrow. Empty. Suddenly I comprehend the emasculating bomb, which fell to sever my penis, to cremate my desire, my child. It was Monday, the sixth of August, 1945. The bomb fell hard and fast, early, cutting through the sun-filtering clouds. At exactly 8:16:43 A.M. my newly deceased baby began to cry.

GETTING THAT OFF MY CHEST was a relief. Seen from my perspective now, I think that letter to Jim resolved one of the three biggest problems I've had to confront in my life. The first was discovering my own sexuality without buckling to outside pressure; the second, alleviated by the letter, was how to explain it all to the man I loved; and the third was the search for my child, his daughter.

I already mentioned how my sexual quest had begun many years before meeting Jim. Particularly significant was my encounter with T, whose asexuality existed in that rigid space where life was neither death nor life, but something intertwined that avoided having to choose one way or the other. Total absence of desire. Clearly, not all those I met while on my quest were victims of Hiroshima, but the first ones were. Returning to my city prompted me to question myself; it's when I felt the need to determine my true sex. That's how I met D. She was plainspoken right from the start, and instead of recounting her sexual adventures, she confessed even more prickly things to me: her fantasies.

D had only experienced one sexual encounter with another person's body, but it was enough for her to realize that the reality of another body didn't satisfy her as much as when she touched herself and reenacted in her mind contact with another being who was incapable of warfare. D didn't want just a tenderhearted man, someone devoted or a good lover. Her sexual preference was clear: she could desire only a man incapable of bearing arms. She was convinced that the most satisfying passion could come exclusively from someone who brought her to orgasm with the peace he also practiced outside of the bedroom. She wanted a mind that was incapable of hatred, a mind from which those feelings had been extirpated, a brain that was missing a part.

I could confirm through her testimonies and similar memories of my own, that one of the aftereffects of the bomb is the permanence of what was taken away. The hole left in D by losing that equanimity when she was still a little girl filled with the weight of that loss as she developed into a woman. And somehow climaxing sexually tied itself to the obsessive need to recover that missing peacefulness.

Things around us didn't disappear altogether because of the explosion, but they lingered as contours full of emptiness, reminding us forever of what the bomb had destroyed. If they had been made invisible, it might not have hurt as much, but seeing the remains of what no longer existed was a daily misery. I remember that after the bomb was dropped, the people closest to the point of impact simply disintegrated, leaving outlines of themselves as nuclear shadows. Their silhouettes remained on the walls against which they had been leaning, the stairs on which they had been sitting, because the radiation acted in different ways depending on the material in its path. So if the radiation had to pass through a person, the surface area the body occupied acted like a stencil. I knew a mother who believed she could recognize her daughter's shadow against her school's wall. For months she spent all her time trying to preserve the silhouette. She sheltered it from the rain and the wind, like someone protecting an archaeological site of cave paintings, so the outline that captured her gazelle's last action wouldn't fade. When the reconstruction of Hiroshima began and they tore down that wall, the mother abandoned the country.

I think it was in John Hersey's piece on Hiroshima where I read the description of the different ways radiation affected bodies depending on the surfaces, or maybe it was in someone's oral testimony, I'm not really sure. But if I remember correctly, there was a man who commented on how strange he thought it was to see a woman dressed in a very tight kimono after the explosion. When he looked closer, he realized that in fact she was naked, so naked there wasn't a centimeter's worth of skin left on her body. But the colors of the kimono, having absorbed and reflected the bomb's heat in different ways, had imprinted the old fabric's flowers onto her body. Reverend Tanimoto spoke of the naked victims. At first they seemed to be dressed in rags, but what looked like clothing was actually ribbons of their own skin dangling like shredded fabric. So nothing that was gone had actually vanished, but instead persisted in the most painful state: absence.

I lived through a scene in the hospital that I have never been able to forget. A little girl was placed beside me where I was laid out for a few weeks after the explosion. A young nurse removed her clothing to evaluate how well her wounds were healing. I watched how sweetly the nurse, who was probably a volunteer from another Japanese city, treated the girl. It had been a while since I'd heard a comforting voice. But when the nurse gingerly removed the girl's shoe, she peeled, like hosiery, the skin of her entire leg off. The doctors had no idea how to treat the wounded. Not even the invaders knew what the physical consequences of the bomb would be, and it took them a long time to figure it out. The nurse burst into sobs, not knowing what to do with the hose; she didn't dare throw it away or put it aside, because surely she must have seen, like me, the leg that was still inside of it. Again, the presence of the absence filled everything to the point of turning us all into a bunch of good-for-nothings, still stuck on caring for things that no longer existed.

So as I was saying, D imagined herself making love to a man whose DNA lacked the gene for violence. Who made love from a place of peace. It was the only sexual experience that brought her pleasure, rising from the absence that she carried everywhere. D's loneliness was mostly affixed to this weight of what was gone, and so too was her peculiar sexual obsession. At the time of the bomb she lived in one of the few cement buildings in Hiroshima. She liked to play at helping her mom whenever she cleaned the windows of their third-floor apartment. She stepped up onto a chair so she could reach up high. They could both see her father swinging her brother in the park below. Her mother dipped the cloth in the bucket, watching the to-and-fro of the swing, and as if she could intuit something, she stopped paying as much attention to D and refocused on what was going on in the park. Pushed from behind by his father, the boy seemed to rush toward them, only to recede again, steadfast in the game. She said the explosion catapulted the boy upward in a last swing, and through the shards of the shattered window she watched her brother transform in the arc of flight from the air to the ground. His entire being blackened in midflight without his ever losing his shape as a boy. It was no longer flesh that was flying, but dust pressed into human form that became a shower of ashes as it fell. She watched the same thing happen to the birds in flight. In the flapping of their wings they went from being birds to being carbon molecules. No fire, no wounds, just birds in their most logical metamorphosis: perpetual weightlessness, the nimblest flight, free of effort and wings. Birds forever became for D the flying shadow of her little brother, always somewhere above her, and perhaps what led her to find orgasm in the peacefulness of painless flight.

———

I wasn't like D. Real men aroused me. When I met Jim, I desired him with everything I had in me. His knowledge of botany, of ornithology, and the way he conveyed it, excited my libido. I had never really considered the more elemental forms of life before, like birds and plants, and to discover them, like a breath of air under the sun, stirred me physically.

That day when we met in the Cloisters at Fort Tryon Park, he brought me to his apartment. We sat on his bed and watched a movie together. I was afraid of what it might lead to. I was nervous to be on a bed with a man that I desired, but I also liked it, because I knew it could all be over in a flash, in that instant of penetration when the thrill of our encounter might fade away. Penetration was similar to expulsion for me. It drove away the chance of a second date, negated the care I took to fix myself up and explain who I am in a dignified way; it expelled me from my own self. I hadn't yet written my letter to Jim, so I wasn't interested in any sexual contact with him. I used to get around things by turning off the light. But it never really worked; it simply put things off because the scars always gave me away. This is what usually happened: If the man caressed my tits gently, he'd feel the stitches from the implants. If in contrast he squeezed them passionately, he'd feel that the texture, the density were off, and know they weren't natural. But breast implants weren't what scared men off, it was the other thing: the artificial vagina that was reconstructed after the explosion, over several procedures that took years to complete. I had all of that on my mind while I lay on the bed with Jim, so I asked him to give me some time, that all I wanted was to be held and to rest together.

I remember Jim talking to me while I leaned my head on his chest. I was so tired and had a hard time paying attention to what he was saying. The words tumbled into the ear that wasn't touching Jim's skin and gathered there inside of me, swinging back and forth in a rhythm that lulled me into a reverie where real life and fiction got mixed together as they do in dreams. The reality was that Jim was very tall, and though I'm of medium stature, beside him I seemed tiny. The reality was that Jim seemed to know all the secrets of botany and ornithology. The reality was that we'd met only a few hours earlier and had ended up watching a movie in his apartment, where I learned the meaning of the first words I had heard him pronounce: *den lilla Aurora*. First he told me about the sun, something like what I wrote at the opening of my testimony, which I copy now, though they aren't the exact words: "The sun strengthens the bones. You'll need it if you spend the winter in this city." And then he said what I only came to understand later: *den lilla Aurora*.

It had happened so quickly. After the Cloisters and the gardens, the subway to his apartment. It was getting dark. First we watched the movie, and then I had to say that I only wanted to rest in his arms. The crucial word for me, which I didn't want to discuss yet, was *sex*, and also *child*, but above all *sex*. His crucial word was *daughter*. And both words came together in a dream because I was so relaxed that I fell asleep while Jim was talking.

Unable to become a mother, I dreamed about my pregnancy until slowly the desire for Jim began to rouse me. I didn't wake up, but I did dream, and I woke up inside of that erotic dream. I was (I dreamed that I was) so tired. I could hardly react to his caresses. I half opened my eyes. Night had come. I calculated by the heaviness in my arms that I must have been asleep for about an hour. I wanted to tell him how tired I was, but words form more slowly than desire. So I accepted. In the space of dreams I could feel, I desired, metamorphosis. He was hard and that hardness entered my flesh still tender from the dreamy lightness. First my neck tensed and I heard a sound escaping through my nose, like a change in matter, like a cold log crackling toward the heat of firewood. And then, as if I were pregnant, I spoke to my daughter, a fetus only a few weeks old. When I woke up, realizing that such a thing could never happen, I jumped right out of the bed and said goodbye to Jim.

When I got home, I wrote something for that unborn girl, mostly images from the dream, stories, and a few of the things Jim had told me about flowers and birds. The experience was so vivid it was as though I had a real vagina. In my dream I told Jim that I didn't want anything plastic inside me and allowed myself to reject one of the things I most envied from those days, but that mostly stuck or tore in artificial vaginas: condoms, forgetting entirely, in my sleep, that a large part of my body was, and is, made of plastic. To date, that was one of the most merciful moments life had ever given me, a vagina by birth, the possibility of saying no to a condom. But it wasn't real. More important, there was another unreal thing in that dream: I had felt maternity in my fake dream-state flesh. I imagined that I was four months pregnant in that dream that took on physical sensations. Don't ask me why four months exactly. Maybe because I'd heard that the fetus is more settled after three months and there is less chance of a miscarriage. Or maybe because I had read a few weeks earlier that the genitals are perfectly distinguishable by then, and though I didn't care whether it was a boy or a girl, what I didn't want was both in the same body and having to blame myself for passing on my sorrow of indetermination. Following this first experience, I felt the same sense of maternity several more times, right up to the very last. I'll come back to that in a little while. Right now I imagine you going back to read everything again in order to catch what I've said about the last event that changed my life for the good while ending other people's lives. But right now I don't want to talk about that. You can go ahead and skip straight to the end, but if you decide to follow the order of things, I'm going to make you wait. If you wouldn't ask gravity to explain why it holds you to the earth, then don't ask me for an explanation either. But let's put this last chapter aside. What's coming now is a transcript of what I wrote to my unborn daughter that first time I felt another life inside of me, thanks in part to the goodwill of Jim, he who was still a stranger to me.

# Fourth Month: 1965

## YOU GASP LIKE A WREN

Before I got pregnant, there were times I didn't notice the little squirt at climax. But ever since I realized you were there three weeks ago, I feel the warmth of the liquid along the walls inside of me and I can imagine the semen of your origins splashing against the water where you are floating, making the little boat rock in the waves. Drink it, daughter, now that you're fortunate enough to absorb it everywhere, since your mouth, your belly button, your anus have yet to be formed. I envy you that. I'm sorry. You haven't even been born yet and already I envy you. Sometimes I don't know in which orifice to receive the fluid, so I change position, undecided, holding who knows what parts of your father, and then, caught in the trance, I make him move, and I don't know how I do it because he's so big and I'm so small by his side. Perhaps he moves on his own, waiting for me to decide. And holds off. Holds off until I can adjust myself and tell him it doesn't matter which organ: here inside, it's fine here. Someday I might beg your pardon for talking to you like this (though I doubt it), but take into account that I'm not your mother yet, and you are no more than a little pea without a princess. A pea without a mattress. No, not a pea. At four months you're a little bigger than that. Rounded, like a four-inch piece of fruit between my legs. And your father's down there. Look! He lifted me onto his shoulders like a little girl and he's running with me through French cloisters. Plenty of flowers and trees. He knows the names of all the plants, down to the most insignificant herbs, and he recites them to me, pointing an enthusiastic finger here and there, even invisible shoots that appear only when he names them, suddenly, like instantaneous flowers, flowers that refuse the tedious gestation of a bud. Shattering the cyclical rubrics of the botanical. I laugh. It's so much fun. I laugh as we run in a circle, dodging the stems that grow beneath the gallery of arches as if they are mines. No, the stems are not mines. We're mines, the weight of a woman and a man running on two single legs, trying to avoid massacring a shrub. Something rubs against my hair. It's the ceiling. The wooden ceiling. I'm so much taller now I have to protect my head. I put a scarf on as if it were a soft helmet, a strong and flexible helmet made of some advanced material. And on his shoulders I reach the center of the cloister. This must be the main tree. It's leaf-laden, and I push the branches from my face.

"It's a yew," says the mouth that speaks beneath my body, "a sacred tree because it's immortal, and before dying, when it's rotting, one of its branches is given space in the already hollow trunk, and the branch grows downward, cleaning the rot away like one of those little fishes that clean the walls of an aquarium."

"The little branch eats the rot?" I ask.

"Yes," the mouth answers, "it's how the branch gets nourishment so that it can continue growing until it reaches the ground and takes hold there, but by then it's no longer only a branch but a healthy root that will sustain the tree for a thousand years more."

"And what did you say the tree was called?" I ask again.

"It's called Aurora." Aurora? All right then, Aurora. That's the name your father gave you when he saw me. *Den lilla Aurora* were

his first words, and his hands touch me in the subway. ("Hey, lady!
What are you looking at? This car isn't made of steel, it's organic
like the wisteria branches climbing the trellis in the park where
the raccoons play. And the families walking beneath it praise the
scent of the flowers. They don't realize that the fragrance is a blend
of the heat of animal pelts, urine, chewed seeds, and the sweat
of the rings around the raccoons' eyes and tails. Lady, don't get
uptight, the ambergris in the perfume you want to buy is whale
vomit.") And he said *Den lilla Aurora* again, giving you a name
before knowing mine, a name with a Swedish adjective because
Swedish is the language of the birds, he said, and it's pronounced
this way: *Dein lilya Aurora*. He said it very slowly—*Dein* (my ear),
*lilya* (my groin), *Aurora*—the strain in his trousers, a vapor, a
gasp in the space between skin and fabric, reduced, in excitement,
to the taut cotton, rained-on, wet fuzz of the flower still on the
branch. And in these unhurried words I had time to tell myself
that I'm allergic to plastic but what does it matter, there's no phar-
macy in this train, and what's more I don't want the time to buy
anything; in these three words there was only time enough to
say that this man must be healthy and I don't admit condoms in
my body and let's go to my place without justifying anything to
him or to me even though we'd met only five minutes ago. And
after we met we watched a movie, and you were newly born into
his big hands on the screen, and he kept saying *Den lilla Aurora*
as he looked at you and I said that if I have a daughter I wouldn't
give her a name because when I was born my father called me
S without ever knowing my real name. And he expected me to
respond every time I heard S. And I didn't respond, but it was
his fault, not mine, for daring to give me a name without knowing me, when I was only seven pounds of bloody flesh. And the
yew leaves graze my face, but I find a clearing inside the tree and
perch a little solider on the shoulders that sustain me. The distance between my two thighs measures the exact width of your

father's neck, which is in the middle of them. I'm so tall. And I'm surrounded by greenery.

And sometimes I feel afraid. So much fear. Afraid that everything will hush up, as spiteful people do, everything will refuse to speak to me or start talking only to the innards, and I'll fall into an aquarium full of mouths opening without language. So I float like a sea bream searching out the eyes of another sea bream in the aquarium's murky waters. The dread is so great that when I see a sea bream I no longer see a fish, but a person mute with fear. That's how I recognize them at the fishmonger's stand, on their bed of ice, the startled look in their eyes before the vision of what was exuded as a word only to emerge as a bubble of air in the water. And how it hurts, so much so that I can't give a name to it without bubbles bursting and emptying out the nothing inside. Only then the people who love me will give me up for lost. They'll file a report, gather the neighbors to search the fields with flashlights in the middle of the night, not knowing that missing people who die mute abandon their human form, change their skin for scales; their bones become the wobbly spines of a dead fish that was never a fish. "Mom, friends," I'd say to them, "the missing who are mute are not underground, but in that common grave of startled eyes and scales that a fishmonger threw into the black bucket of garbage."

But I don't want to talk about that today, *den lilla Aurora,* or whatever your name is, because I'm not in a garbage bucket or in an aquarium, but on the shoulders of a man, in a treetop. And did you know that nightingales are so gutsy they'll attack a cat? And *Tyrannus* is a genus of small birds that will challenge an airplane. They throw themselves against the motors. Those airplanes laden with pesticides flying over fields so low as to clip the grass deserve it. Let the pilots be charred with the flammable poison and the earless insects hear the pop and singe unknowing, or maybe aware that nobody will be fumigating again at least for a week;

they have a whole week (which is a long life) for themselves. And would you just look at that. Here comes a nuthatch. The climbing nuthatch is a neckless bird. He told me why. They don't need a neck because they look for insects while climbing up and down the tree trunk, so they have no reason to look beyond the bark in front of them.

Look over there. One is coming. Crawling up the trunk like a lizard. I take off my shoe and move my foot closer to the scuttling bird. It has an insectivore's long sharp beak. I move my foot closer, gingerly, so as not to startle it, and swing it more or less at the height of your father's belly. I stare at that skinny elongated hummingbird's beak. My foot is right there now. I close my eyes. I hear the bird pecking at the bark and want it to do the same between my toenail and flesh. Get rid of parasites or dead skin cells. But the crawler continues on up the tree, now at eye level. I wonder if it might wash my face like your father does some mornings, his tongue cleaning my eyes, removing the film that dried in the corners at night. But the nuthatch gets lost in one of the branches, and I clean the sandy granules myself. I suck them from my finger, imagining them still in my eyes and the whole of me is the other one's tongue. They dissolve.

And now the fear returns crawling up like a bird, rising with its nose stuck to my legs. The fear that all things shall fall silent. The fear that your father—or anyone else's father, or the father who is nobody's father—will never again hoist me on his shoulders. The fear of going from laughter in the heights to slinking on the ground, to begging for attention like a puppy nipping the pant legs of a hunter who cares only to gaze off at the horizon. But why does it have to be like this? I have nothing to fear right now because your father's hand takes hold of my skirt and hangs it from a little branch, as if setting out damp clothes to air. It's true, I'm not very large, but I sing like a wren. That's what he said: "You gasp like a *wren*."

"And what is a wren?" I ask.

"A wren is a bird whose song is greater than its size." It's true. I chirp. I chirp now as his fingers touch my seed like a bud that dilates the same as you are doing now in my womb, growing. I chirp, and maybe the sound reaches you, padded in the amniotic fluid. But listen, others are chirping too. He is caressing me and I look through half-open lids to see dozens of nests. Dozens. And in each are three or four little birds (how I wish you could see them) holding their beaks open for food. They chirp. They're chirping too. They chirp with beaks like orange smiles, and hundreds of mothers appear to fill their little maws. Wings graze my face as he is touching me, my pink mouth behind his neck tenses in a smile full of water, and it rains over the trunk of this warbling tree.

———

Jim and I spent a few years stumbling around in the fog in our search for Yoro. We were entirely at the mercy of strangers, or if not complete strangers, at least nobody close enough to us to risk sharing confidential information. But one day a package showed up in our mailbox. It was from a friend of Jim's, the one who suggested we travel to Los Alamos. We opened it to find letters that he had copied, but without their envelopes, and a note explaining that for security reasons, the letters and their envelopes had been separated and filed away in different places to make the sources more difficult to locate should anyone try to find them. Unfortunately, he hadn't seen the postmarks, which would have allowed us to configure a timetable of Yoro's whereabouts. I don't doubt this friend's sincerity, but it wouldn't be a stretch to think our access to these letters, which he thought he was copying and sending clandestinely, had in fact been planted to placate us, keep us distracted in a never-ending journey that appeased us by the mere fact of keeping us on the move, but that in truth held us captive to a search leading nowhere.

Our friend had searched out the letters that had clues to Yoro's possible origin, which he ran through a database of foster families tied to military projects during those years. Some of this information proved very useful, but in general, he warned, he couldn't guarantee that the letters had actually been sent from these places; it was all the result of mere speculation, trying to decipher the cryptic content of a few sentences. The rest of the pages were from a medical chart with multiple-choice boxes—*never / rarely / sometimes / often / always*—reports sent by Yoro's different foster families, apparently meant to communicate any changes in the state of her health.

I never understood all the secrecy. But eventually I got used to the nomadic nature of Yoro's imposed life and even came to accept it as something natural, since Jim never disputed the notion. I supposed the girl couldn't be adopted because she had a biological mother who must be temporarily unable to care for her, so the only thing left was foster care. But it was a lot trickier to try to reason away all the detailed reports on Yoro's health. Not only her health, but in the words of our friend, "the progress of her health." What did they mean by progress? Progress toward where? Could Yoro be sick? A person like me, who has suffered so much, avoids asking for explanations because you know they can be given only when those who can explain are ready and feel a need. In the worst of times for me, I felt that explanations had a will of their own, so when people asked me for a reason and I couldn't come up with one, it wasn't because I didn't want to, or not always, but because the life cycle from infancy to adulthood and the release of what could be explained hadn't been completed yet. But Jim's case was different. He hadn't explained things to me, he said, because he (and this included me) was held back by a threat. When the package arrived, he said he'd been waiting for the letters anxiously, since they'd granted him one right in exchange for keeping it all to himself: to be kept up-to-date regularly on Yoro's state. But the letters had come all at once and through an unexpected channel, a friend calling in a favor, and without addresses, deciphered solely on the friend's speculation, together with a note informing us that Yoro had not been relocated this time because apparently she'd disappeared. Jim could have broken his silence that day and explained many things to me, but now I realize there were other reasons at work, personal reasons that went far beyond a soldier's vow of silence.

Yoro was sixteen at the time she disappeared, lost not only to us and to her other families, but also to those charged with her guardianship, military top brass I imagined, though now I suspect, as I began to at that point, that her custody had fallen to civil servants who treated her life like one more administrative drawer to close with relief at day's end. If finding her had ever been truly vital for us before, from that moment forward it became vital for her too; she was too young to be left on her own or in bad company.

Jim quickly shuffled through the letters. As I said, many were responses to some kind of medical questionnaire. At first I didn't understand anything. It looked like the standard multiple-choice form that requires you to check boxes. Next to each of the questions was a space for comments and observations, and another longer space for the same purpose at the end of the document. They'd all been left blank, though. Nobody had offered additional observations. And a quick comparison showed that all the checks, or all the answers, coincided, meaning there'd been zero changes in Yoro's condition, so she must have grown up healthy. I can't recall the precise questions anymore, but what I do remember was being struck with a sense of dread when I realized that every single question focused on the side effects of a very specific thing, something with which I was all too well acquainted: radioactivity. So Yoro was another victim of my own disease, radioactive contamination.

THERE WAS NO TIME TO WASTE. I remember how anxious we felt now. If our lives had already been committed to finding Yoro, we now realized that returning to everyday life was impossible until we did; there could be no inner life, no living for each other. Not because our relationship had deteriorated in any way, but because it had transformed into something else; we were no longer merely a couple, we had become a search-and-rescue team. Nothing mattered to us that wasn't focused on Yoro's whereabouts. Not even food. No time was wasted talking about food; we just ate whatever occurred to us to put on a plate that day. Our love prevailed, but now it had a focal point beyond individual feelings, and kept our band of two tight. Our lives were governed by the need to conserve, not waste a thing—not the heat of our bed, not a single calorie in superfluous efforts that didn't sustain this single purpose. And so we prepared for our next journey on our friend's advice and on what conclusions we had been able to draw.

We arrived on a September evening. It was the first time we had ever stepped foot in Europe. Lyon, France. The airport taxi left us off downtown. Everything was dark, save the intermittent headlights that lit the streets every once in a while. We walked along the bank of one of the city's two rivers. The streetlamps were out, and the houses were steeped in shadows. We walked in silence along a row of small houses with candles in the windows. These hundreds of flames alone lit up the town—ancient light, medieval, cave-like—the light of my childhood, of the walks through the dark with my grandfather, dogs barking in distant fields, when flames burning the rice were the only source of nocturnal light. We could just make out a hill at the end of this strand of little flames, an even darker mass farther in the distance, crowned by an illumined basilica. The whole structure bathed in yellow. It was the only artificial light. The following day someone in the market explained the reason for that ceremonious darkness. The basilica was Notre-Dame de Fourvière, and every September a pilgrimage takes place, a river of men, women, and children carrying the candles that have lit their windows at home for a week. Four centuries adoring the Virgin who spared them from the epidemic that devastated Europe. Four hundred years of flames in silent thankfulness for saving them from the plague.

Walking among those candles was hard for me. The city was welcoming me with the only thing that might seem familiar to me in a European city. The candles reminded me of the paper lanterns my parents and I used to place in the waters of the Motoyasu River when I was a child, together with hundreds of people who gathered for the Toro Nagashi ceremony, commending our little floating lights to guide the souls of our dead. They were beautiful memories, but I'd distanced myself from them a long time ago because they were inevitably tied to traumatic ones too, since the river had turned into something very different after the attack on Hiroshima. It became a symbol of the city's tragedy, the place where the wounded, in flames, had thrown themselves, or where thousands of cadavers had been dumped afterward. For several days, more bodies than water flowed down the Motoyasu River of my hometown of Hiroshima, and a person could cross it by skipping from one corpse to another without even getting wet. There were so many people at the first service commemorating the explosion, and so many who wished to place their lanterns in the water that volunteers had to wade into the river up to their waists to deposit the little floating lights, and despite the river's current that carried them off, they were so numerous there wasn't room enough along the stretch of river near the Genbaku Dome, the only building lit up, offering a vision of its metal frame. It was the only structure that hadn't buckled under the explosion, standing close to a mile from the center of the detonation, and being a government building, it seemed—lit up like that, destroyed but still imposing with its fleshless dome—not unlike the basilica that welcomed us from the darkness of that tiny French town. These memories were painful ones, especially given that all there was in Lyon's river was water, no lights floating in the current, no messages written on rice paper to continue guiding my beloved parents, my neighbors, all the people who had faded away beside me in the hospital after the attack. The river in Lyon seemed to me to lack compassion, to be selfish. A river that fails to carry messages for our ancestors has always seemed to me like a waste of water's communicative faculty.

On the second day, Jim and I went into a small boutique and bought a little music box. They didn't have the melody I was looking for. The salesperson insisted that I buy a waltz I hadn't ever heard before. I still don't know the name of the piece of music. When I agreed, the salesperson didn't want to charge me. I forgot about the box until it was time to go to sleep. I saw it on the nightstand in the hostel when I crawled into bed. I opened it. I cranked the little handle and the music trickled out. Back in New York, for months I turned that little handle every night before falling asleep. Its music brought back memories: our nighttime trek from doorway to doorway; sleeping in sheets fragrant with southern lavender, wondering if Yoro had ever fallen asleep with the same scent of purple fields; the little cuts in my fingers from shucking oyster after oyster for lunch, adding a sort of aphrodisiac element to the vigor of the steps we were taking forward; the woman who saw me crying as I sat on a step in the middle of the block and who told me to stand up, then gave me a hug before continuing on her way.

I cried bitterly on several occasions, and whenever the sorrow overtook me in a public setting, I would just sit down until it went away, because I didn't want Jim to know how deeply the lack of traces of Yoro was consuming me, to the point where I wasn't sure how much longer I could stand it. But the music from that little box reminded me more than anything of the strolls I took with my guide, a wizened blind man who showed me the city, its labyrinths, and what became over time the symbol of that frustrated trip: the so-called traboules, secret passageways that connect one street with another, which used to be an effective way of dodging the authorities. These hidden corridors, invisible from the outside, allowed a person to disappear and then reappear in a parallel street like magic. That's exactly how I felt in that place because every time it seemed we were getting closer to Yoro, things suddenly emptied out, as if from one instant to the next she'd gone from being in front of me to being in a parallel street, the passageway to which I couldn't locate. The door finally swung open and then closed again on her nonexistence, since the place we were looking for was now an empty lot, no building, nothing but a huge warren of cats.

———

As I was exploring my sexuality, S was the most significant person to cross my path, and she's become a beloved friend over the years as we've continued to be close up to today. I met her before Jim, when connecting with like-minded people or others in my situation was as important to me as maternity.

S's place in this story involves more than her role in my personal life. She is woven into the narrative itself, since she is the one who gave me the weapon of my crime, the matériel of my offense, and something far more crucial besides. My first intention is that the reader who is not you, sir, may have the chance to know S, since besides being a wonderful friend and the element who brings my story to a close, she is one of the most fascinating women I've ever met.

It was the season of rains in Japan. I remember I had just turned twenty-two. The rain was falling in that slanted way that makes an umbrella useless. I found refuge in an archway to avoid getting drenched, telling myself it would be the last time I ran out of the apartment in a storm like that. But then I recalled the Tokyo apartment I was living in at that time, nearly bare, and on second thought I figured nothing could be worse than staying inside those four dreary walls. I couldn't have been more than five minutes on that corner when a wheelchair-bound neighbor came up behind me and rudely ordered me to move along and stop making puddles with my sopping clothes. "No problem," I responded, "at least I can walk," and I took off. I hadn't noticed the presence of someone else there, S, who mentioned when we were outside that if I wanted to get out of the rain, she could show me a business that was to have its grand opening shortly, but that was meant to be clandestine. She piqued my curiosity and I accepted the invitation. When I discovered the nature of her business, in that time and place, a humble neighborhood in Tokyo, it felt like setting foot on another planet.

It was a five-minute walk down a few streets. Houses made of brownish wood, mostly two-story structures, lined either side of the street. The street was so narrow you could peep straight into the facing one, in the style of a ferret sniffing out the interior spaces, nests of atmospheric and corporal humidity. The humidity revealed itself in little clusters of sweating moss growing between the wooden planks in the corners. I stopped to observe one. The moss stored water in its rhizoid down, and as I looked closely at it, I thought of it as a domestic kind of dew that had nothing to do with the crisp cold outside. I brought a bit of the murky green to my tongue and it tasted exactly like wet skin. S saw me do it. At first I felt a little shy, as if I had been caught in an extravagance, but then she tasted a little piece of moss too. As we walked along we tried other mosses, terrestrial and scratchy, that resisted disintegrating in my mouth. I chewed these as if ruminating on what type of place S was taking me to.

We arrived at the shop. Before I even learned my new host's name, S began to explain the series of objects on display. There was something peculiar smack in the center of them all, at the room's axis, a strange-looking object that stood out imposingly like some sort of a belly button: the exact reproduction of a dildo found in Hungary that archaeologists date from the Mesolithic period, some 9,000 years before Christ. There was a little card stuck to the pedestal with the name of the site where it was found, the date, the materials, and measurements, making the dildo a proper ornament for any salon. But its decorative quality by no means reduced its functional use, thanks to the detachable base, which meant it could easily be set to task. Later I found that this smoothly polished stone, almost eight inches long, became the object of desire of certain historians who wished to plumb the enigmas of the Stone Age in passionate paroxysms. As I said, as an element of this testimony and my life's story, the object is more the weapon of my crime than anything else, and though I didn't realize it at the time, I was so drawn to it that I asked S for a silicone replica. Finding out what weapon has been used to commit a murder is of vital importance in finding the murderer. Well, here you have it, confirmed in writing that it existed, because the real one, the one I employed, can no longer be recovered.

I imagine what called my attention to that Mesolithic dildo was the idea that some prehistoric woman or man, with only rudimentary language and something like a hundred and ten centuries before the so-called feminist revolution, had decided to think about her or his sexuality as being outside of the other. How could I not help identifying with that prehistoric act of resistance—I, who have spent my life being defined by the names other people have used to categorize me? But I saw other things in that place S brought me to once I pulled my glance and my thoughts away from that object. For example, something that is now familiar, but there I saw it for the first time. There they were. Life-sized dolls that felt and looked so real I had to check for pores; they seemed so human that even their motionlessness wasn't enough of a contradiction. S told me a close friend of hers, a manufacturer of automata, made them, and she went on to explain that unlike other versions, these ones didn't move because they were made to be passive women, receivers of anything anyone wanted to do to them. The exact price hadn't been listed yet, but they'll be expensive, she said. What's more, they came with the manufacturer's promise that if the owner died within the first two years of cohabitation, the doll would attend the funeral the same as any other mortal unless the deceased left a widow behind, and even in that situation if he had it on record that his wife should recognize the inflatable woman as being a part of the family.

I can't help but go back to the Mesolithic penis. It gives me pleasure, you know? I mean it pleases me to think what I did with it, stick a wick up the urethra to do you know what. Look at that—now you have proof that I am unrepentant. As I'm writing this, all these feelings of love that I've always thought define my character dissolve before the pleasure of that violent scene in my memory. If I had to write my last sentence right this instant, it would be the following: let peace rot. I've got some life yet to live, just enough to go calmly, to reconcile myself with the love that has abounded in me, bar a few exceptions.

S showed me other gadgets that now are relatively easy to find but back then only flabbergasted me. Anal lanterns for lovers of the black hole; stethoscopes that allow you to listen to the friction produced by any object entering the body; vibrating panties designed to go off at random, even at the least expected moments in a twenty-four-hour cycle. S designed sexual objects, so for someone like me who had never seen one before, the revelation was colossal. But this was only a means to an end, financing her main project and what she considered her greatest accomplishment, which was the design and later manufacture of a sweet little object that was an exact replica of her genitalia, a duplicate of her interior landscape, from the lips to the uterus, as true to life as two drops of the same water. It might look like a conventional dildo, but it worked in a different way: to find someone else whose intimate hole was the same size and complexion as her own. She called the mold, the intermediary, the dildo, Solitude. Solitude represented S's longing to find her double, her sexual soulmate, someone who would fondle S as she fondled herself. It goes without saying the solace it provided me to find that S was obviously as lonely as I was. Maybe like me, she too needed to believe in fairy tales every once in a while, in stories of princes and princesses, to find her Cinderella by way of something much more intimate than a magical glass slipper.

S designed many gadgets that today can be found in any sex shop around the world. Vaginal pumps, erectile rings, and a genital enlarger based on the principles of traction lengthwise for men, breadthwise for women, and backdoor orifices for both; double vibrators for simultaneous applications, and others with cone-like ends for anal use, called plugs; prostheses; a wing or a trapeze for aerial postures, with a security belt and instructions manual included; an enema bullet resistant to any type of liquid or any temperature, depending on the moment's sexual mood. Have you tried any of these things, sir? An anal plug, perhaps? A penis enlarger? Did you know the idea that Japanese men have little dicks is just a myth? Personally, penis size isn't an issue for me, but I want to give testimony here that not only do Japanese men not have small dicks, but from what I've been able to gather, theirs are bigger than those of the Americans. Well, you just let me know when you see me whether you've ever tried one of these toys, hey?

All of them, sir, I would have used them all simultaneously on those unspeakable louts. Why does hatred suddenly sweep over me again? Well, as I said, if I'd had any one of these objects on hand, along with the Mesolithic dildo, I wouldn't have flinched, I'd have used all of them at once.

I ask myself now, just how high a temperature can those enema bullets withstand? The package states "any temperature," but what exactly does that mean? Any temperature! Would it endure the temperature of the sun? Could it be that the wholesalers who supplied materials to S didn't realize that since Hiroshima, one has to be a little more careful when talking about temperature? I would have tested it on the flesh of those oafs—exactly how many degrees Fahrenheit can the bullet withstand?—and then I'd have written to the factory asking them to be just a little more precise. You do know that they do these sorts of things in these parts, right? Of course all they use are humble plastic bottles, and it's not the woman who introduces them into the body of the man, but the other way around. Later I'll tell you about Jeanette. No, you're not going to be shocked by reading this. What you must find strange, though, is that it's me, a woman, who thinks this way, as the doer of the deeds. So are you going to add malice to my murder now? Why don't you just go right ahead then, tack it on: add malice, because lack of malice had nothing to do with not having the objects at hand to use them as instruments of pain. Instead it was related to the fact that I was clever enough not to allow hatred to cloud my strategic ability: I'm a woman and I acted alone; they were men and there were more of them; I knew I had to act quickly and surreptitiously. But yes, let's not forget then, add malice to that list of degrees, because you can be perfectly sure that the instant I grabbed the prehistoric phallus, my whole body trembled with the third and final orgasm I had yet to experience. You see, one thing you can't ever call me is frigid. Not only have I had an orgasm as a man and as a woman, but also the primeval orgasm of the human race: the pleasure of the kill.

S SPENT LONG HOURS focused on her genital self-portrait, her vaginal clone, experimenting with different materials to make a mold that would fit the contours of her body and someone else's, something that would identify someone else just like her, following the same system in which DNA announces its carrier. Her table was chock-full of all sorts of materials to this end: fabrics, cardboards, drawings, maps, mirrors . . . everything her own hands needed to set the machine in motion that would find the form—her own and the double's—that S was trying to find, her sexual twin, and after six weeks of studio time and elaboration it would finally come to fruition.

Here you are, sir. Thanks to the research and to S's creativity, I found the perfect weapon without even realizing it, one I hoarded away for many years, the instrument to perform the crime. It was one of the few objects that came with me on every one of my trips. Jim always complained, saying it took up what he considered unnecessary space in our suitcase, and when he asked me why I felt the need to bring it, I never really knew what answer to give him, largely because there really wasn't one. How many trips must I have taken with that thing in my luggage? How many scanners must have detected it to the amusement of airport security agents? Had they known my age these more recent years, they would have had an even better laugh. A young woman with a dildo is a slut, but an older woman with one is a batty slut. Now I have the last laugh, because they failed to grasp the fact that every object has multiple uses. I passed the object through security dozens of times right under their noses. You see, who needs to go to some supermarket to buy a firearm? I was against the possession of firearms, and when I actually needed one, I didn't have to go to some North American supermarket for it, because S had already taught me how to respect the potential inherent in any object—its versatility, how it could be employed for both love and war, like the Mesolithic phallus. Who's to say whether that woman who lived nine thousand years ago used the dildo as a dildo? Maybe she used it to open a wolf's stomach.

I already mentioned how as a teenager, I found the architectural shape that corresponded with my sexual quest to be that of the arched bridge, not the flat kind, because again, the flat surface merely allows the pedestrian to go from one place to another, while the arched bridge goes beyond this primary function by allowing the eyes to glance around at different altitudes, taking in the surrounding environment from multiple levels. I always found the straight line the most complicated idea for a well-defined sexuality. Yet when I met S, I understood that my bridge simile lacked sophistication. And anyway, does a well-defined sexuality even exist? Just as the sun rises and sets in transformation, between two states, changing the light around us, the shapes of things, the intensity of its shine, so the walk across the bridge doesn't depend only on the form of it, but also on the time we're crossing. My sexuality was ambiguous before I met S; my gender, feminine; my sexual orientation had only ever manifested itself toward men. But for some reason meeting S was like an epiphany, because she revealed how ductile sexuality could be. I had thought that changing sexual orientations throughout our lives was the only logical thing; what sense did it make that I, precisely me, who from the anatomical point of view seemed conceived for ambiguity, stayed on the straight and narrow of heterosexuality? S's personality seduced me entirely. If I hadn't met Jim a little while later, S would have become my best sexual partner, if she had wanted it. I never sensed that she was attracted to me, though

I was certainly drawn to her, and she could have kept her desire hidden behind what we often call friendship, as I did. As if a friend couldn't also be your best lover.

———

I don't want to take too long discussing the time Jim and I spent in New York waiting for the next trip. I don't really remember how we prepared for the next trip, which took us to a town just north of Borneo. The guide brought us there and left. He said they'd come for us in three days.

The man who seemed to be the town's ringleader welcomed us. Jim exchanged money for information. We're not sure if for lack of any real information or out of fear, but the man offered Jim other services for the money. In broken English, he asked Jim to follow him. I wanted to accompany them, but the head honcho made me understand in gestures—hitting his chest like a gorilla—that it was a gift only for men. I must admit that these chest poundings meant to marginalize me as a woman struck me as a compliment. You see, sir, I've spent so many years living in the guise of a man, that when I'm finally recognized as a woman, I happily throw the advances women have made in social rights to the wind. Later I found out why the man didn't let me go with them to the tiny house. From what I could see through the window when they went in, it was no more than a dark room. The sun was so bright my eyes had trouble adjusting. But as soon as they did, I could make out the presence of a female orangutan in a bed. I knew she was a female because her lips were painted and she was wearing a blond wig and a pink semitransparent top. She was shaved completely hairless. At first I couldn't figure it out, but when I heard Jim shouting, I understood the nature of the invitation. That's when I strode into the room for a closer look. They had chained her to a steel bed. Her genitalia were inflamed. I'd never seen anyone so mournful in my life. And I deliberately use the word *anyone* because the differences between that animal and a person were completely indiscernible. Her eyes moved to see us without raising her head. I started crying. I wanted to touch her. But I was afraid. I was overwhelmed by panic, a fear of everything. I just couldn't grasp it. Jim embraced me and tried to pull me away. I resisted, but finally allowed myself to be led. The man stayed behind, I imagine to wrangle about the price with his first client. A line of men waited their turn outside the hut.

That night I thought about how different it is to destroy someone little by little or to take them in one fell swoop not to death but to nothingness. Not even a sudden bullet eliminates one's existence entirely because it remains in one's dead body or in the memory of one's loved ones, or in the retinas of strangers who might have crossed one's path only a single time. Only once have I been witness to an act that eradicated life not through death but through a sort of restoration of nothingness. Of course I'm talking about what happened in my hometown. Hiroshima was wiped out in a matter of a few seconds. And you know what? We had been in a state of alertness, we were expecting a brutal attack, and yet the power of the weapon was so new, so colossal, that the survivors' testimonies differ wildly from the testimonies of any survivor of any other attack over the course of history, and the hibakushas, the survivors of Hiroshima, we all coincide on one very particular point: we all thought that day, without exception, that it wasn't only Hiroshima being pulverized but the entire planet, and the majority didn't associate the devastation with an attack—even though we were expecting it—but with the end of the world, the causes of which we couldn't identify. The only thing capable of explaining such an abrupt and radical transformation of everything around us, the landscape utterly decimated, was an apocalypse. You see? Weapons are self-referential bellicose processes in which death is revealed by dying, and survival is revealed by surviving, but there was nothing self-referential about the weapon that destroyed my city, because its power to annihilate achieved something unheard of: self-annihilation. It peeled us away from the idea that someone was attacking us, killing us in the worst possible way, in a fashion that was until then totally unimaginable: they bombarded us as they erased from our brains the idea that we were being bombarded.

After we saw Sandy, we spent the next day going door-to-door, trying to uncover some piece of information that might bring us closer to Yoro. Nothing. That horrific vision, that corner of hell, didn't add a single piece of useful data to our search. Our experience in Los Alamos—where the woman who welcomed us didn't offer any new clues, but at least our mutual distress over Yoro was relieved with her photos and memories—had been the exception. The guide showed up on the third morning to fetch us. We told him to give us until that evening to prepare, and under cover of darkness, we broke into the house and removed Sandy's chains. At first she didn't move. She kept the same position as when she was chained. We didn't dare move her; she was huge, after all, and deep down we were afraid she might lash out at the whole species by pummeling us. A few anxious minutes passed, but then she looked at her wrists and licked the wounds left by the chains, still without looking up. She didn't raise her eyes even when she threw her arms around my neck, which I shuffled off onto Jim because I couldn't support their bulk, and Jim had to sit down on that filthy, humid bed under the weight of them. A few seconds passed by without us knowing quite what to do. We remained silent. I grabbed Sandy's hand, which was soft and very cold; we made as little noise as possible leaving the cabin, and all three of us jumped into the guide's jeep.

As we sped off, we could hear shouting and a random shot was fired. But we were already too far away; no vehicle in the village had the horsepower ours did and nobody came in pursuit. Once the adrenaline's effects had subsided, I rubbed Sandy's lipstick off with a handkerchief and removed the wig and top. She was trembling. Both of us were trembling. I felt fear again. Her body was so massive. What could have happened had she decided to take revenge against humanity by attacking me? An understandable impulse. But Sandy just stared out the window as we distanced ourselves from that horror. She didn't move an inch. Her breath misted the glass and screened out the world. Then she closed her eyes and seemed to fall into such a deep sleep that anyone could have suspected she'd withstood all the torture, the mistreatment, the prostitution, with the sole aim of being able to die free. I bent close to her nose gingerly. She was still breathing. She was only asleep, and I was overcome with joy.

We stayed in Sarawak, a small town in Borneo, for forty-two days before returning to New York. We needed the time to arrange for Sandy to be vaccinated in an orangutan rescue center that worked in association with a center in Ohio. I insisted on taking her to the United States because I'd be able to visit her there several times a year, to assure her complete recovery and eventual return to the jungle where she'd been born, though after so many years of confinement, that possibility seemed remote. A return to her natural habitat would be tricky. Though Sandy was still young, nobody could be sure she'd recover enough to be free again. The physical wounds would scar over, but men had humiliated her, they'd sown the seed of slavery in her, which takes root quickly, grows strong and deep and is difficult to weed out. Most slaves never stop being slaves even once they are free.

I met Brigitte in the rescue center. My interest in non-normative sexualities continued long after I'd come to terms with my own. It was a passive kind of interest, though. I mean, I did not seek out sexual minorities, but my wounds had given me a kind of radar that allowed me to intuit things without necessarily looking for them. Things that might go unnoticed by others were obvious to me. Watching Brigitte interact with the orangutans, I immediately picked up on something that few others would have noticed. I should mention there were other female orangutans like Sandy who'd been used as prostitutes by the workers from the palm oil plantations, and also males who were exploited for boxing. The laws of the wild had been twisted in these false combats so that the orangutan's thumping, which was meant to earn the respect of the weaker ones in their natural habitat, was emptied of meaning and had nothing to do with normal animal behavior, devolving instead into a perverse form of entertainment for humans.

So after I had been introduced to Brigitte and watched her work for a while, I could tell by the way she moved—using a kind of passive scrutiny and intuition—that she felt a particular compassion for the orangutans who had been mutilated in some way. Yes, it was compassion, but there was also something else: pleasure. Brigitte suffered a very uncommon sexual deviation called paraphilia, and I use this term not because I accept the idea of sexual deviancy, but in order to make myself understood. Specifically, she was an acrotomophiliac, someone who gets aroused by amputations. This doesn't necessarily mean she had or ever wanted to have sexual relations with orangutans. But that's not the point. She wasn't, she never would, abuse her position as a caretaker to satisfy a sexual impulse. She shared the information with me because I didn't hide that I had noticed it, and when these things are dealt with in a natural way, it's usually a relief for the person who is suffering in silence. Brigitte forced me to reflect on a comment she made about how most pedophiles never actually touch a single child. According to Brigitte, pedophilia, whether you consider it a sickness or not, isn't something you can really call into question because it unquestionably exists, and in most cases the feeling itself cannot be controlled. What the pedophile can control, though, is acting on that impulse. I thought about how hellish it must be to live that way, in a permanent state of strife with yourself, and it seemed to me like a commendable sacrifice.

Brigitte intuited that she could confide in me. Not long ago, one of those experts in creating labels in the form of Greek words told me that my happiness over the bomb having done a number on my genitals means that I belong to a group of abnormal or psychopathic people. The specialists obviously enjoy classifying people and naming their conditions, creating taxonomies. According to the specialist, I suffered from what is known as apotemnophilia, or body integrity identity disorder. People who suffer from BIID feel incomplete, as if some part of their body were missing, even though they are complete. And the only way to achieve the idealized notion of themselves is by amputating one or more of their limbs. I find it strange that anyone would think that wanting a limb that didn't belong to me, a surfeit limb, removed means I have a disease. I explained all of this to Brigitte. She said her desire to mutilate herself was the result of a traumatic experience. A wartime love affair. She had been a soldier before working in the reserve, and told me her story.

She had been called up for duty, and could hardly remember when she'd signed up enthusiastically because she'd believed in peace, though she couldn't remember ever believing in war either. There she was, dressed in the uniform assigned to her, with all those gadgets. A stockpile of arms. More than anything else, she insisted, there were so many arms, but not to defend the homeland, which she could hardly remember anyway, but to defend her head and her heart. She took off running to provide cover for a companion, with all the steel she was carrying. This was her mission. To protect him. He was more important than she was, they said. More important for the war. More important for peace. "And if you feel the fear of battle"—she recalled their warning them before the soldiers headed out—"remember this: you're already dead." Death is the military's home remedy against fear.

"We were already dead," Brigitte said. So she ran crushed by the weight, sweat clouding her vision, never stopping to wonder if the dead could sweat or see, but knowing the person she was covering did. His life before hers. And so over the weeks and months spent protecting him, she fell madly in love with him. So Brigitte fell into the traps set for him on several occasions; he was more valuable than she was for war, for peace. One day she fell into a deep hole full of bayonets. Who knows how she survived that one, she said. Maybe it was for love. Or maybe it was because, as they had said, she wasn't alive anymore. She preferred to believe it was for love. She lost two fingers. (And when she said that, I glanced at Brigitte's two hands, intact, no wounds or mutilations: "The loss happened inside me," she said, and continued her story.)

She looked up from the hole, and for the first time there he was, holding out his hand to her. He dressed the two holes that had been her fingers. Walking tall is important, she said, so she straightened up and cleaned her firearms as best she could, polishing the metal, everything that could be shined with a little grease and some tender loving care. She wondered if he liked her. In the midst of the horror of war, she was an attractive, well-equipped soldier if ever there was one. "I looked damn good in my silver jacket," she said. So they continued on. When they finally reached the trenches she waited, protecting him until the sandbags and rocks took over for her. During one of these exercises, a hand grenade left her with half an arm. And when I stared perplexed at Brigitte's two good arms, she responded again: "Loss is on the inside." That was the last time I interrupted her story, understanding that Brigitte would have forfeited every one of her limbs, bled to death, but she used allegory, as I did, to protect herself against bleeding words that could never explain her feelings.

She went on with her story. He cured her again. She survived again, and who knew why? Must be for love. Or perhaps she wasn't alive anymore, like they said. But she believed it was love. She walked tall again and smiled at him. The sun reflected her silver jacket. She was an attractive, well-equipped soldier if ever there was one. And they marched on. He followed behind her on the minefields, walking in her footsteps. They crossed many fields, and in one of the last ones, Brigitte lost her leg and half of the other one (*allegory,* I thought, and let her continue on with her story). Again, he tended to her. Since there wasn't much farther to go and she had enough body left to continue covering him, she continued onward. She crawled across the few meters separating them from the ramshackle house where their comrades would eventually find them.

"It's important to stand tall," he said, but when they arrived, she couldn't stand on her own. He helped her, propped her against the wall that was also leaning over. Her silver jacket was brown now, sullied with mud and dust. It hurt her to see it, she said. Waiting for relief, she rolled a bandage in the three fingers she had left and cleaned the jacket till it was gleaming again, and all that was metal gleamed, 90 percent of her body. She still had her face, and abundant chestnut hair under her helmet, an arm and half of the other one, a little bit of leg, and everything was covered in her silvery jacket. Not too bad, and all of it handsome. She smiled and gleamed for three days, at the end of which time, the helicopter arrived. This time she allowed him to go first, since the hands extended were friendly ones. Tied to a harness, she watched him ascend and disappear safely through the door of the mechanical dragonfly. This was the only time she allowed him in front of her, because he was more important than she was, for war and for peace. For her. When it was her turn, the enemy forces broke the copper cable that was pulling her up. She fell, but not more than a few meters. She wasn't hurt. She moved around, trying to catch an angle for the sun to reflect her jacket again, like a mirror, to bid him farewell. It took a lot of effort for her to create the reflection, which she controlled with her own movements, the little circle of light sliding like a restless little animal over the skin of the helicopter. Seeing it move into the distance, she asked herself if he, her love, had even noticed the gleam (her goodbye) from the window. She wondered if she would become the memory of a flash or of an invisible soldier.

When she finished her story, Brigitte said that though her body was intact when the war ended, those days spent protecting her soldier—real, faithful, absolute protection—were like a process of dismembering. She has felt a strong attraction toward people who have had limbs amputated, though she couldn't say whether this attraction was connected to the soldier, whom she never saw again, or the things she sacrificed while she was protecting him. I hugged her when she finished, and suddenly felt more complete in our embrace.

———

It was a girl. I mean in the fourth month of my pregnancy I knew it was a girl. Not because I had a sonogram, as they do today to ascertain a baby's gender—still a new technique at that time—or because Jim's offspring, whom I was obsessed with finding, was a girl. I knew because of my belly's shape. You, sir, like so many other people, may deny my pregnancy; you may think I'm out of my mind or that I'm writing this under the effect of some medication. A woman born with a faulty womb, with a non-reproductive system that is primarily masculine, a dysfunctional penis, testicles—there's no way a woman like that can get pregnant. Fine. I can't deny this biological impossibility, but for now you'll just have to believe me if you want this story to make any sense. Just consider it a psychological pregnancy: I wanted to be a mother so badly that my belly and breasts engorged, similar to what happens to dogs. So as I said, I knew the sex of my baby in the fourth month, the way grandmothers used to: by the spread of my still-tiny belly, which was filling in more along my waist in contrast with how boys are carried, according to old wives' tales, showing a more pointy belly in front, making the pregnant woman look further along than she is, especially when seen from the side. I liked to imagine my daughter that way, growing modestly and taking shape, sticking closer to my ribs instead of outward, more mine than anyone else's, more private than public. I could truly feel her, and since I wasn't crazy, I didn't say a word to Jim. What was happening inside me wasn't connected to the lines of communication that allow us to share things with our significant other, so I knew that trying to offer an explanation would be futile.

We were back in New York, and so physically and morally exhausted that it took us a few months to recuperate. We made a promise to each other that we would give ourselves time to recover, until we got our strength back. Jim had his military pension. It wasn't much, but we could live modestly, and in order to afford the trips, we scouted out odd jobs that gave us sporadic income without a great amount of effort, work we enjoyed, and a needed stimulation because the trips often evoked feelings of frustration, sorrow, and discouragement. So we obliged ourselves to use these times of rest in New York to bounce back and do what we had to during these brief interludes: forget the past, stop thinking about the future, and live in the present, jettisoning bad thoughts. At least that's what we tried to do, usually pretty successfully.

I never realized that each month during the gestation period of my baby had a corresponding cycle of months or years in my own life. Time passed more slowly for my baby girl than it did for my body. While I thought I was the one in charge of her on earth, in fact she was journeying through space, traveling more or less at the speed of light. For her, it was a short trip; for me, it was a protracted one, allowing me time to prepare for whatever the future had in store. So sometimes I imagined my little girl that way, in space, connected to me by way of a long, invisible umbilical cord by which she fed me, she sustained me.

These months that made up my fourth month of pregnancy coincided with a letter from S announcing a visit, and I couldn't have imagined a better time. She stayed for five weeks. Her business had been open for a while now, always operating from underground. She hadn't yet revealed the template for her genitalia, but she seemed content, full of hope and very beautiful. I discarded the idea of telling S about my pregnancy. I think she would have gone along with me, she would have seen it, but I didn't know how to explain it to her. I was experiencing a process of metamorphosis and regarded it with an overwhelming feeling of estrangement. My body's transformation was an ultimate act of freedom, the most significant I'd ever allowed myself because it originated in desire. It astonished me, after spending so much money on plastic surgery that this gratuitous development I imagined was taking place inside me, the life I wanted to germinate, without me or anyone else intervening in how it took shape. I didn't have the language for it. I liked to think that for once in my life it wasn't other people who left me speechless, but instead a piece of myself, that breathed only because I did, that grew only because I nourished myself. It was my greatest love, and yet at times I also felt the need to protect myself from that part of me, desire become pregnancy that only I could distinguish, and that kept my tongue in check, which I needed in order to share the news with S.

Though I still lacked the necessary tools to describe my transformation to S, I did let her in on another project, thinking she would be the best companion to accompany me to some classes I had started taking several years before. I had the idea when I underwent breast augmentation, which in my case required a full implant. During the consultation process I met other women who were undergoing mammoplasty. Generally, they had to wait longer than I did, endure more tests, because most of them were cancer survivors who had undergone mastectomies. I could feel their disapproval when they found out I was having the same procedure as they were, but to offset the more visible features of my sexuality. The women considered the right to reconstruct a once-existing breast trumped the right to choose having breasts you had lacked from birth. Though I could understand their way of thinking, I found it completely pedestrian. I knew it wasn't worth discussing with them, but one day I came up with an idea that could ease the discomfort of the months between having their breasts amputated and the reconstructive surgery. I tried it as a pilot project, and it worked. Before sharing the idea, I ask you to keep one thing in mind—which, I think, proved its usefulness—that the women involved had suffered a great loss of self-esteem. Even today, the scars from a mastectomy are devastating, but they were much worse then. These women had never been exposed to images of these kinds of scars before—not in photos, advertisements, or campaigns against cancer—so the first time they ever saw these kinds of scars was the day they finally removed the bandages in front of the mirror after having tried a few times earlier without being able to, precisely to avoid seeing that hideous naught outlined by a gash. The sight was always such a shock that it took a long time to dare look at themselves again, let alone allow anyone else to.

S carefully listened to the project I had developed a few years earlier. I told her how damaging these types of procedures were for a person's self-esteem and showed her the practical applications of my plan. I told her to have a seat while I went to look for something. I came back with an oval mass of silicone they'd given me in the hospital and explained that this was one of the temporary prostheses that were worn in the bra during the waiting period before the procedure. Thanks to the prosthesis, nobody could tell that a clothed woman was lacking a breast. It was such a relief that many women even slept with the prosthesis, even showered wearing a bra, so as not to have to see the amputated area even for a second. But I was interested in finding a way to make these women feel comfortable with their bodies again. How could I convince them that after surviving cancer, they weren't any worse off than healthy women with two breasts? Breasts—I used to tell them—end up sagging. Some women think their breasts are too small; others wish they were not so big. I tried to defend what I still think is true, what in fact I can prove after a few years: the body is not a static thing; it changes, it can be transformed. I didn't see any reason why the burdens of age or saggy breasts were any easier to accept than the effects of cancer. Old age, when it comes down to it, is also an illness. A healthy woman should accept her body with or without scars. I used myself as an example. I was born with a gender that my parents negated. This was a problem because my body wasn't my body, but someone else's that others had chosen for me.

Once I was finished explaining to S the nature of the silicone I held in my hands, I put on some dance music, turned the volume up, and started playing with the prosthesis as if it were a piece of equipment used in rhythmic gymnastics. I'll admit I've never been a great dancer, but my body's flexibility and years of yoga and qigong compensated for my lack of proper dance training. I lay on my back, arched my body to form a circle, and let the silicone roll down to my neck. For a second I asked myself if my bodily transformation, being something in my head, was visible only to me or if S could see the little swelling of my midriff, but it was the effect of the hormones I'd been taking for years, which at times would make certain areas traditionally associated with fertility swell, like my hips, abdomen, and breasts. Within limits, chemistry helped me mimic a woman's natural cycles. The hormones turned me from a flat piece of limestone into the Venus of Willendorf, a little less full-bodied perhaps, but still with some nice curves. I imagined myself, a fossil become flesh, in some museum somewhere generations into the future, an exemplary contour of the twentieth century, being explained in the voice of some android guide: "This is H, the Hormone-Fed Venus of Hiroshima. Found by X at Site X. Material: organic." But as I was saying, that day I was with S, dancing to the music with the prosthesis, I was tossing it up in the air and grabbing it with my feet. S was amazed as she watched me move, quick and agile as a cat, focused on that apparatus meant to be hugging my torso but instead making it fly and then slither down different parts of my body. The prosthesis rolled across my belly button, my forehead, my groin, like a breast moving around free of any divine decision or doctor who fixed it one single place. And that's how the idea came about for dance classes designed for women convalescing from a mastectomy. The prosthesis became a means for strengthening their backs, arms, and glutes. If later they chose to attach it to their chests, then fine, but women needed to raise their self-esteem, and not with a motionless plastic ball but by improving their bodies in ways we are all capable of doing. When I saw that project through for the first time, I was proud to hear some of the patients say they were even more comfortable with their bodies than before the operation. They felt healthier, stronger, more in control of their movements, and as a result, a whole lot sexier.

S loved the idea, so over the course of her stay in New York, she helped me look for women who could benefit from these dances. These classes became a source of income for me, to finance the next trip, and something else. Dancing with them took me away from things. My mind melded with the mass of translucent silicone I was playing with, and everything around me, everything that meant anything, I could see it all reflected there, contained within, and only there. Nothing else mattered to me at that moment. But at night, despite the heat of Jim's body, or maybe because of it, I mourned not being able to share my feeling of being pregnant. I had trouble sleeping. I felt ridiculous helping other women when I wasn't able to express something so fundamental for fear of being misunderstood not by just anybody but by Jim himself, the person I loved more than anything else in life. On nights like those I remembered how many times in the past I had toyed with the idea of adoption, which I always ended up deciding against because I considered it a next best thing to becoming a mother. Maybe—I thought before feeling pregnant—if I had been physically incapable of conceiving, I would have adopted a child. But what obsessed me so much was being denied the possibility, to the point of not wanting to break the connection between maternity and the process of gestation. For that same reason, I spent years feeling stupid every time I stopped to think about how much effort, how much sadness, how much of my life was devoted to searching for someone else's daughter. After I had mulled over these thoughts, lying in bed beside Jim, optimism would descend and carry me off to sleep, when I would touch my belly and say that all this was in the past, and that there was something worse than not being able to announce my pregnancy to Jim: and that was not having anything to announce at all, the absence of my baby, a baby that certainly for me was developing like something real.

Aware as I was that Jim and I had to respect our compulsory downtime in this search that at times governed our lives to an absurd degree, I contacted the hospital where years back I had met the first mastectomy patients, and the director, who remembered me fondly since she had been able to measure the positive effects of my dance sessions as part of post-op therapy, gave me the opportunity to visit the hospital and present the project again, together with S.

BUT THESE NEEDED MONTHS of respite weren't going to last long. The same thing always ended up happening: when I finally caught my breath, this would trigger an internal mechanism and send me back to my efforts as part of the search-and-rescue team. During the first few days of reactivating our efforts, I would be able to see better, hear better, smell better, as if I really were a mother in whom nature had opened up channels of perception for better protecting her young. Searching again. Tracking, pursuing. I simply couldn't last more than six months without setting out afresh on Yoro's trail. Sometimes I behaved as though I were her real biological mother, whom not even Jim could tell me about, since according to him, the parents' biological identity had always remained a secret. That feeling would come back from time to time, and I'd feel a prick of shame again; there I was, off chasing after a stranger's child, when my pregnancy seemed so evident to me, as though I wasn't satisfied with the daughter who was growing in my own womb. If I'd considered myself a maternity mendicant before I got pregnant, like someone obviously incomplete and formed only by crumbs of the crumbs, now I started to feel insatiable, a woman hungry for new children, her own, a sort of Saturn devouring her babies as she gave birth to them, hunting them down only to continue the search. That's why I was very cautious about showing my feelings for Yoro even to Jim, the anxiety that overwhelmed me by the news of her ever more horrifying disappearance.

The next door to knock on was the lighthouse at the Ilha da Queimada Grande, an island off the coast of Brazil. Of all our trips, this one has been burned into my memory as a first descent into hell. The lighthouse was the only building on the entire island, and according to rumors there were five snakes per square meter, unique in the world, whose venom was so potent it could kill a person within an hour. The rumors also said that the wife and daughter of the last keeper had died after being bitten by these snakes and that he lived huddled up in their memory without leaving the tower, even though the lighthouse had been fully automated for safety reasons since the early twentieth century. Of course the dates meant that the man we were going to visit couldn't be the same keeper, and yet the stories they told on the continent assured us that it was the same man. In any case there we were, on a Zodiac manned by two men from the Brazilian coast guard and a doctor who carried an antidote in case of an accident.

From our launch, Queimada Grande looked like paradise. Everything was green, and the lighthouse rose like the lone indicator of human presence. But the moment I touched that ground I felt as though my strength had been sapped—all my hopes, my desire to live, and even my libido, which I feel whenever I look at Jim and visualize a fantasy . . . gone. My body was drained of energy, not only to meet the new battery of frustrations in the lighthouse but even to take the least step forward. I felt distanced from myself, seeing everything from the outside as I walked, dragging my feet, apathetic. The first thing I noticed was the underbrush. If the first man in line didn't cut a trail through the brambles and branches with a machete, it would have been impossible to move forward. We wore boots that reached our knees to avoid snakebites. But my attention was fixed on the trees. There were hundreds of snakeskins dangling from the branches. That's how I felt, like the sloughed-off skin of a snake, skin whose soul had crawled nice and far away, just like my genitals; hadn't I spent half my life asking myself where my penis ended up after the explosion? Though it was a part of me I had never wanted, the idea of losing that piece of myself, without knowing what had happened to it, whether it had been buried or whether it had disintegrated, continued to cause me anxiety. I think since I'd hated my penis and considered—when I had it—self-mutilation, there was a kind of guilt attached to its loss that might be similar to having abandoned a dog. I often recall the figure of Antigone, that beautiful young Greek woman who risked and lost her life trying to bury her brother, whose punishment had been exactly that: that he not be buried, but rot at the mercy of the wind and the vermin, the dogs, the vultures. The problem is that whatever we don't bury or burn or even find is able to haunt us for the rest of our lives. The people who disappear never die; their presence haunts us. I would have preferred to find my penis, to be able to mourn over it, caress it one last time, bury it to know that it is truly dead; but this way, my penis continues to haunt me to this very day. I feel pity for that little lump of my flesh. So this island seemed painfully familiar to me, the empty skins reminding me so much of an image that has plagued me in my dreams since those hospital days: my penis searching for me through the ruins of Hiroshima like a blind lizard, like a legless dog. That repetitive nightmare, over and over: lizard, blind, ruins, dog. In Hiroshima.


THE SLOUGHED SKINS were so noticeable on the island that surely they diverted the attention of the live snakes stalking us from their hiding places. *That's right,* I thought. In the boat they told us that the snakes hid in the trees because it's there they found their principal source of food: the birds. That's why there were skeletons of birds scattered all over the place—among the bushes, on the ground, in the trees.

When we reached the lighthouse, one of the men knocked at the door and shouted the name of the superfluous lighthouse keeper: "Flavio, open up! We brought some food, and there are some people who would like to see you."

I wasn't expecting anything. Not even that he would open the door, let alone that the man would be able to give us any information on Yoro. But the door opened slowly, heavily, with the loud screeching of salt-rusted iron scratching the floor. There stood another person before us, as sluggish as I was, who silently let us in. The five of us looked at him, checked around us. We were at the entrance of the lighthouse's very narrow landing. Looking up, all we saw was a long spiral staircase leading up to some space from which little pieces of plaster would tumble every now and then. Each one of the lighthouse's cracks or crevices was sealed with duct tape or cemented over to keep—I imagine—reptiles and rats from sneaking in. And there was garbage everywhere. Tons of garbage, mostly tins of food tossed around the floor. By contrast, Flavio seemed spruced up and tidy, tall, with an athletic build, but mute. My tongue was tied too, so it was Jim who asked about Yoro, moving a step forward into the refuge.

Flavio said nothing. He just walked by us. He fought with the rust-covered green door and disappeared outside. The coast guard officer who had commandeered the launch tried to hold him back as the rest of us stared out at him from inside the lighthouse, but he stopped when he saw Flavio throw himself down and roll around in the underbrush like a flea-bitten animal. He was barefoot, shirtless, and in a land where snakes are as abundant as ants; it was only a matter of minutes before he encountered one. We heard a howl of pain and the officer ran outside to fetch him, lifted him in his arms, and brought him back into the lighthouse. They closed the door behind them. We all turned to the doctor, but the doctor admitted then that he was really a dentist and had no idea what was in the medical kit; someone had given it to him like a prop for playing the role of doctor. We opened the kit, but nobody knew what we were looking at. There were bandages, plenty of gauze bandages, and a bottle that by its smell turned out to be nothing more than alcohol. Nothing that could be an antidote.

Two little red puncture wounds just below Flavio's knee dripped blood. Even the most ill-informed person would know that if he had been bitten near the ankle, the poison would take longer to reach his heart. But now there was less distance for it to travel, which gave the venom an advantage. If it took an hour for one of the bites to finish off a man, then this one would take half a leg less. Jim made a tourniquet to slow the venom's pace and we used a sheet as a stretcher to transport Flavio to the boat. The leg swelled up immediately. It was the first time since Hiroshima that I'd seen an organ three times its normal size. Everything reminded me of the horror of that day. The serpent skins like my sex, my empty penis. The swollen lump of what only minutes before had been healthy and strong. The distortion of what had once been something else entirely. Flavio kept silent. He stared up at the sky, motionless, as if he were sedated. I too felt numb, like a walking automaton, unconcerned that the way back was as dangerous as the way there had been, the same number of poisonous snakes and a dentist without an antidote.

The day was sweltering, and not even the breeze of the speeding boat could relieve the heat. We were all sweating. We radioed for a boat to come out and meet us with the serum. Jim loosened the tourniquet every ten minutes so that the blood could irrigate the leg enough so that necrosis didn't set in, but he did it against the opinion of one of the officers, who said the only alternative was to cut the leg off right then and there, though I have no idea how he figured we could do that without a doctor and proper instruments. The venom, being a strong anticoagulant, made blood seep like water from the two red puncture wounds, but the consensus was to allow it to bleed out because some of the poison would be removed that way. Flavio's calmness was good because it kept his pulse steady, which slowed the toxin's race to his heart. He couldn't be allowed to sleep, so the crew kept talking to him, though he seemed completely unperturbed. Neither the fear nor the pain had upset him. He seemed no different after the bite than he did before, except that he had started to tremble in spite of the heat. He was dripping with sweat, his hair was soaked, but he trembled like he was lying on a sheet of ice. When the medical boat arrived they administered the serum, an anti-inflammatory drug, analgesics, and an antibiotic. On the way to the hospital, Flavio's sweat turned rancid and sour-smelling.

We spent a week there, visiting the hospital every day, hoping Flavio might tell us something once he recovered, might offer some clue as to where Yoro had come from or gone—at the very least a story, an anecdote, a memory, another photo. Anything would make the journey, the effort, the hope, worth it. Gestures of brotherhood, acts of compassion or understanding, they had the soothing effect of smoothing out the difficulties we'd face in preparing for the next step of the way. So we bore witness to the process of recovery. The leg turned a deep, intense shade of green. It took his body three days to neutralize the venom. Black and blue marks appeared over his arms and legs from the difficulties of coagulation, but the most impressive of all was the huge lump that formed around the wound itself. And for me that was it, I didn't need another thing to finally make my mind up, to throw in the towel—me, someone who cringed whenever I saw a bulge, a cyst, a tumor, even a mere sty. The trip was a fiasco. Too many things had yanked me back to memories of Hiroshima, and how I too had lived in anticipation of bulges, in my case seeping with radiation. When the doctor lanced Flavio's flesh, a huge mound of pus oozed out. But the lumps on my body, the ones I waited for with trepidation, couldn't be extracted. They were like manifestations of a venomous tubercle that brought in its life, death.

Flavio spoke not a single word over all the days we spent there waiting, and the only time he got out of bed by himself was to go to the bathroom, sliding silently from under the sheets to crawl along the ground. As I had supposed from the beginning, there was nothing to be done in that place. Flavio had turned forever into a snake himself.

THAT LAST TRIP RUINED ME. I'd grown accustomed to delicate health, but never had I felt the fear of death so near. Not even in the months leading up to Little Boy had I known that panic of sudden death. The fear of dying used to come in the form of a panic attack from time to time, but feeling it could happen in a split second, just like that, was a new sensation. During the days following the explosion and for years afterward, many of the hibakushas went to bed at night never to wake up again, even though they had survived and apparently been able to enter the ranks of those who can envision a ripe old age. I always knew I belonged to the same at-risk group, but the panic that gripped my mind from time to time never actually found purchase in my spirit; it continued along its path while I attended the specific remedies of the little or medium-sized illnesses that I patched up with Band-Aids. But the episode with Flavio triggered a deep-seated fear inside of me, a wick just waiting for the flame. Who could've imagined that a stranger, a man-serpent who'd never hurt me beyond the infliction of his silence, would spark the fear of sudden death, like a virus, like dying without being able to say goodbye, not even to myself. But there was a certain logic to it after all, seeing how an invisible evil occupied that man, how the venom expressed itself by deforming his body, reminding me that in a day, an hour, a minute my sick body could transubstantiate. Though my soul yearned to live, though it yearned to love and loved so much, it was no more than a wounded bird subject not to other people's care, but to the whim of some superior being who insisted on testing its existence through nonexistence.

Though conscious of the fact that others were in a situation similar to mine, I nevertheless felt as though I were unique to my species. That feeling I had first experienced in the Natural History Museum in London only got worse when I realized there was nothing else like me there, not among the specimens bottled in formaldehyde, not among the people who were accompanying me. It isn't that I thought of myself as some special case among victims; I felt as though I truly was the only member of a different race, like the strange creature pecking its way out of an egg from a different planet who is condemned to live among humans with-out any knowledge of its own species, its life expectancy, precisely what I most craved to know. I was an alien raised without a father or a mother, with nobody whose DNA was remotely similar, a person with more questions than answers, principal of which was that key piece of information about time: When was I supposed to die? How long do people of my race live? Eighty years? One hundred, two hundred? I was a stranger among a strange race, and at times I thought I hadn't the slightest indication of what might become of my own flesh.

I entered a period of neurosis unlike any I'd ever experienced before, which manifested mostly in the guise of thanatophobia (I'd come to know this word well), or fear of death. By day I took tip-top care of myself as always, without developing any special kind of hypochondria or self-protecting habits, but at night the fear would become night terrors, fear of death in my sleep. At first I would wake up in a sweat and shake Jim until his voice, like a mother's gentle pinch, let me know I wasn't alone, I wasn't dead. I recalled what Jim told me about his time on the Death Ship, *Oryoku Maru,* how madness showed itself in the prisoners' obsession with touching the bodies of others in the darkness, des-perately, as a means for grabbing on to life, on to any life, if not their own, at least whichever one they could feel. The lack of sleep kept me drowsy by day, and when the afternoon arrived with the threat of another night of non-absence, I would load myself up with coffee to keep sleep at bay and stay awake as long as I could. Then I began altering my schedule. I started to sleep by day and stay awake at night. Since everyone else slept at night, nobody would come to my aid if my life began slipping discreetly through the cracks while I was asleep. Of course I felt terribly lonely, but I could believe in things like my pulse, my breath. They were a small part of New York's beating heart, the throb of its inhabit-ants, and if that pulse, that breath should fail me, some other person, some other piece of the huge puzzle would come to my rescue; as long as that person, of course, wasn't lethargic, hands tied by that simulacrum of death that is sleep. But all my remedies morphed according to the logic of my illness, and after weeks trying to avoid the night, I figured my best bet was going back to sleeping with Jim, since if there was anyone on the face of this earth who loved me, it was him, and if anyone was capable of feeling, even in sleep, that I was slipping away, it would also be him. So before I resigned myself to slumber, we would hug each other, though it always took me hours to finally nod off. At first I would remain motionless so as not to bother him; but then I'd toss and turn, so afraid of losing life.

Depending on the season, I would focus on one possible illness or another, but the cause of death that I feared the longest was a cerebral embolism. I was obsessed with these lumps, the tumors that appear out of our sight in hibakushas. I started dreading internal tumors or ones that were obstructing an artery in my brain, a blood clot that wasn't allowing the blood to circulate. I compelled Jim to set the alarm for three or four in the morning, for him to ask me a question he knew I could answer. So the alarm would go off, he would ask me completely obvious things like what my grandmother's name or my favorite food was, and if I didn't know the answers, my neurotic supposition was that it was because my brain wasn't working properly, in which case Jim was supposed to wake me up entirely and make sure I wasn't at risk of death. Things got so absurd that I'd ask him to test me with questions like "What color is Santiago's white horse?" or some such with the answer incorporated into the question, meaning Jim should really be alarmed if I couldn't respond and take immediate measures against the impending catastrophe.

It was a difficult time for Jim, not only for how uncomfortable it was to have his sleep cycles upended, but mostly because the lack of physical and mental rest was having an effect on my moods by day. When Jim received news of an unexpected trip because of an inheritance, the situation only got worse. I didn't want him to go, but understood the importance of the issue at hand and decided to stay behind, figuring that perhaps being alone for the eight days the trip lasted might shock me into recovery.

The first night I spent on the couch, and it was so dreadful that I couldn't bear the thought of a second. Even through the fog of my neurosis I was aware of being psychologically unstable and hoped it was just a bad period that eventually would pass. I never felt the need to share my state with a friend, so it was nearly impossible for me to reach out now and ask someone to spend long nights with me on tenterhooks, going through the ceremony of waking me up and asking me some obvious question so I could sleep, even if fitfully. So I spent seven deranged days, each one feeling as though it had lasted ten—hence seventy days consumed without recognizing myself in any of them, because the only way I could reconcile my fear of sleeping alone was by sleeping with a man every day.

It wasn't hard to do. I hadn't gussied myself up for a long time, an act that inevitably raised my self-esteem. The neurosis hadn't affected me physically, despite the signs of panic that like face powder deepen wrinkles, clog pores, and dull the complexion by removing all hints of light. So I spent the days preparing myself for the nightly hunt, then searching out and finally choosing my prey. Back at the apartment, we would drink ourselves tipsy, and I would take him to bed, asking to be awoken in a few hours, promising that at that time, once I was sober enough, I would make him very happy. Same as Scheherazade, who was able to postpone death night after night by keeping Sultan Shahryar's curiosity piqued with the promise of finishing her story the next day, always the next day, so I postponed my death with a much more vulgar promise of intercourse, the only alarm clock I could improvise under the circumstances of Jim's unexpected trip. The stranger's orgasm became the literary technique that gave an element of suspense to my story, what would keep me alive. I felt pleasure, but the indication that I was awake and safe was the moans of the other upon ejaculation, and the sudden contact of liquid on my belly or back, which allowed me to continue sleeping peacefully. My alarm-clock men compensated me for whatever physical rejection I felt over a strange and undesired body. It didn't matter much to me whether those men recognized the peculiarities of my vagina or not. All I cared about was not dying in my sleep. My terror was real. I was convinced that the way my brain and my heart reacted when I fell asleep was the same as when a person faced death. I would have paid any price for my life, and that sort of prostitution wasn't even the furthest I was willing to go.

# Fifth Month: 1969

## A HELL OF ICE

While I was walking along the sidewalk the morning of the day Jim was supposed to arrive, reminding myself not to forget to buy his favorite tea, I happened to raise my glance and catch sight of M, our neighbor—it's still so sharp in my mind—approaching me from about fifty-five yards down the street. I had warned Jim that I was going to disconnect the phone when he left; I was in such a state of anxiety that I didn't want to add more stress over having to wait for the phone to ring. The instant I saw M's face, still in the distance, I knew. I hadn't yet remembered that she was our emergency contact. My reaction was intuitive, prompted perhaps by the mix of gravity and compassion I perceived not in her face—she was still too far away—but in her gestures. So I knew even before knowing. Jim was dead. Before the neighbor reached me, I had fainted. How many times since that day have I wished I could have remained in that limbo of unconsciousness and never had to suffer the news to be confirmed, if only to slumber in the realm of doubt eternally, at least until death came to kiss me awake in its own domain. Had I suspected what was to come, I would have shut my eyes and never cut that little string to the slumbering brain, just let my eyes remain closed. But destiny turned the screw another notch and the string snapped; my eyes opened and I came to. The news was confirmed. He'd been in a car accident with part of his family; they had survived. M offered to accompany me to Jim's hometown, Minneapolis, so I wouldn't have to travel alone, though she'd have to get back quickly for work.

So Minneapolis it was, Jim's birthplace, as if he'd gone back to his hometown to close his circle of life. I thought I'd never return to my birthplace, and even less so to die. These were some of the thoughts I had while in the serene cloud of tranquilizers M gave me to get through the trip. I was so sedated on the plane that I felt a fleeting moment of euphoria and even giggled at my bereavement; it all seemed as trivial as a passing rain shower. It was one of the happiest moments of my life. So this was the pleasure of drugs, I thought, and though I was too overmedicated to hold a conversation, thoughts flew around in my mind that had nothing to do with Jim, future plans I'd made a long time ago, projects; or more mundane things, such as whether I had remembered to pack my face cream. I'd become so disconnected that I suddenly unbuckled my seat belt, imagining I was pregnant again, but now in the ninth month and about to give birth. After that fright, I moved on to a more pleasant hallucination. I'd heard that during the first few months of life, a fetus's skin is so permeable that it's no more than amniotic fluid. I found this connection between what's on the outside and what's on the inside surprising. My daughter, this daughter I thought of as a solid, was really composed of the liquid in which she was floating, my liquid. And by extension, in the airplane I felt as though I was part of everything around me: passengers, seats, machinery, and mites. I imagined myself as a fetus in the belly of a colossal bird, totally connected with everything taking place in its body. I felt every little crack, smelled every scent, even noticed the exhaustion evidenced by the dark circles under the eyes of the woman looking at herself in the bathroom mirror. Mine too was the sense of humor of the flight attendant who catered to me with a smile I knew was forced because we were one and the same thing, particles floating in a single element passing through us, constituting us. I was screw, turbine, and cables.

I slowly returned to myself again from within the plane's excess of serenity as the effects of the anxiolytics began to fade. H in pain. Jimless H. Homeless H. I was now detached from the rest, no longer passengers and machinery, plane food. I was back to being me, conscious of the fact that others would interpret anything I said as a sign of madness; they hadn't experienced what I had, they didn't know we could be one single thing. So after the narcotics wore off, my house seemed empty, without that ancestral fire that some call *family* but I would have to call *never*.

It was thirty degrees below zero in Minneapolis when we deplaned. Residents were given daily updates on how many minutes one could be exposed to the elements before freezing to death. M and I immediately ducked into one of those buildings whose escalators whisk you to an underground tunnel system so you don't have to walk at street level. Thus I began my descent into the catacombs, which I deem my second descent into hell, a frozen netherworld. The city's winter was like a prelude to the significance of receiving a beloved's body gone cold. Passageways that are always inside or underground, an ever-present nip in conversations, chitchat gone chilly and sluggish from frost on the tongue or muffled by clunky parkas—all of it acting as a perfect mirror for the journey to the morgue. All of it a spine-tingling anticipation of what I was about to face. And I wasn't wrong; when I walked into that frozen room I found nothing strange about it. The city had already prepared me for that moment.

Jim's family—his parents, sister, and niece—were as indifferent as ever. They allowed me to decide what to do with the body, and in keeping with Jim's wishes, I chose cremation so that later I could scatter the ashes in a place that had meant something to him, a place I had yet to select or perhaps I had yet to decide on. It all happened so suddenly I hadn't had time yet to work out the details.

Perhaps to escape the wintriness around me, my mind wandered to a spot engraved in my memory, recourse for when I needed warmth. So while waiting in the hospital for the last administrative details to be ironed out, I recalled a story I had overheard once, which surely lasted only a few minutes, though it felt to me like an eternity. I was recovering in the hospital after the bomb when a man told his story to a patient in a bed a short distance away from me. He had returned home a week after the detonation to find a woman's pelvis in his yard, the yard being all that was left of the building where he had lived. But it wasn't the sight of it that had caused him such a commotion, he said. What kept him awake at night, what he had to relive over and over again like torture, was when he picked up the pelvis to throw it in the Dumpster, and it scorched his hand. Seven days later, and it was still blistering hot.

Not only did the idea of that heat send me back to my days convalescing, but also waiting in the hospital with Jim's family inevitably tied one situation to the other. I thought back to my own recovery period, how I felt my pelvis burning thanks to that man's story, and it made me wonder if for some reason the pelvic bones, the box around the genitals, conserve heat better than others. But I lost my appetite for sex after the bomb. The only way I had responded to the sexual urge, being so young at the time, was by masturbating. But the last carnal fire I'd experienced in my genitalia was a feverish one, not a sexual one. This was meaningful to me, so much so that I'd shared it with Jim, and I felt gratified to have had the chance to tell him so many things. I'd discussed those first days of semiconsciousness with him, when I

experienced states of delirium, when I panicked over the consequences of my new state as it filtered through my healing process:
my feelings remained the same, I was still attracted to boys, but
my libido had completely vanished. Lost like a leg. Since I was
aware of the cases of amputees who'd continued to feel the presence of a severed limb, I expected to experience phantom limb
syndrome. I anticipated it for years, not realizing that phantom
limb syndrome usually appears shortly after the loss. So I fan-
cied myself fortunate in that one aspect. Feeling a leg that is no
longer there doesn't serve much of a purpose, since the phantom
leg can't step out or supplement the other. In contrast, I liked to
tell myself, so full of hope, the perception of an amputated sexual
organ just might tickle out an orgasm (for being incorporeal). As
I slowly took leave of that hope, I was overcome with the desire
for one last go. I suffered many syndromes, but phantom limb
was not one of them. In my case it was utterly gone, amputated,
like a Greek sculpture that conveys pain in its beauty: the Venus
de Milo's impossible embrace. Years later in the Vatican, on one
of the few trips I took for pleasure in my entire life, I stood con-
templating the Apollo Belvedere. And it dawned on me that my
sorrow wasn't fixated on the loss of a woman's arm, but on the
absence of a penis, with whose loss came a certain sense of relief.

I slept alone that first night in Minneapolis. I rested deeply,
as I hadn't in weeks. But I would never have slept so hard had I
known that Jim's premature death took with it a fact he would
have shared with me, I think, had he lived long enough to figure
out a way to do it. Since I didn't suspect Jim of keeping a crucial
secret from me, for the next few days my thoughts continued to
revolve around past memories. For some odd reason, everything
reminded me of Hiroshima. Even standing with Jim's family before the cremation furnace took me back to my childhood. It's
hard for me to describe in detail, I was so young at the time, but
I had a picture of myself in a hiding place, observing a ritual I

wasn't allowed to attend. My aunt had died a few days earlier, and from my hiding place, I sneaked a look at the post-cremation ceremony, something very different from the Western ritual. The relatives stood in a circle around my aunt's incinerated body. I recall just a bit of the ceremony, which I corroborated many years later when I was old enough to understand the symbolic rite. The body held its shape; that is to say, even though it was taken from the cremation chamber, the perfect calibration of temperatures maintained the shape of the body in embers without its pulverizing, as when a log in the fireplace holds its form until the moment you nick it, when it disintegrates into dust. I watched each relative, one by one, use chopsticks to pick out little leftover shards of bone and place them in an urn. When I thought back on this, it astonished me to see them passing the shards along, from one set of chopsticks to another, since my mother always insisted that chopsticks are private utensils and nothing ever should be passed with them from one person to another at the table. It was one of my mother's most zealous rules; Japanese chopsticks are an intimate extension of oneself. If I recall correctly, they started with the foot and moved up to finish with the bones in the head. I would later learn the significance of this: this way the body didn't enter the urn upside down.

This brings me now to a scene I witnessed a few weeks ago. I was on my way home, waiting for the next subway train, which was running late. There were rats scurrying over the tracks, nosing the trash scattered here and there. I could tell by how carefree they behaved that the train wouldn't be coming within the next few minutes. So I sneaked a look around, seeing other people waiting, like me, on the platform. My glance was met by a pair of eyes brimming with tears. None had fallen yet, but they were on the verge. The eyes belonged to an adolescent girl who in her sadness was handing something to her mother. The bundle measured about a foot and a half long. I could tell its contents were delicate by how gently the daughter's hands conveyed the parcel. It was drizzling aboveground, so they had improvised a raincoat for it, using a plastic bag. The mother took the bundle in her trembling hands, but before she could fit the bundle to her chest, the daughter grabbed it back nervously in a gesture that seemed almost violent. The mother snatched it back from her daughter and looked at her defiantly as she hugged the bundle close. Then the daughter cried, and the mother closed her eyes. Mother and daughter, widow and orphan, fighting like animals over the ashes of husband and father.

There I stood now, holding my own urn. Once I had it in my arms, I said goodbye to Jim's family and called a cab to take me to the airport. We passed by a park blanketed in a layer of snow and I asked the driver to stop the car and wait for me. I felt like I was having a panic attack and needed to breathe some fresh air. I sat on a bench where the driver couldn't see me. I put on my hat and scarf. It was unbearably cold, so cold that even dressed in thermal gear a person would suffer hypothermia before long. The anxiety, the cold, or both together made it very hard to breathe. I couldn't detect the scent of my exhaled breath as it collected in my woolen scarf. It dawned on me that this wasn't new, that I hadn't been able to smell a thing during those last days I had spent with Jim either. Nothing. I'd somehow wandered into a world without odors. I used to tell Jim that thanks to him I'd learned how to love my own scent. I could smell myself on him and I liked it. But it had become impossible for me to perceive my own scent in this frozen place. But what scent? Where? On whose skin? It was as if Jim had carted off my olfactory sense without my permission, something he'd helped me develop so I could smell the angles of my own body. I'd now become a sanitized woman, a deodorant against my own self, a nose located eleven yards away from my face. I stared down at the urn on my lap. I held it between the heavy gloves, which were so thick I couldn't even feel the contours of the urn. So I took one off and touched the ceramic, already dusted with frost.

The curve of the urn was like the contour of a pregnancy and I pressed it as tightly as I could against my belly. For a split second it felt as though they weren't Jim's ashes in my hands, but Jim himself in the period of gestation. Jim inside that urn, rounded like a five-month belly. Jim's first kicks. His baby teeth aren't visible yet, but they're in place, just beneath his gums. His skin is still pink because of the absence of fatty tissue. Jim in my womb, doing a little somersault in response to the last times someone other than him had penetrated me.

I could have frozen to death in the cold, but he roused me. I looked at the ring Jim had given me on my finger. We never actually married, but he gave me a ruby about a year after we met, a symbol of new blood, of rebirth. I never knew whether Jim was alluding to our shared luck at having found each other, or the newness of my life with him, now that I'd finally achieved my sexuality. And I realized there in that frozen park that I would never know the answer, never could I be sure whether the ruby was a symbol for both of us or only me alone, always alone, despite all Jim had done to make me feel that he was and always would be my companion. I was about to put my glove back on and return to the cab when I noticed how red my hand had become from the cold, and how it was beginning to swell, in part because of my circulatory problems. I touched the ring. I hesitated a bit and my hand swelled a bit more, enough that the finger now felt the pressure of the ring. I had my answer. The ring hugged my flesh and told me that the red stone was a symbol for life, his and mine. At least that's what I chose to believe then. I was sorry I hadn't ever shared the news of my pregnancy with him, even if he might have interpreted it as a sign of instability, or what it surely was, the physical materialization of my desire to become a mother. Take it as he would, it was me, this was me and my desire, and I should have told him. I put my glove on and returned to the cab.

WHEN I GOT BACK TO NEW YORK, I was able to sleep a second time without panicking. Though despair filled every nook and cranny of my bed, Jim's absence now acted as a substitute for my death phobia. If each one of the days he had been away had seemed like ten days to me then, now after his death, each day felt equivalent to ten weeks. Life now transpired in a kind of slow motion. And it finally dawned on me one night that the last penis to enter my body wasn't Jim's. Not even one of the last seven of them had been Jim's. I felt like puking. I ran to the shower, soaped up, and scrubbed my whole body, as if so many days later, there could still have been some trace of unwelcome skin left. But everything dragged, everything moved so slowly. Those men's tongues licked my skin at a snail's pace, and left deliberate trails of saliva. I clutched a vase Jim had given me. I felt like smashing it against the wall. But I couldn't. The rage bubbling up inside me didn't show itself with sufficient energy. Even my anger was numbed. It was a submissive rage, cowardly, incapable of gathering even the ferocity to destroy a simple vase and provide a moment's respite.

AND SO BEGAN A PERIOD of loneliness similar only to the loneliness I felt being shut up in the body that had been imposed on me. My life with Jim had taught me what great love could be, but I'd also become relatively comfortable, had stopped struggling with the question of whether I should be alone or if I should find someone for whom my past and my present were supportable. During ten years at Jim's side I had enjoyed near completeness, but it had produced a kind of collateral damage, such as what happens when a person who has experienced turbulent times finally relaxes and lets herself go with the flow. Thinking back on how hard I struggled in the distant past as compared with these latter times with Jim, I realized I had become someone else entirely, someone much cozier, more on the side of those against whom I used to have to raise my voice to be heard. In the end, I guess, it came down to my collusion with the strong, the putative conventional people who led heterosexual lifestyles in plain sight. In that process I'd lost one of the defining structures of my life, feeling empathy for the weak, a sisterly tie to those invisible men and women. After Jim died, my condition began to collapse again. I was back to debating whether to remain single or otherwise be forced to explain until I couldn't stand to hear myself speak about who I was and what could be expected of my wounds.

These feelings were of themselves difficult to process, but in Jim's absence the real challenge was the feeling that Yoro, the daughter I'd taken as my own after spending so many years searching for her, was also dead to me now. It's true I still had my own secret unspecified or imaginary daughter, but for a time I felt as though my belly had stopped growing too. Just as I had impregnated myself, I was now dis-impregnated. I wonder what you call those creatures, if they exist, who don't need a partner to reproduce, and don't need one to undo it either. I'm not talking about abortion but about going backward to the time before gestation. Jim's death triggered a double abortion all at once. I felt hollow. Empty inside and out, with nothing to give and no desire to receive a thing. Logically, Jim had made it very clear on several occasions that his only wish, should anything happen to him, was that I continue looking for Yoro. But for the first time in all these years I felt disconnected. It's not that I didn't love her; it's that she felt dead to me, or unborn. I was sterile again, cut off from that girl as if the scissors that had cut off Jim's life had snipped the umbilical cord that tied me to her too, or perhaps Jim and the umbilical cord had been one and the same thing. For a very long time I reneged on my promise to continue looking for his girl and on my second promise too: that I would never allow anything or anybody to devastate me again. Jim had insisted on this over and over again, made me promise him constantly, almost like an obsession. Or maybe he simply saw what I couldn't: my utter and continuing state of vulnerability, as if I was dangling from the end of an unraveling rope that could snap me into the void at any given moment. And that's precisely where I fell, into the void.

For several months I did absolutely nothing. I slept most of the day away and spent the rest of my time on the couch. Even the most commonplace tasks of my daily routine became epic challenges. Basic needs were an uphill struggle; a simple shower took the whole day. I couldn't get food down my throat. I forced myself to swallow purees because anything solid made me gag, the tiniest pieces stuck; my angst contracted the muscles in my throat. I was so isolated I was succumbing to agoraphobia and unable even to go shopping. F, an old friend of Jim's, picked things up for me once a week.

One day when F came to deliver my weekly supplies, I opened the door to find her standing there with a dog in her arms. She told me someone had abandoned it at the entrance to the supermarket with a note on its collar saying the dog had been vaccinated, that she was a good dog, but the owners could no longer take care of her. The note also gave her age: twelve years old. She was a very old dog. F figured some company might do me good, though I think her true purpose was to force me out of the house in the guise of a daily walk with the dog. To F's surprise, as she eyed me skeptically from the doorway, I accepted. I hadn't yet considered the matter of daily walks, and the reason I decided to keep the dog came from something I'd been mulling over for some time. I was convinced that my life was coming to a quick end. I'd lost my desire to live, I felt irrelevant, and in some way

I recognized myself in that old dog. Jim's death had aged me so much despite my relative youth. So I kept the dog on the assumption that neither one of us had much time left, which is also why I told F never to buy family-sized items, only enough to last seven days. Why spend money on food that was going to outlast me? Of course I never laid it out to F in those terms, but that was nevertheless my rationale.

In fact, the whole notion of an expiration date really caught my fancy. On my last birthday, just after Jim died, S sent me a beautiful plant by courier. It was gigantic. The trunk was so thick it looked more like a small tree. I loved the thoughtfulness of her gesture, but the plant quickly turned into a source of anxiety. I had a bit of a green thumb and began to worry that if I cared for the plant the way I knew I should, it too was going to outlive me. I obsessed over what would happen to the plant when I was gone, who was going to water it. F was already such a big help; I didn't want to add things to her list, like the ridiculous inheritance of caring for a plant.

So I accepted the dog because she was old. I tried to ration the purchase of one food item more carefully than the rest: eggs. I ordered them only three at a time because if something was to happen to me, which I was beginning to foresee, I didn't want anyone to encounter the stink of a rotten egg before they found my body. The matter consumed me so fully that every once in a while I would jump out of bed to make sure I hadn't left an egg outside the refrigerator. There was no logic to the obsession, which is usually the case. I knew perfectly well that the eggs were in the fridge, but the overwhelming fear obliged me to get out of bed and check once, twice, even three or four times. That's how much I fretted over the idea that someone might confuse the odor of a rotten egg with that of my dead body. Rotten eggs were the overt symbol of my dysfunctional ovaries, and I couldn't abide that someone's last image of me could be linked in any way to that deficiency, which made me feel as much distress throughout my life as the penis I could never bury.

Though, as it happened, the little dog liked eggs, so my order increased from three to six per week. Someone told me eggs were good for a dog's coat, so I fed them to her raw, though I never noticed any difference; the animal's fur was simply not very pleasant. She kept me company, though it took us a while to get used to each other. She was a little cranky and claimed areas of the apartment I wasn't allowed to cross without her growling at me. The bathroom was her favorite spot of all, which she turned into a sort of lair. I figured maybe it was the humidity that attracted her; she seemed to be a water-loving dog. But there came a point when she started to spend all her time in the bathroom, and her growling intensified whenever I tried to enter it. I imagine her previous owners mustn't have fed her very well, because within a few days she had begun to gain weight. I concluded it was due to eating all those eggs.

From time to time I'd admire my little tree, which continued to produce flowers, and had to admit I had a way with plants. The blossoms were reddish pink, like a cherry tree. It made me think back to the springs of my childhood, when my parents used to take me to the cherry blossom festival in April. All of that seemed so distant now. Another life. And seeing those flowers on my tree also made me gloomy. I worried that whoever kept the plant might find it a nuisance to constantly have to sweep the floor of fallen leaves. I felt like I was raising something only to abandon it in its youth, when it was healthy and in full bloom. But with the dog I sensed exactly the opposite. The dog's weariness—exhaustion like mine—and the boundless need for sleep that accompanies the end of all our lives, her quirkiness, even her smell (I grew up in a rural area and knew that youthful things, whether flesh or stone, always have a different smell) told me that I would outlive her, that I wasn't caring for this animal to abandon her, but to bury her. It's the least one can do for the elderly, I thought. I'll place cherry blossoms on her grave. I prepared myself mentally. It was a joyful thought. Following Jim's death, all acts seemed definitive to me now, and emotion was limited to either sorrow or joy, thinking the experience might never come again. An elderly person's die contains only two ciphers: sorrow and joy. Once tossed and scrutinized, the die presents only a single option; the die of dotage makes no allowance for indecision, offers no time to question whether one is happy or sad, no lull in the process of development, such as at other periods in a person's life when a radical emotion can be cultivated.

One day the dog started to bark. It was the first time she'd ever barked at me; till then all she had done was growl. She was in the bathroom and seemed to want to be lifted into the bathtub. *Idiosyncrasies of old age,* I thought. Since she was so hefty now, I built her a little stack of books to get some purchase and jump in herself. It was hard to know what she wanted, but I opened the faucet for her and took care to adjust the water temperature to lukewarm, since it was chilly in the apartment. I plugged up the drain, and soon the water covered her paws. She seemed to like it. She lay down in the water. Then I shut off the faucet and sat down to observe her. She looked even bigger wet, resting there on her side. I figured she was enjoying it and maybe it wasn't just a peculiarity, but something her previous owners did and that she'd grown accustomed to, which made me think how little it would amuse me to put up with the idiosyncrasies of strangers.

But something was happening. The expression in the dog's eyes had altered. She was observing things differently. It seemed as though she was finally welcoming me into my own home for the first time. And her belly began shifting. I didn't want to understand, but I did. She licked her vulva, which was underwater, but I didn't dare remove the plug. Finally a little sac was expelled, and she bit into it with her teeth. The first puppy was born. It blew raspberries with its muzzle and agitated its tiny paws in the water. It looked like a little hedgehog in a lake. I picked the puppy up and wrapped it in a towel; I could feel it trembling and wasn't sure whether it was because of my hands or because the newborn was cold. Three more puppies emerged. Identical. Or at least it seemed that way. I waited a few minutes after the last one came. The bathwater was red. The placentas were floating, broken into segments like the frayed membrane of a giant egg. The dog wanted out of the bathtub. It was difficult for her to move. But the puppies were in the towel outside the tub, and that seemed to give her strength enough to jump out. She started licking them. It seemed so odd to me that an old dog like her could have puppies. For a second, the idea of my maternity fluttered through my head, even though I had sworn never to go back there. It passed quickly and I asked the dog something. I don't remember exactly how I said it, but I was worried about who would take care of the litter and the tree when I was no longer around.

AS F HAD CALCULATED, the responsibility of walking the dog fell on me. I'd been so engrossed in this idea of expiration that such a basic task as that hadn't occurred to me immediately, and the first times out were hellish. After Jim's death, I became utterly consumed by agoraphobia. I had no alternative, and the way my body reacted when I went outside gave me a good sense of what must happen in a person's heart when she is facing the experience of her death. The day I die, the final beats of my heart, the last syllables of the muscle as it takes leave of me won't sound foreign to my ear; they'll be the echoes that reverberate from the scars left by the cardiac lesions of that period of time. When I opened the door and stepped out on the sidewalk, the buildings on either side of the street seemed to bow and then meet up high, creating a kind of dome blocking out the sky. It was like stepping through a cylinder. I had to walk very slowly, clutching at the curved facades so as not to fall. I don't know if you've ever seen one of those circles or wheels in an amusement park that you walk through while the rest of the contraption continues rotating. Well, it was something like that, only this time the circle wasn't three feet long, but a cylinder of indefinite length. In spite of my psychological and physical malaise, and regardless of whether that spatial curve was actually there or not, I knew somehow that none of it was real, or at least I wasn't experiencing the same reality shared by other pedestrians around me. What I mean is that I could tell the difference between what I was seeing and what others around me were seeing, what was real for me and what was real for everyone else.

This awareness had positive and negative consequences. On the positive side, since I was aware that all of this was taking place in my own head, I wasn't completely bonkers, thinking everyone else but me was wrong. It helped to know that I was still sane enough to realize I had a problem. But the symptoms, the suffering, and the adrenaline were so overwhelming that it felt like being locked in a cage with a hungry tiger. Let's say I could feel its breath on the nape of my neck, its teeth breaking my skin, the wound now bleeding, and though I didn't see the tiger, that didn't mean it wasn't crouching there, just behind me. My perception, emotions, and body were off-balance, but the neuronal network was healthy, which had a negative effect too: I was living in a world that was uniquely mine, a world that only I could see, so the loneliness became excruciating. But above and beyond the loneliness was my knowledge that other people couldn't see the streets curving as I did, which only heightened my unease because it obliged me to conceal what was happening to me. Anyone can appreciate how hard it is to stay vertical on a sloping sidewalk, struggling to avoid falling flat on your face, without giving yourself away to other people who do not have this problem.

My new pal forced me outside to face these difficulties, which

I knew might be beneficial in the long run, and I felt safer having a leash to grab on to in the meantime. The leash gave me stability; it was like a flexible walking stick. After months without stepping across the threshold of the front door, I felt fortified by this extra bit of support. My mother used to love telling her friends how when I was little, the first year I was able to walk, I needed a newspaper to do it. With the newspaper in my hand I could walk, I could go down the stairs, I could run, but as soon as they took it away, I'd fall. Who could have imagined that so many years later I'd need to learn to walk again, this time with a dog's leash and my sense of sight? Who could've imagined I'd end up with an aversion to newspapers because, as you know, war isn't visible without them? If one country is preparing to bomb another one and they want the media to cover it, they go to the newspapers to find out what day will give them the maximum audience, which is the best to launch the first projectile. The press organizes the calendar of massacres; it contributes the opening shot for the marathon of war. What made me feel safe as a baby now makes me embarrassed.

There was nothing random about being flooded with memories of my early childhood. Watching the dog give birth may have triggered it, or perhaps being so utterly isolated sparked the maternal instinct as a means of new companionship, but what matters is that for the first time since Jim died, I could feel the heft of my pregnancy again, and I could pick back up where my mind had left off, at the five-month mark. Yet there was something different this time. What was growing inside of me had a name, a familiar presence, a perfectly defined identity: it was Yoro. And whenever I felt the need to talk to my belly I would use that name, knowing that a fetus's tiny eardrums are already formed by the fifth month. Thus Yoro could hear what those other than Jim hadn't cared to listen to—both my heart and me, my voice, H, the mute letter who decided then and there to speak to Jim's daughter, to mine, to Yoro, who I was sure was listening with her tiny ears, and maybe even sucking her thumb.

Though now I had company thanks to my pregnancy, I was still going through a lot. I stayed outside only long enough for the dog to relieve herself. Whenever I felt dizzy, I would stop and sit on the stairs of some doorway and pretend I was adjusting the dog's collar or tying a shoe, only to undo it later and tie it again somewhere else. The most important thing was to avoid conversation at all costs; I didn't trust that I could control the situation and chitchat like normal. But not everything was negative. I knew the fetus could perceive the variations in light through my body at five months, and when the sun shone, it relieved me to know that Yoro was also discovering something beautiful: light filtered through my skin. Once the dog had done her business, I would go back home, stretch out on the sofa alone, and close my eyes for a few minutes, feeling safe, at home, on firm ground, and I'd relax. The walls in my apartment were always straight and the necessity to pretend was over.

Clearly, I'd heard that the support of a psychiatrist or psychologist could be very helpful under these circumstances. But I still couldn't bring myself to use public transportation or walk more than a few blocks at a stretch; I thought it was best to give myself a little time until I could make an office visit. Meanwhile, I began fantasizing about the figure of a psychologist as a panacea. I recall those days as being happy ones, with the possibility of a cure bringing a new sense of hope. Having seen the sunlight again, even if only for a brief period while walking the dog, I could picture something I failed to believe in until then and had only regarded with utter apathy: my recovery.

# Sixth Month:

## LOST IN MY BRAIN

A few tiny steps led to a few more, and though it proved challenging, I was able to walk for the first time into a psychiatrist's office, that of Dr. Z, who had come highly recommended. I spent hours thinking about how to properly explain to him my issues, my phobias, and my despair over Jim's absence. I had a hard time ordering my thoughts, and it was even worse trying to figure an effective way of expressing them to a stranger. But I did my best, trying to make the doctor's job easier by shaping my story into a useful tool for my recovery. After listening to my litany of symptoms, the doctor looked as if he'd just woken up and asked about my relationship with my father as a young girl, as if he hadn't heard a thing I'd said. I couldn't find the connection, since one of the few things I was sure of is that my situation was owed to a very real concern, the death of a loved one, just as my previous crises were inevitably tied to the very specific circumstances of having to renounce maternity or my sexual identity. But I answered his questions thoughtfully, despite feeling dubious that my relationship with my father in childhood had anything to do with the issue at hand, trusting the word of so many people who had assured me their recovery began right here, within these four walls. Surely they can't all be mistaken, I told myself.

Well, I learned that it's possible for everyone but oneself to be mistaken. That gentleman lacked the intelligence to analyze a single thing. He diagnosed the problem I was already perfectly aware of, which is what brought me to his office in the first place—depression—and said I needed proper medication as soon as possible. He referred me to a psychologist for group therapy. I asked if medication was really necessary and wanted to know how he felt it was going to cure me. He said yes, absolutely, in answer to the first question, and our dear Dr. Z had no idea how to respond to the second one; he simply looked at me snarkily, as when someone tries to make up for his lack of knowledge by dismissing your question as ridiculous.

After six months of treatment I knew exactly what kind of method the doctor was using: trial and error. A perfectly unscientific method. He changed my medication according to the secondary effects the different pills had on me. It didn't take a rocket scientist to read the brochures and appreciate that each medication was geared specifically to treat different types of problems. But all he was doing was looking for one that would just shut me up and was free of side effects. So I went through periods when I lost my appetite entirely and periods of binge eating. In six months I went from weighing 110 pounds to 155, and from 155 to 104. Apparently, they couldn't find the right medication, the drug that would sedate the sorrow away with minimal collateral damage; a sorrow that eventually would have gone away.

A friend recommended that I see another specialist. There was a caveat, though: it took an hour by train to get to the specialist's office, and for me the action of walking to the subway, riding the subway, then walking from the subway to the office was the equivalent of drenching myself in cow's blood and jumping into a shark-infested sea. But prey to the magical thinking one tends to embrace in times of weakness, I decided that because he was so far away, he was a better psychologist, similar to the notion that the best sorcerer is the one who requires the greatest effort to reach, with challenges and tests to realize along the way. That's how I became part of Dr. O's practice. The O could also be thought of as a 0, as in Dr. Zero. What should have been an hour's commute was actually three, thanks to all the times I had to exit the subway, with intense panic attacks and vomiting. Certainly the experience heightened my sense of sacrifice, making me believe it meant something special, that by overcoming so many obstacles I was activating a kind of positive reinforcement. Dr. Zero's diagnosis for the same set of symptoms was entirely different, a variant species of bipolar disorder that also required medication, in this case a mood stabilizer. It didn't take me as long this time to refuse more medication. I changed doctors once again.

Over the next three months I was diagnosed with as many different illnesses as doctors consulted: three, Drs. E, W, and B, respectively. Just imagine that for a bellyache, one doctor diagnoses liver cancer and the second appendicitis, and the third assures you it's only gas, and each wants to treat you immediately with a liver transplant, an operation to remove your appendix, or a few simple pills. Well, that's psychiatry for you. Of the three, Drs. W and B caused me the most distress.

Since Dr. W had no idea what sort of diagnosis to make, he tried to work backward, first choosing an illness and then offering up a tray full of symptoms. Over the four months I visited his practice, Dr. W would habitually ask me if I heard voices. Dr. W had chosen schizophrenia as my disorder and was simply waiting for me to manifest the major symptoms in order to send me to a psychiatrist who would share the pharmaceutical company's profits by way of the insurance company. Since I never heard voices, my answer was always no, but the doctor asked so many times it made me feel as though the specialist had already come up with his diagnosis and the absence of voices was all that stood in the way of verification. He was so insistent about the supposed hallucinations that in one way or another, he held me responsible for screwing up the treatment. So pretty soon I started to question myself, doubting whether the voices I actually heard, the same ones that everyone else heard, were real, and worried that they were just figments of my imagination. So when a cashier's voice came over the loudspeakers in a supermarket, I would go to pieces thinking it was one of the voices the doctor was waiting for, and so I would timorously ask someone to repeat what the voice had said. And sure enough, the other people could parrot back the voice's announcement. Exactly what I had heard myself. Unquestionably the voices I heard were real and meant for everyone, not just me, but I had to suffer weeks of second-guessing myself and dread before I finally told the doctor I was never coming back to his practice again.

As for Dr. B, he suggested a method that triggered a considerable problem for me. I told him how I got up several times in the night to make sure the eggs were stored properly because if I forget to put them in the refrigerator and subsequently died, someone worried about me might come into the apartment with the firemen or the police several days later, and I was afraid they might mistake the stench of rotten eggs for that of my body. I also explained my obsession with eggs was tied to the pain I felt over not being able to have children and to a comment I once heard a vegan make that when you eat an egg you are eating a hen's period, which served only to remind me that I'd never had regular periods in my life. Of course by now I was savvy enough to know better than to speak about my phantom pregnancy. Dr. B ordered me to write down twenty times on a piece of paper exactly what I'd told him about this obsession and close with a sentence: *The eggs we eat are not hens' periods.* I couldn't understand the therapeutic advantages of this method, but did it anyway. Instead of getting out of bed each time the compulsion struck, I wrote *The eggs we eat are not hens' periods* over and over again. After writing this hundreds of times, I went from being obsessed about eggs at night to thinking about them at all hours of the day. The repetitive writing had only bolstered my fear. Months later, when the obsession subsided thanks to the therapeutic effects of the passage of time, I sent a note to the doctor that consisted of a single phrase: *Your eggs are nothing but a hen's period.*

Something had intrigued me since I started looking for psychological help, and I wondered how it was possible that methods created for Western brains were used to analyze brains like mine, which are shaped in a society with entirely different moral, aesthetic, civil, and legal codes. I was relieved to find I wasn't the only person to consider the issue. A small group of psychologists and sociologists with a bit of common sense criticized the phenomenon, employing the English term *weird,* an acronym for Western, educated, industrialized, rich, and democratic societies, to call attention to the fact that the studies were produced—and still are—based exclusively on people from Western societies who could be categorized as cultivated, industrialized, rich, and democratic. So the word *weird* called into question the legitimacy of studies applying pseudoscientific methods and, more dangerously, medications, in which 96 percent of the cases were drawn from a group that represented only 12 percent of the world population. The supposed mass therapeutic method was based on the study of this minority (*weird* for how scarce they were, not for the symptom indicators), a group to which I definitely did not belong.

Not a single one of the doctors I saw helped me get any better, and I was continually amazed by the audacity with which they tried to tell me how I felt. They actually used sentences like "You're much better" or "You've had a relapse this week." Even while everything was collapsing around me, the sidewalks and streetlamps and sky curling round my head, how could I be persuaded that anybody else knew how I was feeling except me? And yet there they were, all those diplomas on the wall, charging me a fortune to tell me what I, and nobody better than I, could possibly know. It was the last straw for me, this pretense that they could intuit other people's feelings. I remember feeling truly shaken once by a case. During the hours I spent in Dr. B's office, I had time to get to know and grow fond of other patients in the waiting room. One young man was elegant, well read, and lonely. He told me how at certain critical times during his illness he heard voices that according to others existed only for him. He admitted this symptom had to be controlled in some patients, but in his case it wasn't necessary, he said. The voices others heard were often insulting or frightening, while in his case they only said nice things and in many ways they were his only company. Months later, I heard he'd committed suicide. They'd taken away the only voices that spoke to him. The medication had taken effect.

As a result, above and beyond my normal fears, what now flourished was my phobia of psychiatric or psychological practices. It would have been silly to go to a psychologist to be treated for a phobia against psychologists, though according to them, this is entirely possible. They would employ, if I'm not mistaken, implosive therapy, a behavior therapy that exposes a patient to the feared stimulus ("anxiety-arousing situations," I think is the phrase they use, with those fake airs of erudition) without an escape route. As things stand right now, and for the good of the therapist, may I never find myself locked in a room with one of them.

Regardless, I didn't make the final decision to leave off therapy and medication. I didn't have the willpower to give anything up. Though I had to hear as many diagnoses as therapists I visited, they all concurred on the date when I could finally consider myself cured. I remember it perfectly; it was April 7, the day my medical insurance expired. I was still a little woozy at the time, but realized I'd finally put an end to an ongoing process of ignorant speculation that'd had nothing to do with science, and for months I'd been incapacitated for thinking and for physical exercise, since the medications left me feeling lethargic and floppy.


IMAGINE BEING LUCID ENOUGH during an episode of madness to know the thoughts gripping you are the product of your neurosis and not what is commonly accepted as reality. It's a hard thing to accomplish, but imagine, if only for a second, reaching the level of awareness that allows you to figure out that your head is playing tricks on you by using the rationality of that very same head. But this kind of lucidity—an advantage I've been lucky to have—isn't enough. The second step is inevitable, which is to ask for help. And that's just what I did. I asked for help. And since the psychologists offered none, I turned to friends. But there was a problem with that. When I picked up the telephone, desperate, begging frantically for someone to come and fetch me, to embrace me, to relieve me if only with the bullet I wasn't resolute enough to use on my own; when I called someone to scream for help and that person was willing, saying, "Yes, I'm on my way. Calm down, everything is going to be all right. Just let me know where you are and I'll be right there," I could never say where I was. Of course I don't mean literally; I knew my address—what city I was in, the name of my street, the number of my apartment—but I didn't know where I was in my own head, where it was that I had gotten lost.

Later I was astounded to find a book that dealt with exactly what I'm trying to explain. The title is *My Stroke of Insight,* and the author gives a personal testimony of having survived a stroke. In some languages the title was translated in a more revealing way, something like *A Rush of Illumination.* There's a reason this book is particularly exceptional, and it's that the author, Jill Bolte Taylor, is a neuroanatomist and impassioned brain researcher who specialized in strokes, so she was able to experience (from the section of her brain that remained unscathed) the stroke as it happened in real time, even with evident fascination, since she was now able to understand from the inside the reaction of her brain, this organ to which she'd devoted so many years of research, projects, and dreams. What was the likelihood that a person who had sacrificed so much to comprehend the nature of a stroke, a bona fide expert, would herself succumb to that specific condition? So there she was, dying, while experimenting on an organ that neither she nor her colleagues had ever been able to experiment on before: not a monkey's brain or a dead person's brain, but a live brain, and not any old live brain, but her own.

One of the things that fascinated me the most was how Bolte Taylor discussed certain thoughts she'd had at the exact moment the stroke took place. She was home alone and needed to ask for help. So she had to call someone—I don't remember who, maybe her mother or someone at the hospital—and she had to get the phone number from the list of contacts in her cell phone. It was the single most important phone number she'd ever call, because her life depended on it. Yet she couldn't recognize the letters in the contact list; if I remember correctly, she couldn't recognize either letters or numbers as signs. Here's what impressed me so much. At one point she knew that all the information she'd accumulated since her childhood (including the phone number) was there in hundreds of little drawers in her brain, and she was aware that it was all misplaced now. Everything she'd registered throughout her life was someplace, but how could she know which one of those numerous drawers held the precise information she needed just then, the information that would allow her to ask for help? That's how I felt, only in my case I wasn't looking for a telephone number. I was looking for the spot where I had gotten lost. Which one of the drawers, of those hundreds of drawers surrounding me in the labyrinth of passageways, could I open to find myself huddled inside, cheerfully surprised that I had actually found myself? Desperate, furious, and hopeful at times, I spent a long time opening and closing drawers—one day, then another, and another, and every one of the nights. Eventually I pooped out, was completely spent trying to locate myself. And I knew that nobody could help me because I wasn't able to say in which of those drawers I could be found.

That's when I hit rock bottom, sir, because once I'd realized that my brain was playing tricks on me, figuring it out by way of that same trickster brain, and after accepting that I needed help, and after selecting the friend who would push me the hardest, who could pluck me out of wherever I was, I was astonished to find myself confronting the worst fear of all: not knowing where I was. This is what happened. Picture the long, winding furrows that make up our brain's gray matter—I think they're called cerebral convolutions—as if they composed a skein of organic wool. Well, that's where I was, inside the skein, asking for help, it's true, but not very resourcefully. I was still in the grips of agoraphobia, cowed by even the smallest tasks, like walking down the street. I dressed and went outside expecting to get my due for the mere act of walking down the street: death. I honestly believed that death was waiting for me outside. I didn't even think about the dog or the tree. My only option was to walk and to die. So that's what I did. I went outside.

I REACHED THE PARK near my apartment by clutching at everything, grasping at the walls at times, as if I were blind or drunk. I remember the grass was sprouting green. It was springtime. I had trimmed my own hair the day before, from what little still grew beneath my wig, as if trying to delay nature's resurrection, the change of season after the snows. Grass in the park, shorter hair on my scalp, because I wanted to express the following: flowers, squirrels, hibernating animals, wait till I recover for rebirth, wait for me so that I can watch you. But they hadn't waited. There were the trees, shameless, blossoming, in spring, while I hadn't left winter yet. Enwai—my name for New York—was in full bloom. And that's how I began walking, expecting to die. I crossed the park without leaning on anything, free, evolved: from a simian woman to *woman erectus,* convinced the city would be the last place my feet would ever touch, my eyes would ever see, my badly wounded head would ever appreciate. Enwai was like Yoro's first sonogram, and I absorbed it all with a blend of expectation and fear, while Yoro, in my womb, revealed the genesis of New York as I meandered along, her heart beating hard and fast, what's expected of a six-month-old fetus or a city in continuous gestation, never completely born: the unborn city.

I began at the intestines. A jumble of streets in a mile-long stretch from north to south, from Delancey Street to what would become Ground Zero, and a two-mile ambit east to west from the Williamsburg Bridge to Broadway. Everything was spinning around me. I was giddy and nauseated, probably due to morning sickness, but I continued forward. They call these guts Chinatown, it breaks the grid of the body, and there can be no straight lines or squares between the stomach and the anus. I've always thought that chaos is a product of time, of complexity, and that's why I found it incredible that Yoro, being as yet so simple, so unfinished, could already have such disorder in her belly, this tangle that impeded any view of the beginning or the end. The first time I dared enter a store in this neighborhood, they told me, "We don't accept credit cards. All business here is done in cash." The big intestine doesn't want to pay taxes for what the mouth, and not it, enjoyed; or maybe Yoro's digestive tract was still immature, unable to digest the type of sophistication that came with credit and banks over palpable, jingling cash. My baby's functions weren't developed, I think, beyond absorbing the tiny amounts of amniotic fluid she drank from me. That day was a holiday in Chinatown, and there was a parade in the street. I followed behind a long red Chinese paper dragon that skipped and slithered beneath the firmament. How lucky, I thought. How lucky to be able to lift off the ground. How lucky it would be to fly with my heavy belly, with the lightness of a balloon or a planet held by laws one doesn't even need to know. Free, no references. The dragon had huge yellow scales like flames, supported by all the big and little hands of people celebrating the festival, walking in procession through the digestive galleries, the visceral tubes digesting chicken feet at all hours, orangy pig snouts, starfish, frogs, a variety of aphrodisiac powders from many different creatures who in their best days ran across the windy Asian prairies on four legs.

Enwai is the name she gave herself, that's why I call her that, though it's all been forgotten and now everyone calls her New York. They insist on emblazoning *NY*, her initials, on mugs. NY is also the name of a state, which tourists wear inscribed on T-shirts—*I ♥NY*—to splash a bit of style across their chests, not realizing that the heart doesn't symbolize their love for the city, it represents the pulse of the city thumping between their skin and the cotton fabric. Even now, when I think back to that walk through Enwai, I feel like saying "Listen up, folks, be careful with that heart. It's not just a sticker or a patch. It's my little girl's muscle, or an island they call (by way of that obsession for naming everything) Manhattan, of which only a third is asphalt, steel, machinery; so look out, because in the other two thirds, every year come March, organic matter is developed, like a boy, a rose, an ovary." But I don't want to get sidetracked by other things. I was talking about that walk I took, wandering through Enwai on the third Sunday of a month of March, when I saw Yoro, who in that month had developed—besides her intestines—her head, her brain, her lungs, and her left arm.

Walking, I was surviving so far longer than I had expected,

but anxiety affected my breathing enough that to get away from the crowds, I sneaked into a narrow alley. I would have liked to ignore the fact that Yoro had an appendix. At that point in time they were considered useless, and sailors had them removed before embarking on a voyage lasting months, to avoid the risk of the appendix's becoming saturated with noxious residues or bursting when they were far from land. As soon as I caught my breath again I went down to catch the subway. I found a seat, but a lot of people were standing. It was a sunny day, women were wearing dresses and skirts again, and nearly everyone's legs were bare, like a great forest of white and black trunks that in brushing against one another after months of cold gave off the electricity of a stranger's skin. Others in the subway brushed against me lightly. After such a long time, that whisk of another human's skin comforted me. How little it took to bring joy, no more than the brush of anonymous skin.

Surprised by my unexpected resilience, I got off at the stop where Enwai touched the sky: where the head resided. It's festooned with garlands of flowers and a river. It too was given a name: the New York Botanical Garden. You can see the whole thing from an airplane, or from the eye of the falcon who has nested there for several years now. But I saw the whole thing on foot that day. The bare-leafed trees were covered in hundreds of buds in all stages, from being invisible to blossoming. The garden is equipped with a laboratory that specializes in plant chemistry; samples of the DNA of all the plants growing there are stored in case one day they should succumb. So Enwai is wearing a tiara that is like its own planet, an arched natural reserve where the most unassuming life-forms find refuge, from oaks to lichens. Freezers there store the genetic information of extinct species. But Enwai never displays these icy chambers. Quite the contrary, she keeps them hidden in the tiara where virgin nature protects the machinery of her survival. If I live long enough to see Yoro born and growing up, I thought, I'll comb her hair in the same tender manner this garden is cared for every day, a garden whose existence could be the key to New York's reforestation.

This is how Enwai's metamorphosis was taking place, whose quickening I could sense in myself at the time, and spring was undoubtedly in the air, because I found her head inside her lungs. I was in Central Park, where Enwai's organic system was fighting to gain ground from the mechanical system. Here Enwai thinks as she breathes in and remembers as she breathes out. The main neuron spins and spins at the center of the park, around Sixty-fifth Street: a carousel with fifty-seven wooden horses. I perched atop a white one. The organ music played for three and a half minutes, the time it takes for the merry-go-round to twirl around seven times. The black horse rose and fell, rose and fell, rose and fell. Its mouth was open, as if it were whinnying with glee at the pleasure of copulating with the flesh-and-blood mule who a hundred years ago, beneath these very wooden horses, spent her life tugging the carousel around, huffing and puffing, ever more exhausted, round and round in so many circles: the carousel's, the memories of Jim, my life.

Enwai's development didn't end there with that walk, because year after year she continues to manifest signs of biological regeneration. More proof: expansion, Enwai's colonization of live cells, what the city of New York considers its most recent urban acquisition. The High Line, the unused raised train tracks that are now a panoramic garden. One's view pierces between the buildings all the way to the port as easily as the sea receiving a tongue of land jutting into it. The vegetation is lush now that the tracks are completely hidden. The stone-eyed mayor thinks this is a garden, but it's skin. Just as skin dresses bone, so meadow grows over iron. First, the greenery covered Fourteenth to Twentieth Streets—Enwai's left humerus—and then from Twentieth to Thirtieth Streets—the ulna and the radius. When the hand appears, what were once rails will be fresh green skin from shoulder to fingertips. Maybe then I'll be able to see my girl, not only me but everyone else too; maybe right now, laid out like a grassy blanket soft enough that anyone strolling across might feel called to caress it, kick off their shoes, showing the respect of a good shepherd toward pastureland. These are merely images; don't think I confuse signified and signifier. Today Yoro is a woman you will know in time. The pasture, the prairie, they aren't Yoro, but if Yoro had an ideogram, it would be something garden fresh and good for all humankind.

That whole day I thought wandering around and dying were one and the same thing. But I lived in Enwai, I resisted there, and now I felt spring arrive with Yoro's first little kicks. The sun was still warm in the late afternoon. I found an out-of-the-way corner of that green lung, wriggled out of my dress, and lay down. I could smell it. I smelled the green. Grass was growing in Enwai, and for the first time since the bomb in Hiroshima, my hair was beginning to grow. A few months later, at forty-two, I could feel the weight of my own hair. A little while later I learned that during this stage of pregnancy, a fine soft down grows to protect the fetus's skin, which still lacks fatty tissue. It's called lanugo. That day the same brownish grass sprouted over Yoro and me, like a new down.

# Seventh Month:

## IRRATIONAL NUMBER

But spring ended for me the same day it began. And three years would go by before I ever saw it again. I quit looking outside of myself during that time, because Yoro was developing inside of me, though I felt very bad for having put off the search that had been so important to the man I'd loved more than anything. But it didn't upset me enough, because my despair carried me to the heights of selfishness.

Let me try to summarize the most important events in my life during those three wintry years. My dog died, but I kept one of her puppies. I mention it because you'll soon see how holding on to that puppy's leash is what nudged me toward a brighter period. But it took three years of winter first, and though I would never have believed it possible, my agoraphobia intensified. That's when I met a man I'll call Irrational Number. The name suits him because to this day I still can't figure how many decimals he had. He was like an infinite man; all the subtle features that make up a person's individual character, in his case, were hidden from me. It's impossible to choose a word or two or even one hundred words that could possibly portray him. That's why I use the analogy of irrational numbers, an allusion to that one Greek who discovered them and in return was drowned at sea, as the legend goes. My man, my Irrational Number, had also been tossed from a boat, or more precisely from society. In the manner of Hippasus of Metapontum, he had committed an audacious act of equivalent magnitude.

First let me tell you the story of Hippasus, in case you aren't familiar with it, so you understand the association. The plucky Greek dared to measure the diagonal of a simple square, each side 1 unit long—that is, the square root of 2—and show that the result was not a natural number, nor rational, but in fact a number with apparently infinite and random decimals. He'd effectively discovered incommensurability, deemed heretical by Pythagoras, he who had defined the perfection of the universe, music, and harmony in whole numbers or fractions. Hippasus confronted the Pythagoreans with the difficulty of measuring the universe. It was a blow to the mathematical ego. How to measure the geometry of the world if you can't even measure the diagonal of a square?

The audacity of my Irrational Number—an eminent white ex-professor of English literature who taught in his home state of Georgia, who had just been released from prison a few months earlier—was to beat a white man to a pulp for trying to stop a black woman from entering a public bathroom. It's true the Jim Crow laws of racial segregation had been declared unconstitutional a decade earlier, but the white population in the southern states took a long time to accede to the rationale of a universe that had been built on black foundations. That year several black and Hispanic women filed legal complaints after visiting their doctors because they couldn't seem to get pregnant, only to find that their infertility was due to surgeons who had taken advantage of earlier procedures to tie their Fallopian tubes without their consent. The United States was practicing eugenics some forty years before the Nazis, the regime the Americans had denounced for, among other reasons, carrying out certain practices to better the race, practices which the great father had been developing. So my man wasn't simply punching another white man, but the state itself. And that meant expulsion from the university, and what to him was much more serious, an end to his sincere vocation of teaching.

A mutual friend introduced us, and we first got to know each other through letters. It wasn't difficult to forewarn him about my pregnancy. Even though my, I calculated, seven-month belly was now showing, I let him know it was a psychological pregnancy. I knew somatization was the only way to explain to other people why the pregnancy was lasting so many years: I had gotten myself pregnant. I'd already read about similar cases. A woman in Austria insisted and made her husband believe that she was pregnant with triplets for nine months, her belly had grown so large. When the birth was overdue, they finally discovered that the only thing in her uterus was a giant balloon of unfulfilled desire. It made me so sad to read how they had to return all the gifts they'd received, not for one child but for three, and how they sealed the room so as not to have to confront the loss of their babies every day, because however imaginary the pregnancy was, it was also real. I used these cases as justifications, subjecting myself once again to the academic to be moderately accepted.

Meeting him in a public space was more problematic; it brought into relief my bruised state of mind. To skirt that obstacle, pleading shyness, I suggested a dark place, a movie theater, as the site of our first date. I planned everything in a way that would help me feel as relaxed as possible. A movie theater was just the spot, a dark, enclosed space. I arranged the hour, the row, and the seat. He would get there first. I would enter only once the lights had been dimmed. I would look for the seat and settle in beside him. I cautioned that I would be nervous, a normal reaction given the buildup of desire spread throughout the letters I had written him. And that's how everything went that day. I was so nervous that I sat down without even checking to see if it was him, as if I were some random spectator. I stared at the screen in front of me, and wished I had that cubist eye, the one in my left temple that would allow me to see his complete profile and the screen all at once, without his detecting my furtive glances. I needed to calm down, I thought, he must be nervous too, but for a different reason: he was a lot older than me. I had already said in a letter that I thought age was meaningless. I could have told him that Jim had been several years older than me too. But instead I wrote that life is too short, why should I limit myself to loving someone who just so happened to have been born in the same decade as me? I count like the French, and if he had been eighty years old, I would have said, "Oh, how nice. Four times twenty." That's what I was thinking when he turned to me and we greeted each other in whispers. It all happened slowly, with a measured beginning, very deliberate, as in the verse: "not exposed, but behind a veil / are breasts desirable." I left before the lights came back on, as we had arranged. And so our first date took place between two illuminations. Grateful for the gift of blindness, unfettered by the sense of sight, I gave him four more senses to employ, following a recipe I'd sent in writing beforehand, which he obeyed step by step, delicately, affectionately, while the movie lasted. This was my recipe:

MAIN INGREDIENT:

1 pound of abstraction (repeat six times: "The only two people in this room are her and me.")

FOR SMELL:

Look to the right of your seat. I will be there. Place your mouth at the highest tip of my ear, on the exterior, right at what is called the helix (look it up for greater precision). No tongue. Bite it, or better yet, lightly press your teeth on the nerves three or four times.

Then quickly drop your nose along my neck. My excitement will continue downward at the same pace, and when your nose reaches my cleavage, the smell will already be there. But keep in mind that it's not just my smell. It's ours.

FOR SOUND:

Suck a few of your fingers and slip your hand under my sweater to reach my sternum. It's important to do it quickly because your fingers should be wet. Apply them to my skin as if they were electrodes. The wetness will conduct electricity, which accelerates the pulse. Use the pads of your fingers as if they were ears and listen to the pulse.

FOR TOUCH:

Place a bread crumb, which I will give you, in your mouth. Warm it up until it begins to disintegrate, some ten seconds. Look for my belly button and place the little mush there. Let it sit for a minute until I can feel the ball of salivated bread in my scar. Remove it and feel the texture. It's a texture similar to what you may appreciate tomorrow when we lie naked and share our bodies' liquors. It will be the kingdom of heaven. The place where a woman sprinkled yeast, hiding it in three measures of flour, and the world arose.

FOR TASTE:

Place your tongue on my tongue. Stir it around and pour out the pound of abstraction all at once: "The only two people in this room are her and me." Repeat it three times to yourself: "The only two people in this room are her and me."

Now that I felt a little surer of myself, we had our second date in a lighted place. We arranged to meet in the pub in front of my house, where I arrived having to overcome the customary obstacle of those few yards that to me were like quicksand. It was spacious enough, with huge wooden tables and long wooden benches on which people would randomly take a seat as they came in. I remember what I had on because it was the first time I'd made myself up in a while. I was wearing a very simple red shirt with a plunging neckline, dark pants, and heels, and I wore my hair down—black, long, natural. My new hair, newly born, quickly became my sterling feature, and I was so proud of it. It let me believe I'd been cured of that latent disease, radioactivity, I'd been afraid of triggering all these years and am still in wait for.

HE WAS ALREADY THERE when I arrived. So I asked for a beer to settle my nerves. I hadn't drunk alcohol in a very long time, and I think I am intolerant to ethanol, which modern science has shown often has a strong effect on people of Asian origin. So a single beer launched me into a state of euphoria that made me react eagerly to Irrational Number's hands on my thighs. We had barely seen each other's faces, and yet there I was sitting on his lap. What attracted me most was his size, not because I felt any special attraction to large men, but because it reminded me of Jim. When I sat on his legs and later, when he got up to ask for another beer, I could see other people respected him for the mere fact that he was so tall and robust, even were tolerant of our public show of affection, which was usually reserved for the private sphere at a time and especially in a place as reserved and puritan as that was. But his mind was as troubled as mine was, and though on that second date neither of us could have imagined it, the way we clutched each other, the immediate connection we experienced, the feeling that we completed each other (almost always false), the hunger we felt not for a day but for an entire lifetime beside a relative stranger—all these were signs that something was off, that we were both hollow and needed to be filled. Unfortunately no man, no woman, no child, no friend, no army can fill someone else's loneliness. The only way to appease loneliness is by embracing it, accommodating it in some non-threatening place. Just leave it alone, let it live in peace, breathe; don't fight with it or try to deploy things outside its territory like loves, friendships, companionships, since the kingdom of loneliness abides, and any attempt to fight against it will only turn it back against you.

Irrational Number and I made love that night. I didn't have to explain the peculiarities of my vagina. He just entered me, and I thought if that man, who was born in one of the most racist enclaves of the entire planet, was capable of allying himself precisely with the people he had been educated against, then he'd also know how to connect with my sexual difference, a minority in the vaginal universe. And that's how it went. He entered me, saw me, and was unperturbed. He got up later and I watched him, a Viking, over six and a half feet tall. So white. So blond. His build wasn't perfect, but it was so commanding it was impossible not to admire the energy nature had invested in constructing him. He came back a minute later with four beers. He put my head on his chest and told me to sleep, that he just wanted to look at me as he drank. Admittedly, I can't remember other moments more peaceful than that; I wasn't accustomed to that pleasant feeling of having a man admire my body that way.

That's how it went that night and how it continued to go for several more in the following months. We made love and he forfeited his sleep while I let exhaustion carry me off to that vaporous place smelling of sex, beer, and sweaty hair. And not only hair but down too, since my pubic hair had grown back, and I think more abundantly than normal from what I could see in photos or comparing with friends. It was curly, so its length was measured by thickness, and to me it was a sign of life that I would never have cut, though I allowed him to do it while he kissed me, fascinated, with as much tenderness and respect as when he talked about black writers.

I KNOW I SHOULD wrap this up soon. It seems inevitable now that the verdict will come down on me. I can sense judgment drawing ever closer, as if my ear were to the ground and I could hear the sound of the approaching train. So I'll move on to the most relevant point for closing the story, but before I do, allow me to include some pages I wrote to Jim. In all seriousness, you don't deserve access to this part of the story, the most personal part, and I can imagine that none of it really matters to you anyway, even if to fulfill some perverse curiosity. Familiar as you are with the taste of blood, you don't understand the value of stories. All you crave is to feed again off that human flesh you ripped from a neighbor one day, and in so doing lost the chance of ever being a person again. You've been hunting for that taste ever since—a taste for cash, for the protein of banknotes. Skip as many pages as you want. If I transcribe a few of my letters to Jim here it's only to leave this world hoping one single reader might comprehend. One person's regard is healing enough for me. You know? I don't give a hoot about happiness anymore. I used to think that knowing Yoro is safe would suffice; that I could die in peace. But it didn't happen that way. Now that I know where she is, have touched her, kissed her, saved her, now that I know that she'll survive not only me but probably you too, I will admit her love made me want to live as long as she is alive. And now I'm sad. Of course I am. But I don't fight that sadness. Yes, the right to happiness exists. But not the duty. I relinquish my right. Today.

Tomorrow. Who knows, maybe tomorrow I'll be happy again. Or maybe I won't ever be.

BUT BEFORE I TRANSCRIBE my letters to Jim, let me just give an account of what I am observing right now. The sea isn't visible from the cabin, but I can see the river. A broad, muddy river. I can see it from the terrace. The friend of mine who built it has good taste and a steady hand. The sun peeks from behind the trellis, but it doesn't prick, and it creates shadows laced with flowers I've never seen anywhere but in Africa. They look like fruit. There's a baobab just to the side. I remember the legend about this tree. It was so beautiful that the gods punished it by turning it upside down, burying its flowers, its leafy branches, and its treetop. That's what they did to Yoro for a long time, the most beautiful of them all; she was born and grew in the earth, alongside diamonds and gold. But I pulled her from the ground and placed her straight up. I put her on an airplane and now she's in safety, far away from you, from this earth made miserable by the hands of foreigners. Yoro is missing the vision I have right now, this Africa whose sacred trees are upside down, but I know she'll get accustomed to her new earth like I did, another transplanted woman.

Fifteen years in Africa. Who would have thought I would land in this place fifteen years and a handful of days ago, and stay so long? My whole life I thought I would die young, from some manifestation of radiation poisoning, and here I am, writing from illness, that's true, but my only diagnosis is old age. Dotage, that sickness I never thought I'd experience after all those sleepless nights shrouded in the panic of dying. Suffering now from old age, I write from a hidden cabin looking out over sights that are golden to my eyes, accompanied by the constant buzzing of life, night and day, sounds of animals and at times even plants that crackle as they grow. Of course it had to take place here, where human life began, where despite the exploitation they're subjected to, the land and its people resist annihilation.

I'm having breakfast and writing here on the terrace. Looking out over a stretch of river that is teeming with hippopotami. If I wanted to disappear, all I'd have to do is walk into the water. But I don't want to do anything like that right now. Every morning in this beautiful land is another sun. The roots of the trees are strong, deep, and able to hold straight to nourish themselves. The baobab roots help; they sustain the earth with the strength of their flowers that open to subterranean fauna, offering leaves and petals for nests. I remember those joyful days. But who isn't happy in the spring, even when it feels like winter? Now my tired old body won't admit any more resurrections.

So here, now you can read some of the pages I wrote to Jim, which made me feel closer to him, at least while I was writing them:

*Jim my love, Irrational Number lives on the sixteenth floor of a building in Harlem. Gradually, I got used to staying there and not going out, the same as in our own apartment. He has several reproductions of William Blake's watercolors on the walls. The one titled* Pity *hangs just above what is now my bed too, a huge one that overwhelms the size of a so-called marriage bed. Blake painted an androgynous figure on horseback flying through the air, holding a baby and lowering its eyes toward a woman lying on the ground with her arms over her breasts, looking up. Irrational Number interprets the watercolors for me. Not only Blake's visual or written work, but also the simplest words Blake uses. Blake uses language in a virginal way, allowing himself to be moved by the singular aura each word has the first time you hear it, and conveying—to me, like I imagine he did with his students—that quiver of primordial significance. The piece hanging over our bed, he told me, was inspired by a few verses in Shakespeare's* Macbeth, *which Blake alludes to from the very title, a word that means mercifulness or compassion. I never wrote out the verses and I can't transcribe them now by memory, but seeing the watercolor evokes them very precisely. They show a naked baby boy as a symbol of compassion and an angel meant to express horror before everyone's eyes, until the number of tears shed drowns the wind; but by contrast the voice of whoever is speaking—Macbeth, I imagine—is distressed by having such towering ambition, so excessive a drive, that when he mounts the horse of good intentions, he always ends up falling off the other side.*

*I don't think I'd be able to recollect the meaning if it weren't for hearing the verses when I saw the image, and feeling the empathy in the words, imagining myself a rider trying to flee the rancor and hatred, having seen the eyes of compassion, yearning to carry what is reflected in them to others like new links in a chain of kindheartedness, but I too always leap too far, overreach, and fall off into that territory where nothing I do matters or signifies, that no-man's-land where one is drained by the sieve of one's own intentions, regardless of how good one is. Now, for instance, aren't I giving you too much information, Jim? Should I skip over my amorous adventures with other men? I've been talking to you about someone else for weeks now. I think in spilling the details I'm confirming the fact that you can no longer hear me, even though I don't want to face up to that. Now I can appreciate the need for secrets. Keeping something hidden implies respect. Absolute sincerity is incompatible with life, with love. If only I had the desire to hide things from you, it would mean you're still alive to me. If someday I feel the need to restrain myself in my writing for fear you might find something out, it'd mean you weren't dead after all, and I'd leave this diary, throw your impostor's ashes into the garbage, take a shower, moisturize my skin, and run out to welcome you.*

*But I was talking about Blake. Pity is what I need more than anything else. The world's pity, the pity of some other, even a single one, and pity for myself, to love myself even though I haven't accomplished anything in my life, nothing beyond changing my body, loving a few people, and looking for your daughter, a girl who not for a single second of her life has ever had me in her thoughts, since she doesn't even know I exist. I can no longer tell whether that girl is the same one I am carrying inside. My pregnancy no longer seems like a miracle to me, not even an achievement; birth eludes me. I'm beginning to feel as if it's no more than a punishment, that I'm a Sisyphus watching how the stone he's lugged to the top of the mountain insists on rolling back down again. Only what in Greek myth is a stone, in real life is me. I'm the gargantuan rock I bear; the gargantuan rock I've created so as not to be alone.*

*When I consider the few things I've actually accomplished in my life, I can't help but wonder where I'm going to get the strength to pull myself out of the well I'm in. I have no faith or hope in a future or in the tenderness of your love, which is now stored in the past; nor do I have the will to inhabit the present. For years, I think, I've lived like a puppeteer; all my energy has gone into making something move, something that is lifeless without me, but that has only the appearance of being alive with me. More than anything else, I feel exhausted. I wonder when the puppet will free itself so it can hold me up, pull the strings that move my back, my ankles, my head— especially my head. It seems as though every time I wake up, I am forced to organize these strings that have touched nothing but my hands and the ground, to separate and clean the strings that I'm dragging, with the sole purpose that if one day my puppet should return me the favor and pull me up, make me*

*jump or fly or run or trip, it doesn't find the strings in a tangle.*
*But that day is slow in coming, and for that reason, my love,*
*sometimes I consider cutting the strings. Of course I think*
*about it. Cutting the strings and forever falling like a stick*
*and a piece of cloth to be shunted about and broken by the tip*
*of some random passerby's shoe, nobody imagining that there at*
*one time a brain had fired and a heart thumped. How easy it*
*would be to disconnect myself, and yet how difficult it is to grab*
*the scissors and cut those strings if not of life, at least of motion.*

*One simple act is what separates my life from my death, one*
*stroke of the scissors, something a toothy rat could accomplish.*
*How can it be that the only thing keeping such dissimilar states*
*apart from each other is no more than an artless nip or nibble?*
*Why now, when I've emptied my life of all value, does it still*
*have enough consequence to suck me dry just trying to keep my*
*breath kindled—all that effort to feed myself, wash myself, put*
*my hair up, turn the lights on or off? Why is so much sacrifice*
*needed just to maintain something that is supposed to be so*
*valuable but in fact can be obliterated just like that, in a snap?*
*It seems so strange to me, once I've decided I don't want to live*
*anymore, that people who see me in the subway or walking*
*down the street aren't able to distinguish how little I want to*
*be alive in comparison with others. How can such an enormous*
*decision be invisible to others or not alter their perception of me*
*somehow? I contemplate all these things, and yet, you see, I'm*
*alive, and not only that—sometimes I'm overcome with a sense*
*of rage that leads me to consider not cutting my own strings,*
*but perhaps one day, who knows when, cutting the strings of*
*others.*

*Piety. Blake's watercolor speaks of piety and that's why*
*I like it, and that's surely why Irrational Number chose it*
*to watch over me while I slept. His devotion to these pious*
*images is not in vain, in the purely pagan or religious senses*

*of the word; while piety in this work is rendered artistically as something traditionally religious, Irrational Number sees it as full of personal connotations. He's always been avid to know the genealogies of words and feelings, so a few weeks ago he told me a story derived from his commitment to the ideas of empathy and compassion, which is supported by other pictorial works representing piety. It's one of the most beautiful stories anyone has ever told me since you went quiet, with two main characters: a man in chains, usually an elderly one, in what invariably appears to be a prison; and a woman substantially younger than him placing her breast in the old man's mouth. When Irrational Number explained who the characters were, I understood the tale to constitute the simplest act of kindness. Let me tell you the story. I think several versions exist, but they all share the same outline. A man is sentenced to death by starvation for an unspecified crime. He's allowed to receive visits in the jail by his daughter, but permission is granted with a single condition: the daughter is not allowed to bring in food of any kind. Time goes by and the man shows no signs of dying, so the warden begins suspecting foul play. He can't fathom what's keeping him alive, since the girl, as he himself corroborates with every visit, hasn't brought a single form of nutrition. One afternoon he decides to spy on them and finally discovers what is afoot: the daughter, who had given birth a few weeks earlier, has been breastfeeding her father. The authorities, far from being outraged, take the act as a symbol of what would later be known as Roman charity and free the father—the father whom the daughter had transformed, through her charity, into her baby.*

*I've ruminated often on the image of the jailed old man ever since Irrational Number told me that story, particularly when he went out to buy something or walk the dog, and I felt even lonelier. I felt as miserable as I possibly could: old man and*

*lonely woman, or lonely man and old woman, two sorrows
and opposing genders, the kind that produce friction when they
grate against each other, like a square wheel in the soul, rusty
and timeworn. This was another period of descending into
hell. I find it hard to keep track of them anymore, and it doesn't
really matter because instead of descents into hell, they are like
numerous hells spread over the same floor. A colossal floor with
rooms all on the same level, each one with its signature brand
of suffering so unlike the rest that its very newness is what
makes it seem like you're falling again. That one was, as far as I
remember, the third hell to the right.*

*Irrational Number tried to get me out of the house on several
occasions during that time, but I always rebuffed his efforts.
I just couldn't. This continued until the morning he came up
with an idea. He said that if I preferred not to walk, he would
carry me on his back. At first it seemed a ridiculous notion. As
you can see, I'm still reluctant to act the fool, I who have had to
forgo my fear of ridicule so many times when people judged as
extravagant or shameful attitudes that were wholly innate to
me, intrinsic features of my nature, simply the way my mother
brought me into the world—features that for a long time (as
you well know) I was able to conserve.*

*So I left the house today on someone else's back, holding on
to his neck like a little girl clutching her father's horse. If only
you could have seen the way people stared. Him so huge and
me with my big old belly in between, whose growth I have
paused. Neither the gawping or my weight fazed him in the
least. He also held the dog's leash in his right hand, the dog
who kept pace with us and was ostensibly the only normal
thing about us. Remember that Bernini sculpture? Of Aeneas
when he escaped from Troy carrying his father on his shoulder,
and his son beside, so tiny in comparison to that sort of fleshy
spiral crowned by the old man's head? That's how I imagined*

*others would see our little cluster. The tiny dog nearly invisible, me atop Irrational Number, in an attempt to escape a city in flames that only I could see. It's a strange feeling to walk so high above everyone else. Not only could I observe the streets again after so long—the people, the cars—but I saw it all from a height way above what I would on my own two legs. Today I took it all in from Irrational Number's height of nearly six feet nine. I'd never have imagined how much the sight of things changed from a foot's difference in height. I didn't see individuals so much as groups, multitudes. Irrational Number explained not long ago how he had to put up with his schoolmates teasing him and poking fun all the time, treating him like a heartless giant, but he didn't remember the hilarity coming from one person or two, but as a single hoot from a multitude below. I don't think he sees singularity, only collective behaviors that steal into one person the same as they could steal into another. That's why the beating he gave that man that sent him to jail hadn't been a personal thing, he said, but a beating meted out to a body that symbolized the many together who constitute racism.*

*Our neighborhood in Harlem is fairly dangerous. The people there don't like white people, and for good reason. And that's how we walked around the place, like a huge bundle that couldn't possibly go unnoticed. They say that in moments of danger the last thing you should show is weakness, but I'm not so sure I agree. For me at least, it's always been the other way around. I think the best self-defense is showing the other cheek, like the Christians are always going on about. In my case, mounted like that on his back, like an appendage of someone else's body, not using my own legs for motion, I gave off an enormous sense of dereliction, same as that which emanated from our underprivileged neighborhood. So I didn't feel out of place and nobody looked at me like a foreigner; it wasn't the*

*color of my skin but my fragility that made me similar to them,
to people white society was trying to undermine.*

*I'm writing you from bed now, Jim, recovering from a bump
on the head. Yesterday was Thanksgiving. I woke up especially
cheerful. It was a day for hanging around the house, and
socially it justified my not going out and being able to spend
the next twenty-four hours amid these walls with all the sense
of security they provide. Strangely, even though you think
you don't care what other people think or are used to being
criticized, it's still lovely to feel that you are part of the crowd
the few times they let you feel as though you fit in.*

*That morning we heard an all-too-familiar story on the
radio: how the police abuse and murder of the black population
goes unpunished. That's what happens in our neighborhood,
where abuse of power is so entrenched in the system that
protesting doesn't make a dent in anything. But dissent and
conflict need outlets, and those conduits include gang violence
and hatred, robbery and muggings, which, though at times
economically motivated, are inevitably amplified or justified
by race. But yesterday something happened, the straw that
broke the camel's back. People poured into the streets in droves
to protest. The last straw was the news that the (clearly) white
policeman who riddled a (clearly) black man's body with bullets
six months ago won't be put on trial. It's just one more case that
proves the utter impunity the police enjoy in the United States
whenever the bull's-eye happens to be black. In this case, an
unarmed fifteen-year-old boy.*

*Irrational Number and I were cooking our Thanksgiving
bird when we heard the news, now with a warning that
disturbances were expected, and riots. Thanksgiving. You know
I've always liked this holiday for a simple reason: because I
like its name. Do you remember, Jim, how you always laughed*

*at me when I said that? But it's true that I've always taken advantage of the day to thank people whom I may have failed to appreciate properly in the rush of everyday life or because I was being insensitive or simply selfish. Yesterday I felt the tension in Irrational Number's hands, the rage on his face when the news broke. The raw turkey, recently plucked, was atop the kitchen table, and I could see him eyeing the cavity emptied of offal. I asked what he was staring at so intently. He replied that he was trying to remember a recipe. I was tickled that he would follow my lead after coming up with that recipe on our first date at the movies. I responded saying all the ingredients were already there on the table: apples, bacon, corn, bread crumbs, cranberry sauce, sweet potatoes, chicken broth. But he said his recipe was for something else, and marched out of the apartment to pick up a few of the ingredients we were lacking. He returned a little while later and placed what he called the fixings on the table:*

> *A glass bottle*
> *A funnel*
> *Gasoline*
> *Motor oil*
> *A rag*
> *Insulating tape*
> *A lighter*

*Hands atremble and anger visible in his every gesture, Irrational Number stuffed that turkey with his particular fixings, tied it with a string, and left part of the rag hanging out. And finally it dawned on me. The rag was exactly what it looked like—a wick—and the bird had been transformed into a Molotov cocktail. He taped it up, strapping the wick to the freshly plucked skin. He told me to put on some gloves, dark glasses, and a hat to protect me from his own peculiar turkey roast, and then he disguised himself too. I fell silent. I got it. But above all, I fell silent. That's how the judicial system works when dealing with a black life. It falls silent. Not to perseverate over insignificant things. But above all, it falls silent, and that silence is what allows the grand jury to holler, to condemn. Not the criminal, but the victim, the person who is dead, the black person, the black father and mother of the black person, of that black person: the dead center of the bull's-eye.*

*So yes, yesterday was Thanksgiving. We commemorated the day the Indians nourished the white settlers, thus saving their lives. The very Indians who are now all packed off and secluded in out-of-the-way reservations like animals on the brink of extinction. We heard shouting—the riots were under way. We went outside. Me, once again, on his back. I watched from on high as an enraged mob took to the streets. Their reactions were logical, violent. The police were also on the scene, shoring up the streets with barricades. Irrational Number carried his turkey in a bag. He'd have to use it soon to avoid blowing ourselves up. At one point he handed it up to me. I took hold of it, and keeping everything in mind he had told me when preparing the bird, I launched it at an angle that was between thirty degrees (so it would splatter as widely as possible) and forty-five (to gain distance). I felt a blow to my head. I'd been hit with a rock that was surely meant for the police. I was only semiconscious when I watched our stuffed turkey, the Molotov turkey, suspended in the air for a few seconds. It wasn't falling.*

*Despite everything's being in motion around me, I was able to pinpoint the image of the turkey. I heard the sound of its skin being pierced from within by the first ejected feather, with its quill, the central skeleton, all so clean and straight. Then I heard the rest of the quills being ejected like heads of wheat morphing into many-colored feathers, red ones, blue ones, green* and yellow. It was dazzling to watch, suspended like that in midair, so richly hued. It wasn't even a turkey anymore. It was a quetzal, the bird that dies if kept in captivity. It spread its wings, soaring gracefully, emptying the drippings of its belly over the multitude. I opened my mouth to catch a drop on my tongue. No death, only metamorphosis. A blend of white and black skins in a Dalmatian race. Both things at once now, white and black. The bird flew into the distance, voiding little drops like missiles that germinated a stunning race of mutts, a breed of humans with a thousand different bloods. Yesterday, on Thanksgiving, I witnessed that human amalgam as I fainted. When I came to, I wished so hard that the policeman treating my wound while we waited for the ambulance to arrive were black-and-white-skinned. I guess it'll be a while yet before that happens, my love, and I suspect my time is nearly up. There's barely enough time left even to dream about this race of the thousand purebloods.

After a few days at home recovering from the head wound, Irrational Number thought some fresh air would do me good. He arranged everything, even packed my suitcases, and we headed out. It's the longest trip I've taken since your death, you see, and we didn't even leave the state of New York. After we drove nearly four hours, Irrational Number finally stopped at the Montauk esplanade, just at the tip of Long Island a little west of the lighthouse, the same place we went crab fishing that one time, do you remember? We'd gone out in the wee hours and came back around eight in the morning. Irrational Number rented a cabin there for a month, which is where I'm writing now, about two hundred yards from where the car is parked. The place is still famous for its remarkable marine landscapes, but what really impressed me when I got out of the car that Sunday, even more than the ocean, was how thick *the grass is, and its light green color, which gave an impression of youthfulness. You bet—it was springtime again. After such a long time I could change seasons again, even if it was only a fleeting sensation of feeling the freshness of dew on my ankles. I expected my response to be short-lived, but in truth I was overcome all day long by the thrill of freshness, by a certain kind of joy. I tried to take a step forward, and though I couldn't, I didn't feel anguished. Just as he had promised, Irrational Number picked me up and put me on his back so I could straddle that huge lover again, the lover who cares for me in my feebleness, in my heartache over having lost you, Jim, and the never-ending pregnancy that is now scaring me, haunting my nightmares, incised with an image of Yoro. Irrational Number takes charge of everything and trots along with all the extra burden as if with his gait he was dusting off the layer of grime that has been settling over everything during my time of confinement.*

*We get up early every day. The dog goes out to wander about on its own and doesn't come back until nightfall. We drink fresh milk for breakfast. Everything here seems green and new. Not only the grass everywhere, but also the fresh cow's milk, the dark blue sea, and the sound of the birds. Even my name seems green to me, and so more alive, more sonorous. Irrational Number is my white horse during the day, my trotting horse at night. At times when we're asleep, when a cracked window bursts open from a gust of wind, I take advantage of the moment to caress him and he doesn't move, his sleep is so profound. He's exhausted from carrying me on our walks. I'm so grateful to him. I love him.*

*Do you mind that I love him? It's a different kind of love than the love I felt for you. I would never write to him after he dies because, to be honest, he's a necessary crutch in my life, and if I wasn't ill, I don't know if I'd love him the way that*

*I do now. It's different, was different, with you. I loved you, Jim, in sickness and in health. Loving in health is what the priests say, as if it were something so easy, but it's actually the more difficult of the two. Sickness, not health, is what bonds humans so intensely, and sickness is what is imprinting Irrational Number on me, like atomic shadows, the silhouettes of the victims that were carved onto the surfaces of things during the explosion. Like the friction of water that polishes a swimmer's body, I noticed how my body was conforming to the space left by that man's body whenever I dismounted. It's as if my bones were beginning to grow again. Don't they say that if a woman is young enough, she might grow an inch or two during pregnancy? I am not young, but it's the feeling I get when I'm on him and he moves while I remain still, and there I am, growing on top of him. Maybe it's a false sense of physical development, but when I look at my full body in a mirror, I can make out the shape of an absence between my legs. When we separate and I move around the cabin on my own as he rests or walks about a few hours unencumbered by me, I don't feel solitary as long as I remember how the shape of his back remains impressed in the curve of my inner thighs. When he returns from his outing, I run to the door to welcome him. We put on or take off our pajamas, and I can smell the scent of the fields in his clothes, and all the aromas of my horse.*

*I'm happy. We're happy. Who isn't happy in the spring, even though it's winter? But it is spring.*

*That's what I was writing yesterday when I interrupted myself, because I saw him hanging his head. You might think it's normal for such a tall man to hold his head like that when he looks at someone my size. But it was the ground he was looking at the whole time, just staring straight at the ground. I tried to justify his attitude, reason it away as if it was just a symptom of his bliss, looking down like that as something contrary to sadness. A downcast glance—I said to convince myself—is a way of noticing a fresh footprint, or the utmost present of all present moments, a blade of grass just sprouting up through the surface when two steps earlier it was still belowground. One looks up at the sky and there's no birth there. An awakening, perhaps, but that's something entirely different. The sun that rises again is an old man born millions of years ago. It takes focusing on small details to observe birth, and most often looking down at the ground—where a mushroom burgeons, or an ant colony—or hearing the little audible crack a butterfly makes when breaking out of the cocoon. I thought he was able to observe all of it and feel the joy of each new birth. I mounted him again, to live out yet another day on top of him. We were a few hours into a long walk by the time it occurred to me that my heft and I were all he had in life. It scared me to suddenly find myself thinking such a thing, how geocentric of me, what a narcissistic idea that another life needed to revolve around me, some obtuse medieval asteroid.*

*I fell asleep, my head resting on his shoulder, and when I woke up, we were passing through an area we hadn't visited before. I realized that he was not celebrating anything at all. You have no idea what went down. He started walking in fits and starts like a blind person who hadn't been born blind, but had lost his eyes for lack of use. The blindness of lassitude. His once blue and twinkling eyes were now hollows. Though I felt bad for him, I appreciated how despite his obvious despair, he was still willing to lug me around for the dose of fresh air that little by little was helping me recover. The landscape changed in a second. The day became night when the sun was still high in the sky. The roots of the trees became more visible. They rose up from the earth searching for light. The wind was light, yet trees were snapping, since the roots didn't have the strength to sustain them. Trees fell over entirely. Fallen trees and trees*

*tumbling all around till we reached the swamp. I suddenly
realized I had to get off him or our combined weight would
cause us to sink. Perhaps if I had dismounted when we entered
the quagmire, if I had stood on my own two feet, things might
have happened differently, but when I finally roused myself
to try, it was without any luck. I was so completely fused
with him we had become elements of a single centaur, and
how could I separate the animal from the human without
killing myself, without killing him? Neither did I detect in
time that song of the equine siren whose melody lures horses
bearing gratuitous burdens into the depths of mud. Blind and
bemired in the muck, I got wind of the woeful music. From its
invisible score sprang the fountain of eternal sludge. Writing
this now, Jim, I can hear the same music, a circular melody
like the vortex of mud that sucked him down. My trotting
man. I feel him so close, as if he were somewhere down below.
Might I be writing you from a few yards above his cross? How
ghastly.*

*Sadness may not be the right word to define my feelings
in that swamp. It was a kind of feeling that didn't have a
counter. A sentiment without antonyms. Happiness was not its
opposite; instead, the feeling was so absolute it disallowed even
the thought of a shade to its blackness. I lowered my head. I
remember he stopped. He just froze. Instantaneously. I pleaded
for him to keep moving, but he wouldn't budge, smack in the
middle of a bog that reached his knees, the surface just beneath
my toes. He spoke not a word. I was so frightened I couldn't
own up to my responsibility, and before I dared peel myself
away, I preferred to blame it on the music, its tempo, andante
moderato, that melody as light as it was heavy, like flour,
which thickens with liquid into a mass. I tried to shake him
up, intensify his pulse, his breathing, whatever would speed up
his slackening pace. I whispered quickly in his ear. I shouted. I*

*encouraged him. I pulled at his shirt. But he wouldn't dislodge himself. Solid as a marble slab.*

*Then we started to sink. When the mud reached the level of his groin, it covered my ankles; up to his waist it was at my knees; up to his chest it reached my chest too. I was terrified. He was sinking and taking me with him. The surface of the mud rose like a tide darkening the earth with the sea. I watched his white skin stain from the bottom up till it reached his neck. My white man was growing dark. Only then did I finally dismount, not so much to help him as to avoid being carried along with him. For some reason, I didn't sink. It was as if he was in quicksand and I was on solid ground. For the first time in ages, I was more stable than someone else, and when I snapped into action and tried to rescue him, it was for him, not just for me. But it was too late. I pulled at his wrists so hard I'm sure it must have hurt him. He mouthed words without making any noise, trying to accommodate his tongue as if this muscle had also become weak. For a few minutes I thought that was all he wanted. To accommodate his tongue seemed like his last wish as he was sinking.*

*The mud reached his lips and I pulled even harder. I could hear the music in my head moving at the same slow yet brisk pace, like a bad horse pulling my good horse to the bottom of the mire. I sobbed. I insulted him. Then I asked him to forgive me for having overburdened him. I begged him to react and told him I would never mount him again. I promised that he would recover his ability to resist without me. I pulled his hair; I did everything I could. And when the soft black sands covered his teeth and his nose and his vacant eyes and the last curve of his white ears, I hated him. He'd pulled me out of the trench I'd hidden in, that kitchen of my own despair, for this? Once he'd disappeared entirely, once all that was left of him were a few thick bubbles of heavy air, the remnant of what had been in his lungs, I was all alone again. Alone in the middle of that swamp. I cursed him for leaving me that way again, and for taking my four legs away. Then I cursed myself.*

*I never reported his disappearance. If they'd found his cadaver, they would have looked for a weapon, and I'm afraid the weapon had been me, the excessive encumbrance of my body's 110 pounds. What weighs more—my father asked me when I was young—a pound of straw or a pound of iron? I always answered straw. There was no way that he could make me see how a pound weighs a pound regardless of the material. I realize he was right now, because even as a child I intuited my destiny or my chastisement: to lug around a sack full of iron strands when everyone else saw straw. Since nobody could see or suspect that I was carrying a satchel full of iron, nobody could relieve me. Your death, Jim, added more iron to my satchel. Exhausted, I ended up imposing it on Irrational Number. But in the end he couldn't take the added weight. My colossal man of lead was gone, my heavy horse. The shape of him left in the curve of my two lonely thighs, I'm writing you now a little livelier perhaps, but not too much.*

*Once I'd lost all my trust in psychology and its servant, psychiatry, I had to get over my agoraphobia, Jim, without anyone else's help. I went back to our apartment. Since I had to walk my dog, little by little I started going farther away from home, just as I had before with its mother. So two generations of dogs had become familiar with my depression, though this last bout now appears to be allowing me to rise above the surface and breathe a little fresh air, after breathing the same stale air for so long, my lungs being like those fountains that recycle water over and over again, with a sign that reads NOT POTABLE WATER. DO NOT DRINK. That's how I've been breathing over these years, a closed circuit of air recirculating in my lungs without ever renewing itself.* TOXIC AIR. DO NOT BREATHE. *So that's what I decided: I needed to learn how to stop breathing so that little by little I could open up to some fresh air. That's how this new phase began.*

*I don't know if you recall, from wherever you are now, the sports center between the apartment and the park where they were constructing an Olympic pool just when you left for Minneapolis. When I passed by the other day, I noticed the poster announcing open registration for apnea school. Nobody I asked knew what the sport of apnea is, but I remember the legends my mother used to tell me about women in my country who would dive down deep into the sea to hunt for pearls, tankless, using only their lungs. I've always known there was one thing I could count on since I was orphaned early in life and had to survive on my own, as you know, first as a boy and then as a girl. One thing never failed me, even gave me the audacity to question my gender, my sexual identity—the first marker people use to distinguish between individuals. This one tool I trusted so much is my intuition, which is connected to the wellness of my body and to pleasure, and is what drives my natural predilection for things that are not only pleasant but also good for me. By the same token, this intuition is what guided me to giving the sport a try.*

*I consulted with our general practitioner. I hadn't wanted to see him again after losing you. So I had changed doctors. I couldn't bear to give him the news. But when I walked into his clinic, he saw me and approached me to say that he had already heard the news. He seemed sorry and sad, but also visibly happy to see me again. You know? People think it's better not to raise the subject with the loved ones of the deceased. When I lost you, people stopped talking to me about you. After the first days passed, there were days, even weeks, when it felt like you died all over again; that you died every day, over and over. At first I wasn't sure where the feeling was coming from, but soon enough I figured it out. You were being killed on a daily basis, Jim, by the silence that had absorbed the place of your name. All the chitchat about everyday things was lost on me at that time. Your death brought absolute depth to any conversation, like apnea, and that obliged me either to talk plainly about your death or else about topics that involved nonexistence, perhaps subjects that many people find painful to discuss, but it was in them that I could see the representation of your emptiness. I needed to talk about you as much as I needed to use your toothbrush—which by the way, you forgot at home—brushing until my gums would bleed. You see? All that nonsense about not mentioning the noose in the house of a hanged man is a big lie. I needed to talk about the noose and its texture, who manufactured it, how the neighbor hanged himself in exactly the same way. More than anything else, I needed to talk about the hanged person. I wanted to talk about my departed one, and if I couldn't talk about my own, at least let me talk about other deceased people or about death itself, any subject that really allowed me to talk about you. I would have loved for everyone who knew you to come over, not to keep quiet or to see me in grief, but to say your name. I would have been grateful if the fireman who removed you from the tangle of the car's steel had described your last look to me. But it didn't happen that way.*

*Only one person actually brought you up to me. It was our neighbor M's youngest daughter. One afternoon as we were having a snack in one of the few get-togethers with friends I participated in, the girl asked if she could play with one of the toy soldiers in your collection. I saw her mother shoot her a glance that said,* Lower your eyes and be quiet. *That's when I broke down and started to cry and told them all to leave. I'm sure that even today they all think it was because*

*of the girl, that she'd hurt my feelings without meaning to,
when they were really at fault, treating me as if you'd never
existed, burning the memory of you—which is the soul—and
tossing away before my very eyes the ashes that are your soul
in the urn where your body's ashes already were. That's what
people who won't talk about the dead achieve: they cremate
the soul. So that's why, as I was saying, the day I walked into
our doctor's office, I was happy that he brought up an anecdote
about you before even asking me what I needed. He loves you
a lot, our doctor, and surely that's why he also needs to continue
talking about you. Yet in view of my ongoing panic attacks, he
suggested that I not try to practice apnea, since he thinks being
underwater and holding my breath will only exacerbate the
moments of angst. But I told him that I have this intuition,
which holds the same weight for me as the word* knowledge,
*that this sport will help me control a key piece of the always
confusing puzzle of mechanisms that trigger a panic attack:
breathing.*

*That's right. Apnea, the voluntary cessation of breathing
whose primordial objective is to allow us to reach the great
depths of the ocean, is an exceptional means for relaxation.
The goal is to spend a maximum amount of time submerged
in water, and you learn a series of techniques that help you
consume the least amount of oxygen possible. Oxygen is precisely
what I have too much of, because when I'm feeling afraid,
anxious, or panicked, I hyperventilate, which produces vertigo
and intensifies the unease. Let me explain in the present tense
what I learned today, the first day, because apnea is lived in
present time or, what is the same thing, indefinite time. The
minutes before immersion are vital. It's when you begin the
controlled breathing and expansion of all parts of the body.
Once you're in the water, you have to avoid attaching to any
single thought. They tell you it's very important, and I wonder*

*how am I not going to think if I live tangled in your net?*
*Apparently, the more complex the thought, the more oxygen it*
*consumes in the brain. Thinking drains you. That's why it's*
*good to allow mental images to pass by, similar to when you're*
*a passenger in a moving car. The landscape goes by without*
*your having to hold on to a single tree or a mountain or a*
*church. Everything gets a little easier. That's it. I find my own*
*mechanism. I close my eyes and see your image: you're greeting*
*me like in one of those books that you can thumb through*
*quickly to animate the illustration. I keep flipping. I can't stop,*
*because if I do, you become static again, which is death. I don't*
*pay attention to details. I don't have time to stare at your eyes,*
*your mouth, your arms, because the pages flit by so quickly, but*
*I see your motion, intangible but alive. After watching you*
*greet me, I show up in the book too. You kiss me, you take off*
*my clothes, you caress me, suck me, penetrate me, hug me, pick*
*me up. We're in the shower: you soap me, rinse me off, dry me.*
*We get dressed and walk out the door. To have supper. Not to*
*die. To have oysters and wine. It's not a bad way to begin the*
*first day: not grabbing on to you, but to your movement.*

*I continue listening carefully to the trainer, sitting beside my*
*companions around a small pool next to the main one. The*
*water in the little pool is somewhat warmer, which allows*
*you to last longer because the cold also makes the body use*
*more oxygen. We're a group of twelve, counting me. After the*
*trainer's brief presentation, we get in the waist-deep water.*
*He asks us to form a circle, holding hands. We're supposed to*
*relax and take a deep breath of air before floating facedown*
*on the surface. So I take in as much air as I can and float*
*facedown, following his instructions. I know the world record*
*is seven minutes. How I envy those seven minutes of peace. But*
*it doesn't matter. It's the first day. Except for another friend,*

*all the rest are still submerged when I come up for breath. Following the security protocol, I don't break the circle and I squeeze my two companions' hands every thirty seconds, the left hand of one and the right of the other. They respond by squeezing my hands the same way. They're fine. They're still floating facedown and they're fine. I think I'll never forget the image of them floating like that, in a circle, completely relaxed and in a brotherhood of suspension, there in the same liquid. For the first time in a very long while I am dread-free, happy, and serene, and in good company, a circle of strangers. And for the first time in many months, Yoro kicks again. Here she is, resuming the pregnancy today, the same day I'm learning how to breathe less. I think Yoro will be like me, a woman accustomed to making fish from bread, wine from water. These weren't divine miracles; they were the work of a good man who, like us, did the best he could with the little he had.*

*I touch my belly while in the water. There, I feel her move. I know that by this point, Yoro inhabits the larger part of the uterus and there's less amniotic fluid, so I think it's peculiar that the pregnancy should show again just when I'm submerged in water. As my internal liquid decreases, the external liquid, all the water in the pool, surrounds me and contains me; while I learn how to moderate the need to breathe, my baby's lungs are almost prepared to learn about air. I think back to my cousin's pregnancy after the bomb, her belly shrinking after the sixth month, as if from remorse, as if saying, "I refuse to be in this world," walking backward down the path from fetus to sperm, from sperm back into the nothing. Something to the contrary takes place in the pool, as if I am the one who is walking backward, who moves from being a woman to becoming an embryo, while our Yoro foists herself on the world, gets stronger, expands, and goes in search of the boundless waters that extend* beyond the walls of my uterus. Exactly like reliving one's own gestation. I've never stopped cursing the terrible moment when the embryo who became me decided to choose both sexes, but I feel as though for the first time I'm reconciling with my own self; I now realize that the life without form that I was months before I was born shared the same beating heart with the one that has been doing all the judging. So now I understand how silly it is for me to be cursing my own seed's indecisiveness at the forking path between male and female because the person didn't make the decision, the decision was made for the person. Slipping into that prenatal unconscious allows me to take responsibility for my own nature, the same way I eventually took responsibility for choosing my sexual identity, which has never changed.

It still takes me about three times longer to follow the route from my apartment to the pool, because every once in a while I have to sit down on the first stair I can find to allow my anxiety to ebb. But it never happens when I get out of the pool, when I take a step and breathe normally. These return trips remind me of my previous life, how regardless of the pain I could think freely without that sticky mass of disquietude clouding my judgment, making me think, mistakenly, as I had a thousand times, that I was going to die right there in the middle of the street.

The exercises in the pool allow me to experience new sensations with my body. For example, when I'm underwater, holding a companion's hand in keeping with the safety rules, I can feel his or her pulse in my fingertips. First it's a normal pulse, and little by little I can feel it slow down and enter the stage of extreme relaxation. The heartbeat decelerates, like a tiny flame going out little by little. And now I'm discovering the definitive cure for my fear of death, because when the heart abates and there's more space between beats, I'm the one who *decides whether to breathe and, in spite of it all, choose the surface. By raising my head above water I'm confirming my commitment to life, overcoming death with every immersion. The sea magnifies that feeling; the water pressure in the deep feels like an embrace, a physical manifestation of someone welcoming me down there, someone who would welcome me forever if that's what I would want. But I don't anymore, and with each breath when I break the surface, I am giving birth to myself again. So I return to the stories my mother told me as a child, about those women from our land who dove without tanks, looking for mollusks, abalone, algae, sponges, octopuses, and if they got very lucky, pearls.*

*I wonder if this natural penchant for deep-sea diving doesn't have its origin in those stories, or maybe it's because of my grandmothers, who were born in the village of Wagu on the Shima Peninsula in Mie Prefecture, a place known over the centuries for its female divers, who still today use the same techniques as two thousand years ago, the first recorded activity, which have been passed down from mothers to daughters over the generations. When I imagine those women descending, naked, into the cold waters of the Pacific, it makes me feel as though my training is a canard, almost an act of snobbery, and because of my roots I think I have a right to travel to Wagu one day, once I've recovered, to put faces, voices, and movement to the legends that my mother used to tell.*

*Apnea may not have freed me of heartache, but it did help lighten the load of what terrified me so much. The sea and the outdoors had already begun to cure me during my time with Irrational Number, and now those years of dysfunction were coming to an end. Being in nature protected me from the swindling psychologists and precluded the machinations of society, allowing me the chance to turn over a new leaf. My*

*addiction to pseudoscience ended. Now I know for a fact that*
*people survive many deaths, and whenever I hear a homeless*
*person shouting in the street, disturbed, it's as if that person is*
*using my same voice.*

*Now that I'm back on my feet, I want to go somewhere for*
*pleasure; it'll be the first trip since you died, Jim. It's an odd*
*notion, going somewhere that has nothing do with finding*
*Yoro. Somehow it feels like a betrayal of the promise I made to*
*you to continue looking for her, and the certainty that I carry*
*her inside me doesn't really alleviate the feeling that I am*
*not keeping my word. After all, in the end I'm not breaking*
*my water or anything of the sort because (yes, from time to*
*time I'm aware of it) I'm not really pregnant. It's only in*
*fleeting moments of optimism that I tell myself perhaps this*
*interminable gestation is real, that maybe it got its start with*
*the radiation sickness I've always been on the lookout for, as a*
*kind of positive sickness that doesn't end in death but in birth.*
*If as they say, there are still three-headed rabbits, why couldn't*
*my situation be just another nuclear anomaly? Wouldn't it be*
*a nice radioactive aftereffect? My desire made the flesh of my*
*flesh, my baby. So I prepared my trip, allowing myself to play*
*around with the notion that at any given moment I could go*
*into labor.*

*It's August 1977. I arrive in the village of Wagu during the*
*women's fishing season, which runs from March to September.*
*My dog is with me. There must be something in her genes*
*because this animal, like her mother, had puppies late in life.*
*She suckled for such a long time that her nipples are sizable.*
*It's a little strange to see such a clear mark of suckling in a dog*
*obviously up there in age. I thought about that when I saw the*
*amas—that's what the divers are called—going in and coming*
*out of the sea, always naked, regardless of age, the very youthful*

*amas—apprentices who begin diving at thirteen, called*
kachido—*keeping closer to the shore and the veteran divers,
called* funado, *reaching depths of close to a hundred feet with a
single breath.*

*Perched on a rock in Wagu, I observed a group of amas
on the sand, warming themselves in the sun before going
back into the sea. It's the first time I saw for myself that these
women actually exist. I strolled along the streets of the fishing
village before catching this scene. There wasn't a single car. The
way they speak, the way they walk, it all seems so much more
relaxed than Hiroshima, my hometown. It's as if everything
is marked by a natural clock from dawn to dusk, and though
they are strict about all things that have to do with their labor
in the sea, life is still much more flexible and easygoing and in
touch with the natural course of a day and not built on a work
schedule that hides people from the sun, in an office, a factory,
or at home. One woman in a corner caught my attention. She
was sitting on a small bench scarfing down raw clams and
seemed to invite me to initiate a conversation, so I asked if she
sold the seafood she was eating. She must have been around
thirty years old, and said she was just recovering strength from
the morning dive to be ready again for the afternoon. She was
an ama who had separated herself from the group to eat in
peace, missing out this once on the news they share during these
times of rest, when the town's women come out to help them
restore their strength like a great big family where the sea—
despite the danger, the cold, and all the effort—is almost like a
man shared among them. It was that clam-devouring woman
who pointed out their diving spot along the coast, and a great
rock on which a few minutes later I would watch her cohort
lying in the sun.*

*When I saw a small boat approaching the beach, I imagined
the women would board it for the afternoon dive, so I jumped*

down and ran. I didn't have time to consider what I wanted to
say to them. When I got there, I saw the same woman I had
spoken to earlier and asked her if I might be allowed to board
the boat with her group. None of them liked the idea when they
heard my proposition. Though my clothes were perfectly casual
for any normal city, in that village where everything seemed
to follow the dictates of the sea, I was clearly overdressed. But
work was at hand, there was no time to waste, and eventually
they allowed me on board.

My new friend's name is Tokumi. Except for a kind of
fundoshi *that covered her pubic area and left her buttocks
exposed, Tokumi was completely naked, as were the rest of the
women. In the few minutes it took the boat to reach the diving
spot, Tokumi explained that she had recently been promoted
to* funado, *which means she'd become part of the group of
veterans, the ones who belong to a higher rank thanks to their
skillfulness, and now she usually fishes at a medium depth of
eighty feet, though at times she goes much deeper. After a year
of apnea training, I'd reached the respectable maximum depth
of a hundred feet, but I know that to descend and ascend is
not the same as to descend, work, and ascend. One needs a
great amount of physical and mental talent to work like that
in water whose temperature never goes above sixty degrees
Fahrenheit.*

As soon as we arrived at the diving spot, they all leaped into
the water equipped with nothing but goggles, fins, a kaigane
for scraping mollusks from the rocks, and a basket to collect the
quarry, which also served as a buoy to help them rest between
dives. The fastest way for the divers to reach the bottom is
to carry iron or stones, and to return to the surface they tug
twice on a cord tied to their waists like a lifeline, and the ship's
captain, the only man on the expedition, pulls them up to
facilitate their ascension.

*I watched from the boat how the divers went up and down, grabbing on to a single basket, throwing their catch into it while preparing to go back down. Between dives they would make a noise when they breathed that was so beautiful, it alone was worth all the sacrifice to be there. They breathed in a special way in order to fill their lungs with more air, which produced a kind of whistle. To hear one of them is remarkable. But to hear three or four at the same time is astounding, because each one emits a different tone in their whistling. I counted Tokumi's dives between one whistle and another, and tallied up to forty, which was more than she had done in the morning.*

*Those sounds, the sounds of a body submerging itself every few minutes, the smell and taste of green tea that spilled from the pot the captain would refill whenever it was empty, and the slight bobbing of the boat brought pleasure to four of the senses: sight, sound, smell, and taste. Each one of these networks had been activated, except for the sense of touch. And yet I didn't need to touch a thing or be touched by anybody in order to feel sexually aroused after such a long time. I felt excited and attracted to the cluster of women or, more precisely, to the women who were in the water at that precise moment. So I got up, grabbed a pair of goggles that had been left in the boat, undressed, and jumped into the sea. The captain said something, but I didn't understand and he didn't get in my way. The water was a lot colder than I had expected. I started swimming away from where the divers were in order to warm up, trying not to disrupt them at work. Once I got used to the water, I returned to where the group was and looked for Tokumi. Seeing all those nude women swimming about with fins seemed like the utmost freedom within the enslavement that is work. Natural bodies, each one in its own shape, not being hidden but not flaunted either, in a group where nobody lorded over anyone else, each one restricted by nothing more than the capacity of their lungs. It was the freedom that excited me. I knew the importance of being able to take off one's clothes without fearing reprisals. If only I could become like one of those women, I think now, after all the identity that was denied me, the operations that were never completely successful; if someone were to give me a normal body, my body, I would look for an occupation that allowed me to be naked most of the time. I'd show up at the bank to receive your life insurance payout, naked. Did you ever notice how dull and gloomy the employees are at our bank branch? All that time counting money they can't spend mustn't be very good for them. I would waltz in bare naked and make myself a tanga with those dollar bills right on the spot; oh, so sorry, I mean a clitanga.* Clitanga . . . *Oh, look at that, I didn't mean to say the name of an animal. Everyone would be staring at me by then. "What're you all looking at?" I'd say. "Has nobody ever seen a clitanga before? Clitangas are pets from the Pacific regions; they feed off small crustaceans."*

*My fake breasts didn't change shape when I submerged myself in the water. The other women's breasts lifted, were ductile, as alive as any other marine creature. I didn't want to break the group up, creeping like spiders along the marine floor with their knives, so I decided to take advantage of the day to do my own set of immersions.*

*By the length of the cables I gauged that the amas were working at around sixty feet, but one group was busy in a basin just a little farther down whose intense color of blue, a blue verging on black, gave a sense of increased depth. I positioned myself where the surface coincided with the opening of the basin and began to descend, a few feet more with every new immersion. When I would surface and breathe, I'd grab on to the boat for a few minutes and then dive again. Fully relaxed, I crossed beyond the level where the group of amas worked and lost myself in that black hole. I wasn't sure exactly how many feet down I was reaching, but for at least half of the descent I didn't need to move in order to fall, since the body starts falling on its own as the depth increases. The effect triggers at fifty to sixty-five feet, so back at the surface, when I could think clearly, I calculated the depth of my dive at somewhere in the area of 115 feet. This was unquestionably too much for me, especially since I didn't have a spotter, but the call of the depths, which had always enthralled me, was powerful and I felt compelled to dive again, to gain if only a few more feet with each plunge. The pressure squeezed my lungs, and my body, free of breathing, was so receptive that I felt a sense of the whole in each of the parts; in my fingertips, in my belly button, in my throat. I was alive again. My heart put distance between one beat and another, and allowed me to slip into that space where you hear the pulse descend like an echo saying goodbye, growing weaker and weaker. The sound of a heart in repose. Silence, I told myself, don't think, your heart is at rest. The last echoes were almost inaudible, but I remained motionless several feet down because I know that before the echo gets lost completely, the human angel would appear, warning me that it was time to surface. Usually I could feel it tickle softly the nape of my neck, the breath of life that called me back upward. But for some reason the angel didn't show up that time or I didn't hear it. The lack of oxygen and the pleasure of it lured me into that most dangerous state: the feeling that I could live without air. And so I fell into the abyss, with a pleasurable feeling of immense serenity.*

*I felt warmth in my skin and a hot liquid in my mouth. I opened my eyes to see Tokumi's face. She was holding my head to raise me up and give me some tea to drink. I understood. I* had passed out while diving. But that's not all. Before passing out, I must surely have experienced what divers know as the narcosis of the deep, they said. I forgot to surface because I was experiencing the kind of euphoria certain narcotics produce, which occurs when nitrogen is exposed to high pressures. I told the amas exactly what had happened, how at first I felt a sort of happiness that made me think I didn't need air anymore, I belonged there now, in that aquatic environment. So I just continued diving, not even considering surfacing, completely oblivious to the state I was in.

The next thing I remember was seeing, as I was falling to the bottom of the basin, all of them, the amas, around me. At first I thought it was so strange, but as is true when you are under the influence of certain drugs, you don't question what you are seeing. In the space of a minute's time I lived in a much vaster world, like in a dream. At one point I saw my new companions looking at me with expressions of wonder through the glass of their goggles. They opened their eyes, as if trying to say there was some sort of danger behind me. So I looked around and saw a huge whale vagina. It was astonishingly beautiful, so much more than human ones, a slightly paler shade of pink, and more slippery in texture, like fresh ice. I wanted to gesture to the amas so they could observe it with me, but they were unperturbed, floating like creatures from this underwater world daunted by nothing but the danger I was in. I stared at the vagina, which was like a huge heart beating as it engorged; she's in heat, I thought, and when I looked back at the amas, it was me this time who had to alert them with my eyes and point with my finger for them to look behind them. A male, about a hundred meters away, was speeding toward the female just behind me. The amas darted, disappeared, and I had to swim with every ounce of strength from my position between the male and the female so as not to be crushed in the heat of *those two cetacean bellies. When I finished telling my story, still caught in the emotion of the scene, it was hard to accept that it hadn't really happened. It's true that hallucinations happen rather often at certain depths and under certain conditions. It's also true that I'd once heard Jacques Mayol mention this same danger of being flattened by the desire of two cetaceans. Still to this day, Jim, I'm not entirely sure that it didn't actually happen, and that the amas, in order to protect the world that is their birthright, chose to keep it hidden from me.*

# Eighth Month: 1978-1999

*Always alone, my love, but since I was so close to Tokyo, I decided I might as well pay a visit to S. She'd already told me in our correspondence that her business was thriving and she'd even given it a new name: A Thousand Bloods. I think the name is brilliant. In fact I've put a lot of thought into this idea of purity through bastard blood, from the blend, the mongrel, the mixed race. There was a second when I thought maybe S had heard me mention it sometime. But no matter, wherever the idea came from, the name is perfect for her business, especially when you think of how the AIDS scourge is making people afraid of fraternizing, first among the same sex, but now among heterosexuals too. S added a second part to her sign that reads A THOUSAND BLOODS. The addition, written between parentheses, reads Yes to AIDS. It's meant to contradict these countrywide publicity campaigns with a supposedly global reach that read No to AIDS. The media picked up on the slogan, and her enterprise came out of hiding as a business that caters to large minorities. Some people may see her Yes to*

AIDS *as offensive, an unnecessary provocation, especially those who aren't sick or who think they're out of the disease's reach, but AIDS persists, and it endures in the people who suffer it. If you say no to* AIDS, *it means you are denying that the disease exists. All that such an unfortunate slogan accomplishes is that the carrier interprets the* no *to be hostile toward the person suffering from* AIDS; *you don't marginalize the sickness but the person who is sick. You can't imagine the number of people diagnosed with the virus who have been in contact with S to thank her for this resounding* yes, *which means inclusion for them, and of course, a way of resisting the illness through acceptance.*

*S introduced me to the first person I've ever met from a continent that you and I never visited: Africa. S is, like me, a seeker of identities, though her motivations are different from mine. Singularity is to her like finding a new treasure every time she encounters it. Wealth, luxury, and social standing mesmerize some people; K's only wish is to ascend to spiritual realization by way of that spiral staircase whose every step represents a distinctive style: sexuality. It's the singular that is so attractive to her. So, as I was saying, S conveyed the* Yes *to* AIDS *message to the first African woman I'd ever met. Her name is K. She's from Bamako, a city in Mali. When S introduced me to her, I had no idea where to place Mali in Africa. S spent years working out the administrative details that would allow K to travel to Japan. The woman had been repudiated in her country because female circumcision, the removal of the clitoris, had made her unable to give birth. And I say specifically* give birth, *because she is able to conceive; it's just that when K is in labor, for some reason the babies die in that transit between the tenuous light inside and the brightness outside. From what I was able to find out, cases like hers are relatively common and are not generally reason enough to force a woman to leave her country entirely, since some of them are able to find help and survive in cities that are far enough away from their hometowns. What pushed this woman into such a radical break and prompted her to leave her country, her language, and her customs behind was another tragic occurrence. Her most recent and botched attempt at giving birth had resulted in the creation of a fistula, which is a conduit, a hole, uniting her vagina with her urethra and her rectum. This means she has to deal with the perpetual incontinence of her bodily fluids, producing a stench that leads to not only moral but also physical rejection. Even if she had received a helping hand, she would still probably have been rejected by others simply for a reason that, though callous and inhumane, is at the same time very human: she stinks to high heaven.*

*K has been in Tokyo for only a few days. They're going to operate on her fistula next week, and luckily it's a relatively simple operation. I noticed how she stays far away from everyone; it's hard for her to believe that the diapers and smell-neutralizing creams available in Tokyo actually do their job. S had already explained her problem before she introduced us and I wanted to respect her need for distance, though I would have liked to give her a hug right from the get-go. I don't know if I ever told you, my love, but I'm not put off by odors. Not that I like them, mind you, it's just that they don't seem to bother me as much as they do other people, and certainly if I feel fond of someone, a bad smell isn't enough to keep me from giving him or her a hug. You know how often one homeless person reeking of perspiration and old piss can empty out an entire subway car in New York. People cover their noses and mouths with a hand or a scarf and stay that way till the next stop, when everyone scuttles over to the next car. They don't care whether the homeless person feels humiliated by all the rejection.* Take a shower, *they think, without taking into consideration all the reasons that a person doesn't wash himself or herself. If exorbitant hospital bills left me homeless, I don't think I'd ever wash up, I'd waltz my stench around all the public places. That's why I never cover my nose. Of course the smell bothers me, but it's not offensive, and above all, it opens my sensory canals to a new perception: that smell, whomever it's coming from, is always the same; it's a democratic smell. When we're clean, we all smell different. But when we're piss-stained and sweaty, we all smell the same. I don't like our common odor very much, but it nonetheless offers an unusual and mentally satisfying experience. There are things that do make me sick, like seeing some lady hold her nose ostentatiously over a stupid smell. So yes, no question, if I didn't have a home and lived on the street, I would let layers and layers of stench accumulate too, just to make sure I couldn't be confused with all those people clutching their noses while kissing any old ass necessary to make the money to buy the perfumes that camouflage their spite.*

*K is twenty years old now; she was mutilated when she was nine. One night her mother and aunt woke her up. Stroking her hair, they told her how for the next few days she would eat better than her brothers and she would receive special attentions. She didn't understand. Everything was so quiet, her mother and aunt spoke in whispers the whole time. So she was already frightened before knowing what was going to happen to her. For the first time, she was afraid of a family member, though deep down, she told S, she understood that they would do to her what they'd already done to her older sister and other girls in town. She'd often heard how the act was necessary so that nothing bad would happen to her family. After telling her she should be happy because she would be treated with deference for the next few days, that she was becoming a woman now, they held her down, opened her legs, and sliced off her clitoris. The*

*pain was so severe that to this day she can't stand the sound of*
*someone crying out in agony. They used acacia needles to sew*
*her up, which was even more excruciating, and she screamed*
*until she passed out.*

    *K spent the next month in bed following the amputation.*
*The slightest movement made the pain worse. The hemorrhages*
*were so abundant she became anemic. She panicked every time*
*she had to urinate, the pain was so excruciating; as a result*
*her bladder swelled to the point of bursting. The more details*
*S and K gave, the more I realized K's experiences mirror my*
*own painful ones. Both of us suffered the extirpation of the*
*organ that originates as a hermaphroditic core and defines*
*itself around the seventh week of gestation as either a penis or*
*a clitoris, a procedure that goes beyond what a young girl can*
*bear physically, beyond what an adult can bear psychologically.*
*Though I had writhed in pain in Hiroshima and she in*
*Bamako, we both shared the same dearth of care. Nothing for*
*the pain. Nothing for the scarring. Nothing to alleviate the*
*dread. Not even the fact that her town was at peace and her*
*family and neighbors safe differentiated our experiences because*
*when you are facing affliction on that scale, it's hard to take*
*stock of what's happening outside of you. It's not that it didn't*
*matter to me whether my family was alive or dead, it's that*
*at the time I was nothing more than a throbbing piece of skin*
*covered in sores, pus, and burns and burning up with fever.*
*The absolute pain, when it comes, was the only family that*
*matters; pain that is my mother, my father, my siblings, my*
*whole country. Only when the pain was alleviated could I think*
*about all of them, the real ones, the blood of my blood, about*
*whether they were alive or dead. And they were. Forever dead.*

*Meeting K in A Thousand Bloods made me consider the*
*importance of blood, since she was so connected with it. Not*

*in the sense of the blood that spills as a result of an amputated organ, but of the blood that transmits, that circulates or flows to carry a message. It reminded me of your bout of malaria in Burma. I would get so worried whenever your fever spiked over something as simple as a cold, thinking it was a new episode. And I'd begin trembling as if I were the sick person and not you. I imagined the guilty mosquito had to be a female anopheles, because only the females suck blood in order to hatch their eggs. I cursed that female who could activate the illness in your liver, circulate it throughout your body, messenger it through the bloodstream.*

*S and K were talking about something—I can't remember what. I had taken a seat and was just watching them. I fixated on K's corneas. I could see they were red from exhaustion or maybe from another urinary tract infection. Blood in her corneas too. Yoro, Yoro, Yoro, goddamn it forever. The blood of your blood that has bled out of me over so many years of searching. Can there be any greater waste of time than looking for something? Love, yes, of course, one looks out of love, but in the meantime you don't love anything else but what is not there. Which is absurd. Looking for love, instead of simply loving the person who is present, who is not hiding away, who doesn't require that you waste years following her trail. That's why if I could jump from blood to blood, Jim, if I could live in other people's lives, I would be faithful to you. I would be unfaithful (again). I would get bored like the thick blood of a slothful man. I would bleed wood and not think of anything but the material of the trees. A carpenter. I would be a carpenter, and then I'd be the bird that bleeds the bark. I would also be the bullet of a hunter that slices through a deer. Fleeting. The blood of gunpowder shot by someone else's hand. Sliding smoothly through hair, skin, flesh—my last destiny, warm body, animal, burying me in its middle, distancing me from the loneliness of a cold grave. I would drip in a grove. I get to know you anew. I would close like your glottis that hinders my blood from dripping down your throat. I would open it like I used to open my glottis to swallow your germinating saliva. I imagine now how it works on my organism. Your saliva germinates reeds that wave in the currents inside of me, in my esophagus, my guts, the soft walls of my stomach. Fields of tails like elongated blossoms in the springtime of a body that gets its light through your saliva. Photosynthesis. Erosynthesis. While you sleep, I would trap insects with my tongue to spread over your wound. I would forget you. I would believe in peace. I would make war. I would make love in wartime. I would be the index finger that pokes an eggshell to learn the taste of yellow. I would live crouched in the ghostly pyramid only for the pleasure of relaxing my muscles—strong, red—when that beam of light illuminates it for thirty seconds each year. And every once in a while—and I mean once in a while—I would be me again, same as I could be anyone else. Me now, me then, and me in my remote past, inhabiting the simultaneity of my infant's crawl, my first steps, with the search, always the search for your blood: Yoro. Goddamn you forever, Yoro.*

*I don't curse Yoro when I feel her inside of me. Because then she's also blood of my blood, this blood that instantly transmits the message that I'm pregnant, and it doesn't matter much whether I am or am not, because the message is repeated for weeks in each and every beat of my heart, tirelessly, over and over again, reverberating in me like Morse code in a submarine. Certainly this is our first inner call of life. There it is, connecting. I suppose these signals are felt most clearly in pregnancy, this perpetual repetition notifying of a transformation in course, which doesn't originate in a person's own body, but in someone else's, one that is invading you, the blood of your blood that nonetheless inhabits you as a different being.*

*Everyone around a pregnant woman caters to her and cares for her as if they were protecting their own mother's fetus. How odd. It's a type of invasion felt by few men, unless they experience a metamorphosis themselves. Anyone who's written about metamorphosis wrote about pregnancy. A cockroach, a swan, a bull, golden rain. If I had lived my entire life in isolation, and one day someone told me that another body would sprout from my own, I might find the idea of turning into a cockroach far more plausible. We clutch our heads when they talk about magic, but we've normalized pregnancy to the point of making it banal. Not me. I say: this can only be magical, and because it is, I'm often overwhelmed by the same fear as the person who woke up one day transformed into a cockroach. I find myself controlling my thoughts from time to time as if this blood transmitted information through the internal communication system to the still-premature brain that would allow it to pick up on what I'm thinking.*

*What happens when I doubt my daughter's existence? Would her DNA somehow register it as contempt, as if I didn't believe in her or want her? What happens when I don't care to live, not even for her? How unbearable it would be to not have secrets. At times I've felt hatred, thinking she's a kind of vigilante, a spy. But then I feel guilty, worried that my scorn might somehow impede her growth. And again I think about your blood. The blood of your father, now circulating through me. And the blood of your family too. That sister of yours, whom I've never liked very much, is also my sister as long as you are circulating inside of me. The blood that raises the alarm when something is wrong, though only when I believe I'm pregnant, of course; the daily scrutiny for blood after each pee. I go back to thinking it doesn't really matter if my pregnancy is a lie, because that fear is there, the fear of bleeding. Perhaps the fear of bleeding is the fear of accepting the fact that my*

*little girl doesn't really exist, and the blood is then the sign
of the termination of my fantasy. And then there's the blood
flowing through the umbilical cord as my belly button begins
fading away. Me, who was always stuck to my mother's skirts,
I feel as though I'm cutting the umbilical cord that ties me to
my mother every time I glance at my belly button. Maybe
the last trace of cord that ties us to our mothers is cut in order
to make the new cord that ties us to our daughter. You see, the
cord that tied me to my mother, the cord that even her death
in Hiroshima couldn't cut, is now being severed by life. Life is
by far the strongest explosion. Will I feel my body spit out the
plug of blood that signals an approaching birth? I imagine it
would be released like a clot, like a plug, like what happens in
the morning during a period when the blood's been retained all
night, thickening, getting darker from the pressure. I wanted to
feel that release so badly. And I was so afraid that it was never
going to happen.*

Sir, allow me now to call your attention to the fact that I am
once again addressing you directly. I will now move my testimony
forward.

A torrential rain has begun, and it's unlikely that anyone will
come looking for me while it lasts. The roads will be impassable
for a few more days after it abates, as you can imagine. But by
then I'll be ready to come to you instead; I'll turn myself in. So
for now there's plenty of time to enjoy telling my story. Truth be
told? I don't care whether you're interested in what I'm about to
say, but what else is there to do in this lodge if I can't leave? All I
can do is play with the only other person here with me now, in one
form or another: you. So let the game begin. Do you remember
my saying that there were details about my life you could understand only if I doled the information out morsel by morsel? What
I meant is that if I were to tell you all the particulars of what had

impacted me the most in one fell narrative swoop, or more specifically *the* single greatest incident after the bomb at Hiroshima, you wouldn't fully appreciate it. No doubt you would grasp it as information. That's not hard to do. But what I'm trying to do is drench you in the details. I want you to soak up every drop of my happiness, sir. That's why now, in this savage rain, I'm beginning my game, a game of riddles, and here's your first clue:

Rain.

Drop after drop it's been saturating you throughout this story, without your ever noticing. Do you feel capable right now of gathering all the little written droplets together to tell me which is the particularly significant event that I wish to highlight now? I suspect not. So let me just crack the window a sliver, enough for the water to christen the text lightly as I plow on. Let's see if maybe, just maybe, you'll figure out what all the fuss is about. If you puzzle it out before I have to reveal it, you'll have won the game, in which case let me congratulate you beforehand.

Remember my friend S's sex toy store, where I got my crime weapon? Let me tell you it thrived, which allowed her to buy the space next door to set up a library accessible through a small door, so the murmuring of clients wouldn't disturb the readers' need for silence. At first I thought it was strange how much effort she put into gathering such a large number of books and buying a space that was elegant and comfortable, with wooden tables and individual lamps for each reader, because I didn't see the logical connection between the store and the library or couldn't justify the need for a reading space so close to a sex shop, seemingly an unusual juxtaposition. Yet whenever I went from the shop to the library or back, I never felt a gap between the two, only a soft transition to and fro, and soon I discovered a simple explanation precisely through reading. Our genitalia are not our bodies' most erogenous zone, and neither is our skin; it's our brain. That's why I'd always gotten so aroused by reading books that had nothing ostensibly erotic about them. It was the primeval sexual organ that got so excited, activated by the challenge of thought, which at the same time activated my desire. I bet you still have no idea where I want to take you with all of this? And I say, "I want to take you," because I wouldn't mind if you won the game—it would make you a worthy rival. So let's see now, another clue, one little drop after another of rain:

The brain, the most erotic organ in the body.

If you've accepted my challenge to play, it's because you're interested, and so in a way it could be said that you are interested in me, as the other player. Arousing another's curiosity is not an easy task. I presume it means you attribute a certain amount of intelligence to me. Thank you. This is precisely the case. I am an intelligent woman. So the question is, are you suitably intelligent to read between my lines? If so, this acumen will allow you to reach a climax before I have to explain. Just as in S's library, I'm the book that attracts your attention, but also the book that foresees my ending.

I spent many hours in the library. There were days when you could say I was content, but invariably I was lonely. A while had passed since Jim's death, and with his death, the abandonment of the outer search for Yoro (not the inner one, which I always carried with me). What I just wrote between parentheses could serve as another clue, expressed in this way: I carried Yoro inside of me. But let me continue—this last bit might get clearer toward the end of my story. I felt as though my love for Jim, the love we shared, belonged to another life. I felt disconnected from those past times. And yet, though my life was in many ways a new life, I still bore the same emptiness as before. I felt the gravity of eight months' worth of gestation, while still feeling the absence. My belly showed as full as it was deserted. Read this quote, which I'm copying from one of my notebooks, a quote Okakura attributed to the Chinese philosopher Lao-Tzu, probably paraphrasing slightly:

"A room is valuable not because of the walls or the ceiling, but for the emptiness that the walls and ceiling enclose. The utility of a pitcher of water is in the emptiness that can contain the water, not in the shape of the pitcher or the material of which it's made. The emptiness is able to do this because it contains everything."

I would think of myself as a pitcher at times, whose hollowness was meaningless, a pitcher without water, a pitcher full of water, but water that would never break before I went into labor, that didn't keep my clay moist. There was no water for someone who thought that with me they might quench their thirst.

Third clue:

Emptiness can do everything, because it contains everything.

Under those circumstances, reading helped relieve my aloneness, but not just any kind of reading. I read mostly testimonies of people like me who had put into writing their reflections on absolute forms of isolation. Knowing that other people had gone through similar things made me feel I had companions, even if they were dead. As I write this, I realize that it might seem a little gloomy to feel that the dead are still with us, but the mere act of reading how other people have gone through situations like mine before brought them back to life for me, before me. I felt these others place a fraternal hand on my shoulder as I read what they wrote years or even centuries ago. Did you know that in some countries they are already studying the best way to warn the citizens of the future, people from other worlds millions of years ahead of us in time, about how truly hazardous the stockpiles of nuclear waste are? Language will have morphed completely by then, so how can we possibly take preventive measures against the dangers of nuclear waste for people who will be born or come to Earth for a visit thousands of generations hence? Fortunately life on Earth is still so young that as it stands today, we can understand almost all of what has been carried forward in written testimony. So how could I help but feel as though someone dead for only a few centuries shares my same era on Earth? If someone happens to read me a thousand years in the future, they'll still understand me. You see? Two thousand years hence they'll still appreciate this story, and yet it's pretty clear they wouldn't judge me the same way you are judging me now. Your law is worth nothing over time. Nothing. I'm not even going to trot out that hoary comparison with grains of sand. Your law isn't worth a grain of sand. My words are so much grander than your law. Anyone's words will outlast the law by thousands of years. Even the words of people who don't know how to read, illiterates, will last longer than your current laws. Language is what I think gives cohesion to a single generation, a family.

When I was at my worst, I kept in mind all those people who thanks to their written testimonies accompanied me despite being dead. Perhaps they had died precisely because they couldn't abide being isolated and misunderstood. So at times I thought of myself as being strong, a survivor—because I was alive—barred from the world that knew me best, the netherworld, whose doors you are opening to me. Thanks. Aren't you just the gentleman? I won't hide the fact that at times I feel self-pity and don't want to "go gentle into that good night." How woozy I get when I think of the passing of time nowadays.

With me in mind, S stocked a book that contained the beautiful and explicit testimony of what they used to call a hermaphrodite, one who at baptism was forced to take the name of a girl: Adelaide Herculine Barbin.

This man was born on November 8, 1838, in the French village of Saint-Jean-d'Angély, though his diaries were published only a few years ago for the first time. I was moved by how he dealt with the main issue, his intersexuality, but there was something deeper at work: how honest he was in telling his story, the simplicity and purity he demonstrated in a century that saw what Herculine Barbin was as a public disgrace. Herculine was uncannily aware of his tragic destiny from early childhood, when nobody, not even he, could appreciate how exceptional his body was. He foresaw his own tragedy and yet was still able to love. Just like me.

Herculine describes somewhere in the diary how his doctor, who was aware that he was more man than woman in his adolescence, commented on how accurate his godmother had been by insisting on calling him Camille. Camille is both a masculine and a feminine name. So at least one person noticed that Herculine Barbin's gender was undetermined at birth. The same thing happened to me when I was born and my gender was considered ambiguous, though I didn't have a godmother who called me by a name that reflected who I ultimately would be. The whole naming business has always obsessed me. Honestly, I've never understood why we have to spend our entire lives with a single name given to us by someone else. A person's name is the most sacred thing of all. It sees us through our entire lives, personifying us to everyone else, and for that reason it's something we should be able to choose ourselves. Countries have rituals of all varieties, but not a single ceremony that allows us to confirm or reject the name we were given at birth. We haven't even opened our eyes yet, and someone has engraved the name inflicted on us on a marble slab. Me, I refuse to accept it. I will be the one to choose what name goes on my tombstone. Please, leave it at *H, for Hiroshima.* You'll never know my birth name. My gender and name were imposed on me, the outcome of a mistaken assumption, like a bad bet in a game of cards. But it was my life being wagered, not just money, when I was no more than a lump of defenseless flesh that surely could sense her parents' disappointment at not being able to pridefully proclaim the key words of the event: "It's a boy!" or "It's a girl!" Maybe I noticed the disillusionment while I was still wrapped in my mother's warmth, the silence or the shame of whoever tried to imagine me outside of that undefined limbo.

The book included a medical report written in 1860 by a Dr. Chesnet, who detailed the state of Herculine—who was customarily known as Alexina—when Herculine visited his practice at the age of twenty-two because of sharp pains that were probably caused by inguinal testicles, meaning testicles that never fell and so remained invisible. The doctor's report was originally published in the *Annales d'hygiène publique et de médicine légale*, and I unapologetically tore the reproduction of this report out of the book because I couldn't help feeling as though it belonged to me even though it didn't exactly correspond with my case. I didn't have access to any other kind of official report on my body. So here's the fourth hint, it's a little more self-explanatory:

I never had access to any kind of report on my body.

The report said the following about Herculine:

[. . .] has brown hair and measures 1.59 centimeters. Her facial features are not well defined and appear undecided between those of a man and a woman. The voice is feminine, but there are times in conversation or in coughing when deeper, more masculine timbres resonate. The upper lip is covered in a fine down: there are whiskers on the chin and cheeks, especially on the left-hand side. Her chest is that of a man's, flat and without the manifestation of breasts. There's never been menstruation, to the great frustration of her mother and family doctor, who wasn't able to bring on the flow. The upper limbs are not rounded, as is characteristic in well-formed females; they are quite dark and slightly hairy. The pelvis and hips are a man's. The upper pubic region is covered in black hair that is growing thicker. Opening the thighs one can see a longitudinal slit, which extends from the mons Venus to the anus. There is a peniform body on the upper part that is about four or five centimeters long from the point of insertion to the free tip, which is made up of a glans that is covered by a foreskin that is slightly flat in the upper part and that has never been perforated. This small member, as far from the dimension of the clitoris as it is from a penis in its normal state can, according to Alexina, engorge, stiffen, and grow. However the erection must be very limited, as the imperfect penis is held from the inside by a sort of frenum membrane that allows only the glans to be freestanding.

WHAT REALLY CAUGHT MY INTEREST in this part of the report was how they describe Herculine's genitalia as a "member" whose dimensions make it as far from being a clitoris as a penis. That's exactly my case. A baby stuck halfway between clitoris and penis. But isn't that just like a baby? A being that is neither male nor female? Why not keep the status open till it's time for the baby to develop physically and decide an identity for itself? But no, for some odd reason gender is rendered definitively like a judge's ruling: boy or girl, lad or lass, male or female, old lady or old man.

But like me, Herculine knew perfectly well in her own mind and heart that she was only attracted to one sex. Herculine liked women. She felt like a man, though she was raised as a girl, a woman, surrounded by girlfriends until well after puberty, finding work as a governess in an all-girls school, where she met her first love, one of the headmistress's daughters. She fantasized about marrying her and envied men who had that right. They slept together every night, and her companion's mother thought it merely a platonic friendship and felt stirred by their devotion. In her diaries, Herculine doesn't go into detail about the sexual side of the affair with her young friend, but it's clear that they are in love with each other and sexually active. So it was strange for me to read a medical report written eight years later by another doctor, E. Goujon, included in the *Journal de l'anatomie et de la physiologie de l'homme,* referring to Herculine's case as being an example of "imperfect hermaphroditism." What does it mean to be *imperfect?* Has anyone ever recorded a case of *perfect* hermaphroditism in the history of medicine? If hermaphroditism can be considered a fusion of the masculine and feminine, then Herculine was perfect—taking into account the data given in the report a few years later—since "the shape of the individual's external genitalia allowed him, though he seemed manifestly masculine, to take on the role of either man or woman during coitus." Though ejaculation hadn't taken place through the penis because, according to these reports, it didn't have an orifice, but instead through the vagina, the latter, at the same time, allowed for penetration. Fifth or sixth hint, I've lost track:

Ejaculation didn't take place through the penis.

But something else impressed me in the medical report—something fascinating, encouraging, and beautiful: Herculine produced sperm. Though she never realized it. It was discovered in the postmortem report done by microscope when Herculine's corpse showed up the age of twenty-nine, in a flea-bitten room in a boardinghouse in Paris. He died of carbon monoxide asphyxiation. He committed suicide, or you could say, they pushed him to suicide. After he successfully changed his legal status, after he moved to Paris to avoid the neighbors' gossip, after he lived through so many struggles and dreams, he finally set out on a new life; but by then it was too late. His friends turned their backs on him. Society had accepted her and raised her as a woman, but it didn't have the means for his inclusion as a man. Not even in a bustling capital like Paris was Herculine able to hide how singular a creature he was. Finding that Herculine had produced sperm made me feel deeply compassionate, that—finally—the man might have chosen a different future for himself if only he'd known. He might have managed to bring to fruition all that had been denied him in the first part of his life—building a future with a family, producing and raising descendants—and seen his dreams come true. But now he was dead, friendless, having pinned his hopes on Paris because he felt inconspicuous there. How much does loneliness have to weigh for a man to prefer obscurity? How painful Herculine's loneliness must have been to prefer invisibility over noticing how other people—walking by, chatting with him— could see him but didn't include him? Obviously he preferred the thought that he wasn't included because he was out of sight, instead of facing the fact that he wasn't included precisely because they saw him. That man loved, coveted life, dared leave the protection of womanhood to change his identity, but failed. For years he asked for help. He left the job for which he was so manifestly prepared, as a governess, to work as a waiter, went hungry, "left no door unknocked," as he wrote to himself. Everything that had been like a song to life at the beginning of his diaries became death at the end. He considered himself dead long before he took his life. That's why I despaired over reading that he had sperm. I wonder what might have happened had he known that life, the life he naturally loved and wanted to prolong, didn't have to end with him?

The most poignant element of Herculine's testimony—later Abel's—was how honest she had been with herself, how her strength of character allowed her to resist the hypocrisy of the social milieu. Reading the diaries, I knew that Abel had been proud of himself when he died. I found comfort in that. It's often more than I can hope for, and it encouraged me to think that if this man figured out how to validate himself a century ago when all he received was reproach, then I too should find a way to vindicate my singular maternity. At the very least, I now counted on a strong, faithful companion: him, Abel Herculine.

The last clue:

My maternity has been vindicated.

Game over. If by now you still don't know what I'm talking about, it's not for a lack of clues. You must be one of those who read a sheet of paper where the clue is written as if the paper itself were the object they're trying to find. A sheet of paper is not a clue. A sheet of paper is not an object. The paper is only a suggestion, like smoke is a suggestion, telling you that fire must be lurking somewhere. But to think that smoke, which should lead you to fire, is contained in the clues alone is also a mistake because, as you know, smoke disperses into the air. How could I possibly contain it in a piece of paper? This whole game has been smoke, so don't focus on the explicit clues alone.

If you haven't located the fire, then I've won. I ask that you allow me one wish before I die, though I don't expect you to accede to it: I ask that you permit someone else to read my account. Remember what I said: empathy, the fondness of a single reader, is enough to heal me. If anyone else is reading me now, it means you've granted my last wish. I am grateful.

# Ninth Month: 1999–2011

After a long sojourn in Tokyo, I decided to return to New York, expecting a peaceful old age. I hadn't set foot in my apartment for several years. I was anxious about a number of things, afraid I might collapse the minute I opened the door as I perceived Jim's smell. And I was simply concerned about what kind of condition the place would be in after the series of renters. I had no idea yet that the morning, whose skies were as clear and bright as the ones on that fourth of August in Hiroshima, would usher in a whole new period in my life, perhaps the final one.

The first thing I attended to when I walked in was the correspondence I'd received from institutions or distant friends who hadn't known I was in Tokyo. I fingered through the envelopes until I came across the word *Yoro* on a return address. You can imagine how startled I was to see Yoro's name as a sender for the first time. So many years desiring a child before Jim, then so many years looking for Yoro after she became my own daughter through my love for Jim, followed by subsequent years of not looking for her anymore because I felt she was inside of me (or who knows, maybe so as not to have Jim on my mind every second of every day), and suddenly there is her name on an envelope. Her name! And that's all—there was no last name, no address. But on closer scrutiny, I saw that the stamp was from Zaire. I mean from right here where I'm writing you now, the Democratic Republic of the Congo.

I've traveled to so many different countries thanks to Jim, yet our outings never lasted long enough for me to adapt myself to the rhythm of true travelers, the people who unpack their suitcases on the other side of the world feeling perfectly at home in the new land by the time they first brush their teeth. The most important thing, though, is that I was completely resistant to the charms of new places; I was a little like a mule with blinders on. I kept my eyes straight ahead, and the only thing I ever saw was Yoro. For the rest—the exotic foods, the friendliness or hostility of the locals in whatever place, the country's history, its landscapes—none of it mattered to me one whit. So my travels did not help me get to know the world. In fact, they had no repercussions whatsoever on my personal growth, nor did they offer me anything by way of a cosmopolitan attitude, which made me always feel a little unsure of myself outside of Hiroshima, Tokyo, or New York. I clocked so many miles looking forever at the same horizon: Yoro. And then I stopped looking for her and stopped traveling. I stayed put in Tokyo. Until now, back in New York, when I saw her name on an envelope sent from a country I'd never stopped to consider in my life, and a slew of thoughts came rushing into my mind so suddenly that I had to sit right down on the sofa for I can't say how long, not opening the envelope or even looking around, not taking stock of that space where I had lived with Jim for so many years, full of my belongings, his belongings, and the furniture we'd chosen together.

When I think back on it, for a split second I must have felt something akin to gratefulness, even a jolt of giddiness, since the letter had reached its destination, and it was still recent. Other than that, only questions came to the fore, posthaste and one after the other, so chaotically that I couldn't stop to analyze a single one through to a conclusion. I was sixty-six years old then. I'd already gone through a lot—everything you've read till now. I'd suffered quite a bit. At my age, then, I'd already reconciled myself to the idea of living out the rest of my life quietly. And yet here's that man calling me right back again so passionately—no, more passionately than ever. Even before I opened that envelope, with nothing more than a name as a return address, Yoro was calling out to me for help, and I was sure it was the only thing she could do, call out from a country I was perfectly unfamiliar with, about which I hadn't the slightest opinion, except that if there was one place I imagined being the diametrical opposite of my own culture, it was Africa. Aside from my encounter with K, the young woman from Mali whom I had met in Tokyo, Africa had always been an imaginary place for me. It wasn't real, and I could have died thinking as much, without even considering the reality of an entire continent that I'd relegated to fiction and fantasy. How was I going to face a trip like that on my own? Is Yoro really asking for help in her letter or—worse still—requesting that I go to fetch her there? Maybe it was just the opposite; maybe she wanted to come visit me?

Even now, when I think back on that time, it still puts me so much on edge that I've overlooked an important detail: Yoro didn't know I existed. So the letter must have been addressed to Jim. That basic point hadn't even crossed my mind as I sat there those first few minutes holding the envelope in my unsteady hand: I didn't exist for Yoro. In any case, I opened it and read it. So many things happened in those five minutes after reading the letter. I screamed, I cried, I broke the pitcher Jim had given me as a gift, that had never broken on its own, the pitcher no renter had dropped in all these years, that continued reminding me not only of Jim's absence but of the absence of everything else, of Yoro, of my own self. I felt like tearing the letter to shreds, forgetting it. But instead I folded it away and kept it on me at all times. That day I entered my ninth month of pregnancy, which would still last for a long time, but it gave me one advantage: I could now take fewer precautions, move around in the shower without the fear of slipping. I felt less heavy because Yoro was no longer growing inside of me. Now she was on the outside and I had to find her to cut the umbilical cord, to rock her in the cradle and sing a lullaby in the name of Jim's love.

WHEN YOU READ what Yoro wrote in the following pages, sir, try to imagine what it all meant to me. Then read the letter from the point of view of the future as you know it, and you'll see that if it doesn't absolve me entirely, at least it justifies my acts. I spent the first part of my life focused on Yoro, and the second half, my years in Africa, looking for her, afraid that I might die before I found her or didn't find her in time. Let's just say that when I got there and found out what happened, nothing else mattered. I don't know how to explain it. I wanted and I want to spend my old age with Yoro, but the great mission of my life, to hug her and hold her, had already been accomplished. So the hatred I felt then for the people who had hurt her far outweighed the possibility of being able to swallow that hatred in order to spend the years or months left of my life with her, which some might consider a more thoughtful response. It was a strange feeling for me.

Thinking rationally, anyone might conclude that my responsibility was to stay with her, shower her with Jim's and my love, try to make up for everything she'd lost, all those years of silence. But when I had the occasion to exact revenge, to avenge her—indeed, not just her—I did, even knowing that it meant separation, and this time forever, and that I would be subject to your brand of justice. But you know something? I believe I was kept apart from

Yoro for a reason, something that was determined by the fate imposed upon us. Because, tell me, what was I going to do once I found her? Pretend I'm Jim? Pretend I'm finally a fulfilled mother? Pretend to be playing house at my age? Pretend to be killing time exchanging life stories and circumstances, everything we didn't know about each other, like two old friends reencountering each other? People throw out empty expressions all the time, like *we're making up for lost time* or *we're just catching up*. I might have unthinkingly used catchphrases like those before running into Yoro, but now I was aware of them, I realized how a catchphrase is but a euphemism that hides what these sentences really are: vacuous words empty of meaning. You can't make up for lost time and you can't catch up for one very simple reason: we are so much more than random pieces of data.

In fact, I'd say 90 percent of what we are is not merely information, but has to do more with the senses. I could tell Yoro how being constantly frustrated while searching for her, and then losing Jim, had made me a recluse for a number of years; that walking outside was like stepping into a spinning tunnel; that for years I truly felt her in my belly, sensed her growing there. I could tell her all of that and much more, but would it help her to comprehend my love? No. And though it isn't the case in this situation, data can be falsified. Why? Precisely because data is empty of meaning: it's interchangeable, superfluous. What matters is saying while you are physically present with the other: "Yoro, here I am. Feel in this embrace all the weight of the life I've spent looking for you." And it's true that in the culture I grew up in, physical contact is not customary, not even in extreme cases, but I've been a hybrid for a very long time. It doesn't matter; modify it if you want, morph it into some gesture instead of a hug, and it'll still mean the same thing. What doesn't work is raw information.

Had I plenty of life yet before me, I could fill it with facts and figures, shared experiences alongside her, and it has value, this shared future, but for the three days I have left in the world, I preferred to guarantee that nobody else will fall prey to the hands that abused Yoro in the name of peace. I may not dress in uniform, sir, or carry a name as slick or unctuous as that greasy pizza of military men and mozzarella, but I do have power, the same as anyone else, and it's a pretty remarkable power, simpler than you can imagine before you actually wield it: the power to take a life. And that's what I did: no need to hide behind a flag of peace, which they rape each time they rape a woman. I alone am enough. So once I embraced Yoro, I knew it was all she needed to understand what she needed to understand. Yoro acknowledges everything, she acknowledges us, she acknowledges Jim and me. We needed nothing else. Ours was an atavistic attraction, an attraction that connected us from an ancient place where we recognized each other without being conscious, without knowing what it was that bound us to each other so tightly. I allowed myself to become a criminal because I sensed that everything was spilling over now. At my age. You see? No time for regret, much less a desire for it.

So go ahead now, read Yoro's letter below to see what it was that I read that day, which according to the date stamp had been sent a month and a half earlier:

*Dear Dad:*

*In a few minutes, a friend and confidante will come to take this letter and send it clandestinely. Things aren't easy here— I've been trying to smuggle this letter out for years. Till now I'd only written it in my head so nobody else could find it. Everything happened so abruptly, they just came to tell me that it's now or never, my chance has come; so let me go straight to the most urgent point. I'm somewhere in Zaire. Look for me. Do you still remember me? You're all that I have. All the other foster families have turned a blind eye. I don't know if you're aware, but I lived with five different families. A new family every two years. You're the only one I stayed with for a longer period of time, those first five years of my life. The address on this letter is the one you obliged me to memorize. I've lived hoping against hope that you haven't moved. Each one of the families took really good care of me, I can't deny that, and I missed each one of them when I left, but your love is what I remember the most. I don't know if perhaps I'm idealizing things because I was so little. I'm frightened to think you might be dead or that you've killed me off in your heart, where I remember once being.*

*I don't know where they are keeping me, Dad. I know only that they brought me to Zaire, which I think is a gigantic place and so unstable they had to change the name. Now I think it's called the Democratic Republic of the Congo. But I can't say for sure because I live underground. Some of my companions who share this underground confinement say that pretty soon they're going to take us to Namibia. They say there's uranium there and people die in the open-air mines where it's extracted; we die here buried in the earth, pulling minerals from its guts. At least they get to see the sky every day. When this letter reaches you, I will probably be here or someplace in Namibia. But since you're in the military, I thought you might figure out a way to find me. I don't know how I got here. I was with my last family one day, and the next I knew I was being loaded on a plane to I don't know where, with a bodyguard, and then another plane, and another. They made me work doing things that I don't want to talk about here, I wouldn't know how. And then they sent me to a mine, and here I am. It's a clue, of course, but they say that in this country there are many mines like this one, so it's not much information for you to go on. I heard we're in a coltan mine near Goma, but I'm not entirely sure. One of the ways they torture us is by lying to us about where we are, using a different name every once in a while to confuse us. We can't ever be sure of anything we're told. Only what we see. Which is mostly death. So many of my companions here have died, and nobody says anything when they do. Sometimes they just leave them where they fall, as if they aren't in the way. Eventually they end up in the earth covered by the stones we excavate with our bare hands. We are our own mass grave.*

*For a while my families would send reports about my health. I don't know who wanted them. They'd ask me questions all the time. My whole life, a long battery of tests. I don't know what it is they expect me to come down with, but now I really am beginning to feel weak, and for the first time I'm afraid it might have something to do with the disease everyone has been waiting for. If it is, and if it's serious, I want to die close to you, Papa. I'm saying goodbye before they come to take the letter. I pray it makes it to you. I'm waiting for you. Please don't forget me. Besides, Papa, I'm pregnant, my belly is growing even in the miserable conditions here, working in the tunnels fourteen hours a day. I'm so frightened. I want this child, even though it's the result of rape. It was one of the armed men, though all the men guarding the mine are armed. This particular mine, though, is also an arms reserve.*

*At first I wanted to get rid of the baby. I've never wanted to be a mother, and less so after being raped. I'm not so young anymore either. I must be around thirty-nine. More than half of those years were spent underground. Like a dead woman. I'd pull the baby out myself, but I don't know how to do it and I'm afraid. Now it's the only thing that keeps me company. If you make it here and don't find me, please look for him or her. To make it all easier, I decided to give the baby a name, my same name, whether it's a boy or a girl: Yoro. There's a Spanish guard here who once told me that Yoro means to cry*

*in his language, but it's written in a different way. If anyone*
*deserves this name, it's me. I've cried an ocean. Please, I beg*
*of you, if you can't locate me, please find your grandson or*
*granddaughter, who will have my same name, and give him*
*or her the chance to live to contradict it. I've already cried*
*for myself and for the baby, and for the children of his or her*
*children. I've never, ever forgotten you. You are my true father.*
   *Your daughter,*
   *Yoro*

I was sixty-six years old when I read that letter. I'd just returned to New York to rest, to stay put in the home I had once
shared with Jim and to take care of myself while I waited—as I
had always waited—for the definitive fatal disease to come and
take me. I had reached this age and lived calmly, fear-free. But
that letter shaved years away. Her cry for help rejuvenated me,
which shouldn't be confused with feeling happier, more beautiful,
or more agile than before. What it did was throw me back into
the tunnel of fear from many years before. The distress came from
knowing that I would go after her, and in order to find her I had
to be alive, and I had to remain alive for a good while longer, and
to remain alive a good while longer I had to feel again the fear
of death, the fear that I might not get there in time. A double
fear, since again I knew it wasn't only about me anymore, but
about two of us: her and me. This anxiety brought me strength
more than anything else. The strength to stand up for myself and
for her, Yoro, whom I could feel again inside of me. At sixty-six
years of age I finally felt the heaviness of an advanced-stage pregnancy. Nine months. I was a terribly strong old pregnant woman.
I remembered my mother. When I was little she told me she'd
wanted to give me a little brother, and that she and my father
had tried for a long time but were never successful. She said it re-
gretfully; almost embarrassed, as if apologizing for having denied

me a playmate, a companion with whom to share my troubles or achievements later in life, when she was no longer around, someone with whom to grieve her death. She was very intuitive, my mother. It was if she could foresee that I would be left alone too early. A brother, if he had survived the bomb, would certainly have been a great help in my life. A heart that loved the same mother I did, a pair of eyes that shared a vision of all the pain my eyes have seen, a sense of joy that would have relieved some of the melancholy that had weighed me down since I was a little girl.

MY MOTHER USED TO SAY that the only way to attain something was by visualizing yourself with it, seeing yourself together with what you desire. Yoro's letter made me grasp those words fully. Thanks to the letter I could now truly see myself with Yoro for the first time. Did it mean I had her? That I would find her in the end? This pregnancy on the verge of birth is what brought my mother to mind. Coincidentally, yesterday was her birthday, and I realized I had forgotten to think about her and wish her well, which was strange for me. Yoro melded with her in my mind and I began putting things together. I thought how true it was that my mother hadn't been able to get pregnant again, but when she curled me inside her uterus like a little pink woolen sweater, she had also gestated another little girl, who was inside of me. So I was born pregnant. It's why I felt pregnant so many years later. It's why, truly, I've been pregnant my whole life. Pregnant—the day I read the letter—at sixty-six years of age. And that's why, too, I've resisted, why I recovered from what anyone else would have solved with a bullet, a rope, or a knife. I withstood thanks to the daughter my mother gestated inside me to keep me company. Now I can be alone because I know I never really am, no matter what it looks like to other people, no matter what it looks like to me. So that's why I take such good care of myself and drink alcohol only on special occasions. I avoid eating unhealthy things, don't puff on cigarettes, and stay away from drugs. That's why I've chosen carefully the people who can enter my body. That's why I use my claws when attacked. That's why in spite of everything and without really knowing why, I never chose death, nor would I give my life up for someone else, not even my mother if she were still alive, or Jim, though at times I've thought that for him I would.

No, I would never have given my life up for anyone because I'm not a single person, I'm two. There's a girl inside of me, I knew when I read the letter; there's a little girl I knew was Yoro. Yoro was inside of me, not since birth but from before I was born, from when I was being formed, the process that brought me from embryo to fetus, and from fetus to baby. This was my mother's treasure and greatest gift, even though I wasn't aware of it yet: my strength. She is my strength; it is she who gives me extraordinary energy. People wondered how I could be so alive, despite my age. Don't overdo it, people said, not knowing what I was carrying inside. Today I'm more aware of this than ever. And you'll be too when I'm ready to tell you about it. I was one body with two hearts, one body cupped inside of another. That must be why my little dog would approach my belly and rub her ears against it like a stethoscope. She must have heard Yoro's beating heart, and the dog would whimper and Yoro must have liked the closeness of the animal too. I could tell when something charmed her because I'd close my eyes and feel so light that I would soar like an eagle at rest, an eagle nested in the flight of another eagle. I saw that image so many times. That's the strength, the high flight and se-renity. My mother's gift. Sixty-six years of pregnancy that I never interrupted because, though at times it may have been a burden to carry so much life, I could never have aborted my mother's daughter. Yesterday was her birthday and I hadn't even thought about her. I closed my eyes, clutching Yoro's letter in my hand, and expressed myself more or less in these terms:

"Mama, it was your birthday yesterday. I was far away and couldn't celebrate with you. But I appreciate the astuteness you've shared with me throughout my life. My little girl and I, our daughter and I, love you with all the potency of our two hearts that beat to your beauty and generosity."

THAT LETTER GAVE ME the vigor I needed to look for Yoro, to give birth, but I grew unsettled as I began preparing for the trip. I was confronting this without Jim for the first time. And as if dealing with this at my age wasn't daunting enough, the letter shook me up in another way. As you must have read, Yoro explained she was about to be taken to mine uranium. Uranium. The central ingredient of the bombs that annihilated Hiroshima and Nagasaki. Uranium. In my little girl's hands. It's a relatively abundant material in the earth's crust, but can only be mined cost-effectively in regions where there is a high concentration of it, and where nobody cares about the ensuing environmental contamination from the extraction process, neither the country's government nor the international companies that hold mining rights. Which is to say, this type of mining takes place only in the trash dumps of the world, the landscapes that are of no interest to anyone, the air that can be poisoned because the lungs they fill belong to people who have no value whatsoever, the neglected class. Nuclear energy is much cleaner—I've heard it said so often—but believe me, I know something about uranium, and I know that, aside from the risks of accidents in nuclear power plants located in developed countries, the most polluting phase is the first one, the site of extraction, not only for the environment and nearby cities, but also for the hands of the people who mine it without knowing they're being murdered. Even if the workers knew their lives were at risk, they'd continue extracting the uranium because death by starvation seems more imminent than death by radiation poisoning. You can feel hunger—it pricks every day—but radiation poisoning is a silent killer. Besides, you know that in Africa there are always more workers than jobs. A thousand ants for each tiny crumb of bread. If they don't explain the risks of exposure, it's not for fear of being left without laborers, only that there's no time to waste; the white queen orders them to extract material, no break. Time isn't only gold in Africa. It's more valuable than that. Time is uranium. Africans aren't informed about the hows and the whys of the death that is coming because the need to fill their bellies, or their sons' or daughters' or parents' bellies, is far more urgent. Starvation, that physiological law, doesn't hide; on the contrary, it is made manifest. Radiation, on the other hand, is the way death satiates its own hunger: silence.

Uranium. Just the name to me was like something straight out of hell, like Uranus, that god, son and husband of Gaea, Mother Earth. Uranium changed my life. It took my parents, grandparents, and friends away; decimated my city; destroyed my country; insulted the human race. Yet there it was, to all countries the most coveted gold, radioactive gold that Yoro was now extracting, handling, someplace in Africa. In an African mine, where no doubt the process didn't follow any safety measures for workers, who are in reality slaves, as I came to see for myself later on.

I'll skip the details of my preparation for the Africa sojourn. First, because I have to finish this testimony today. And anyway, let me just say that it's not about the journey for me. Whenever I go somewhere, be it short distances on foot or long ones by train, I go directly from the departure scene to the arrival scene. The in-between is always like a big empty space I sneak into so I can find my own world. I'm not interested in itineraries, only where I come from and where I'm going, which in my case are not existential issues but practical ones.

So I will limit myself to saying that I made it to a desert worn out by one of these mines, the Rössing mine in Namibia. It had taken a few weeks for me to get all the details together, so I decided to start in this country, where Yoro had said in her letter they were going to take her. If I didn't find her there, I would continue on to the Congo.

The Rössing mine is in the Namib Desert some thirty-eight miles from Swakopmund, the German colonial city where I am today, where, as I learned in my previous stay, the residents like to brag about their buildings and wide streets with fairy-tale houses in the shade of palm trees planted rigidly equidistant from one another, scrupulously aligned, like teeth adjusted by the best German orthodontist. They are proud of their urban design, but also of the special attention the Germans paid to the population as compared with other colonizers. Apparently they built schools. What good folk, those Germans. What they don't tell you is that the schools were just for white people. But I didn't see any schools in Swakopmund, only the slave labor camps, the first testing grounds for the concentration camps the Germans would later bring to Europe, along with the eyes, brains, and other organs of Africans preserved in formaldehyde for racial studies. Just a few years ago, Germany finally returned the skeletons they'd taken. Now the descendants of the colonialists pat the shoulders of Africans who lost their grandparents, greeting them like buddies; they surf together in the sand dunes of that desert and invite their international friends to come and record them speaking North American slang with their state-of-the-art cameras. A friend of mine told me not long ago about two members of the United Nations peacekeeping forces who surfed the dunes or more like staggered down them on a kind of board. I thought it was nearly as ridiculous as their ill-named *peace mission,* which not even staggeringly have they actually been able to complete.

The Namib Desert is the most important tourist attraction and the country's greatest source of revenue, more so even than the mines. Swakopmund is a major tourist enclave, bordered on one side by the icy, though striking, vistas of the Atlantic coast, and on the other three sides by the Namib Desert. The climate is cloudy and humid, and the legion of ships that get beached in the fog along the coast are an attraction in and of themselves, uncanny shipwrecks that people on land, adults and children, pick apart to sell off the materials until there's nothing left. Tourism, one of the country's few sources of revenue, is being put at risk by the uranium being exported to the UK, France, the United States, and my country, Japan. So why should I care about any of this at this stage in my life? I guess if I'm writing about it, it's because it still matters to me, but let me get back to what I really care about: Yoro, whom I hoped to locate in the desert mine.

A villager in one of the last places I went explained the effects of the desert invasion through an interpreter. That's how I came to understand the value of that great esplanade of shifting sands before the mine was built. Multinational companies defended their actions by saying it was a perfect spot, a nothing in the middle of nowhere. As if the nothing was not as valuable, or even more priceless, than the something, the populated, the city. Ignoramuses. Because of them, the desert is losing its presence. They made the necessary nothing disappear, that indispensable place for insignificant plants and animals that were and are going extinct, essential for the survival of nearby villages and tourism. The relentless racket of heavy machinery and its constant beeping every few seconds supplanted the silence. The emptiness, a mythical place for those coming from far away and a fundamental physical space for those living nearby, was filled up with trucks and roads that coiled into an enormous spiral descending level by level to below the ground, a kilometer-wide oval where thousands of hands scrabbled in search of the cancerous substance.

The man who acted as my interpreter placed a tiny reptile that looked like a pink chameleon in the palm of my hand. It was one of only a few of that species that were left, or at least the villagers said they no longer found them in the sand as they had before. I don't think I've ever seen such a beautiful creature. Its mouth was turned up in a permanent smile, but its skin was what caught my eye, so fine it seemed translucent. Looking closer, I realized that what at first I thought were the pastel tones of its skin—bluish orange, a very soft green—were in fact the colors of its internal organs, which were visible underneath. I thought of that legend of the old queen of Brittany whose skin was so delicate, so white, that when she drank red wine, her throat went blue with each swallow. How could such a delicate creature resist the harsh desert light, the direct rays of the sun that a few minutes earlier had turned my arms, my hands, my unprotected skin all red and patchy? How could that little animal—seemingly unformed, still inside the egg—survive in such a severe environment? A land scorched by the ruthless sun was its habitat, and yet it couldn't survive something ostensibly so much less powerful than the king of the solar system: the human touch.

One day the locals observed the arrival of vast quantities of heavy machinery: trucks, equipment of all makes and models, technologies they'd never heard of or seen before. The British company Rio Tinto had been working the mines since the seventies. They had promised to build schools, create jobs, and provide better infrastructure for the population, and over the years they've done exactly nothing to better the lives or the standard of living of the locals. The only thing that rose was the death toll from direct and indirect contamination. The workers labored for a pittance and the uranium profits were siphoned out of the country or stolen by the government officials who signed away the mine's exploitation rights. A few years later, in 1978, a sort of prefabricated city grew up some ten miles away from the mine for the Rössing laborers. They christened it Arandis. To visit the mine and the settlement was for me like a new descent into hell, as you'll see in my chronicle of events. As I mentioned earlier, the hell in my life hasn't been organized as levels one below the other, but horizontally, on the same plane, like a huge flat surface on which each door opened onto a different version of suffering. I'd never seen it as a gradation of pain going from lesser to greater, though each form of misery seemed worse than the last, even if it wasn't, as a result of the newness in the form of pain. But what I saw in Rössing was like an authentic classical descent into Avernus, and being belowground added to the feeling of perversity. For once, an inferno into which I was thrown fit the traditional subterranean image.

ARANDIS REMINDED ME of Los Alamos, not only because its infrastructure broke the desert landscape, but because of the inexorable sun, the heat suffocating everything like an allegorical representation of what was being cooked up there, the atomic material. A rudimentary cardboard and wire sign on the way into the housing zone read WELCOME TO ARANDIS. It was something like a bad joke, welcoming one to a place that could scarcely be differentiated from the work camp barracks. The atmosphere was laden with despair. The way the building materials had been arranged made the settlement a far more soulless place than Los Alamos. People were there simply to earn their daily bread—literally, the bread for one day, not the bread for two days. All the hope had been sucked out of the place. The air was grimy and bleak, unlike in the North American camp.

Not a soul could be found outside the tiny shacks. They were all working in the mine. Within an hour I was there. The hellish oval yawning under an open sky, the great pit where so many black people worked, as Yoro had explained in her letter. I remember reading her words and thinking how working here must have been a bit better, at least in comparison with toiling in the subterranean galleries. But when I walked into Rössing, I was overcome with pity for Yoro because of the blistering sun she would have had to endure there. So again I proved my case that data alone can't be trusted at all. I would never have believed that there was something worse than suffocating in a tunnel until I experienced that heat: being scorched by the free-falling rays of sunlight that burn more than the skin—the stomach, the throat, the nostrils, other organs. To me, it was like the sinister prank of a superior being: an invisible cloak of fire laid out between the blue sky and our heads, held in place by the unremitting breath of a dragon condemned to immobility, not allowed to fly an inch into the open air. I couldn't find a single white face among the black ones. After I had paid the negotiated fee, they let me walk down to the mine's first level. I could now see down into it and into that upside-down cone used to extract the sterile material that would be separated from the mineral.

The scaled terraces of Peruvian farmlands came to mind; those terraced plots that follow the natural curves of a mountain. The shapes were similar, but the colors were wildly different. In Peru, everything was green; in Arandis, it was all yellow. A massive film of yellow powder coated everything, even the lungs, though you couldn't see it, and of course the workers weren't told about this. Soon, though, any connection between the living terraces of Peru and these fell away. This was an open-air mine contaminating the atmosphere and the surface and subterranean waters. It was destroying or extinguishing the local flora and fauna and dismembering the landscape. The simple thought that Yoro could be there made my heart skip a beat in my chest, though knowing she might be in some other mine, far away from me, also brought a sense of panic. My anxiety was exacerbated by a sun that blistered my skin even under my clothes, even though I was covered and wearing a hat. Some workers wore helmets, but the majority went unprotected. There was no water anywhere, even though sweat streamed from everyone's face. No one ever looked up, either from force of habit or to avoid the impact of the sun shining straight in their faces. In that awful space, the land's once-beloved sun had become a source of humiliation, like the foremen who obliged them to work with heads hanging; the work didn't allow for hats or even shirts. The blackness of their skin was tinged with red.

It was too much for me, at my age, to take in all that horror in a single day. I felt a wave of fatigue and had to sit down on a rock by myself, crestfallen and all choked up, with no idea how or where to begin. Though I took care to sit in something akin to shade, I still had never experienced heat like that. It was like the summer at the dead center of all summers. My vision clouded and I remained transfixed like that for minutes that felt like eternity. I'm aware of what happens in these processes. I knew the sun's heat was beginning to damage my cells, to clog the invisible ancestral passageways all over my skin. Only once had I felt comparable temperatures, though less intense. It happened in America, when I was with S in Teotihuacán. Both experiences of extreme heat fused somehow, and the weariness brought me back there, or maybe it was the dizziness or a need to escape or stay put, but I relived, collapsed into, that day in Mexico.

A man was holding a prickly pear leaf in his hand beneath a colossal sun. It was an edible cactus, and he told us to look closely at the little white dots. I brought my face a little closer and listened as he explained what they were: "They're the eggs of cochineals, which reproduce on the leaves of this species of cactus."

The man gingerly removed an egg with a very thin stick and

placed it on a piece of paper. He poked it and a red stain spread over the white paper. Then he drew a garnet-colored circle with the same stick. Finally he jabbed the cactus leaf, extracted a kind of sap, and covered the stain with it. "Now," he said, "the prickly pear juice protects the color. It helps to dry and fix the blood."

I touched the circle with my fingertip. It was perfectly dry. I pulled my finger away, startled. Maybe I saw a mirror inside the red circle that reflected back to me my own dehydrating self because it was high noon—noon in the mine and noon in Mexico. The temperature was still on the rise, but was it in the mine or in Mexico? I couldn't remember because the little tails of fatty acids were melting, the cells moving more fluidly, the sperm liberated from their reproductive burden. But other, much less benign things were happening too. Membranes were being damaged and breaking into tiny pieces, pieces that were replicas of elements of me, multiplied, reduced, infinitesimally; and so the multiple breasts, knees, ankles—visible only under a microscope—that scuttled here and there, similar to those lizard tails I used to see when I survived Hiroshima, started thrashing around again and again and again, never locating the body. This is what was happening to the people I was watching. As in Mexico. It was the death of proteins. And I wanted contact with other flesh, other liquids, other sweat, because the body always finds a way to communicate. I felt that in Teotihuacán, but not in the mine; in the mine, all I felt was heat and decay.

The man in Teotihuacán took out another plant. It looked like a thistle. "It's called chicalote," I heard him say, and he bled it too. Its sap was yellow, and he used it to draw the rays around the sun. Animal blood and vegetable blood. This plant was similar to the one I saw in the Namib Desert, a place so dry that who could imagine a flower growing there whose scent could be appreciated in all its intensity from several yards away.

I looked at the circle the man had drawn, the rays, and raised my eyes to look at L, in front of me, from behind my glasses. S had introduced us the day before and he had offered to accompany us. I liked him. L was also admiring the painted circle and didn't realize I was looking at him and musing. But I didn't think the way I thought about everything else, but

> with the kind of thought
> that isn't linear
> like the Avenue of the Dead,
> but alive,
> circular,
> running the perimeter over and over
> of the circumference that tied the tail
> of the eyes I used to see him, with the mouth,
> of the eyes he used to elude me.
> Circular thought also like the mine,
> spiral,
> curling,
> toward the inside.

We left the man working on the drawing he had started, sitting in a chair under the full force of the sun. The heat didn't seem to bother him, dark flesh whose long shadow projected over the earth like a clock hand that ticked for everyone but him. Ticked for everyone but especially for me, knowing I had been given a single day beside L. I could feel the little fleeting hand of time, an intangible hand that couldn't be grabbed or held back. The horror of the shadow, always the shadow, the awkward tracing that mistakenly interprets the arms opening in an embrace and projects instead a cross on the wall; the body that might have delivered her will never pass before it, never.

"I'm thirsty," I said. I asked L for water. I had been sweating, had lost salts and electrolytes.

I drank less than I needed, thinking (hoping) we still had a lot of ground to cover. And I hadn't paid attention to the sunburn that was becoming more and more visible, though I did notice what was going on inside me, the blood vessels dilating, trying to irrigate as much surface area as possible to bring cooler blood to the deeper tissues. I wiped my brow with my hand and detected the activities of that army of microscopic mechanisms organizing themselves to alleviate the effects of the heat.

L took me to a place where, he said, they could hear us from very far away even if we didn't raise our voices. From there, the feathered chieftain would address the crowd. I whispered something to J to give this amazing acoustic phenomenon a try: "Can you hear me?"

Nothing. L couldn't hear me. But a person in the distance, someone walking toward the valley's horizon, appeared to turn around. What a strange place, where closeness protected itself with an operculum, an organic door, like that tiny plate a sea snail uses to close its aperture after retracting into its shell; that lid that is shaped like an ear, though it's deaf, covering the ears of the mollusk in its shell. Isolating it.

The sun continued to scald (it was Mexico, it was the mine, it was Hiroshima) more and more, and my immune system persisted in announcing my biological response in ever deepening shades of red. But it was a chain of the deaf: L couldn't hear me. Yoro can't hear me.

> since neither did I hear the process
> destroying me
> inside,
> that fatal snap

of the cellular RNA.
Nobody heard anything.
We were too near.

IT WASN'T SO HARD to climb the stairs of the highest pyramid, the one dedicated to the sun. A lot easier than I expected. Far easier than descending into the mine. That's what they say: the descent is more difficult than the ascent. People were resting in different spots around the pyramid, not everyone suffering from a lack of energy but more from a kind of halfheartedness passed down from their parents or the parents of their parents, like a dust accumulating over their long or short lives and passed from generation to generation, a genetics of apathy, a sort of contagion spreading this indolence from one to another, loosening the legs and the will, purging the words of tension.

It wasn't difficult to climb up the pyramid, but it was hard to accept that the view from the top didn't allow one to see beyond the people. A large group of people gathered around a preacher all raised their arms. The red of my shoulders had begun to descend upward and ascend downward; there was no order to anything anymore, like a fire that spreads itself following the whim of the winds. The mine was that upside-down pyramid, and the people there extended their arms, but instead of raising them to the sky, toward God, they lowered them to the minerals underground.

I moved in full knowledge that the cells were setting loose an altered material due to the ultraviolet radiation, drawing from the neighboring healthy cells an inflammatory response meant to remove the cells the sun had damaged. Though the lesions weren't painful yet, I was beginning to feel woozy, and like the healthy cells, I wanted to be free of the presence of these damaged people. So I asked L if we could jump the fence. The fence had been put in place to keep tourists from leaving the group, pushing the limits of safety, of decorum, of the history they'd just been told. An insolent divider separating what was accessible from what was not. I pleaded: "Let's jump." And we did. And we didn't have to walk anymore, because other things were walking over us. Not people, because there were no people on the other side. There were massive lightweight blocks of stone; there were those little plants that asked for so little and stuck like lichens to our shoes, same as the desert rocks. The vertigo of the genuine. It was peace. It was shared loneliness. And after the silence, laughter. I painted something on the palm of my hand: "We laughed here, and we rested."

We got into the car after seeing the pyramids. So yes, we were both beginning to feel the sting of the burns, though I had it worse, being so fair-skinned. The heat in that closed-in space, the excitement, the tight skin urgently needing a salve or another person's saliva or maybe just a caress . . . all of it, all that was lacking, on four wheels, in a blind car or just a selfish one, both of us realizing it had to stop right there, that we needed water.

At a stop sign we looked at each other and pointed out our burns.

"You're sunburnt," L said.

"You too," I responded.

He was dark-skinned and I was very fair-skinned, but the difference in skin color doesn't matter in regard to the sun's passage, the cellular massacre, the regeneration. Pigmentation, individual genetic makeup—a sunburn allows any passerby to notice the nice coincidence:

> Both of us came from the same place,
> both of us were exposed,
> both of us had walked together
> and unprotected.

But all we had was a single day. And the end was nigh. My thoughts still whirled like the wind inside a tornado, moving without having to break the loop of desire that attracts everything toward it. But sadly, time imposes its own form; time then and now doesn't move in circles like my thoughts. Time continued to be (or appeared to be) linear like the Miccaotli, that Avenue of the Dead that only a few hours before we strolled together, unwittingly or perhaps knowingly carrying ourselves along its stretch. A mile-long walk in the heat, with something much heavier than death in tow: the burden of self-sacrifice, the rejection of a gift that we would never be offered again.

Before returning to the hotel where S and I were staying, L and I drank a beverage from a can—no glass, no table or chairs. Just the two of us, two cans, sitting on a bench in a plaza whose perimeter came to a close with the first church of New Spain. The circle's only light was a very dim streetlamp, like a cigarette in the mouth of a giant who took pity on us and embraced us. We rested our backs against the colossus. It was warm. But the silence had already begun to settle, not the uncomfortable kind resulting from a lack of words, but the coming glaciation after an entire age (an entire day) of heat.

We arrived at the hotel, our heads drooping as if to protect ourselves from a nocturnal sun. The burgeoning inflammation hurt. The heat had carried desire to those spots the sun hadn't seen, hadn't touched, that we hadn't seen or caressed either. The heat had drenched us like a liquid—our backs, our lips, our throats, our genitals. I asked for more water.

Water.
Water to cool the burns.
Water to part the waters of red breasts.
Water to drown the sweet word (stay)
that shouldn't be pronounced,

because only one day, or so we believed,
had been given to us.

And our skin hurt so much (or the desire, one and the same)
that we embraced in front of the hotel, like two irresponsible
people, ignoring or misinterpreting our screaming cells—lame,
one-armed, blind—that asked us, begged us, to rejuvenate all the
members who fell from the cliff of the two hundred and eight
stairs of sun.

We moved away from each other, foretelling sorrowfully the
closing of the wounds. Neither one of us was going to use cold
compresses, cortisone creams, anti-inflammatories. What for?
Cellular death is irreversible. We knew that even once we were
scarred over, when the blisters appeared and burst and then dried
out, returning the skin to its winter shade, it'll continue to smart.

When I opened my eyes, I saw that I was on another level of
the mine. My forehead was fiery. Nobody had come to help me.
There was a tiny bruise on my forearm. The slaves—I insist that
*slavery* is the only word to use for this—hadn't come to my aid
either, not even to put me back into the shade. I got up as best I
could. Me, an old woman. Me, nearly lifeless from the heat. Me,
missing that Mexican lover who never was but whom I brought to
mind once again while immersed in the mine.

Once I'd resuscitated myself—when all is said and done, something I'm rather used to doing—I located the interpreter again
and we started asking the laborers about Yoro. I didn't have a
recent photograph of her, but I had one thing working in my favor:
her fair skin and Asian features. Luckily for me and for Yoro,
nobody in that place could distinguish Japanese features from
Chinese. China hadn't yet sunk its claws into the mine or sent
Chinese prisoners there to work off their crimes through forced
labor, as they did later in certain African operations, with reduced
sentences for the prisoners if they finished doing their time in

Africa. Unfortunately, in most of the cases when Chinese prisoners consented to work in Africa, they were condemning themselves to a death sentence they hadn't received in China. So that
was my only advantage: Yoro's physical difference from the other
workers. The people we asked said nobody there fit her description, and they'd instantly segue into nervous complaints about the
working conditions, always keeping their voices low. They asked
for money and help, screaming in silence, really screaming for
help in whispers. The people who worked there, they said, got sick.
The foreman assured them it was because they smoked and drank
alcohol, but that wasn't a plausible explanation, since only a small
minority of them drank and smoked. There was something else
going on, they said; all they wanted was to know what it was.
Neither the directors nor the mining company's doctors admitted
the negative effects of radioactive dust, which some of the miners
were exposed to twenty-four hours a day.

Sometime later, when demonstrations outside the mines became widespread, mostly by antinuclear groups, it came out that
the so-called daily controls meant to measure radioactivity levels
were actually done only once a year. According to the mining
companies' spokesmen, the registered data showed radioactivity
levels below the danger zone. But independent experts warned
about the danger of never being at the zero point, and since radioactivity is cumulative, daily exposure to the ingredient that supplied countries with nuclear arms, uranium—at levels far below
dangerous for short periods but always above the zero point—was
a trigger for illnesses.

So here I was in Africa so many years after Hiroshima, yet
another place where doctors obeyed orders that were clearly inhumane: they colluded in hiding the diseases from the people
who were sick, allowing them to continue working under conditions that were killing them off little by little every day. Hundreds of pawns worked like that, dying for some foreign king in

this endless rummaging around, the relentless burrowing under death's sun.

YORO WASN'T IN RÖSSING, nor had she ever passed through. Either she hadn't arrived yet or she'd been misinformed or misled when she wrote her letter. Or maybe she was dead. The thought of her being a casualty didn't dampen my plans, though; I had pledged the rest of my life to looking for her. I would die in Africa. My spirits flagged at times, of course, but they'd been at rock bottom for so long that however low they dipped now, it was never enough to throw in the towel. I'd gotten so used to my ration of sadness that no additional misery would be enough to take me down much further. You could say that my ongoing sorrow was like a maintenance dose. I learned the mechanics of extreme pain: a tightrope walker's cord, on which the acrobat, the wounded person, isn't worried about losing his balance. Balance isn't the problem for people whose only worry is an acrobatic move that's difficult for them: instead, it's reaffirming the will to stay on the cord, to live. That's the secret, don't ever get off; the body's weight keeps the cord from lifting higher, and pain tends to elevate us, only to let us fall like dead weight from the sky. Very early on I learned to get off the ground where the ants roved, the predators, the dogs, who'd run straight toward the smell of my torn flesh. That wire was my place, some ten feet high. No running with the pack, on firm ground—I had to concentrate all my efforts on resigning myself to walking that tightrope. Of course it was uncomfortable, but one learns to live with discomfort. The trick was not to go so high that if I fell I would break every bone in my body or die once and for all. That's why I've always acted this way, accommodating, discreet, trying to make discomfort my natural territory, a tightrope walker, at the same time aware that those ten feet above the ground are what give me an upper hand:

I could leap from on high like a panther pouncing on its prey from a tree branch; attack from a position of ambush, from the invisible heights, the way the bomb fell on me. From that moment on, sir, I no longer lived on my tightrope. The pain is gone. I'm at peace. Now that I'm on the ground, I miss the temptation to jump, but it was revenge that put my feet back on earth.

THE ONLY TWO REFERENCES in Yoro's letter are the Namibian uranium mine and the coltan mine in the Democratic Republic of the Congo. After the Namibia fiasco, and not knowing specifically which of the countless mines there are in Congo, I finally chose one of the best known, in the outskirts of Goma in North Kivu.

I found lodging in a house with views of Lake Kivu. It looks like such a lovely body of water. It looks spotless. But the lake is hell, and I was warned about it when I got there. Close to a thousand feet deep, the lake contains approximately 300 cubic kilometers of carbon dioxide and 60 cubic kilometers of methane, a gas that can become a detonator, especially because it's near Nyiragongo volcano. Which means Lake Kivu is an explosive lake, and if the gas it contains should ever surface, it will expand through the atmosphere and kill off thousands of people by suffocation. Theoretically, this could happen at any time. This doesn't frighten me, though. There's very little that frightens me these days. At sunset, while I was taking in all the apparent beauty of the lake, I thought how if one day it should actually explode, it would blow out the cemetery too: the victims of Rwanda. There's a refugee camp nearby. What can I possibly tell you about this area that you don't already know? When I went to visit the camp a little later, I realized how much the sanctuary was like the lake, only superficially tranquil, because in its guts a group of UN soldiers sporting blue helmets was corroding it to the core, corroding the refugees, especially the female refugees, who carry in their vaginas the best currency for international aid. You bet—the blue of their helmets matches the color of Lake Kivu. A blue to cover up the brown. But I'll take care of those blue helmets a little later.

A few days after I got here, I started measuring distances in time, since the local roads were precarious at best. Miles didn't exist. It is impossible to determine the length of a road that isn't there. So everything around me was measured in time, and even then the length of time was only approximate, since the hours or days it took to get from one place to another depended on the rains, the presence or absence of a tree fallen across the road, the sudden appearance of an illegal improvised roadblock or a bullet, which of course suspended time.

But the day we set out for the mine I could calculate both distance and time thanks to other factors indicating the nearness to our destination: we began passing numbers of people walking with sacks on their backs. Several of them were adolescents and children. By now such sights don't shock me—you can't possibly expect me to get outraged over seeing a child with a sack on his or her back. I would be a hypocrite to argue that this child should go to school if his family is dying of hunger. But coltan is a macabre metal, one of the densest metals on earth, which makes it extremely heavy. A relatively small sack of coltan weighs almost ninety pounds, so you could say, as so many others do, it's a size that even a child could carry, and if they hunch over like that it's because they like to complain. And so we passed hordes of people on the way, stopping often to pay a toll foisted on us by armed groups or the regular army, money extorted to allow them to continue on with the mineral burden they would sell for a few dollars in the city, to be sold in Europe for three hundred a pound. All of this I learned later. No matter, whatever the final tab, nothing justified that daisy chain of horrors originating in the belly of that mine.

Inside the mine. You know what people do inside a mine?

Search. For years, entire lifetimes, they surrender their health, their time, their strength, to searching. An eternal search for something—in this case coltan. Curiously enough, most of the people looking for it have no idea what it's used for. I was searching in the galleries of the mine, surrounded at all times by other people searching. The galleries are built specifically for searching. *If only I had a tunnel to dig in, or a thousand of them,* I thought. But the quest that I had been on thus far had taken place on an immense esplanade, a huge prairie with boundless horizons on all sides, in whose vastness there wasn't a single mineral to clean, pebble to remove cautiously from the earth, ever so tentatively nursing the hope of finding that one valuable material that would please only me.

In some way I envied this trade that has been carried on over the centuries. The laborers in those mines worked without machinery, and the process of extraction was done in a wholly artisanal way—enviable. I imagined that the techniques for finding and extracting the mineral had been passed on from generation to generation, and that the whole enterprise was based on a kind of sustained ancestral authority and communal effort of people of all ages. I in contrast was a solitary miner. Nobody showed me how to excavate, nobody helped me bail the water out of my gallery because, as I said, my gallery was an esplanade, and when water came in, there was no place to chuck it, and I could only wait, drenched, for days, months, years, for it to dry out. I saw the lights they wear on their heads in the mine in Goma and knew they wouldn't have been of any use because I searched in the light of day, and intense sunlight is what damaged my eyesight more and more, not darkness or advanced age. I didn't have the fans the miners use to renew the air in the galleries and protect themselves from gases because I worked outdoors, winding through the variables that are the enemy of any quest: complete freedom, no clues, no suggestions, no guide. The coltan miners kept moving their makeshift fans here and there to breathe better. And how ironic that outside the mine, far from the subterranean galleries, the land known as the world's second lung because of the lushness of its vegetation was in bloom. The miners, me, we were like microbes attacking that lung's alveoli, like others who attacked from above by chopping trees, killing off the population and selling off their lands for a pittance to huge multinational companies, who then used the cheap land for uncontrolled dumping. Poor second lung of the world, mortally wounded, tubercular, pneumonic. I registered several galleries, bolstered every four or five yards by trunks, like catacombs, people who lived cut off from the rest of the world unaware that the fruit of their labor, coltan, was precisely an essential piece of global communication, an essential superconductor for manufacturing mobile telephones, laptops, and state-of-the-art weapons. Coltan was the coin of their sacrifice, served up to finance the wars that killed their fathers, their sons, themselves, living in agony to the death, buried by the coin swathed in earth.

When I left, I saw some of the miners with shallow pans in the river's muddy waters, using the same techniques as gold miners do. At the bottom of the tray were little black and gray pickings: that was coltan. Everything was dark there, not only the material they were quarrying and the inside of the mine, but also outside, the dirty faces, the strange absence of sunlight. I started by asking the workers outside the mine about Yoro, and they passed the same question down the line one by one until it went past the mouth of the tunnel and on down the line inside. The question, my voice, had to go as far as the earth's kidney, I thought, before it came back—hopefully answered in the positive—through the same mouth of the same tunnel where I was sitting on a rock, waiting, with brown water covering my feet and red varicose veins, hidden like the galleries where Yoro might be.

I was afraid that no information would come back out of the tunnel. I recalled the radical silence reigning over Hiroshima the first few days after Little Boy's explosion. The dying in the hospital where I was convalescing stopped moaning. Not even the children cried. There was only a whispering of names. People with their faces blown to pieces looking for their loved ones, a strange experience because it didn't depend on the one looking but on the one being looked for. Documentation, paper, were the first things to burn in the explosion, so the only way of identifying people was by the sound of the voice of the survivor. If the wounded person didn't have the strength or the will to say *Yes, it's me* to the mouth approaching the ear, his or her father, son, would go on forever whispering into the wrong ears. So many years have passed since then, and now I was the person looking for a loved one, waiting for her to identify herself.

My voice finally went out and came back. They hadn't seen a white person working there in the past few years. Getting the answer to that question took so long that I worried the process might take more time than I had left in this world. I was horrified to imagine that receiving the right response—the definitive response, the information I'd spent a lifetime searching for—might take so long that it would reach my worm-riddled ears only when they were unable to hear or send a signal to my amorphous brain, fallen to the bottom of my skull, shrunken or liquefied.

SIR, I HAVE VERY LITTLE TIME LEFT. I'll try to keep it even briefer, and say that despite the many pages I've written, there are certain details I've skipped, especially since they can come for me at any moment now.

I lived that subterranean life for many years. Even when I went outside, the images that flooded my mind belonged to the interior of a mine. You could say that after fifteen years on this continent, I can recognize it only underground. That's my expertise.

What can I tell you about my time in Africa? You were born on a beautiful continent, for the little I've actually seen from the surface, but they're boring holes in it, hollowing out the inside of the continent. One day you'll be sleeping in your bed and wake up suddenly underground, or you'll go to your daughter's room and discover a deep hole when you open the door where the miners are excavating and throwing the useless material atop that little girl whom you tucked into bed and kissed good night just a little while before. You'll be left clutching the doorframe, paralyzed by the vision of a white nightgown disappearing into the brown, the gray, the blue-black flesh of this earth. And from there you'll watch all the horrifying cogs and gears at work. You'll see how the buried body will slip and slide through those tunnels like a recently cast nut along a factory assembly line, where nobody believes they're assembling the weapon that will end up burying you like another nut falling on the same assembly line, and so on and so forth till the continent is nothing but a big factory spitting nuts out so some guy in another hemisphere can destroy things on the cheap.

I remember shortly after arriving being invited to a party where I saw a Belgian artist fashion a sculpture—or that's what he called it—that was highly acclaimed and that, after a while, I associated with the African massacre. Before the eyes of his country's dignitaries and all the people invited to the opening, he grabbed a jerrican full of liquid aluminum and spilled it into the mouth of an ant colony. He waited a few seconds for the liquid to solidify, then dug out a big block of earth, which he cleaned with a pressure hose, exposing the passageways that the ants had excavated. The silver aluminum tunnels showed the beauty of the insect labyrinth, but there was no sign of life there whatsoever. Sometimes I think this will be the only salvation for these lands. A giant sculptor might come along to spill liquid iron into the thousands of tunnels of this human ant colony before it's completely hollowed out and all of us fall to the bottom: men, elephants, snakes, antelopes, monkeys. Though by that time I think I'll be far away from here. I won't be alive, not here or in any other place. But Yoro will. Yoro is already safe, and I laugh at you. I despise you. I feel joy. Nobody will take that joy away from me. Even if they torture me before executing me, I will think: "The torture will last one, two, seven days. But my happiness will last an eternity. It will outlast my body, my conscience, because it will be the sound repeated in a chain, an alpha gorilla pounding his chest to claim his territory, the sound of the rain that comes to fill the crevices left by the parched earth." You have no power over that feeling of mine and it will prevail: happiness, free laughter, the spark in the air, the fall from corporeal confinement.

"THE CONGO ENDS UP CHANGING even the best person," I once heard a UN soldier say. You remember I told you what happened one day on the North American television program *This Is Your Life,* when a victim of Hiroshima and William Sterling Parsons, the commander of the *Enola Gay* who dropped the bomb, were put together on the same set? Well, a few years ago I saw another example that I found as sad as that program. You're perfectly aware, sir, what I'm talking about, but I'm thinking once again of that reader who still has her or his full capacity to empathize, the reader able to feel pain before the suffering of others. To that reader I want to explain that there's a video used to train personnel for the largest international organization in the world, the United Nations. The video I'm referring to is called *To Serve with Pride,* and it has the subtitle "Zero Tolerance for Sexual Exploitation and Abuse." It informs UN bureaucrats about issues anyone belonging to the United Nations should be fully aware of already. The video defines their conception of sexual exploitation. Later, when everything was about to go down, the video became one of the interlocking pieces of the puzzle enabling me to recognize the sinister final image.

Now as I write, I imagine the members of the UN peace mission sitting down with a notebook and, pen in hand, taking notes while they're explaining what they understand to be sexual exploitation. It appears as though it's not such an obvious thing that someone working to defend peace knows what pedophilia is, just to give an example. On several occasions the video ponderously enunciates the rules, such as "payment with money, jobs, goods, or services in exchange for sex is prohibited." The video also describes a few real-life cases as practical illustrations for the theory. And so it tells the case of a sixteen-year-old girl who was brought to Liberia as a prostitute and who was confined there in a place called the Sugar Club. When the girl sees a UN vehicle at the door of the establishment, she thinks she's saved and, relieved, runs to the car to ask for help. The driver rapes her and later informs the owner of the club that the girl had tried to escape. It's like what happens in those popular tales when a princess gets lost in a forest and thinks she's safe when she sees a little house with the lights on. She doesn't realize that it's in the house and not in the forest where the greatest threat lies, or maybe she comes to understand it only when the soldier pulls up his zipper. Another illustrative story on the video: A UN worker gave some cookies to a young girl in exchange for sex: he got her pregnant and subsequently skipped town. The mother got by selling bananas to care for her boy, at less than a dollar a day. The boy was called *mzungu tali tali,* an insult that means "not black or white"; an out-of-the-ordinary child who was denied treatment even by the Congolese doctors, who alleged they couldn't understand the mystery of difference, this mixed body.

There's a sequence in the video that I find particularly disturbing. The sanctimonious voice-over says (I wrote it down word for word in my notebook): "Victims face other consequences besides possible discrimination, the threat of AIDS, or unwanted pregnancies, because the worst of all possible damages is perhaps that of robbing a person of their dignity." It would seem the United Nations also attributes supernatural abilities to itself: it thinks it can take a woman's dignity from her. Those nasty little pieces of work in uniform think dignity is located in a woman's cunt and with their phalluses they wield the power to strip it out.

Should anyone forget or not have caught the message clearly enough, there's a recap at the end, kind of like at the end of a recipe where the cook enumerates the ingredients again. So they insist:

REMEMBER:

No sex in exchange for money, work, goods, or services.
No sex with children.
You have the obligation to denounce sexual abuse or
    exploitation.

MONUSCO. That's the name of the peacekeeping mission specific to the Congo, an acronym for United Nations Organization Stabilization Mission in the Democratic Republic of the Congo. But I think it should be called *mollusk* in English, *mollusque* in French, that slimy creature that recoils and hides when approached. What name do they give your mandate? Oh yes, it's a "monitoring" mandate, meaning they're there to do nothing, maybe play some cards. These missions send soldiers to the Congo for counting the dead and observing. Yes, a big bunch of Peeping Toms, or voyeurs of death in the best-case scenario and, in the worst, perverts.

MONUSCO has airplanes, state-of-the-art technology, and the very best in trucks. In the Congo, people say the mission is there to do nothing, and though the group is flush with resources, they're only good for transporting minerals and doing business with the companies that later sell it on the international market. It's also said that the members of MONUSCO sell arms to rebel factions or exchange them for gold or other precious metals, which means they are the ones financing the armed conflict. They call coltan *blue gold;* I don't know if it's for the color, which is more like black, but knowing what I've come to know, I think it's in honor of the blue helmets the UN soldiers wear. UN Security Council Resolution 1857 grants this organization the responsibility of overseeing and controlling the gold and coltan routes. And behold its undoing. The demise happened the moment they named as judge of the criminals the very criminal himself, the instant United Nations personnel were authorized internationally to control the routes that form part of its own corruption. Sir, you can tell me a thousand and one times that the UN soldiers didn't do anything. I could tell you the same thing: you're absolutely right, they did nothing. But that would be only—how can I put it?—the best-case scenario, when they dedicate themselves to this monitoring work that though useless and entirely cynical is idyllic when compared with other actions.

You can tell me that I'm an old woman, that I'm not as sharp or as quick as a young person. And I would answer that you're right, that today, a day when I'm writing my testimony, I'm very old, but since my mind had stopped for so many years and took a nice long nap, slept in its madness, it's not as worn out as the minds of other people of my same age. Yours surely has never taken a nap in restorative insanity, because the crazy ones, when they do stop reasoning, also stop producing and fall away from the corrupt social mechanisms. I bet you've never wanted to allow your madness to snatch away your ambition. You are very sane. Oh, no doubt about it. You are very sane today, but when you reach my age you'll wipe your drool with a hundred-dollar bill thinking it's a rag.

Now tell me, how can it be that after so many years, European citizens, North American citizens, or citizens of any other country who grant themselves the right to defend human rights—with all their attendant sense of superiority when waving their flags—are able to watch the rebels or soldiers of the regular Congolese army, day in and day out, systematically massacre their girls and women? As you already know, sir, in Africa generally and in the Congo in particular, the family economy is built on women. Men don't work. Women do everything. They are charged with fetching water, washing clothes in the river, finding food. The more fortunate are able to sell a few products gleaned from the earth, and whatever else the rebels allow. Four- and five-year-old girls prepare food for their brothers. When I arrived, I was surprised to find the men so idle, playing cards or sitting on the porches of their homes. So one day it occurred to me to ask one of these men why only women worked. He responded that men are warriors and they can't work because they have to be ready for war at all times. I thought about it again when I heard an intelligent and very good woman say something, a woman I'll call V for *valiant* to cloak her identity. In the Congo, V said, women have become a weapon of war. The rebels know everything depends on women, so they destroy them; they rape them so they can't work for days. Some suffer so much they end up taking their own lives. They don't have to bother killing the women themselves. Systematic rape is enough to ruin this country. So V then told a story to everyone who had come to that informative meeting to address the situation of Congolese women. There were twenty of us. Most were European. You already know the things I've seen and lived through. Well, believe me when I tell you that while listening to V tell her story, I confronted the truth about absolute cruelty for the first time. I felt the same shock, the same sense of disgust, the same impotence, the same desire to scream or to run nowhere and everywhere all at the same time. V told us the following story:

V had a friend, Jeanette, from her same hometown. The rebels kidnapped her together with her five children. They raped and tortured her for a week. At the end of the week, they gave her a room and nursed her back to health. They gave her water; they cured her wounds to the extent possible. They even fed her meat for several days. It had been a long time since Jeanette had eaten meat. Jeanette asked the soldiers why they were taking care of her after having hurt her and wanted to know if they would please let her see her five children. One of the rebels answered: "Now you say you want to see your five children? Now, after we've taken care of you for seven days? Now, after finally eating meat?"

V didn't need any further clarification. She didn't have to say it; all of us who had listened to her story understood what kind of meat Jeanette had been eating. One woman stood up and made her way through the chairs nearly crawling, wobbly. Outside of the little room we heard someone scream, "Please, someone call a doctor!" A boy had just passed out too. Obviously, no doctor ever came, and now that scream of the newly arrived white person seemed so bogus to me. A doctor to alleviate someone's wounded sensitivity? Should he have warned V that her story wasn't appropriate for the general public? No, not only did she not acknowledge it, she wasn't the slightest bit ruffled by our expressions of horror, the scream of someone who surely had to wait for that moment to learn the nature of true pain. V kept still, her hands on the table, grave, looking each one of us in the eye, each and every one of us, and in a very poised tone of voice said, "*Je suis désolée.* I don't mean to wound you, but the Congo needs help."

# Delivery: 2011–2014

Despite what she wrote in her letter, Yoro never left the Congo, though she had changed mines. She went from mining coltan to mining gold at a site controlled by armed groups called Chondo. She was no longer there by the time I arrived, though something happened there that I'd never forget. Outside of the mine there was a man who weighed on a rudimentary scale the gold each miner extracted. He placed a match on one of the scale's little plates, and on the other one, gold. For no reason, right before my eyes, they slit a woman's throat and stole her tiny seed of metal, which passed from the scale to the hands of the man who had slaughtered her. It was the first time I'd ever seen someone's throat being slit. I've often wondered if I'd ever experience it myself; if the circuit linking my eyes to my brain would still function for that last second to see and smell the same earth that would cover me, the ultimate freshness of the root tangling around my waist in a welcoming embrace into the nothing.

The Chondo mine was the third world's bottomless pit. It was the seventh world. There couldn't possibly be anything worse lower down. Though nowadays I believe there is always something deeper down, always something worse, substantial enough to sustain all the strata over a buried surface. I think I never actually saw the sturdy bedrock of hell, and yet how deep I went. When they took me to the Shinkolobwe mine in the Katanga region, the last mine that I would have to see, luckily, I stopped counting hells. It's an endless descent, because in that descent is the journey to death, the journey of the restless wanderer.

You must have an idea already of what they extract in Shinkolobwe. Nobody had to explain it to me beforehand. You know why? Because the closer the jeep got to the mine, the more fragile the vegetation became—more and more frail, drier, yellower, deader and deader. Also the noises indicating the presence of animals grew fewer and fewer until there were none. Silence. Once there, only silence. There was a small artificial lake ahead, which the Belgians, pressured by the Americans, built to conceal what was below. But the dimensions of what lay below the lake were fabulously ambitious, and the mine never ceased its clandestine operation. The mineral was exported through Zambia. Most people said it was copper, others cobalt. Perhaps. But the most valuable resource there was uranium. Uranium, sir. Once again, oh yes, uranium. But what sets this mine apart from Rössing is that this uranium is not some garden-variety uranium. It's the selfsame uranium that fed the bombs of Hiroshima and Nagasaki.

Life's like that sometimes, isn't it? Just when you think you've overcome what hurt you the most, you find yourself in a river whose current isn't taking you to the outlet, but to where it's born, forcing you to flow the course for a second time. That's where I was, smack in the pit that exterminated my city. By day the mine didn't seem to function, but large groups worked there by night extracting the uranium, whisking it out of the country illegally in trucks, passing customs at the border with rigged radioactivity detectors and moving through random controls for a few bucks in bribe money. The inanimate are the only ones with a right to life in this land. People kill each other, animals go extinct, vegetation burns, but the raw material of money abides. The continent of the human rights of the dollar. Human beings are no more than conduits, copper wires. Dollars won't save your life, though if you're alive they allow you to move. He who has money and is alive can move, money guarantees mobility, but not survival—that depends on chance. This took place in 2011. The second night in Shinkolobwe, in a tunnel whose ceiling filtered the radioactive water from the lake, I learned conclusively that Yoro had died. I had expected as much, don't think I hadn't already calculated that likelihood.

I DIDN'T WANT TO TELL YOU about Yoro's death earlier, because I wanted you to read the story following the same steps as I did. So there you go, Yoro was dead, it had happened in 2011, in a tunnel raining the same acid drops that had filled the open mouths of my thirsty Hiroshima. I discovered the news at the end of my life and hereby document it at the end of this testament, which probably has more pages left to write than I have days. Yoro. Dead. But no, I didn't crumble; I'd come undone so many times by now that I lost the capacity to feel that depth of sadness anymore. I'm going to let you in on a secret. I really like to be touched. Poor Jim, I used to bore him to tears asking him over and over again to caress my arms, my hair, and my legs while we were watching a movie or before we fell asleep. I tried to stroke myself to liberate him from my whims, but it was never the same. The only caresses that relaxed me came from someone else's hand. The explanation, or what I tell myself at least, is that the skin processes pleasure only when the origin of a touch is a surprise, when the brain isn't aware of its coming, can't anticipate its intensity, the exact point where or when it's going to take place. The same as sorrow, I think. Sorrow, like the pleasure of a caress, materializes only in virgin territory; for it to take effect it has to happen as if for a first time. In my case, after having experienced a multitude of sorrows, I find that nothing takes me by surprise anymore; I'm an arm, a leg, a piece of hair groped in the same place so many times, I've lost the capacity for despair. Yet I could and can feel joy because despite what I've done, I'm a good woman, and good people never lose their ability to feel joy. The news that Yoro had given birth to a girl didn't compensate for the loss, but it gave me enough joy to continue forward. I'd asked myself so many times if the pregnancy she spoke of in her letter had been carried through to term. The answer was yes. She gave her daughter, as she had promised in the letter Jim could never read, her same name. Yoro, her daughter, Jim's granddaughter. In a sense also my own grand-daughter, only in a sense, or at least that's what I thought before finding out what I'm going to explain now.

What I'm going to tell you now I read in a document given to me by one of Yoro's caregivers in the mine. Yoro had entrusted it to her, afraid someone might try to take her daughter away. The document certified Yoro's last name, a name Jim knew but had always kept hidden from me. He never used the name when refer-ring to her. And when I saw the name, the whole puzzle clicked into place. Sure, it could have been a coincidence. But that didn't even cross my mind. If her name was the same as mine, it was because Yoro was flesh of my flesh, blood of my blood, and my encounter with Jim had been no coincidence. In a flash it all made sense. I watched my entire universe levitate, in a single instant, right before my eyes, the entire meaning of a story lasting years revealed itself. As I said, my encounter with Jim hadn't been off the cuff. Jim had searched me out because I was his daughter's father, her biological father, and when he found me as the true woman that I am, it was only natural that he would fall in love with what was the closest thing of all to Yoro.

This must all seem very complicated to you. But it's not really.

I explained how in the days following the attack and throughout the occupation, the American doctors weren't allowed to treat atomic victims. But they did have other rights. Like the right to carry out experiments. The right to remove a testicle the bomb hadn't damaged and extract the sperm—apparently those little cells were stronger than I was—to inseminate an anonymous womb. Yoro was born, a baby destined from her first day of life to express the consequences of radiation on a fetus, on a child, on an adolescent . . . for however long she lasted. That was the reason for the periodic medical reports the foster families had to send in. But the signs of radiotoxemia had only begun here, in the mines. Yoro's radiation sickness began manifesting itself when she worked with tons of atomic water over her head, extracting from rock the same material that had killed her at birth, but without which she would never have been born. Yoro was a daughter of Oppenheimer; a daughter and later a mother of uranium.

The same woman who showed me the document Yoro had entrusted to her said the only thing Yoro had done the last few days of her life was to pronounce her daughter's name over and over again. As I said, she had given her daughter her own name, hoping to make her identification more probable: Yoro, like *to cry* in Spanish. I'll never forget what Yoro asked in her letter: for Jim to care for Yoro so she could live to contradict the verb *llorar*. For me, Yoro, my daughter, had been fully identified by the fact that they'd given her my name. Who knows if it was motivated by some last-ditch act of compassion toward me as her father or, on the contrary, a complete lack of interest, creativity, or simply scorn, thinking Jim would never want or be able to find me. They thought so little of me that they gave my daughter my last name, like someone who hides in a closet not because they think it's a good hiding place, but because he or she knows that nobody would look there. But Jim looked for me, found me, and revealed who I was. I loved Yoro. I looked for her as if she were my own daughter, never realizing that she actually was, crying over her absence throughout my entire life. Why did Jim hide the fact from me? you might ask. I don't really have an answer for you. Probably the shock of encountering me a woman cast Jim into a knotty process of assimilation, so he must have needed time to work up a way of sharing the news; but death, as you know, took him too soon.

How many times did I wonder what happened to my genitals after the explosion? How many nightmares did I have of my penis and my testicles crawling around looking for me to no avail? Jim knew about it even more than I did. He'd always known. He knew where the precious element of my testicles had gone, what came out of me, my daughter. He was privy to the significant details of my life and he loved me like no other man ever had or ever will: as a woman and as the father of his daughter.

SO, AS I SAID, they told me in the mine that all Yoro the mother did was repeat her own name, which was her daughter's name. In response to any question she gave the same answer: Yoro. And not because she'd gone mad, I'm sure, but hoping to make the name stick as long as possible, so the word would be on every tongue and spread until Jim, having read her message, came to find her. Think of the words she used in her letter: "If you can't find me, please find your grandson or granddaughter, who will have my same name, and please allow her to live to contradict it." I like to think that aside from having a practical motivation, Yoro had inherited my sense of how significant names are. I'm sure attentiveness to names derives from other traditions close to my own. Take the Chinese characters, for instance, used to express *own name*, which are formed by the words *mouth* and *moon*. Some say it's because on the last day of each moon the Imperial Guard would call out the names of the men who were to stand in for their companions for the next few days; others—and this is my favorite explanation—

argue that its etymology derives from something else: the name of a newborn could be whispered by the father to the mother only by moonlight. It was whispered as something sacred. I call myself H, which doesn't mean it's the initial of the name my parents gave me, parents who couldn't even get my gender right. I chose this initial with something very clear in mind. After realizing that Yoro knew the meaning of her Spanish name, I started asking someone from Spain to say certain words. Eventually I asked how they pronounce the word Hiroshima in their language. "Iroshima," they said. "The *h* is silent. We call it the mute letter." It seemed marvelous to find a letter that existed without a voice. It's a letter like me, with a presence, a body, but aphasic. That's how I realized it was my name, the mute one, the one whose city had been razed. I'm H, the mute daughter of mute Hiroshima.

According to the woman at the mine, my daughter wasn't allowed to speak much or my granddaughter either. Baby Yoro had been left unprotected when her mother died. Cannon fodder from the day she was born. To begin with, being the offspring of a black father and an Asian mother, she was neither-nor, *mzungu tali tali*. But she had certain features that set her apart too. Mostly the shape of her eyes and her very long neck. A Burmese guard who had helped her mother for years had placed a few golden rings around her neck as the girl grew to protect her from lions, he said, though he said different things at different times, like how the rings were symbols of nobility in his land. But what lions? And what nobility? Such things don't exist underground.

When Yoro died, baby Yoro was taken to a refugee camp outside of Goma. With my eyes wide open when I arrived in the city, the first thing I saw was prostitution. That's right, alongside all the five-and-dimes, prostitution is how many of the women eke out a living, selling their bodies for food or money. It's why I could never understand this need for soldiers to rape underage girls or pay for sex with them in cookies or Fanta. Later it was explained to me when we arrived in the refugee camp. The soldiers figured these girls were more likely to be healthy; they wanted to avoid catching sexually transmitted diseases. As demand grew, prostitutes began arriving from surrounding areas, as happens in other countries, and set up shop there to satisfy the hankerings of UN people who, however much they try to hide the fact, are a cog in the machine that leads to human trafficking of minors.

There were hundreds of rape victims in that refugee camp, underage and adult women alike, who gave birth to what came to be known as a "MONUC baby," meaning a baby conceived by rape or a criminal sexual transaction on the part of a UN blue helmet. Only girls not young enough to have had their first menstrual cycle were safe from unwanted pregnancy. I could verify it all on my own from firsthand testimonies in situ. Hanging all over the UN's central pavilion were posters with illustrations prohibiting sexual relations with minors. Many women go to the UN for help. Can you imagine what it must feel like for them to encounter all these warnings directed at the peacekeeping staff, posted all around their supposed sanctuary? Just think of the confidence generated by all these posters in the selfsame headquarters of the people who have supposedly come to their country to protect them. It's as if a wounded person showed up at a hospital where the operating room had posters in the halls around it reading "Killing patients is not okay."

A journalist once told me that when soldiers are issued their uniforms, they are also given cards listing ten rules of conduct, one of which is the fact that sexual abuse is prohibited. Just the thought of some soldier, some keeper of the peace, carrying such a card in his pocket disgusts me. Ten rules on a pocket flash card like those learning aids with vocabulary words so you can learn a new language while on the subway or standing in line. A quick memory prompt on a perverse backcloth: it's for memorizing the terrible acts that are prohibited as if they were something new; the word *rape* on a flash card, the verb, was no more than something you had to learn consciously not to do. You study the lesson of "I shouldn't rape" by the same method you employ to learn that in Spanish *mesa* means "table." So you memorize it. And if you happen to forget, all you have to do is pull the card out of your pocket, remind yourself, and start all over again. If it should happen, the important thing is to follow the next step: hide it.

That's how things were in the Congo. You know it perfectly well. Over twenty thousand soldiers came to protect the country in what was the United Nations' most important peacekeeping mission. But they only made the situation far worse. It's said that when the dying ends, so do the jobs, reason enough for soldiers to instigate internal conflicts to keep their double pay: military wages from their countries of origin and from the UN. I think people were hopeful at the outset, but when I walked through that camp, all the refugees wanted to know is when they would finally be left in peace or in war, but without all these peacekeeping forces with their blue helmets. Most victims lacked the resources to accuse their rapists, especially in a country where countless people couldn't even tell you the day or year they were born. The most dedicated personnel did what they could and had even supported the creation of a soldiers' DNA bank to determine the paternity of MONUC babies and to be able to file the appropriate criminal charges. Most soldiers agreed to the idea of a DNA bank, since accusations could be leveled against anyone, even the innocent, though, in general, innocent or not, what happened in the Congo has been the result of a great conspiracy of silence protected by the only organization in the country with money and means.

I ate lunch with the soldiers while I was visiting the refugee camp. The meat—they said while serving me—is Argentine; the cheese is French; the after-lunch coffee, Colombian; and the chocolate, Belgian. Everything was paid for by the UN. The mind, sir, which at times takes us down paths that we're ashamed to acknowledge, played a little trick on me, and I wondered while I ate why the soldiers couldn't show a little decency and pay the girls with some good roast chuck ribs and chocolate, instead of Fanta and cookies. What a shame the Congolese children haven't tasted chocolate. I was mortified when I found myself thinking such a thing. And I thought back to what they had said, that the Congo changes even those with the best of intentions and I felt for an instant closer to the criminals than the victims.

YORO HADN'T GONE UNNOTICED in the refugee camps in Goma. They told me she'd gone to work voluntarily, wearing the rings around her neck, in a sort of zoo or menagerie on the outskirts of the city, built by the great Congolese military chief. Yoro probably thought, rightly, that a zoo is a better refuge than a refugee camp in a place where people had become like beasts.

When I got there, I saw the damages the rebellion had caused the day before. I was sure this was finally it, though, the last link that would bring me to Yoro. The zoo. All I wanted was to get onto the grounds, which when seen from outside were torn apart, full of howling creatures, bloodied. I thought it might be more practical to use the old wad of money instead of a door, always the black market. But there was no need to pay; a fire had razed most of the premises. Later I found out the zoo had been left to the grace of god a while before, a god that didn't exist.

I don't know why I even bother to write what happened once I got into these brand-new ruins because you certainly don't deserve to know. You don't deserve to know how I felt when I found Yoro. Writing even three words that might help you imagine what that moment was like would be a sign that I don't love myself very much. It's a matter of my own heart, something at once so beautiful and so painful that I refuse to waste time explaining to you how my entire life transformed in a single flash. Of course I explained it to my dead Jim as soon as I was calm enough and had the proper distance, which allowed me to write at a remove from the fever of that moment. Below is the letter I wrote to Jim. It's written as if I really thought he could read it. Maybe the merciful, humane reader would like to know the details that preceded the end of my story, if someday you ever want to share this testimony with others and satisfy my last wish. You, sir, can just skip these pages, I wrote them for Jim, so move along to where I explain the only thing you care about in this case, which is my crime.

*The zoo of a city at war, my love. Imagine what that's like, a zoo in a city at war. Impossible to imagine without seeing it. Here you could truly feel people's agony, much more than outside. You can't really appreciate people's death by seeing dead people. I had seen so many dead people already they all seemed the same to me. You can really feel people's death in a derelict zoo; the hanging bellies of the hippopotamus dragging like newborns around a fake pond that's nearly dry; the hoarse orangutan who has been sobbing so disconsolately it lost its voice and now merely opens its mouth wide in a silent scream that punctures your eardrums. Outside the zoo, the dead and the wounded are all the same. United in suffering, people lose their individuality. But in a zoo where animals have been abandoned in their confinement, each species manifests its pain in a different way, within the parameters of its way of being; the way of the bear, the way of the monkey, the way of the lion, the way of each animal in keeping with its nature, like all the facets composing a diamond that is the human heart. I've always known that the creatures inside Noah's ark weren't animals, but the entire spectrum of a person's feelings. He tried to salvage joy and grief in all their variants. That was Noah's work.*

*Oh, if only you could have seen Yoro's eyes, my love . . .*
*You would have fallen in love with her, even though she's*
*your granddaughter, and despite the love you felt for me.*
*I felt a special attraction to her myself. How beautiful our*
*granddaughter is, daughter of my biological daughter, and*
*how good you were to find me, to make me feel like her mother*
*without ever needing to let me in on the secret. You'd have*
*told me eventually, I know that, but it doesn't matter now.*
*It never really mattered because I've moved along the same*
*roads I'd have traveled had I known the truth, and perhaps*
*not knowing made me a little more patient when I told myself:*
*Take heart; don't worry; looking for someone else's daughter*
*isn't so important. But the second I laid eyes on her, I knew*
*for sure that she'd sprung from my own genetic sequence.*
*Some things you know without having to study them. So*
*how important is blood, my love? Can it help us identify*
*the mysteries of the human chromosome? I always thought*
*it couldn't, that blood isn't important, and I still think this*
*because even though I was born defective and wrongly sexed by*
*relatives and doctors, at least I was born of myself. Yet when*
*Yoro looked at me it was as if the little puppy of the little puppy*
*I'd gestated for so many years suddenly recognized me, smelled*
*me, and looked over my body with hunger, maybe looking for*
*the nipple of the woman I wasn't allowed to be when I was*
*born, condemned to the flat chest of a sad man. But Yoro was*
*there, turning me into a mother and a grandmother in one fell*
*swoop. A snap! Everything faded into the background when I*
*saw her. Like in a birthing chamber, only she, newly born, was*
*all that existed. Her presence signified everything. Even you*
*disappeared in those first few moments. The birth, my love, was*
*painless. All the catchphrases mothers use are true: when Yoro*
*was born, all that I had suffered stopped hurting me. It's hard*

*to explain, it's not really that nothing hurt, more like all the suffering somehow transferred into a kind of movie that I could watch scene by scene, but no longer feel.*

*After so many years searching for Yoro, when I finally found her, it was like coming back to you again. Spilling water over your ashes at the foot of a tree to watch how the limbs rise up. All of you, erect. Yoro has your eyes, but with a twinkle of a star that has heated up over years of pressure. There was pressure there. The pressure of war. She was so young, and yet the look in her eyes was on the verge of splintering from rage, from heat. But she was good. She bent down to caress the wizened skin of a crocodile. But the animal didn't move. If it had been a person, I would have thought he was dead, but for a crocodile inertness and sadness are one and the same thing, and sadness, everyone knows, is an evergreen tree.*

*We walked slowly, checking all the cages. Many of them were open. We saw a tiger approaching some fifty yards away. We knew it by its stripes. The stripes were nearly the only thing it had left. Stripes without a tiger. It couldn't walk. It scraped forward with its front paws alone, dragging the back ones so slowly we weren't the least bit alarmed when it got close. When it reached us, it raised a hungry tooth to the sky; that's what its feline strength had been reduced to, a chameleon's failed attempt to catch a fly.*

*Yoro is beautiful, my love, but what really stands out is her kindness. She caressed the iron bars as if they were wounded flesh. She entered the cages with respect, as if not wanting to awaken the dead. We saw a young elephant, still alive. It was lying on its side and it reached out to us with its empty trunk, which reminded me again of the image in my recurring nightmare, shed snakeskin—though now I knew what had happened to my penis, my testicles. All of it was in Yoro. An empty elephant trunk was no longer a symbol of my genitals*

*looking for me all over Hiroshima; now it was just that, an*
*empty elephant trunk. Yoro and I spent many hours together*
*picking whatever grass was left, locating grain and water in*
*other cages. For the elephant. It was so weak. Yoro placed the*
*food in the lobes at the end of the trunk for it to smell, then set*
*it in the elephant's mouth with some water. It was as if she'd*
*grown up taking care of sick elephants. Maybe it was just that.*
*Right now I don't know anything about her. How to ask? I*
*haven't told her who I am yet either. But I believe she knows,*
*Jim, I believe she does. I wish you could see how she looks at*
*me. She knows the same way that I've always known, like*
*you never told me, through the silent communication that runs*
*from body to body. It doesn't matter, though. I will tell her*
*the truth. I have to think about how to go about it. How to*
*explain using words why we have spent a life, the only lives we*
*had, looking for her mother, looking for her. Our only life, Jim.*
*A life dedicated almost exclusively to searching for the treasure*
*you didn't live to find.*

*We spent seven days at the zoo. The first six we traveled*
*on foot. The last, my love, the last, Yoro left on the back of an*
*elephant. If only you could have seen it. The elephant was tame.*
*It stepped around the bodies lying on the ground. I realized when*
*I mounted that seen from above like that, desolation multiplies.*
*That's how I saw the city as a battleground. That's why the*
*kings and the gods deserve less forgiveness, because the higher*
*up you are, the better you see the plain and the easier it is to*
*prevent war.*

*Squalid horses roamed about with their ribs poking out,*
*sniffing the human pasture. They nibbled it. Thousands of years*
*of an herbivore's diet replaced by a carnivorous one. The thing*
*about war is that it makes anything possible. I watched the*
*horses, my love, die without complaint. Their way of showing*
*pain is silence, which isn't the case with other animals. Will*

*I die silent as a horse or will I let out a pig's squeal that in a single blast quells all the silence I've suffered? We trekked through the city for almost an hour before the elephant finally recovered its ancestral memory, raised its trunk to the sky, and shook us off its back with a great trumpeting roar. From the ground we heard its footsteps running away, but it didn't bother to sidestep the vacant-eyed faces of the ones responsible for his captivity. Two helmets cracked in a single footfall. I liked the sound of it. "Peace," it said on one of them. But you can't drain a solid, and the soldier brain, now a liquid thread, might just flow into one of the lagoons of true peace, the peace those soldiers ridiculed. About a year ago, a spoiled little girl in a suit made a feminist speech at the UN headquarters. The candid words of an actress aren't going to change the world. The world is fixed by the tread of an elephant recovering its memory as it races away. You taught me you don't ask for equality using words like* please. *Equality is not even under discussion. That was then. It's different now. The only way to defend black people and women is the tread of an elephant. The world no longer understands words.*

*Jim, my love. Here I am, me, who never believed in life after death, writing to you. You see? My writing is all messy now, because I realize I never told you the crucial part. I should have told you in the beginning that Yoro was one of the attractions in the zoo. Yep. Like another animal. You're asking yourself why, I bet. And I know you're not here, you aren't reading this, it's absurd to be writing to you, and yet I have to find the right words to tell you delicately that Yoro wears five bronze rings around her neck. Almost five pounds of weight on her collarbone. I found her huddled in her cell. A ring around her neck was chained through a loop to one of the bars. "A guard told me that Burma is at war." That was the first thing she said to me. Only afterward did I realize that Burma is where you had suffered too. Is that land still in conflict? You didn't come immediately to mind because when Yoro mentioned Burma, it was meant as some kind of rationalization for the wars. It didn't seem so strange, more like a discreet form of asking forgiveness for all forms of conflict in general. As I said, Yoro's most outstanding feature is kindness. She spoke to me in her mother tongue, Japanese. It's the language her mother taught her as a protection, she told me later, so that nobody would understand them. She was curled into a ball of sadness, all except for her neck, which was tall and straight. There was a tiny cage at her feet. A cricket inside. "An insect and a giraffe woman are alike in one way," she told me. "If you remove one of our rings, we're nothing." I imagine it must be true. The insect would bleed to death, the neck of the woman would break. When I severed the chain that held her in the cage, it took an hour for her to articulate a single word. Then she started to speak.*

*Before explaining what will lead to the end of my life, I have to tell you the story, link by link as Yoro told it to me, of what took her mother, our daughter, from Japan to Africa. It's not about her mother getting sick. As you know, the medical reports the families sent periodically always showed stable results. Yoro was a strong baby, resilient, a healthy adolescent. The top secret project, the test-tube baby created with the hope of observing how weeds flower in it, how the pitiable cypress trees of radiation sickness grow willowy, grew up to be a strong, healthy adolescent, and she remained vigorous for such a long time that she stopped being of interest to the project overseers. So they got rid of her for being healthy. And they sent her to the mines to keep her quiet, with a labor contract that was already breached at signature, where radiation exposure finally took her life. That's how it happened. Everything so simple, and so tough. From Japan to Africa, Jim. We should have come to Africa together. How did it slip by us? The origin.*

*Of the woman. Of Yoro. Today the scar, the keloid on my left cheek in the form of the African continent has more significance than ever, like an outline of that crucial element sought for so many years: Yoro.*

*Later Yoro did tell me who brought her first to the refugee camp in Goma after our daughter died, and then to the zoo, where she wasn't just a tourist attraction, the giraffe woman— something she imagined and accepted. You probably remember, my love, how upset we were over what they did to Sandy, our orangutan in Borneo. Yoro's conditions were similar. So you'll understand what I'm going to do and you'll approve. Luckily, Yoro had recovered her strength a few days later and could point out for me the blue-helmeted peacekeeper who tricked her into the cage.*

*But that's a few days hence. She could hardly speak when we first met, and all she did was sob for the animals that had died in the final battle. We slept together in the cage that first night. Two women in a cage, with another cage that had a cricket inside. I remembered that ancient Chinese custom. The concubines used to sleep to the song of a cricket in a golden cage. I thought a giraffe woman's neck rings were also made of gold. But Yoro had her neck set in tin, and the cricket's cage was made out of little sticks. When you took me to Thailand, the people there said they raised crickets because this insect had an aggressive nature. Do you remember? They used them to fight so people could gamble on them. You gave me a losing cricket as a gift. Its leg was bitten and it couldn't fight anymore. We kept its cage in the backpack. The first night the cricket sang. My love. The first few nights it sang, and when I heard it, I took Yoro's hand in mine so as to sleep with the feeling of your embrace for the first time since you'd gone.*

*I have no idea where the words in this letter will go, but I know that finding Yoro isn't the end of the journey, as we*

*had thought. I couldn't put the end in writing; it would be*
*an unnecessary risk, taking into account that you can't read*
*it. You must know that the risk I'm referring to isn't to Yoro,*
*who is now being looked after by S, my faithful friend. The*
*risk I'm referring to is that I destroy the ending I want for this*
*story. But if everything comes together as planned and if you*
*survived death and you're there somewhere above, there's a*
*good chance I'll be able to tell you all about it myself. I love life.*
*But losing it is a possibility that grows plumper and plumper*
*the farther I move forward on this journey. And you know I've*
*never been good with diets.*

SIR, YORO AND I WAITED a few minutes in a tiny hole beneath the barbed wire surrounding the refugee camp. You, of course, didn't realize that. Yoro knew the place well because that's how they passed food to her from the outside when she lived in the camp, without having to report it to the authorities. Once a week, around midnight, a whistle sounded, and together with five other refugees she would sneak through the hole to fetch the aid some stranger would pass through. I imagined the group of six in the middle of the night—like hungry cats, eagerly answering the call of a voice no matter whose it was. That anonymous charity seemed more appropriate for animals than people, I thought. We heard footsteps a few minutes later and remained in the hole, noiseless. My hand brushed against something hard, coarse; I thought the worst, a cold body, but it was only the root of a tree. I looked above me and didn't see a trunk or a treetop, nothing. I remembered the legend of the baobab, the tree that was punished for being too beautiful, forced to grow downward, underground. There I was with Yoro, in the same stratum as the root of a tree condemned to the blindness of a hedgehog. The most beautiful things in this land never seem to rise above sea level; instead all of it—the moon and the stars, even the birds and the clouds—is underground, buried, and afraid. The dead man and the mountain climber are both underground. How is it possible that someone who in a show of determination, muscle, and the strokes of his pickax reaches the top of a peak, aiming there to find freedom, is never able to see beyond what a dead man sees? When was this continent, over which life runs, flies, and cries out in pleasure, buried so deep? It's important for you to know these things that run through my mind before the end. It's not that you'll understand me any better because of it, but I want it to go on the record that I love life, because it's what places me above you.

While we were waiting in that hole for the people standing close to us to move on, it started to rain. The drops were small, but it was a hard rain. The earth began soaking it up and my hand sunk in a little. I felt another part of the root. Suddenly I was very cold. For a second I was afraid I myself was dead. Then I thought how coldness is a feature of death that only the living can feel. That's when I realized I was alive. At times being dead and being alive seemed only a question of one's deciding whether one was dead or alive. I kept evaluating my state: though we hadn't eaten anything all day, I wasn't hungry. I wasn't thirsty either. I'd had my last meal the day before, a bowl of rice that I shared with Yoro. The last water I drank was also several hours earlier. My mouth was dry, but without thirst. My stomach was empty, but without hunger. It's as though this dryness and this emptiness were destined to remind me that living things need water and food; yet I, feeling their absence, didn't need anything. Nothing. So was I dead? I looked at Yoro and all my doubts evaporated. We were alive. Or maybe that's all it was, a question of deciding that we were alive.

When the people next to the barbed wire left, I saw that Yoro's head was resting sideways on the ground. I didn't want to wait any longer, but she grabbed me by the arm and held me there in the hole. She said the spiders made music when they wove their webs, that the larvae made a sort of purring sound when they grow, like lounging cats. She assured me that these tiny sounds are beautiful and that she had learned how to discern them in the mines. She appreciated these souls that for years were her only company, lives that nobody paid attention to, which were squashed under a foot or simply ignored. Then she told me she was afraid. And something happened then, sir, which I will never be able to forget. Yoro stretched out a hand and I saw what she wanted to show me by the light of my tiny lantern. A flying ant had opened its wings in the palm of her hand, in the form of a cross, and it's not that I'm Christian or believe in many things, but I had to think it was nature's way of sharing our circumstances. A snail left its shell, and after leaving a slippery trail, like a long, continuous kiss, it returned to its shell with its antennas down. A lizard egg cracked so that Yoro could see—and it seemed such an obvious, generous gesture—the spectacle of the creature's premature birth. All these minimal lives were with Yoro. Not a single one of these creatures was on my skin. They were all on Yoro, caressing her in their own way. I think that if Yoro had been able to walk she would have gotten up; thousands of tiny backs would have held her and carried her faceup, looking at the starry sky. But I was there to move her, and after delicately brushing off all that life that had settled on her skin, I finally helped her up, and we moved to the other side of the fence.

It was the dead of night, and the area had become a boggy pit from all the rain. We had to walk with special care so our footfalls didn't make noise splashing in the water. Luckily, the tent we were looking for wasn't too far away from the hole we'd entered and, anyway, in the worst-case scenario, it wasn't likely that anyone not in uniform would be bothered by our presence. Flies don't generally bother other flies—they prefer to bother people, and there weren't any people there because anyone who entered that place was transformed into a black insect that fought over the world's garbage with other black insects. You might think that in the case of a refugee camp, the fence is there to protect those inside from what is on the outside. But that wasn't the case. As I have already explained, many of the refugees were faced there with a war inside of a war, where humanitarian aid was sold at a premium, much higher than on the outside.

Once I spied the pavilion and before Yoro said anything, I knew it was the one we were looking for. It wasn't hard to figure out. It was all lit up, and from outside we heard the sounds of laughter and jolly music I could identify only once we were a little closer. Good old rock 'n' roll; the great Jerry Lee Lewis singing "Great Balls of Fire." That's what was choking me up. You know something? I really did feel like dancing. I don't know if you've ever heard or remember the song. I recall the image of that beautiful man, Jerry Lee Lewis, with his shirt open, his chest young and brawny, playing the piano and shaking a long blond curl to and fro across his forehead, throwing it straight up every time he said "Kiss me baby," a sentence that would cause him to break into a bout of laughter in front of thousands of fans screaming his name. I would have scratched my face over Jerry too. What an irony to find that music coming out of such a filthy tent, the energy of a colossal talent celebrating the gorgeous petulance of youth, of eternal libido, of rock 'n' roll's no to making war. That was the genius of rock stars, the key to their condemnation and commitment, a sort of sportsmanlike spirit that didn't understand differences before the collective euphoria of the mind and body moving to the rhythm.

Yoro pointed to a little soldier who was with two others. It was a grotesque sight, them playing cards with their blue helmets on. Maybe the other two were good guys. To tell you the truth, it didn't even cross my mind. I just felt more and more rage, and the music filled me with a vigor that together with

the indignation morphed into a kind of violence I'd never experienced before. Every time I heard one of those three soldiers
giggle, another ball of fire dropped into my stomach from the
collection of them already accumulated in my throat. You'd be
surprised how many balls of fire fit in a person before they explode. Obviously, I wasn't going to blow myself up. I didn't want
to be the one who exploded. I was joyful; I held my daughter's
hand in mine now, just in time, at the end of my life. The rain
had died down a while back. Yoro's eyes reflected the light in the
tent. Another ball of fire was burning inside. I released Yoro's
hand and walked the perimeter of the tent, dousing the base of
the tarp with fuel. I kept listening to the music: "Kiss me baby,
woo-oooo, feels good." I returned to the spot where I had left
Yoro. I took the weapon from the bag. You may remember I
told you that my friend S gave me the weapon. It was an exact
plastic replica of a Mesolithic dildo, an eight-inch-long penis
some primitive man or woman must have used around eleven
thousand years ago. I found it extraordinary to think that sexual
split away from the other had taken place a hundred and ten
centuries before the so-called feminist revolution. So I asked S
to make a replica before I ever thought of shoving a wick up its
urethra. Positioning the wick, I thought back to years earlier,
on Thanksgiving, when I launched the Molotov turkey during
a Harlem rebellion. I had been repeating over and over again:

*Launch it at an angle somewhere between thirty (so it splatters
wider) and forty-five degrees (so that it travels farther).*

I lit the wick in front of the tent. I watched the fire moving
toward the glans, the inflammable material, and before it reached
the foreskin, I threw that Mesolithic penis inside the tent where
the three soldiers were playing cards and the whole thing went
up in flames within seconds. Jerry Lee Lewis's music went dead
before the screams of the cavemen had ended.

Consider now the first page of my testimony. You already

knew that was the fire, but what you didn't know was everything that happened in my life between the fire that both opens and now closes my testimony. Here it is. Flames devoured the tarpaulin with the voracity of synthetic fiber. I was holding Yoro's hand. I could feel her trembling, almost keeping time with the roaring fire. As if her shuddering could bestow the flames with something sound alone couldn't: substance. Yoro and the flames were like the sternum and spine of a single creature, two integral parts of a whole, like a drum and its stick. With her hand in mine, I could feel the swan-song hiss of a table's soul, of a tin cup, of the metallic tubes that sustained the tent. Though my attention was fixed on these delicate particulars, I wasn't without feeling for the people and things being consumed before us, but I've trained myself to contain the instinct to flee in dire situations, not to cry or try to fix what's beyond solution. I avoided blinking too much. It's like hyperventilating. Keeping the movement of my eyelashes steady saves oxygen, energy, and helps keep my knees from buckling. That's how I could remain standing. That's how I've always been able to hold a person's gaze. Of course I was scared. Of course I felt compassion. But I held myself in check, not only because if I fell, others would consume me, but also because I promised never to move a muscle out of rage or despair. Not a single one. I had promised Jim that. Dwelling on these thoughts helped me keep my promise, observing the heat from a distance when it was so close to my skin. I found serenity in my own way, in the string of memories I tug at whenever I need to salvage some experience that helps me keep my composure. I found it. The string. The string was the death of Quang Duc, the seventy-six-year-old monk who immolated himself in front of me and several other monks on a street in Saigon. He torched himself to find freedom, incinerated himself without altering his meditative posture; not even when the flames had engulfed him entirely did he allow a slightest movement. The other monks and I cried;

some sobbed over him without opposing his will; others asked for help to rescue him for his sake, at the same time against his will, because he was meant to burn to put an end to the persecution, to achieve peace for his brothers, and for others who, like me, have to measure the blinking of their eyelids before a fire. Slowly but surely, I found serenity. The heat of the flaming tarp led me to a distant place, far from the here and now, and rekindled the heat of the monk I had watched immolate himself in Saigon, and the more the tarp burned in the refugee camp, the further away I withdrew, without stirring, toward the moment of Quang Duc's death. Just as Yoro's trembling seemed to give a body to the sound of the flames, so the sobs of we who loved the monk seemed to give sound to the silence, since the burning man said nothing, not a cry, not a hiss to express complaint or pain or reproach.

So without complaint, without pain, without reproach, I ran away from the refugee camp with Yoro, who by that time had learned how to give me kisses and hugs and had called me grandma several times, and other times grandpa.

# ACKNOWLEDGMENTS

I would like to thank Ana Laura Santamaría and Alejandra Toro for giving so much love. To Gloria Noriega, who rescued turtles on a Florida beach and sent me the sounds of the sea while she was doing it. To her I also owe several of the images of beautiful blood that envelops a pregnancy. I am also grateful to María José Villegas Arévalo for always being there and, more important, for always being true. To Sandra Medina Lozano for our friendship since childhood and because she dares to tell me her fears, and her loves, deeply and in detail; she's aware that it's her compassion that protects her. To Isabelle Champaney, who survived getting bit by a snake and thereby gave me the opportunity to thank her for all her help during my French sojourn. To Ana Carmen Martínez, who spent many hours researching the marvelous passageways of someone who is neither a man nor a woman. To José María Cabeza Laínez, who, one night on a Chinese steppe, listened to a father whisper the name of his firstborn son and recounted it to me as if it were something sacred.

To Felipe R. Navarro and Ernesto Calabuig for helping me through the training process that allowed me to swim across the Gibraltar Strait, a crossing without which I would never have been able to write this novel, which I thought up as I was swimming and during the long months of aquatic discipline.

I also want to mention some of the books that I've referenced as I've written this novel, and highlight my gratitude to their authors.

The phrase "the Venus de Milo's impossible embrace" is a verse by Rubén Darío taken from the poem titled "Yo persigo una forma," which is included in *Antología Poética* (Edaf, Madrid, 1988).

"Not exposed, but behind a veil / are breasts desirable" is the translation of a line by Daniel Ingalls of the poem "Rhetoric" by Vallana from *An Anthology of Sanskrit Court Poetry*.

Whenever I mention Project Orion, I'm basing my information on an article published in *Science* on July 9, 1965 (volume 149, number 3680). Titled "Death of a Project," it was written by Freeman J. Dyson.

I also cite excerpts throughout the novel or use data from *Herculine Barbin llamada Alexina B.* (Talasa, Madrid, 2007); *Nagasaki: Las crónicas destruidas por MacArthur* by George Weller (Crítica, Barcelona, 2007); and *Hiroshima* by John Hersey (Vintage, New York, 1989).